The Fallen Kingdom

The Armor of God

Book 2

The Fallen Kingdom

JEFF BOLES

ISBN: 978-1-6653-0770-3 - Paperback
ISBN: 978-1-6653- 0771-0 - Hardcover
eISBN: 978-1-6653- 0772-7 - eBook

Library of Congress Control Number: 2023920663

⊚This paper meets the requirements of ANSI/NISO Z39.48-1992 (Permanence of Paper)

1 0 2 5 2 3

Prologue

A heavy rain cascaded from the ominous black clouds and brilliant flashes of lightning continually lit-up the early evening sky. Each flash was followed with hardly a pause by roars of thunder that shook the very ground. A steady wind blew across the land with an occasional gust that picked up loose objects and carried them away. Not a soul walked the streets this evening, all taking refuge where they could.

Deep within one of the large stone buildings of the village, a lone boy sat at a long wooden table, reading a book by the light of one small candle. The room itself was designed for the singular purpose of study. It was not a large room, barely fifteen feet square. There were easily two hundred books and even more parchments crammed onto the few shelves that lined the walls. There were no decorations, lest you count the dozen or so maps that covered portions of the walls where there were no shelves. The bench upon which the boy sat was less than comfortable and had been worn smooth by countless other people who had sat in the same place as he was over who knows how many decades. There was no fireplace and therefore no source of heat, but the lad was used to the less-than-cozy temperatures. He had spent many days and nights in this room. The room had one doorway, though no door hung from its frame. The boy would occasionally make notes on a piece of paper as he made his way through the book, page after page. He was so intent on his studies that he was not aware that another person had entered the room. He looked up, startled, when a voice broke his concentration.

"Edwin, you have been in this room for the past four hours without a break," the newcomer said. "You need to take a break. Come, let us get something to eat."

"In a bit, Walter," Edwin said, waving off the invitation. "I am not hungry."

Edwin Gallard and Walter Brewster were best friends and like brothers. Both boys were sixteen years old and had known each other the entirety of their lives. While Walter was the son of one of the more influential noblemen in their homeland, Edwin was the third son of the king of their homeland, Nordham. However, in Edwin's mind, he might as well be the son of a mere farmer for the way his father and brothers regarded him. Being third in line to succeed his father to the throne was all but meaningless, and his brothers wasted no opportunity to remind him of his place. Nevertheless, he dedicated many hours and many days to his own education and training. Whether as king of his homeland or in some other capacity, he was determined to be a man of profound influence in the world.

"Although your mind may not remember, I am certain that your stomach has told you many times that you have not eaten anything since this morning. It is now evening. Come, lay aside your learning for a time and let us make our way to the kitchen," Walter urged him. "If you would but take one step into the hall, you would no doubt take notice of the appetite-teasing aroma of a freshly roasted chicken that seems to permeate every nook and cranny of this building, other than this room it would appear."

"I have found something, Walter," Edwin said, looking beyond Walter at the empty doorway, his voice barely rising above a whisper. "Something of great interest."

"It must be extremely interesting to rob you of your otherwise insatiable appetite," Walter replied, his curiosity aroused. "What have you found?"

Edwin rose from the bench and walked past Walter to the doorway. He peered both up and down the hallway to ensure that no other person was within earshot. He turned back to Walter.

"A legend," Edwin said with barely more than a whisper.

"A legend?" Walter asked, not the least bit impressed and somewhat disappointed. "What do you mean a legend? We have had nearly identical childhoods and education, and I can tell you with no uncertainty that there has been no shortage of legends passed on to us, and most of those have simply been fabrications of someone's imagination."

"I assure you, this is no fabrication of imagination," Edwin replied. This is history, of that there is no doubt. It is the kind of history that for whatever reason, certain people wish to remain in secrecy."

"So, tell me of this legend, that we may satisfy your curiosity and then satisfy my grumbling stomach."

"It is best that I show you," Edwin said as he took one more look into the corridor, then after grabbing the small candle from the table, led his friend down several hallways and flights of stairs until they were in what had to be the lowest level of the building. All along the way, Edwin continued to appear paranoid of being detected, as he would periodically stop and listen for any sound that might indicate they were not alone. Finally, he stopped in front of a door that had an ancient looking lock on it. With a final look down the corridor, he reached into his shirt and retrieved a key. He inserted the key into the lock and twisted it. The lock opened and Edwin quickly removed it from the hasp on the door. He pushed the door open.

"Quickly," he said, pulling Walter into the room and closing the door. While the small candle only provided a limited amount of light, it was enough for Walter to see that the room, while only 10 feet square, was full of ancient books and documents. There were also many other items in the room, some appearing to have immense value, not the least of which was a golden breastplate inlaid with three dozen precious stones surrounding a stamped design in the middle of the piece of armor. Despite the aged look of the room, it appeared that it was being well-maintained as there was no dust nor cobwebs present. There was a lone table in the middle of the room and on it sat a large candle which appeared to have been used recently.

"What is all of this?" Walter asked incredulously.

"This, my friend, is history. It is the legend that I have discovered."

"Being that it is behind a locked door, I do not suspect that our presence here would be appreciated by our hosts," Walter said. "I believe we should leave this place, now, before we are discovered."

"Look around you," Edwin urged Walter enthusiastically. "Look around you! Everything in this room goes back hundreds of years. This is all for one family, for one ancient king that at one time ruled from one horizon to the next, and beyond! Look at that breastplate! Surely it was for an especially important man! I could not begin to imagine its value!"

"Okay, I believe you," Walter replied. "Of what importance is that to us? There have been many kings, many rulers since the beginning of time. Some great, some not so great. What makes this king so special that you risk the wrath of those who have welcomed us here and treated us most kindly?"

"The potential reward makes the risk well worthwhile," Edwin replied with a knowing smile. "How many different kingdoms are you aware of that rival our own, kingdoms with which our ancestors have battled over the past two hundred years if not longer? It was only twenty years ago, as my father tells it, that he had to fight off an invasion that nearly took his kingdom." Walter thought for a moment.

"I would say there are at most four kingdoms that would pose any serious threat to our own," he finally answered.

"Imagine one king, one man, ruling not only our kingdom but those others as well," Edwin continued. "There would be no more war, no more threats of invasion, nor more devastation and the needless loss of countless lives. There could be all but endless prosperity and peace."

"And just who would be this king, this overlord, to rule the land?" Walter asked, though he knew the answer.

"Someone who is already entrenched in a royal dynasty," Edwin replied with a mischievous grin, spreading his arms out with his palms facing up.

"You?" Walter asked incredulously. "I know that I need not remind you that you have a father who currently sits on the throne and whose health does not appear to be fading, and you have two older brothers both of whom are eager for the opportunity to inherit their father's throne."

"None of that is of any matter," Edwin replied, shaking his head. "There will come a day that my father's health fails him, and he passes from this existence, and who is to say that my arrogant, condescending brothers do not precede him in death? You have seen Oliver, he is hardly more than a drunkard and glutton, either of which could easily send him to the grave before he sees another year. And Jacob, by his adventurous nature and defiance of danger, scoffs at death daily. One false step and his life could be taken from him in a heartbeat. Death could come to either of them at any time, and there would be no question to it."

Walter understood what his friend was alluding to but did not give voice to his concerns. He did not want his friend to confirm his fears.

"I fail to see what in this room could lead a man to such a destiny," he finally said. "If his line had not died out or been conquered, that ancient king's descendants would remain to this day and be ruling even as we speak. However, we know that to not be the case."

"Do we?" Edwin said. "While his kingdom may have been conquered and his people scattered, how do we know that his line did not endure? How do the people not know that the line continued, though possibly in hiding, waiting for the right time to resurface and once again claim their rightful throne?"

"Where are you going with this?" Walter asked suspiciously. "Either the line has been broken and lost, or it has not. Either way, I seriously doubt that your family's lineage is the same as that of this ancient king."

"Hmm," Edwin grunted with a I know something that you do not know undertone. "Are you sure about that?" He went to reach into his tunic as if to retrieve something when the door to the room burst open and their unauthorized expedition ended abruptly. Edwin immediately dropped his hand.

"Gentlemen," an older man, at least seventy years old with a bald head and full, white beard, addressed the two boys. Behind him were two more men who appeared to be only slightly younger than the first. They were all wearing long flowing black robes with small golden crosses attached to chains around their necks. "I believe we need to have a conversation. You will follow me."

The five men walked in silence back up through the building's corridors and stairways until the older man led them into what appeared to be his personal study room. He walked around a desk and sat in an ornately carved and cushioned wooden chair. The two young boys stood in front of the desk. The other two men stood to either side of the desk. The older man spoke.

"Gentlemen, several weeks ago you were welcomed here with open arms and hearts as you expressed a great desire to enhance your education through study and instruction. As the son of Francis Gallard, king of Nordham, under whose protection this city lies, it was our honor to give you that opportunity. You were shown the areas to which you would have free access, day and night. The lowest level of this building was not one to which you were granted access. Why have you betrayed our trust and entered where you were not permitted?"

"Reverend, truly we did not know that we were not permitted to explore the lower levels," Edwin answered as contritely as possible. "Our curiosity simply overtook us. We beg your forgiveness."

"The lock on the door was not sufficient evidence to indicate that passage was not permitted?" the reverend asked.

"The lock was unsecure," Edwin replied. "It was our intention to secure the lock, but we accidentally leaned on the door, and it opened. Again, we were victims of our curiosity. We shall curtail ourselves in the future."

"Edwin Gallard, I may be an old man, but I am not a fool." He looked at the man to his right. "Sebastian?" The man named Sebastian stepped over to Edwin and before the boy could react, Sebastian reached into one of Edwin's shirt pockets and pulled a key from it. He presented the key to the older man.

"Unsecured, you say," the reverend said as he held the key up for Edwin to see. "I think not. This key has been kept safe in this very room since well before even your father was born. You were seen entering this very private study not long ago, and it was around that same time that I could not find this key. You stole this key with the intention of entering a room for which you had no permission to do so. And, you have just lied to me. Theft and lying are not tolerated here. Therefore, I have no recourse but to send you back to your father and forbid you from entering this place ever again. Perhaps your father will be able to teach you the meaning of honesty and trust, and what it means to be a man. You will leave first thing in the morning."

As the old man finished speaking, as if to place a seal of authentication on his pronouncement, there came an explosion of thunder that rattled the walls. The rumble continued for at least ten seconds. As the sound died away, there was an obvious change in the countenance of Edwin.

"What it means to be a man?" he asked, repeating the reverend's words. "You forget to whom you are speaking, old man. I am Edwin Gallard, son of Francis Gallard, ruler of Nordham, the protector of your city. There is royal blood running through my veins, and I expect to be given the respect that my blood demands. I WILL be given the respect that my blood demands."

"Respect is earned, young Gallard, not demanded," the reverend replied stoically. "You are still a boy, a boy who feels entitled to whatever he desires. We had hoped to teach you otherwise, but our lessons have failed. Now return to your rooms and pack your belongings. At first light, storm or no storm, you will take your leave of this town and never return. You are no longer welcome at the Covenantal Orthodox Church of Christ."

"We shall see about that," Edwin sneered as he and Walter left the priest's study.

"I would say that went about as expected," Walter said as he and Edwin walked back to their room. "I am sure your father will be less than pleased at our unexpected return."

"I do not care," Edwin replied, still fuming. "It will not matter."

"Was satisfying your curiosity worth the humiliation we just endured, because to be quite honest, I saw nothing in that room that was worth us getting kicked out of a church of all places," Walter replied, not hiding the irritation in his voice.

"Oh, it was well worth the harmless chastisement of an old man," Edwin answered. He reached into his tunic and retrieved a piece of paper that had been ripped from a book, an extremely old book, and showed it to Walter. Walter took a moment and looked at the markings on the piece of paper. There was a symbol drawn on the middle of the paper along with a name.

"DuFay?" he said questioningly. "Who is Reginald DuFay?"

Edwin looked at Walter with a wolfish grin. "The legend. And as of this moment, I am his long lost descendent. This place has not seen the last of Edwin Gallard, I promise you that."

Chapter 1

S he moved forward cautiously, the small candle in her hand struggling to provide enough illumination for her to see through the blackness just a few steps ahead. Childhood memories of a dark and enticing playground worked their way from the deep recesses of her mind and with every step she took, the otherwise haunting corridors became a little more familiar. Many years ago, she had abandoned these hallways as a place for fun and adventure as she had grown into a young woman and responsibilities had been thrust upon her. The underground world had become a thing of the past for her and for many, many years she had neither the desire nor reason to return. But things change, and in the matter of only a few days her life and been turned upside down. She now had no choice but to find her way through the black corridors. She had to talk to him. She had to find out for herself.

She paused for a moment as her ears picked up sounds from somewhere deep in the dark. Her heartbeat quickened at the ghostly echoes. She took a few more steps and determined that the echoes were voices. She was close now. Not wanting to be discovered, she set her candle on the ground and eased forward using the fading candlelight and the rough rock walls to guide her on. She turned down a corridor and could see a very faint glow ahead. She continued, and the glow became stronger. The voices also became clearer and with a few more steps the voices were more than just echoes. She could hear the conversation going on. She was close. She peered around a corner and saw King Talbot, Martin, and two guards standing in the corridor. The king was speaking to a fourth person, whose back was to her. She could see that the fourth person's hands were bound behind him.

"I swear by all that is holy, if you do not tell me where she is, I will take your head with my own sword! Now where is my daughter?!"

"I have been down here for two days," the fourth person replied. She immediately recognized Andrew's voice. "How could I possibly know where she is or what has happened to her?"

"It was your plan all along to kidnap her! We already know you have accomplices about the land. Just because you have been behind this door does not mean you had nothing to do with her disappearance. What was your plan? What is it that you want for the return of my daughter?"

"Your majesty," Andrew replied, "if I were a spy, and if it were my intention to kidnap Marie from the beginning, why would I have saved her so many weeks ago and brought her unharmed to you? Have I not had many, many opportunities before now to take her away? You yourself know that after I first arrived, I spent many hours in her company, both here in the castle and riding about your lands. What sense would it make for me to wait until I am imprisoned to have her kidnapped instead of completing such a task myself while I am able to make my own escape?"

"It is not beyond reason that you told your fellow thugs to abduct her if you were imprisoned yourself, and therefore you could use her to get back your freedom."

"But have I demanded to be released? No, I have not because I had nothing to do with her capture! You must look elsewhere for those who took your daughter. I had nothing to do with her abduction. I do not know how I can convince you of this. Perhaps I cannot. But it is the truth. If you release me, I will make every effort to assist you in finding her."

"Release you!?" Talbot roared back. "How big a fool do you think I am? You will remain down here until you rot away or until I decide a more fitting end for a spy and kidnapper." The king turned to Martin.

"Leave one man here and take the other with you. I want every available man searching for my daughter." Talbot turned back to Andrew.

"If any harm comes to my daughter, you will wish you had never been born." With that final statement he turned and disappeared down the corridor along with one of the guards. With a purely evil sneer, Martin loosened Andrew's hands while the second guard stood with the tip of his sword pressing against Andrew's neck.

"Your pet rats await your return," Martin said sarcastically as he shoved Andrew back into the small prison cell. He slammed the door shut, locked it, and headed after the king.

The eavesdropper knew that she somehow had to get around the guard to speak with Andrew. Physically overpowering him was out of the question. She had to find some other way. As she retreated down the corridor a plan began to develop in her mind. It was a risky plan, but she was convinced it would work. It would have to work. She would have to exercise extreme care lest she end up a prisoner, too. She retrieved her candle and worked her way out of the underground maze.

For several hours Andrew played over and over in his mind the conversation with Talbot. The news of Marie's abduction was shocking and surprising. Although he could not be one hundred percent sure at this point, Andrew had a strong suspicion that Martin was involved. Without proof or a convincing argument, it would have been foolish to present such an accusation to the king. As it was, Talbot believed nothing Andrew said. Andrew knew he had to figure a way out of his imprisonment and soon. He had a good feeling of where he might find Marie and time was not his ally. As he contemplated his escape, the small door at the bottom of the cell door, used to ferry food and water in and out of the cell, opened. A tray was slid in, and the small door closed again.

"So, what is for dinner?" Andrew asked the guard lightheartedly.

"For me, roasted chicken. For you, whatever the dogs did not want," the guard growled in reply.

"Sounds delicious," Andrew stated as he retrieved the tray and looked at the food. Although not quite as bad as the guard had described, the food certainly was not the cook's best effort. Tough mutton and stale bread were the meal of the day. Since he was only fed once per day, Andrew did not complain and ate what was given to him. As he finished his food, he heard a loud thump outside his cell, as if someone had fallen. He stood and walked over to the door. There was a small opening, perhaps eight inches wide by three inches tall, in the door five feet off the ground. Andrew peered through the opening, but his line of sight was severely limited. For several minutes there was no movement. Then he was startled when a head of golden blonde hair and sparkling blue eyes moved in front of the door.

"Heather!" Andrew exclaimed, completely surprised. "What are you doing here?"

"I had to come see you," she replied in a desperate tone. "I … I heard that you had been arrested for spying. I did not want to believe it. I could not believe it. I wanted to come down here and ask you myself. I know you would not lie to me. Please tell me the truth, Andrew. Are you a spy?"

"Wait a moment," Andrew replied, ignoring her question. "What happened to the guard?"

"He is but sleeping," Heather answered. "I slipped into the kitchen where the food was being prepared for the guard and yourself. When I was alone, I slipped a concoction into the guard's drink that would make him sleep. He will awaken sometime from now with a terrible headache but that will be the worst of it. Now answer my question, Andrew. Are you a spy?"

"Have I given you any reason to suspect me of being a spy? Have I given anyone any reason to suspect me of being a spy? No, Heather, I am not a spy. I may be a little mysterious at times and guarded about who I am and my past, but I am no spy. Ask your father. He will tell you that I am no spy."

At the mention of her father's name Heather's head lowered and Andrew could tell that something was wrong.

"What is wrong?" Andrew asked concerned, although he feared greatly he knew the answer.

"My father ..." Heather started as she looked up at Andrew with tears in her eyes, "my father is dead."

"Dead?" Andrew repeated. "Your father is dead? When and how did this happen?"

"It was the day after King Talbot had you arrested," Heather answered. "My father's workshop caught on fire and he ... he was inside and was not able to get out." She paused for a moment. "My father was always most cautious about his shop. He had never let a fire get out of control and he never let anything that burned easily close to the fire pit. I do not understand how it happened."

"Is the rest of your family okay?" Andrew asked.

"Yes, nobody else was hurt. The fire happened while my mother and I were at the market and my brother was at the stables. My father had just begun to work when we left."

"Nobody saw what happened?" Andrew asked.

"No. There was nobody around. When we got back home there were some people trying to put the fire out, but they had not been there when it started. When the fire was out, they found ..." She could not finish.

"Curse him!" Andrew shouted as he slammed his fist into the door. "The unbelievable monster! He killed your father!" And then, more sorrowfully, "He killed your father."

"What do you mean?" Heather asked, wiping the tears from her check. "Who killed him?"

Andrew looked at Heather and felt great compassion and sympathy toward her. He could not imagine the hurt that she was feeling. He questioned whether he should tell her of his suspicions, but it was too late. He had to tell her or else lose her trust completely. And he needed her trust.

"Your father told me that three of your former elders died soon after Talbot arrived," Andrew started. "One died in a fire at his home, one was killed after being thrown by a horse, and one drowned in the lake."

"Yes," Heather agreed, "Their deaths were such tragedies. They were great men."

"Did it ever strike anyone as odd that the men who died were three of the four former elders of your village?"

"To my knowledge everyone considered the deaths to be accidents and it was just coincidental that the accidents happened to three elders."

"Did they?" Andrew asked. "Were those truly accidents? Not by your father's account, I can tell you that much. He did not believe that those deaths were accidents and he put forth quite the persuading argument. He was completely convinced that those men were murdered. I believed your father. I believe that the man who killed those elders also killed your father, and for the very same reason."

"Who?" Heather asked eagerly. "Who killed my father?"

Andrew looked her in the eyes and paused momentarily before answering. "I believe it was your king, Talbot. Your father believed it was Talbot who killed the other three men. They were killed because they knew of a secret, of something for which Talbot was searching. Something that was extremely old and especially important, a legend of the land. Talbot was prepared to remove anyone who might stand in his way of obtaining this legend. Your father survived initially because Talbot did not know that he knew of the legend and was seeking it himself. Once Talbot figured out that your father knew of the legend, he had him killed. You yourself said that the circumstances around your father's death were suspect."

"Perhaps, but that does not translate to murder. If I thought for a moment that my father had been killed by another man's hand, there would be revenge taken." Andrew saw something in Heather's eyes that he had never seen, something that was in complete contradiction to her usually soft and harmless demeanor. Heather paused in reflection for a moment then continued. "What is this legend that you speak of? And how did it involve my father?"

Andrew was anxious to find a way out of his cell before someone came back down from the castle, but he indulged Heather with an explanation. "The legend, which I now know is actual history, involves a great king who lived many, many years ago. Six pieces of armament were made in his honor. Through the years his heirs became less and less honorable until the land was invaded and captured by another army. The armor pieces were scattered. Legend has it that when all six pieces are reunited in the hands of the rightful heir of this king, he will lead the land to a level of peace and prosperity that has not been known in hundreds of years. This castle was where the king of legend lived and ruled. Talbot knew of the legend and was seeking the armor. Your father knew of the legend and was seeking the rightful heir. Talbot is not the rightful heir, therefore, he disposes of anyone else who knows of the legend and could contest his claim of descent should he capture all six pieces of armament. The four elders of your village knew of the legend and were seeking clues within these lower levels of the castle. Three of them were killed many years ago. The fourth was protected by keeping clear of the operations of the other three. That is, he was protected until now."

"What changed? How did King Talbot find out of my father's knowledge of the legend?" Heather inquired. Andrew took a big breath before responding. He had to carefully choose his words lest Heather hold him responsible for her father's death.

"The night I had dinner at your home, your father and I conversed for quite a while. I told him of a quest that I was on to discover the rightful heir of the king. It was a quest I began over five years ago, and it was that quest which had led me here. Your father told me that he knew of the legend himself and that he had been searching for clues for many years. That is why he spent so much time scouring the countryside, disappearing for hours at a time. He said that there were clues in these lower levels of the castle but since Talbot had gated the entrance, no one was permitted to come down here. I told your father that I would find a way down here. Your father gave me a key for the gate. Marie and I came down here several nights ago and conducted a search. Somehow Talbot learned of our escapade, I do not know how. Perhaps someone saw us either entering or leaving the gated corridor. Talbot confronted me and asked if your father had given me a key to the lock. I denied any involvement of your father and denied having a key at all. Obviously, Talbot did not believe me. He must have presumed that your father knew of the legend after all and therefore had to be disposed of."

"Why has he not killed you yet? It would only make sense that if he believed my father knew of the legend, he would have assumed you did too and would have killed you."

"Talbot must have some need of me yet. He may suspect that I have one of the pieces of armament and will keep me alive until I tell him where it is."

"You have one of the pieces?" Heather asked.

"Yes, I have the sword. There is a sword, a shield, a breastplate, a helmet, a belt, and boots. I have the sword. Talbot has the shield. I do not know where the breastplate is. The armor cannot fall into the wrong hands! If people follow the wrong leader for the wrong reasons, what peace and freedom there is will quickly fall away."

"Marie came down here with you? If Talbot suspects that you were down here looking for evidence of the legend, and he knows Marie came with you, what will he do with her? Do you think her disappearance has anything to do with your exploration down here?"

"I cannot say for sure. I believe there truly is a spy within your father's administration. I believe he is the one who set me up and convinced Talbot that I am a spy, and he could be the one responsible for Marie's disappearance. I would say this person knows of the legend also. For whatever reason, he has suspected or known that I at least know of the legend and perhaps possess the sword. It was important for him to get me out of the way, and I am certainly out of the way down here. I would be surprised if he did not confront me very soon about what I know. He would also have guessed that Marie knew too much, too, and therefore felt he had to get her out of the way. Perhaps he will use her as leverage against Talbot for some reason. I am greatly concerned that something is brewing outside Talbot's lands and he may soon face an invasion. From whom, I cannot be certain. But there have been too many signs for me to believe otherwise. I must get out of here before Talbot decides to do away with me for good, or the spy comes back and removes me from this existence altogether. I also must get out of here and find Marie. I have a strong feeling of where she is being held captive and I must bring her back before anything bad happens to her."

Heather looked at Andrew for a moment, trying to comprehend everything he had just told her. It was a staggering story with any number of weak points, not the least of which was his claim that her father's death was no accident. She was convinced that Andrew was not lying and believed everything he had said. But that did not mean it was all true. Andrew could be wrong on several fronts. Yet if there was the least chance that her father had indeed been killed, and by Talbot's order, she had to do something. She bent over and retrieved the key to the cell from the unconscious guard's waistband. She cast one last look at Andrew before putting the key in the lock and opening the cell. Andrew stepped out with a great feeling of relief.

"What are you going to do, and how can I help?" she asked.

"First and foremost, I must find Marie. I feel solely responsible for letting her get involved and if anything happens to her, I will hold it against myself for the rest of my days. After that, I do not know. I must deal with this man who set me up as a spy at some point. I must decide what to do about this legend, though my next step is a mystery to me right now. Before anything else, though, I must get out of here. How did you get down here?"

"There is a secret passage that Marie and I found when we were small girls. It is well hidden, and I would venture that few, if any, know of it other than the two of us. We can get out that way and nobody will see us. Follow me."

Heather led the way down the corridor and made several turns into adjacent corridors. They were in an area he and Marie had not ventured into the other night. He was totally lost. They entered a rather plain room that looked no different from any other room. However, in one corner a portion of the wall appeared to be slightly offset. Heather approached this section of the room and after turning sideways, disappeared into a crevice. Andrew stepped forward and inspected the crevice. It was quite well hidden. It would be tough to discern if one did not know it was there. He turned sideways and squeezed his large frame through the opening. After nearly ten minutes of walking Andrew saw a bit of daylight ahead of them. The opening to the passageway was greatly hidden by dense overgrowth on a small hillside in the woods. After ensuring that nobody was around, Heather exited the tunnel and Andrew followed.

"There are two things I must have," Andrew said as he surveyed the surroundings. "I must have my horse, Annon, and I must have the sword that is hidden away in my room. I cannot retrieve either. Can you help me?"

"That will be no problem. Steven works in the stalls. He will be able to bring your horse to you with little suspicion. If anybody questions him, he will simply claim to be exercising the horse. I will also have him help me get your sword. Where is it?"

"It is hidden well-up in the chimney in my room. I doubt that either of you will be able to reach it on your own, so you will have to stand on a stool or something to get it. It is for certain that my room has been searched several times and there is no telling if it will be searched again, therefore you must be extremely careful and watchful. The same goes for Annon. Who knows what eyes are on him and eager to search my belongings in the stall again? Steven must exercise great caution. Nothing can happen to you or him or I will truly never forgive myself. What I am asking of you could put your lives in great danger."

"We will both gladly face the danger if it means avenging the death of my father, one way or another," she replied.

"It may be wise for you, your mother and your brother to leave this land as soon as possible. If your roles are discovered in setting me free the penalty may be great."

"I will discuss that with my mother," Heather answered. "But I doubt she will be willing to leave her home. She is a fighter."

"I can see now where you get that side of you," Andrew said. "But I would feel much better if you and your family were not around here for much longer. I will wait here until you are able to bring Annon and the sword to me."

"It will be after nightfall, but I will return with both. I promise," Heather said confidently, leaving no doubt in Andrew's mind that she would do exactly as she said she would.

They stood there in silence, looking at each other, both feeling a bond forming but unsure as to the extent and nature of the relationship. To Heather, Andrew represented everything she ever wanted in a man. He was honest, loyal, strong, dependable, wise and caring. With but a word she would give him her heart. To Andrew, Heather was a magnificent woman that any sensible man would not hesitate to latch onto and not letting go. He considered himself a sensible man. As much as he longed to give his heart to a woman, though, he felt a hesitance within him. Perhaps it was too soon. Perhaps he just needed more time with her and giving his feelings for her the opportunity to grow. But perhaps it was something else, something that he could not quite define at the moment. Whatever the case, now was neither the time nor place to explore his feelings.

"Go, now," Andrew said as he broke their gaze and pretended to peer into the woods as if to check for danger. "Time is not our friend, and we cannot waste a moment." Without another word Heather simply nodded and disappeared into the dark.

Chapter 2

K ing Talbot, Angus and Malcolm sat around the table in the king's strategy room. Each had a goblet of wine on the table along with a loaf of bread and a cube of cheese. Although the meeting was rather informal, the topic of discussion was quite serious.

"Do you believe what he says to be the truth?" Malcolm asked the king, breaking off a piece of bread.

"He is a shrewd one and very convincing in his arguments," Talbot replied. "However, I will not allow myself to be fooled by well-chosen words. There is much more to Andrew MacLean than he has chosen to reveal to us, be he a spy or otherwise. I am not completely convinced that he participated in the kidnapping of my daughter. We must not forget the men who attacked Marie, Heather and Michelle so many weeks ago, and we must remember that MacLean killed one of them. It is not likely that he would have killed one of his own countrymen. Perhaps those who escaped have returned and completed their original mission. That would be my guess."

"What do you make of his exploration into the lower castle levels?" Angus asked. "Do you believe his story of simple curiosity?"

"Absolutely not," Talbot replied. "He had purpose to be sure. He must know of the DuFay legend. I can think of no other motivation for him venturing down there. For what other reason would he have settled here? He knows of the legend, and he knows that Reginald DuFay reigned from these very foundations hundreds of years ago. What I do not know are his intentions. Does he know who the heir truly is? Does he know that we possess the shield? Does he possess one or more of the other pieces? Is he trying to obtain all six in order to claim the throne of DuFay? We must find answers to these questions and determine his purpose."

"How much do you believe Bergman knew? Is it possible that there are others who know about the legend and could sabotage our goals?" Angus asked.

"I believe Bergman knew everything, even that we have the shield. We should have seen it years ago. He likely told the same to MacLean. Perhaps we should have interrogated Bergman before his 'accident.' Do I believe there are others who know of the DuFay legend? Yes, I do. These families have been on this land for centuries and legends and tales are passed from generation to generation. Such stories die hard. As for how many people know how much, I could not venture a guess. They do not share their legends with outsiders very often."

"What do we do with MacLean?" Angus asked.

"We let him stew for a while in his prison cell," Talbot answered. "We question those whom he spent most of his time around and see if he confided in anybody. And we must search his belongings most thoroughly. If there are any clues regarding the DuFay legend or the location of the other pieces of armor, we must find them. Start your questioning with the Bergman family. Especially the daughter. MacLean has spent much time in her company lately Then question Morecraft and Conner. They have spent a good deal of time with MacLean, also."

"I shall take care of the search and questioning first thing to-morrow," Angus volunteered. "I should have no trouble deter-mining in whom he confided."

"Very well," the king said. "I shall await your report in the afternoon. Malcolm, to you I leave the task of searching the passageways and rooms beneath the castle. Although we have searched those areas most thoroughly in the past, it is possible that MacLean made a discovery of his own. Perhaps he left some sign of his hunting. If he stumbled across anything we missed, I want to know about it."

"As you wish, my lord. I shall conduct the search myself," Malcolm replied.

"What of your daughter?" Angus inquired.

"I have left the search in the hands of Martin," the king answered. "He has dispatched no less than three dozen men to track down her kidnappers and bring her back to me. I would expect to hear from her captors very soon. I am baffled as to why she was abducted. We are not at war with any other country. I can only imagine that she shall be held for a ransom, and we will receive word from her captors soon. I can only hope that is the sole reason for her abduction. I will pay any ransom for her safe return. And then I shall track down her captors and make them wish they had never set foot on our land.

"Gentlemen, we have known all along that the DuFay legend would return home and all we needed do was wait for those pursuing the DuFay Armor. The time is here, and we must do whatever is necessary to secure the throne of DuFay for ourselves. Once the armor is in our hands, there will be no end to our domain. We must pursue our goal with tenacity and determination. All obstacles must be removed. We must prevail. To success!" Talbot said and lifted his goblet of wine. The other two men lifted their goblets and drank to the toast.

Chapter 3

The half-moon hung low in the sky and its eerie glow struggled to penetrate the leafy veil of the forest. An orchestra of frogs and crickets had replaced the symphony of birds and bees, lulling to sleep the inhabitants of the land. A cool, gentle breeze caressed the tops of the trees back and forth, adding its own voice to the nocturnal lullaby. Such a setting should have brought a feeling of peace and serenity to anyone caught in its soothing embrace, however, it could not take away the feelings of anxiety and foreboding that saturated Andrew.

Since Heather had departed to somehow steal Annon away from the stable, Andrew's mind had been consumed with the events of the past few days. First and foremost was the knowledge that his nephew, Donald's son, was now the rightful heir of the DuFay line. It was most ironic that the very thing that had forced him from his homeland could be the thing that required him to return. Andrew did not know if he totally believed the legend that the rightful heir, once reunited with the Armor, would bring peace, prosperity and justice to the land once again. It seemed such a preposterous story, a story that is told to lull children to sleep at night. How could a few pieces of ancient armor make such a difference, and how could people be so gullible as to believe such a legend? However, Andrew knew all too well that people were like sheep, allowing themselves to blindly be led through pastures full of lions and wolves with hardly a second thought. Now he must decide whether to return to

Alexander and bring him into the fray, or let the legend die with Donald. Without his father around, Alexander would be lost and not know what to do.

And then there was the murder of Heather's father. This evil act infuriated Andrew to a degree he had never known. Perhaps Andrew's developing feelings for Heather added to the emotional impact of this tragic event. He had felt a true friendship with Carl Bergman and had come to consider the man a comrade in an ancient mystery. Had it not been for Carl, Andrew might never have made his awesome discovery. Andrew vowed that the man responsible for Carl's death would taste the steel of his sword.

Finally, though no less powerful than everything else, was the kidnapping of Marie. Andrew was convinced that Martin had a hand in her abduction. Whether he did it himself or allowed others to and then covered their tracks, Martin had some responsibility in the matter. Andrew could not think of a solid motive for Martin's actions, though. It was as if Martin had a vendetta against him, a personal animosity with origins unknown to Andrew. If he indeed had some involvement with the kidnapping of Marie, then it would prove that Martin's objectives went farther than getting Andrew out of the way. It would then have something to do with the kingdom, with Talbot. That would mean that Martin was the spy, not Andrew.

Andrew's mind was not so occupied that he did not hear voices floating toward him on the soft evening breeze. He withdrew a few more steps into the shadows of the forest, not knowing if it was Heather returning or if his escape had been discovered and the voices belonged to those in search of him.

Despite all that was flooding his mind, Andrew had become concerned with the time that had elapsed since Heather's departure. She should have returned much sooner than now. Each minute that ticked by added to his anxiety. The voices became louder and as they drew closer, Andrew could tell that they belonged to two men. He was expecting Heather to return alone.

This was not a good sign. He stood as still as the large oak tree behind which he hid.

"This is madness," Andrew heard one voice complain as the riders approached. "He could be anywhere. Finding a man in the middle of the night when he could be hiding anywhere is plain madness."

"Quit your complaining," the other voice replied. "You had nothing better to do this evening than ride around the countryside. At least it is not cold and raining."

"True, but it certainly is not as warm as the tavern, and I doubt there are hot-blooded waitresses waiting behind these trees to bring us mug after mug of ale until we cannot but stumble our way back home."

"You have been drinking too much of that stuff as it is," the second voice countered. "You needed a break in order to clear your head. Besides, I have noticed that growing bulge under your shirt. Missing a night of ale-drinking will do your stomach good."

"Keep your eyes off my stomach, lad, and keep them on the women. Perhaps then you would not go home alone every night," the first voice retorted. "This must be where she said she left him. He has to be around here somewhere."

"Perhaps he tired of waiting and headed on by himself," the second voice replied. "At least we know in which direction he would have headed. We could track him down and would probably have an easier time tomorrow than finding him tonight."

"MacLean!" the first voice called out. "MacLean! Show yourself!" There was no response.

"He must be far away by now," the second voice said. "We are wasting our time. I say we return home, get a good night's sleep and start north in the morning."

"If you were expecting that beautiful blond to come back to you on a night as romantic as this, would you be so quick to leave?"

"Ah, you have a point there. I would venture that he is hiding behind one of these trees with a nice blanket spread out, waiting for the return of such a lovely young lady."

"If you indeed are waiting for Heather to return," the first voice boomed out, "you are going to be sorely disappointed. She will not be returning to meet you this evening."

"Andrew, drag your scraggly carcass out here. I am tired of Lawrence's shouts that could wake the dead."

After having listened to the voices for a minute, Andrew knew that the two strangers were none other than his friends, Lawrence and Louis. However, he was still unsure of their intentions. Not having a sword with him put him at a severe disadvantage should a confrontation erupt. He decided to remain under the cover of the forest but to respond nonetheless.

"Louis is right. That stomach of yours could afford to miss a night or two at the tavern."

"Let me worry about how much I eat and drink. Where are you?"

"Close enough for us to speak and not offend Louis' soft ears."

"Show yourself, MacLean," Louis ordered, ignoring Andrew's remark. "What have you to gain by concealing yourself?"

"Where is Heather?" Andrew asked, remaining in the shadows of the night. "If she has come to any harm, it will not go well with you."

"Harm Heather? What in the world would possess us to harm Heather?" Lawrence asked.

"Again, I will ask you, where is Heather? Why are you here instead of her?" Andrew asked in reply.

"Heather is at home trying to console her mother and brother. Did she not tell you that her father passed away? She also did not wish to be traveling out late at night by herself, therefore she asked us to come and meet you instead," Lawrence replied.

"Forgive me if I appear skeptical," Andrew replied. "What reason did she give you for coming out to meet me?"

"To bring you a friend," Louis responded. "If you do not want your horse then we will be happy to take him back to the stables. Either come out of the woods and get him or stay in your shadows. We are tiring of this game."

"Annon?" Andrew asked in response. He whistled loudly, and his stallion whinnied in answer. However, that did not convince Andrew of the reason for Lawrence and Louis having taken Heather's place in meeting him. "That is the only reason you are here, to bring Annon to me?"

"That, and a little matter of finding Marie and bringing her home," Lawrence answered. That reply brought Andrew out of the woods, although with much caution and care. He scanned the surrounding area to be certain that his two friends were alone then walked over to Annon. His horse was fully saddled and appeared ready for a trip of several days. Unfortunately, he did not see the DuFay sword. This concerned him greatly.

"What did Heather tell you?" Andrew asked as he walked around Annon once again, trying to keep his horse between him and his two friends in the event their intentions were indeed foul.

"She told us why you were imprisoned and that she helped you escape because she did not believe you to be a spy. For the record, we do not believe you to be a spy either. She said that you believed you could find Marie and bring her back home and that she needed to take your horse to you. We have known Marie since she was a young girl and will do anything to get her back. Therefore, we told Heather that we would bring your horse to you and help you bring Marie back to her father."

"That is all she told you?" Andrew asked. "She did not say anything else?"

"That is all she said," Louis confirmed.

"How did all of this come about?" Andrew asked. "Did she seek you out and tell you all of this?"

"We were headed to the tavern for a little evening refreshment when we saw her walking down the way with Annon. This seemed very odd considering your imprisonment, therefore we asked her what she was doing. She was reluctant to say anything at first, but Louis here can be very persistent and persuasive. Few women can resist his charms," Lawrence replied with a slide smirk at Louis.

"It is true," Louis agreed. "Give me five minutes with any young lady around here and I will know who her first kiss was. Then again, most of the time that would be me anyway so it may not be a fair test."

"I do not care about young ladies and their first kiss," Andrew replied. "I care about what has happened this evening and what is going to happen next. You swear here and now that what you have told me is the truth and you have left nothing out?"

"Your paranoia is becoming quite annoying, Andrew, and is bordering on insulting," Lawrence stated with irritation in his voice. "Have either of us ever given you any reason to doubt our honesty or our friendship? In all this time you have been here, in our company, on nearly a daily basis have we ever dealt with you in any way other than as trusting friends?"

For a fleeting moment Andrew recalled the Skills Contest and how Louis had not exactly been an honest competitor. Outside of that experience, Louis had never said or done anything that Andrew considered dishonest or tainted with animosity.

"No. You have always offered most fair friendship," Andrew conceded.

"Then do not doubt us here and now. Come, take your horse, and let us be on our way to rescue a damsel in distress," Lawrence said. "The gratitude of the king will be most immense. Let Louis and I join the elite club of heroes in the village, a club which at this time has you alone as its sole member."

Despite the caution that still tugged at Andrew's conscience, he decided that he would trust his two friends. He took Annon's reins in his hand and leaped up onto the stallion's sturdy back.

"Forgive my doubts, my friends. Imprisonment has left me in a foul mood. Let us take to the road as friends and return as heroes," Andrew said as he nudged Annon in the ribs and tugged the reins gently to the left.

"So, tell us your theory on who took Marie and where she is," Lawrence said as he and Louis fell in beside Andrew "I am most curious to say the least."

"What do you know about Martin?" Andrew asked in reply.

"Martin?" Louis stated. "You believe Martin is involved in this?"

"Not just involved. I believe he plays a major role in Marie's abduction," Andrew answered.

"That is a serious accusation," Louis said. "While I do not consider Martin to be a friend, I certainly have never seen anything in him that would give any indication of him being an abductor of women."

"What evidence do you have of his involvement?" Lawrence asked.

"There are a number of things that have happened in recent weeks that support my suspicion," Andrew replied. "Mostly circumstantial evidence but when you put together enough little pieces, they form a big picture. I have my instincts as well and I trust them more than any physical evidence I could find."

"Evidence aside, what could his motivation be?" Louis asked. "Is it a ransom that he is seeking?"

"I do not believe his motivation is money," Andrew responded. "I believe he has a greater motivation than that."

"What greater motivation is there besides money?" Louis inquired.

"Power. Prestige," Andrew answered. "Some men are capable of terrible things in order to obtain and keep power."

"What do you believe, that he will demand Talbot's throne in return for Marie?" Lawrence asked.

"No, he will not do that," Andrew said. "The people would no sooner follow him than a pig in a field. He would have to be properly granted a position by someone higher in power than him. A position gained through overt blackmail would be a position that held no power."

"Tell us your theory," Lawrence said. "Tell us how Martin plans on using Marie to gain power without using her as a bargaining chip. Tell us where Martin has taken her. Tell us something that makes sense."

"Lawrence, do you remember a couple of weeks ago the day you and I jousted in the field?" Andrew asked.

"Please, Andrew, to the point! I remember very well that day and how I put you in your place," Lawrence answered. "What does this have to do with what we are now discussing?"

"As we were returning to the village, we saw Martin and his men riding north," Andrew continued. "While you elected to visit the blacksmith, I followed Martin. After a time of riding, he and his men planted a sign along the road that warned of a plague to the north and declared the area off-limits. Martin and his men continued riding north. Nobody around here knew of this supposed plague other than Talbot. If there was a deadly plague do you not think that other people around here would know about it? Do you not think that men would be posted to ensure that travelers did not bring that plague into the village? Yet that has not happened. There is nothing preventing someone from that supposedly foul and festered land coming here and infecting us all."

"And this tells you what?" Louis asked.

"It tells me that there is no plague to the north. It tells me that Martin and his men have a reason for not wanting people to venture beyond a certain point in the road to the north. It tells me that there is something there that is important and worth investigating. It tells me that this is where Martin has taken Marie and therefore it is where we must go."

"And just how far might this place be to which we are traveling?" Lawrence asked.

"That, my friends, remains a mystery," Andrew answered. "However, I would not think it more than two days' ride."

"Okay, now that we have the 'where' part resolved, at least in theory, why not continue and convince us of the 'why' part?" Lawrence said. "Let us get back to the whole issue of Martin wanting some kind of power and prestige."

"I am still working on that one," Andrew admitted. "Martin

could have kidnapped her on behalf of someone else, someone who would be in a position to grant him that which he desires."

"It would be possible for him to force her to marry him and then have her father killed," Louis suggested. "She would inherit his throne, which would mean that Martin would come into power along with her."

"Louis, could you see anybody forcing Marie to do anything against her will?" Lawrence asked before Andrew could answer.

"No, I do not think that to be the case," Andrew said. "Martin would have to deal with Angus and Malcolm and while Malcolm might not be a challenge, Angus most certainly would. What of rivals to Talbot? Have there been any murmurings against him as of late? Has there been word of another king desiring to take over Talbot's lands?"

"None of which I have heard," Lawrence responded. "Every king has enemies, of course, but I have not heard of any planned aggression against Talbot."

"Nor would you until it happens in all likelihood," Andrew stated. "An army could be but a day's ride away before you knew of its existence and intentions."

"You said you thought that we would ride perhaps two days before finding out where Martin has taken Marie," Louis said. "Is this what you think that scenario to be? Do you believe we will find an army two days out?"

"It is difficult to say," Andrew answered. "My theories sound reasonable, but they are only theories. I would not be surprised, though, if an army is exactly what we find."

"I still believe that it is Martin's intention to hold Marie for ransom," Louis said. "He knows that Talbot would pay any price to get back his only child and heir to his throne."

"I would hope that it is that simple," Andrew responded. "That scenario would certainly be most favorable for everyone involved."

"What made Talbot suspect you of being a spy in the first

place?" Lawrence asked, changing the subject. "I thought you were held high in his eyes."

"I believe Martin concocted certain events that gave the appearance of me being a spy and convinced the king of just that."

"Again, with Martin?" Louis asked. "What do you have against this man?"

"The question is not what do I have against him, the question is what does he have against me?" Andrew replied. "I have felt his eye of suspicion on me since I first arrived here. He held no trust in me when I told him of the attack on Marie, Heather and Michelle even though our descriptions of the events were identical. I cannot tell you how many times I have caught him out of the corner of my eye, watching my every move from a distance. He brought a man to Talbot, supposedly a spy, who in turn pretended to know me as a fellow spy. I had never seen this man before. Martin presented to Talbot some very frail evidence that linked me to this man. Indeed, the evidence was so thin as to be transparent. The king chose to believe Martin's accusations and evidence and had me thrown in the dungeon. It was some time after that when Talbot visited me and demanded to know where Marie was. Naturally, I was shocked to learn of her abduction. I would venture that in the past two days nobody has seen Martin in the village."

"It is not as though I make it a point to seek him out on a daily basis, therefore I could not testify to his whereabouts," Lawrence stated.

"Then return to the village and see for yourself while I continue on his trail," Andrew retorted.

"No need to get testy," Lawrence replied. "I did not say that I did not believe you. As your friend, I do believe you. Besides, if I were to return to the village I might have to stop by the tavern and have a few mugs of ale out of spite."

"And some cheese," Louis joked.

"Ah yes, that would be nice," Lawrence replied laughing.

"We will ride for a few hours, at least an hour or so beyond the warning sign, and then stop for the night," Andrew informed them, ignoring his friends' attempts at humor. "We will continue on at first light and hopefully within another day or so find Martin and where he is hiding Marie."

"I hope it is that simple," Lawrence replied. "I hope it is that simple."

Chapter 4

With no gentleness of urging, Marie was pulled out of the tent wherein she had been held captive for the past two days and into the fading light of the day. A heavily armed sentry took position in front of her and another behind her and the threesome started marching across the tent-strewn field. As Marie looked around the encampment, she could tell that this was an army in preparation for war. Spears and swords were being sharpened, arrows were being fabricated by the dozens, and men all around her were jousting and practicing their combat maneuvers despite the near end of the day. There was not much conversation to be heard, only the clanging of metal as swords beat against shields and each other. The air was saturated with intensity.

After a few minutes of walking, the lead sentry stopped in front of a large tent, a tent that was markedly different than all the other tents she had thus far seen not only in size but also in decoration. The structure itself had to be thirty feet wide at least and no less deep. The ornate fabrics and pennants fluttering in the wind were bright and new and reminded Marie of her father's own décor. She then understood that this was the tent of a man of power, of authority, and likely of royalty. Two more sentries stood outside the entrance to this royal dwelling and as Marie and her escorts stopped, one of the sentries disappeared into the tent. After about fifteen seconds he re-emerged and waived Marie inside. While her two escorts remained outside, Marie hesitantly stepped forward and into the tent.

The inside of the tent was incredibly lavish. The gold and green color scheme enveloped nearly every aspect of the interior of the tent. There was a beautifully crafted sofa with two matching chairs off to one side of the tent. The furniture's upholstery was a bright gold color with fabulous patterns sewn into the fabric. The cushions on the furniture were made of a silky, dark green material with gold, lacey trim. All around the walls of the tent hung tapestries that sparkled in the glow of the candles spread all about the interior. A sweet aroma filled the air and Marie spotted a small bowl on a stand in a corner of the tent in which something was smoldering. A faint wisp of smoke curled into the air from the bowl. Off to one side of the tenant, opposite the sofa and chairs, was a six-foot long table upon which rested several books and rolled-up parchments. Near the back of the tent was a large and comfortable looking armchair, decorated no less boldly than the rest of the tent's interior. For about sixty seconds Marie was left to herself to take in her surroundings. Then, from behind the large chair at the rear of the tent, hidden by a large veil, a flap opened, and someone entered the room. As he stepped into sight Marie could tell from the way he was dressed and the way that he walked that this was his tent. His clothes were anything but ordinary and his demeanor was anything but common. Without a word yet with his eyes on Marie, he stepped around the chair and lowered himself into its cushiony comfort. Marie kept her eyes on the man, not flinching and not looking away. She would not be intimidated. Finally, the man spoke.

"Young Lady Talbot, my tent is graced by your presence."

"Your tent is graced by my presence?" Marie repeated incredulously. "Do you greet all of your kidnap victims with such compliments?"

"To be truthful, never before have I taken someone from their home against their will, but desperate times call for desperate measures."

"As you know who I am, I believe it only polite that I have your name," Marie said. "And then I would know why you chose to have me abducted. I warn you, if any harm befalls me, you shall regret it dearly."

"As for my name, that shall come in good time. It is of little importance here and now. Regarding your safety, well, that shall be up to you. If you are helpful, you shall be none the worse for wear for the experience."

"I would that I could say the same for you. However, my father shall command a heavy price from you for this audacious act," Marie stated boldly.

"No, I do not believe that will be the case. In fact, it is I who will command a heavy price from him," the man replied.

"I am to be held for ransom?" Marie asked. "Is that what this is all about?"

"A ransom of sort," the man replied. "Not a ransom of money but we shall get to that later. First, I have a few questions I would like to put forth to you. If you are fair with me and cooperate fully, no harm shall befall you. If you prove to be resistive and stubborn, well, it will be a different fate for you."

"I will have you know that I will never say or do anything that will cause any harm to come to my father. You know who I am, that much is true, but I shall tell you nothing that will make easier whatever foul plans you have against my father."

"Actually, the situation is quite the contrary. The information I seek is not such that will aid me in a violent confrontation with your father and his kingdom. The information I seek will hopefully aid in the avoidance of a violent clash. I do not wish to enjoin your father in battle and waste the lives of hundreds of brave warriors. I hope to avoid it."

"That should be easy enough," Marie replied. "Simply release me, withdraw your army and return to your homeland. If no harm has come to me, as you have promised, then my father will not pursue you. You will have avoided conflict."

"No," the man replied as if in thought, "I do not think that is the course to be followed. My intentions follow a different path."

"And just what are those intentions?" Marie asked. "You have stated that your intention is not a monetary ransom. What is it then?"

"I shall answer that question in due time. For now, I have a few questions of my own, and I trust you will be cooperative and answer fully."

"Put your trust where you best see fit. Ask your questions," Marie replied.

"What does the name DuFay mean to you?" the man asked.

"DuFay?" Marie repeated. "I do not know anybody by that name."

"I know you do not know anybody by that name," the man continued. "That was not my question. Please listen carefully because I do not enjoy repeating myself. What does the name DuFay mean to you?"

"That name has no meaning to me," Marie lied in response, looking the man in the eye.

"Are you certain of that?" he asked.

"Please listen carefully because I do not enjoy repeating myself," Marie replied sarcastically. "That name has no meaning to me."

"I was told that you could be very stubborn, and very bold. It is quite a thin line separating the two," the man stated, not allowing himself to get angered by Marie's sarcasm. "You are a feisty one."

"You have not seen my feisty side, not yet," Marie replied.

The man simply gazed at her for a few moments with a slight smirk on his face. He took his time in asking his next question.

"Some time ago a man showed up in your village, a stranger who rescued you from some rather unsavory men with unsavory intentions," he finally said and looked at her as if expecting a response.

"I am sorry, was that a question?" Marie asked innocently.

"His name is MacLean. Andrew MacLean. What do you know about him?"

"I know that he rescued my friends and me and saved our honor if not our lives."

"What else do you know about him?" the man continued.

"Could you be more specific?" Marie asked. "I am better at answering specific questions than just generalities."

"Do you know where he is from?" the man asked.

"No, I do not," Marie answered.

"Do you know why he came to your village?"

"No, I do not," Marie answered.

"Do you know why he has tarried so long in your village?"

"No, I do not," she repeated.

"You certainly know very little about a man around whom you have spent so much time," the man stated knowingly. "What could you possibly have discussed in all the time you spent together if not where he was from, why he came to your village, and why he has stayed all this time?"

Marie's first inclination was to deny having spent much time around Andrew at all, but her instincts told her that this man obviously had eyes in her father's land and to deny spending time with Andrew would be a transparent lie.

"Andrew is a very private person," she replied which was the truth, but the only truth she would allow at this time. "He did not discuss anything about himself, though I gathered that his past had been one of trials and tribulations. He claimed to be simply a man wandering the lands, looking for a place to call home. That was it. The rest of the time he was content to discuss topics such as philosophy, politics, my childhood, things such as those."

"Philosophy and politics," the man repeated. "Yes, Andrew has always been one to express his opinions in those areas."

"You know him?" Marie asked, surprised.

"Indeed, I know him," the man replied. "I have known him for many, many years. In fact, he was in my service for quite a long time before turning on me."

"You are Gallard," Marie said thoughtfully, then immediately regretted her loose tongue.

"Ah, so he has indeed told you something of his past," the king said without any surprise in his voice. "And here I was beginning to trust you," he added sarcastically. "I believe you know much, much more than you are admitting, which is basically nothing." Gallard's voice took an edge to it that was less than friendly. "I highly recommend that you reconsider your uncooperative attitude."

"You wish to know what I know about Andrew? Then I shall tell you what I know about him," Marie said with bravado in her voice, trying to keep from acting intimidated. "He is a brave man with a strong, moral character. He sees right from wrong and good from bad. He is a man who can be trusted and who is loyal. It was not he who turned against you, it was you who turned against him."

"Ah, so he did tell you about the sword after all," Gallard said knowingly.

"Sword?" Marie asked with the most genuine expression of puzzlement she could muster. "Why would he tell me about his sword? Is there something special about it?"

"Young Lady Talbot, do not continue playing games with me and do not insult my intelligence."

"Truly, you have me perplexed," she continued. "I have seen his sword and it appears no more or less special than any other sword. It is quite ordinary and unimpressive to be honest."

"If MacLean told you of our bitter departing, as it is quite obvious that he did, then you know of what sword I speak," Gallard said.

"My lord," Marie said respectfully, not wanting to antagonize Gallard any farther, "MacLean told me that you ordered him to shed the blood of a man guilty of no crime other than failing to bow low enough to you for your satisfaction. You then ordered other men to slay him but after a very intense battle he fought his way to freedom. That is why he fled his home some years back."

"Why did you not admit this earlier?" Gallard asked.

"Because your highness did not ask me if I knew why Andrew had left his homeland. You asked if I knew where he was from, and in truth I do not know. You asked me why he came to our village and in truth I do not know. My best guess would be chance. You asked me why he has tarried in our village so long and to the best of my knowledge he has found the land and people to his liking. He recently acquired some good land and has captured the eye of an especially nice young lady. He has no reason to leave."

"If indeed this is the story MacLean provided to you regarding the commencement of his five-year journey, which I highly doubt is the case, then he is quite the liar. No, I suspect that you are still being less than truthful."

Marie knew that the last thing she should do was admit to knowing anything about the sword. Once Gallard was certain that she had knowledge of it there was no telling to what lengths he would go in order to ascertain just how much she know. She felt that her best defense was to continue pleading ignorance of the sword.

"Perhaps the good king would find it favorable to inform me of the true cause of the chasm between the two of you, if it is not as I was told," she said politely.

"MacLean stole something of great value and importance from me," Gallard replied, "and I will have it back."

"You need an entire army to retrieve this stolen item?" Marie asked. "Andrew is a good fighter to be sure, but I do believe an entire army is a bit much even for him."

"The army is not for him," Gallard said. "It is for your father should he not deliver MacLean and his possessions to me."

"And that is why you have stolen me away. Andrew is the ransom, and I am the security that will ensure my father complies with your demands," Marie said, putting the pieces of the puzzle together.

"If your father does indeed comply with this demand, I will return you to him unharmed and I will remove my army from this land. If he does not comply, well, my men are not training just for show," Gallard said.

"What if Andrew elects to run again instead of allowing himself to be offered to you on a plate?" Marie asked. "From what I know about him, he is not likely to be anxious to see your face again."

"The dungeon in which he is being held holds little room for him to run," Gallard said with a smile on his face.

"Dungeon?" Marie asked, puzzled. "Andrew is in the dungeon?"

"Ah, yes, you would not know about that, would you? I believe you were taken away before word of his imprisonment could reach your ears," Gallard replied. "He was convicted of being a spy and sent to the dungeon beneath the castle. I believe you are familiar with that part of the castle, no? You did have a recent late-night stroll down there after all. Anyway, the evidence against him was quite strong, or so I heard."

"How do you know this?" Marie asked, puzzled.

"I have exceptionally strong eyes and ears," Gallard replied smugly. "They see and hear things from great distances."

"Spies," Marie surmised. "You have spies watching my father."

"Apparently I am not the only one," Gallard responded. "It would appear that your father has captured one certainly not loyal to me."

"Andrew is no spy," Marie said firmly.

"And yet you supposedly know so little about him," Gallard taunted. "I will let you go and rest in comfort this night and consider what you have told me, and what you will tell me, when we resume our chat in the morn. Mark my words, young princess, if you are not true with me tomorrow, I guarantee that this will be the last night of comfort you have for an exceptionally long time. Guard!" A sentry immediately entered the tent. "Take the lady back to her tent and ensure that she stays there through the night. Nobody is to enter the tent without my express orders. Do you understand?"

"Yes, my lord," the man replied and took Marie by the arm. Without another word he led her out of the tent. As soon as they were gone the flap at the rear of the tent opened and Walter, Gallard's military advisor, and Martin walked in.

"Do you believe she truly knows of the sword?" Walter asked the king.

"Yes, I believe she knows of it and much more," Gallard answered.

"Of course she does," Martin said. "That is why she and MacLean searched the bowels of Talbot's castle. That is why she sent a messenger to the professor in Habersham. They have spent much time together and I can assure you none of it has been of a romantic nature. They share a secret, and that secret is the legend of the DuFay Armor."

"We shall summon her again in the morning and determine exactly how much she knows no matter what methods we must employ. We must know where the sword is and if anybody else knows of it," Gallard said.

"I shall return to Talbot and keep my eyes and ears open," Martin said. "My instincts tell me that MacLean has brought no other soul into his confidence."

"And what of the shield?" Gallard asked. "I assume that it remains under Talbot's close watch?"

"That it does, my lord," Martin replied. "He has it well stowed and secured."

"Perhaps the life of his daughter shall loosen his grip on it," the king thought aloud. "After we interrogate the young princess again tomorrow, we shall learn whether or not she knows that her father possesses the shield. Perhaps there is a way we can steal it away from him and avoid a long, violent confrontation. I do not wish to have a chaotic scene like last time when the sword was within our grasp yet slipped away," Gallard said as he stared toward the front of the tent in deep thought. "I will not make the same mistake twice."

"Then by your leave I shall return to my duties as Talbot's Captain of the Guard and learn what more I may about the shield and the sword," Martin said as he bowed to Gallard.

"You have my leave," the king replied. Martin quickly left the tent.

"Do you believe Talbot will relinquish the shield to save his daughter's life?" Walter asked.

"I certainly hope so," Gallard replied. He reached to a large chest on the floor beside the table and opened the heavy wooden lid. After pulling aside a soft fabric covering, he hefted out a magnificent looking piece of body armor and set it on the table. "One way or the other, though, we shall have the sword and the shield and be that much closer to our ultimate goal: The crown of DuFay."

Chapter 5

T he small fires within the encampment twinkled like fireflies in the darkness when viewed from far away. The activity in the camp gradually dwindled as the men returned to their tents for the remainder of the night. From their hidden viewpoint on a knoll five hundred yards from the camp Andrew, Lawrence and Louis quietly watched the serene scene. They had come upon the camp just before dusk and had taken up a position that would keep them hidden yet allow them to watch the camp.

"What shall we do now?" Louis asked. "Perhaps just wander into the camp and start asking where the kidnapped princess is being held?"

"Wander into the camp, yes," Andrew replied, "but asking where Marie is being held will not be necessary. It will not be difficult to determine in which tent she is incarcerated."

"I had my suspicions that you were insane, but this just proves it," Lawrence said to Andrew. "You plan on just walking into the encampment of a well-armed and well-trained army and prying around without raising a hair of suspicion?"

"That is the plan," Andrew answered confidently.

"Yes, I see how this could work," Lawrence said as if deep in thought. "All we need to do is retrieve our cloaks of invisibility from our saddle bags and simply walk into and around the camp. We will not be seen. What an ingenious plan! Louis, did you remember to bring the cloaks of invisibility?"

"I looked for them but could not find them," Louis answered, going along with the joke. "That is the drawback of the cloaks being invisible."

"Then we shall find three more," Andrew said without pause.

"Oh, and you know where to find invisible cloaks?" Louis asked sarcastically.

"I have brought you this far. Do you now doubt me?" Andrew asked him, smiling.

"I only doubt your sanity, not your ability," Louis replied. "So where are these cloaks?"

"Right there," Andrew said, pointing to three men who apparently were leaving the camp to go on patrol.

"I do not suppose they will be giving up those cloaks voluntarily?" Lawrence asked, though he knew the answer.

"I believe it is time to see just how much you have learned from your training," Andrew replied with a wide grin as he strolled over to Annon and jumped onto the horse's back. "We shall wait by the road and when the men approach, we will ask them for their clothes. If they have any intelligence and wish to save their lives, they will do as we bid. If they do not, we at least gave them a choice in the matter."

Lawrence and Louis gave each other a questioning look but without a word mounted their horses and followed Andrew.

Gallard's patrol followed the main road out of the camp and into the wilderness. Being well trained they spoke little, instead keeping their eyes and ears alert for anything that might threaten the secrecy of the army. While this was a path these three men had followed any number of times, they did not allow boredom to creep into their routine. Being chosen for patrol duty was an honor, for the safety of the men in the camp could very well be held in the hands of the men on patrol. The road in front of them meandered across a grassy plain before snaking its way through a very sparse forested area. A few large boulders and clumps of trees bordered the road on either side. It was truly the unwary traveler that the patrol was meant to be on watch for, anyone who might discover the existence of the army by accident and report its presence to Talbot. A chorus of crickets and frogs sung to the men as they slowly proceeded down the road.

The patrol was well out of sight of the army when a lone figure on a horse appeared in the road fifty yards before them. The three men on patrol slowly approached the figure. Each man held his horse's reins in one hand while the other gripped his sword.

"You must turn back, friend," one of the men said with an air of authority. "It is too dangerous to go any farther. There is a deadly plague in this land. If you proceed down this road, it will certainly be at the risk of your life."

"Your warning is appreciated," Andrew replied. "However, I have most urgent business down this road, and I must take the risk. If you will pardon me, I shall be on my way." He nudged his horse in its ribs, and it started to move forward.

"I am afraid we cannot allow that," the man who had spoken before informed the rider. "You must realize that it is for your own good. We are under direct orders from King Talbot to not allow anybody to pass any farther along this road. You must turn back and find another route to your destination."

"As I said before, my business is urgent and there is no time for me to find another route. I appreciate the concern of your king, however, I must take responsibility for my own life." And then Andrew added as a warning, "Just as you must take responsibility for your own life."

"It is not my life that is in jeopardy this evening, stranger," the man replied. He was startled to hear a voice answer from the road behind him.

"That may be a bit of a presumptuous statement," Lawrence said as he and Louis blocked the road behind the patrol. While the lead patrolman kept his eyes on Andrew in front of him, his two companions whirled around to face Lawrence and Louis.

"We can do this the easy way or the difficult way," Andrew addressed the man in front of him. "The easy way is that the three of you dismount and disrobe. We shall bind and gag the three of you, go about our business, and then when we return, we shall give your clothes back to you and allow you to accompany us back to our village. No harm will come to you. The hard way is that you resist, we fight, we take your clothes anyway, and one or more of you will likely lose his life in the process. I beg of you, choose the easy way."

The man in the lead of the patrol drew his sword and pointed it at Andrew. "You shall not pass, you shall not take our clothes, and you shall never return to your village."

"You had to choose the hard way," Andrew said as he, too, drew his sword. "I was afraid of that." With a hard kick to his ribs Annon reared up and leaped forward toward the horse and rider in front of him, intent on running them over if they did not move. The rider yanked his horse's reins to the left while digging his heals into the horses' sides, prompting the beast to bolt forward and to the left. As the horses passed each other the swords of the two men met with ferocious force and nearly knocked both men to the ground. They immediately turned their horses for another pass. Being well trained, both horses knew instinctively what to do and after quick turns charged forward again. The stillness of the night air was once again shattered by the clanging of metal on metal as the swords bounced off each other. Lawrence and Louis sat firmly on their horses with swords drawn, looking as menacing as they could. The two men in front of them also sat with swords drawn but made no move to attack. Their horses fidgeted nervously, ready to engage but obediently waiting for their masters' orders. Neither side desired to initiate an attack, apparently waiting to see the outcome of the duel between their leaders.

The battle between the two men raged on and eventually Gallard's man was knocked from his horse. He quickly jumped to his feet and faced Andrew, ready for another onslaught. Andrew dismounted and carefully approached his adversary. When less than ten feet separated the warriors, they engaged in a fast and furious fight. Their swords clashed together again and again. Punches were thrown to heads and midsections when the men got too close to each other. One man would make advances and the other would fight him off, then the roles were reversed. The battle raged on for ten long minutes. It was obvious that the men were equals when it came to fighting. It was as if they could somehow anticipate the other's next move and make their own move to thwart whatever attack came their way. The men pulled back for a moment, both gathering his thoughts and analyzing the battle thus far, searching for a weakness in his opponent's defense, looking for a way to end the fight. While Lawrence and Louis had watched the battle with much admiration, their opponents had never moved their well-trained eyes from them. Finally, Lawrence broke the silence.

"MacLean, as it seems that you are unable to dispatch of your opponent on your own, Louis and I would be happy to lend you a hand after disposing of these two gentlemen blocking our way."

"Tend to your own concerns," Andrew replied without taking his eyes off the man in front of him. "I shall take care of my own business soon enough."

"MacLean?" his opponent said with a tone of recognition. "Your name is MacLean?"

"That it is," Andrew replied. "Andrew MacLean. Do you feel better knowing the name of the man who shall best you in battle this night?"

"It is not possible," the man said, slightly bewildered. "I knew an Andrew MacLean once, but he was killed in battle more than five years ago. Yet there is so much familiarity in your voice and fighting technique it is as if you are his ghost."

"I am no ghost," Andrew replied, "I can assure you of that." As he spoke with the man, Andrew's memory tugged at his thoughts. He could not help but feel something familiar about this man, too.

"What region do you hail from?" the man asked.

"It has been many years since I was last there, but I once called Nordham my home," Andrew replied. His fighting instincts begged him to cease conversation and continue the melee, but he had to find out who this man was who seemed to know him.

"You had a brother, did you not?" the man asked.

"I had a brother," Andrew confirmed. "He was killed in battle the day I left my homeland."

"It truly is you," the man said as he lowered his sword. "I do not know how it can be, but it is. Andrew, do you not recognize me?"

Andrew looked at the stranger as he, too, lowered his guard a bit, but the darkness of the night made it difficult to see the man's face. He took a step forward, but his body remained tense, ready for battle. "There is something familiar about you, that much I will admit, but the darkness hides your face too well. Tell me your name, stranger."

"Andrew, it is I, your brother Donald!"

Suddenly the veil was lifted, and Andrew knew that it was indeed his brother standing in front of him. How this could be Andrew did not know, for he had seen Donald killed on the battlefield. But there was no doubt in his mind that the man before him was most certainly his brother.

"Donald?" Andrew asked, bewildered. "How can it be you? I saw you killed on the battlefield that day. I saw that man stab you in the back and I saw you fall to the ground."

"Yes, I was stabbed in the back, and I did fall but the blow was not fatal. It took several weeks for me to recover from the injury but as you can see, I did recover." Donald approached Andrew until they were but two steps apart. "I was told that you were killed as well."

"Not that my life was not threatened closely but I managed to escape serious injury." Andrew took another step forward and looked closely at Donald. So much had happened in the past five years that he did not know where to start or what to say. "I cannot believe that you are alive." He stepped forward and embraced his brother who returned the gesture. "My brother," he said as he fought back tears. After several seconds, the men parted.

"Where have you been these past five years?" Donald asked. "If you were not killed, why did you not return home? Why did you leave?"

"It is a long story," Andrew replied, "and I am afraid we do not have much time. Is that Gallard's army encamped in the field?"

"None other," Donald answered.

"What is his purpose? Is he planning an attack on Talbot?"

"That is the word. Gallard believes that Talbot has been ordering assassinations of some of Gallard's nobles in order to weaken Gallard's kingdom in front of an all-out assault. Therefore, the king has ordered a pre-emptive strike against Talbot."

"A plausible story, though I doubt its sincerity. I know that Talbot is capable of murder, but I did not know that he would stretch his hand so far," Andrew said.

"You know Talbot?" Donald asked, surprised.

"I have been living in his village for several months," Andrew admitted. "I have spoken with him on numerous occasions. Yes, I know Talbot."

At this confession Donald took a step back. "What is your purpose this evening, Andrew?" he asked.

Andrew looked past Donald to Lawrence and Louis. "If the two of you are finished exchanging pleasantries with those two men haul your mangy carcasses over here. It is time that you learned why we are here."

"I thought the purpose was quite clear, to rescue a young maiden," Lawrence retorted as he and Louis dismounted. Donald's companions looked at him questioningly and he gave them a short nod, indicating that everything was okay. They, too, dismounted and joined the circle.

"The story goes beyond that," Andrew replied. "Let me tell you why she was abducted to begin with." With those words

Andrew launched into a story of legend and betrayal, of greed and corruption, and the events that had consumed the past five years of his life.

52

Chapter 6

As Andrew finished his tale the men around him sat in silence, filled with questions, doubts, and suspicions. He expected nothing less considering the intricate and complicated nature of the issues at hand. Without any physical evidence, namely the DuFay sword which apparently was still hidden in Talbot's castle, convincing the others of the truthfulness of his tale was difficult at best and impossible at worst. However, he knew that the many years growing up with Donald would certainly vouch for his integrity with his brother. He did not feel as confident when it came to Lawrence and Louis, though. Despite the many hours he had spent in their company, the deepest of trust can take years to develop. They had spent many, many years under the influence of Talbot and had no reason to doubt his integrity and honesty. Going against him was his many years in Gallard's service. He was definitely caught in the middle and did not know how the situation would turn, but he knew that he needed Donald, Lawrence and Louis in order to rescue Marie and possibly thwart a war. He was afraid that even if Donald believed him and went along with him, the two men with Donald could prove to be a big obstacle.

"So," Donald said, breaking the silence that had engulfed the group after Andrew had finished his tale. "You believe that I am the heir of a king who ruled hundreds of years ago. And to think that the last time I spoke with you, you were quite sane."

"I firmly believe that what I have told you is the truth," Andrew replied. "The pieces of the puzzle all fit together. What better proof do you need than the very emblem burned into your forearm?"

"Andrew, there is nothing royal about this scar," Donald argued. "It is something that has been passed on in my family from one generation to the next. It is tradition."

"Have you never thought why?" Andrew countered. "What other families do you know of whose eldest son is branded in this way? I have traveled through many countries and seen many peoples but have never seen anything like this."

"That proves nothing," Donald argued. "It is simply a family tradition that started long ago. Father informed me that the MacLean clan was once a powerful clan, long ago, and this was our way of identifying with our history. It is not suspicious that no other family with whom you have had personal contact practices a similar ritual. Besides, if this brand is given to the eldest son alone, why was the brand given to you after it was given to me?"

"As for that I can but offer a theory," Andrew replied. "I am a bit older than you are. Since your father formally adopted me into his family and made me his legal son, perhaps he felt that it was only proper that as his eldest son, I receive the mark."

"I am sorry, Andrew, but this is beyond believable. There would have to be much evidence to back your story and you have none," Donald stated.

"There is evidence, Donald. It is in the deepest parts of Talbot's castle. I intend to return there not only to retrieve my sword but to bring out this evidence that Talbot has successfully hidden for many, many years," Andrew replied.

"This man may be your brother, but he is not your blood," one of Donald's companions spoke up. "You cannot put your trust in him. He is nothing more than a spy of Talbot. Talbot has learned of our army and our impending attack, and he has sent these three men to determine our strength. Rescuing his daughter is probably of secondary importance. That man has cruelly assassinated several of our prominent leaders. I doubt that sacrificing his daughter would cause him to think twice."

"Think about it for a moment, Marcus," Donald replied. "If they were spies, why did they reveal themselves to us? They could have let us continue on our patrol and we would have never known of their presence."

"It was their intention to kill us and steal our clothes so they could sneak into our camp," Marcus replied. "They said so themselves, do you not remember? Do not be so enthralled with discovering that your brother is alive and being reunited that you throw wisdom to the wind."

"Do not concern yourself with my wisdom," Donald spat back. "I have not risen to my position by virtue of stupidity."

"Donald, why would Gallard tell you that I was slain in battle when it is rather obvious that I was not?" Andrew asked. "I will tell you why. He knew that he could not tell you the truth. He knew that you would not believe that I simply walked away or turned my back on my fellow countrymen for no reason, especially after having obtained the position I had back then. And you would not have believed that I was capable of defying the king and turning on him for some mere material possession. His only two options were to tell you the truth or tell you that I was killed in battle. He knew that I would never return and would venture as far from home as I could to avoid him, and therefore your chances of ever seeing me again would be few at best. His very lie about my fate should tell you that he had something to hide, and if he was not concealing this truth that I have relayed to you then what was he concealing?"

"I do not know," Donald said, his thoughts whirling through his head.

"That is quite a fantastic story, Andrew," Lawrence said, trying to ease the rising tension. "Although I must admit, I knew there was something deeper to you than you had let on. After all, there was never any doubt that Marie was not spending all of that time around you on account of your looks and personality."

"It is good that you can joke about this, Lawrence, but I am greatly concerned with this story," Louis countered. "Andrew has no less than accused Talbot of murder and conspiracy, and murder of your own father. In all the years we have been in the service of Talbot, not once have I ever seen or heard anything that would cast any doubt on his honesty and integrity."

"Nor I, I must admit," Lawrence answered. "Andrew, how do you expect us to believe these things that you are saying? We have known King Talbot nearly all our lives. He has always been fair and just. The land has prospered under him, and the people are happy. What you say is more than difficult to believe."

"I realize that, my friend. Perhaps if I had time to retrieve the sword it would lend credence to my confession. However, we do not have time for that. Does not the abduction of Marie convince you? Does not what she and I found in the bowels of the castle convince you? Does not the untimely death of Carl Bergman convince you?" Andrew replied.

"All of that is circumstantial," Lawrence replied, playing the Devil's advocate. "Marie's abduction could very well be nothing more than Gallard trying to weaken Talbot in advance of a simple invasion to take over his kingdom. We do not even know if Gallard is truly responsible for the kidnapping of Marie, or that Martin is the one who consummated the act. As for what you found in the castle, we have only your word and interpretation of what you found. And then as for the death of Bergman, while most unfortunate and sad, accidents do happen and people die. My father's death was an accident, of that I have no reason to doubt. Then as for the sword, we could not know by simply looking at it that it was anything special."

"Gallard is indeed responsible for the abduction of this young lady," Donald said. "I have seen her. I do not know this Martin person you have described, although on two separate occasions I caught a brief glimpse of men I do not know in Talbot's company. It is quite possible that this Martin intentionally remains out of sight of anyone other than Gallard and his closest advisors. That would make sense if he were a spy."

"So Gallard had Marie kidnapped," Louis said. "That does not prove the rest of your story."

"No, it does not on its own," Andrew admitted. "But not long ago, when I was suspicious of your appearance in the stead of Heather, I recall Lawrence asking me if the two of you had said or done anything in the time we have known each other that should cause me to doubt your motives, to doubt your honesty, or to doubt your friendship. Now I ask you the same question: Have I ever done anything that would lead you to doubt my integrity or my friendship? What I have told you is true, my friends."

Lawrence and Louis looked at each other. They knew Andrew had a point. In the months they had known him he had proven to have the most integrity and honesty of any man they had previously known. His deep confidence in himself and what he said was very convincing.

"No, you have never said or done anything that lacked total truthfulness," Lawrence admitted. "In fact, it has always been a bit annoying if nothing else, would you not agree, Louis?"

"I heartily agree with that," Louis answered. "Your integrity has been beyond question," he said to Andrew.

"Then do not turn a deaf ear to what I am saying right now," Andrew pleaded.

"I will go this far," Lawrence said. "We shall rescue Marie and listen to what she has to say in the matter. If her story supports yours, then we shall believe you without a doubt. If her story does not support yours, well, I am afraid that you will not be returning to retrieve this sword you claim to have hidden."

"Fair enough," Andrew answered. "However, there are a few theories I have not shared with Marie due to their sensitive nature and I would hope that you would respect my judgment in these matters. I have not told her that her father possesses the shield. I have not told her that her father may very well have murdered the former elders of the village. And I have not told her that I believe her father is intent on possessing the DuFay Armor in order to claim lordship of not only his land but every other known land in this region."

"Pray tell, what HAVE you told her?" Louis asked.

"She knows where and how I obtained the sword. She has seen it with her own eyes," Andrew answered. "She knows of the legend and that Donald is the heir, although at the time of this discovery I believed he was dead and shared that with her. She knows that her father's castle was once the dwelling place of Reginald DuFay. She may have other suspicions concerning me and my quest but if so, she has kept them to herself. There will be a time when she will learn the entire truth, but I wish to put off that day as long as I can."

"Then it is agreed," Lawrence said. "We shall leave it to you to explain those theories to her in due time."

"What do you propose to do?" Donald asked.

"My only concern here and now is rescuing Marie and returning her to her father," Andrew answered. "After that goal is accomplished, I will have to determine a way to convince Talbot I am not a spy, retrieve my sword, and somehow prevent an all-out war."

"And somehow convince him and Gallard that Donald here is the heir of the DuFay line, and they should relinquish their kingdoms to him," Lawrence added. "That should be a simple task."

"I will assist you in rescuing Marie," Louis said, "but that is as far as I am willing to go. When we return home, I will report to the king and urge him to prepare for war. My allegiance is to King Richard, not to you or to any supposed heir of a man who has been dead for hundreds of years."

"That is all I ask at this time," Andrew replied. "Rescuing Marie is our one and only goal this evening." He turned to face his brother. "So, what is your final decision, my brother?"

Donald looked intently at Andrew as indecision raced through his mind. He had always been able to trust his brother without hesitation, yet this story was complex and confusing. There had to be some measure of corroboration to Andrew's tale before he could believe it totally, though. His loyalty to King Gallard was beyond question. After having spent nearly twenty-five years in the king's service with not the smallest bit of evidence of sinister intentions on Gallard's part, he could not throw his allegiance away in a heartbeat to follow a brother whom he had not seen in five years. There had to be a way of proving Andrew's story, or at least finding additional support for it, without breaking his loyalty to Gallard.

"This is what I shall do," he finally answered. "I shall pay a visit to this young lady whom Gallard has taken prisoner. If her story matches yours then I shall believe you and help free her. If her story does not match yours then I will at least give you the opportunity to turn your back and run away as you did over five years ago."

"You cannot seriously be considering this?" Marcus asked incredulously. "We need to take these men into custody as spies and take them to the king."

"You may try," Lawrence said as he took a couple of steps back and grasped the hilt of his sword. Louis did likewise. Donald's two companions did the same.

"Marcus, Sean, stand down!" Donald ordered. "There will be no blood-shed, not at this time."

"You are about to commit treason!" Sean spat at Donald. "We will not stand idly by while you betray our king!"

"Listen to me!" Donald replied, taking several steps forward to separate his men from Lawrence and Louis. "I will go down and question this woman. If she proves Andrew false, then I shall return with a squad of men and take these men into custody. If she proves Andrew true, then that will show us Gallard cannot be trusted."

"I trust Gallard," Marcus replied. "I do not care about the lies your brother has told you and I do not care what a prisoner of the king's has to say. If you assist them in freeing the prisoner, you will be guilty of treason. We must take them to Gallard and let him determine their fate, which I am sure will be one fitting for spies."

"Do not do this, Marcus," Donald warned. "You will not be committing treason by allowing me the opportunity to go down and speak with Marie."

"No, we will be giving you the opportunity to return with a whole regiment of your men to take us into custody," Louis stated, his grip on his sword becoming firmer. "I for one do not find that an acceptable strategy."

"You will be taken into custody, or you will die," Sean retorted, drawing his sword. "Donald, you must decide where your loyalty lies. You are either with your king or you are against him."

Marcus drew his sword, too, which in turn prompted Lawrence and Louis to draw theirs and take fighting positions.

"Lawrence! Louis! Hold!" Andrew yelled.

"Andrew, we have wasted enough time with talk," Lawrence replied. "The longer Marie is in custody the more likely she will come to harm. We have given these men a fair chance. If we must fight our way through them then we will do so. I am through with talk."

Andrew could not have felt more helpless. Not only was he not able to completely convince his brother of his story, he could not convince Lawrence and Louis either. And now that the men seemed intent on fighting, there was nothing he could do to prevent a melee. He had been afraid of this very scenario and now it was unfolding in front of him. He did not want to fight Donald again, nor did he want to fight his friends. Bloodshed was the last thing he wanted this evening, but it looked unavoidable. He looked at Donald, but Donald looked just as much at a loss as Andrew.

"Do not kill them," Andrew finally said, trying to control the battle that would not be put off. "Disarm them, nothing more."

"We shall see about that," Louis said. In unison he and Lawrence bolted forward, covering the few yards between them and their adversaries in a heartbeat. The metal-on-metal clash echoed through the forest as Marcus and Sean stepped forward and swung their swords to meet those of Lawrence and Louis. The fighting was intense, but brief. In less than two minutes Marcus and Sean were on the ground with the tips of Louis and Lawrence's swords at their necks.

"Disarmed and alive," Lawrence said with a smirk, his breathing only slightly heavier than normal from the short workout.

"And here I did not believe that you had been paying attention during your training all these past weeks," Andrew said, relieved that no blood had been shed.

"Now that you have my two men at bay, what is your intention?" Donald asked, still very unsure of what was going to happen.

"This is the plan," Andrew answered. "Lawrence and I will exchange clothes with these two men. We will accompany you through the camp and to Marie's tent. You will proceed with your questioning of her. Once she has convinced you of my story, at least in so much as she knows of it, you will allow Lawrence and me to leave with her. Whether you come with us or not will be your decision."

"What about Marcus and Sean?" Donald asked.

"We will bind and gag them, and Louis will stay here and keep watch."

"Donald," Marcus said, wary of Lawrence's sword at his neck. "You cannot do this. This is treason!"

"When Lawrence and I return with Marie we will take your friends with us as far as a day's ride. We will then release them," Andrew finished.

"They will return and let Gallard know Talbot is aware of his army," Lawrence warned Andrew. "That will ruin any chance of Talbot launching a surprise attack against him."

"We will not murder them," Andrew replied. "And we will not take them to Talbot to be hung as spies."

"Andrew," Louis said, "they are the enemy. If they captured us, they would not hesitate one breath to take us to their king and they would not give a second thought as to our end. It is not for us to decide what fate King Talbot should hand to his enemies. Our duty is to protect our land, our families, and our king. Turning these men loose will accomplish none of that."

Andrew pondered the dilemma for a few moments. He knew that taking the men to Talbot would indeed be their end and although he was convinced that Donald believed him to a certain degree, he knew that his brother would not allow his two comrades to be taken away to certain death. He also knew that Lawrence and Louis would not allow the men to be released so they could warn their king. Somehow, they had to keep the men in custody without taking them to Talbot.

"We shall hide the men," Andrew proposed.

"And where exactly do you wish to hide them?" Lawrence inquired.

"By now my escape from Talbot's prison has been discovered. There is no longer any reason for the king to venture into the bowels of the castle. When you tell him of Gallard's approaching army his attention, and that of every person in his administration, will certainly be focused thereon. We shall place them in Talbot's prison. The men will be well hidden and safe, for the time being."

"You do not wish to give custody of my men to your king, yet you wish to imprison them in his prison?" Donald asked incredulously. "Beneath his very feet?"

"You are insane!" Sean spat at Andrew.

"I understand all too well how unpleasant the thought of imprisonment is," Andrew replied. "But the thought of death is much less pleasant. Those are your only options. Temporary imprisonment, or permanent death. At least with imprisonment there is always a chance you may escape and become free again. Once you are dead, though, there is no coming back."

"Before settling on this issue, there is one nearer at hand to be decided first," Donald said. "We must first determine just how much truth is in your story and that shall be decided once I have spoken with your lady friend. Only then will we know in which direction our futures lay." Donald turned to his two friends. "Marcus, Sean, I know you do not agree with this, but there are mysteries here which prudence dictates we investigate. Should Andrew's tale turn out to be false, I shall have him and Lawrence taken into custody and I shall return with a dozen men and free you. Should Andrew's tale turn out to be true, then I can no longer fight for Gallard. We will return and follow Andrew's plan." He turned back to Andrew. "You DO have a plan that extends beyond locking my men up, do you not?"

"I am working on it," Andrew said with a sly grin.

"I would urge you to stay here and continue formulating your plan," Donald replied. "Despite your absence of five years and the dark of night, it is not entirely beyond reason that your face may be recognized. That would effectively destroy your mission."

"What manner of fools do you take us for?" Lawrence asked. "Do you believe for one moment that we will allow you to return to your king and bring a legion back to cut us down?"

"He is right," Louis chimed in. "Andrew, despite what trust you have in your brother, Lawrence and I cannot share that trust. He must not go alone."

"I have to go," Andrew replied. "I cannot but feel responsible for her being kidnapped. It is my responsibility to free her. And even that aside, if we are discovered I would stand a decent chance of remaining alive since Gallard undoubtedly wants the sword. If you or Lawrence went instead of me and were discovered, you would not live to see dawn."

"Do not doubt our ability to remain in the shadows and avoid discovery," Lawrence said to Andrew. "Not all of our training over the years has been hand-to-hand combat. Both of us have the skills to keep our presence and identity secrets. One of us should take your place and go down to the camp. That way we will be certain that neither Donald nor you have any tricks up your sleeve."

"Let us not waste more time arguing this point," Andrew replied, conceding the argument reluctantly but necessarily. "Lawrence, you will go instead of me. I will remain here watching over these two men. Donald will locate Marie and verify my story, at least to the extent of what Marie knows. If you can sneak her away, then do so and bring her back here. If the risk is too great, leave her and come back to this spot. We will then devise another plan for rescuing her. Is that acceptable to everyone?"

"I can live with that plan," Louis answered.

"I find it agreeable as well," Lawrence concurred.

"Donald?" Andrew asked, turning to his brother.

"If Lawrence and Louis can contain themselves and follow my lead then I am certain our actions will remain in secret," Donald replied.

"Then it is settled," Andrew said firmly. "Lawrence, Louis, I believe you have a wardrobe change waiting for you."

"That we do," Lawrence replied, looking back to the men on the ground in front of him. "Marcus, Sean, do not take this the wrong way, but I believe it is time you took your clothes off."

With anger and contempt shooting from their eyes, Marcus and Sean hesitated only a few seconds before reaching down to commence disrobing.

Chapter 7

L awrence, Louis and Donald approached the outskirts of the camp. There had been little if any conversation between them as they nudged their horses down the road.

"So, we are to just ride into camp while avoiding detection, interrogate a kidnapped princess who is certain to be well guarded, and then escape from an encampment of thousands of trained soldiers without being seen while this princess rides along with one of us in her flowing dress?" Lawrence stated dubiously. "Does that about sum it up?"

"Aye, that pretty much covers it," Donald replied. "As long as you can maintain your composure, I am confident we can accomplish our mission."

"Maintain my composure?" Lawrence replied a little defensively. "Now what exactly do you mean by that?"

"I do not mean that as an insult," Donald answered. "You are a passionate man, I can see that. Passionate people tend to act more on their passions and less on their intellect from time to time. This young lady is a friend of yours I take it. Your passion for her safety may move you to actions that your intellect would otherwise give you pause, and in doing so may compromise our mission and safety. If you are able to keep your passion in check and maintain your composure, our chances of success are much, much better."

"Now there is no doubt in my mind that you and Andrew are brothers," Lawrence said with a touch of sarcasm. "What you just said sounds exactly like something he would say."

"Now it is you who insults me," Donald replied lightly. "Andrew was never the wiser of the two of us."

"Again, something Andrew would say," Lawrence stated shaking his head. "How could anybody stand you two growing up?"

"I tend to think of myself as somewhat passionate as well," Louis grumbled from behind Donald and Lawrence.

"We are approaching the outer sentry post," Donald said in a hushed voice, changing the subject and becoming serious. "Our first test."

"Wonderful," Lawrence replied as he spotted the two sentries posted along the road. "Could we not have simply chosen a dark, unguarded side of the camp and stole into the camp unseen? This is an unnecessary risk. We should stay in the shadows."

"The shadows are being watched, my friend," Donald replied. "Gallard keeps unseen guards around the perimeter of the camp, and nobody knows where those men are stationed. We would surely be discovered if we attempted to sneak into camp. No, the shadows are not for us. We have to stay in the light to avoid being seen."

The trio approached the sentries and one of the men on foot stepped forward, sword in hand. The second sentry stood off to the side, close to his horse, in the event that those who approached were not friendly and he was forced to gallop into camp and raise the alarm. The man with the sword raised his left hand, motioning the men on horseback to stop.

"Who goes there?" the sentry demanded.

"I am Donald MacLean," Donald answered. "We are returning from patrol. Let us pass."

"And you?" the sentry asked, turning his attention to Lawrence. "What is your name?"

"Marcus Fordham," Lawrence lied without pause.

"You there, in the rear, what is your name?" he asked Louis.

"Sean Lancaster," Louis replied.

"Wait here," the man answered. He walked over to a small tent and retrieved a booklet. He then moved several steps over next to a post in the ground that held a lantern about seven feet off the ground. He flipped through a few pages, then paused and read something scribbled in the booklet. After a few seconds he looked over to his partner and gave a brief nod of his head. His partner hoisted himself onto the back of the horse.

"You are returning from patrol," the sentry stated, turning back to Donald. "The logbook states that a patrol passed this point hardly two hours ago. That seems a bit shorter of a patrol than usual, would you not agree?"

"Patrols vary in length of time and in distance," Donald replied. "This throws off any spies that may be watching us. Do you wish a spy to be able to know exactly when and where our patrols are at all times?"

The sentry looked at the three riders and despite a nagging suspicion, he waived them on. "You may continue," he instructed and stepped back off the road.

The trio continued down the road and crossed an old wooden bridge that spanned a small but fast-running river. The first tents of the main camp were still a couple of hundred yards in the distance. They were long out of earshot of the guard post before any of them spoke, and it was Donald who broke the silence.

"You see? Not a problem," he said with a slight smile.

"Now that the first hurdle has been cleared, what next?" Lawrence asked.

"This time of the evening there should be very little activity in the camp," Donald replied. "We should be able to walk to the prisoner's tent without raising concern. Once there I should be able to talk my way past the guards. I will question Lady Talbot. If her answers corroborate Andrew's story, we shall take her with us. If her answers do not satisfy me, then events shall unfold in a manner not much to your liking, I dare say."

"I do not doubt that you will be able to talk your way past the guards into the tent," Lawrence said, "but as for leaving the tent with Marie, I have my doubts about that."

"Yes, there would be little chance of me being able to take her away. Getting in should not be a problem but getting out with her may not be easy. I could represent that I am to take her to Gallard for questioning, but that would seem very suspicious at this time of the night."

"Correct me if I am wrong, but does that not present a bit of an obstacle to our plan of rescuing her?" Louis asked sarcastically.

"It could," Donald replied casually.

"Before we put both legs into the pot of boiling water, I would like to make one more observation," Lawrence said. "There will likely be four of us leaving the camp, but we have only three horses. Unless I miss my guess, we will not exactly have time to saddle up another horse before what I assume will be a most hurried exodus."

"Marie will have to ride double with one of us until we reach the sentry post along the road. We will grab one of their horses and continue from there."

"Will it not be a little suspicious if someone sees three men and a princess riding through camp in the middle of the night?" Louis asked.

"They will not see three men and a princess. They will see four men," Donald replied. "We have a number of young men in our army. I will borrow a set of clothes that should come close to fitting the princess. If everything goes well, she will change into those clothes and the four of us will walk out of the camp just as us three will walk in. Anybody who sees us will see three men and a boy."

"And the men guarding Marie's tent?" Lawrence asked. "What is your plan there?"

"I will approach the tent. You and Louis will position yourselves behind the tent, out of sight of the guards. I will speak with the guards and hopefully get them to let me into the tent. After I speak with the lady, I will exit the tent. If she has confirmed Andrew's story and is believable, and if there is nobody else in the area, I will say, "I am satisfied." Upon that signal you and Louis will subdue the guards, though very quietly. A hard knock on the back of their heads should do the trick. We will drag them into the tent and bind and gag them. The lady will change clothes and the four of us will walk away. If for some reason the alarm is raised, then we will ride like the devil and hope we get away."

"And if you do not say, 'I am satisfied?'" Louis asked.

"Then your worries will have just begun," Donald said matter-of-factly. "We are entering the camp. Follow my lead. Do not speak unless it is absolutely necessary."

The men dismounted their horses and guided them through the encampment. The glowing embers in makeshift firepits provided an eerie glow around the camp. The smell of smoldering wood filled the air and smoke from the fire pits hovered amongst the tents. Occasionally the shadow of a figure could be seen walking around the tents, but nobody approached the trio. Sounds of heavy snoring seemed to fill nearly every tent they passed. Though they were being as quiet as possible, to Lawrence it seemed as though they were making enough noise to wake the dead. His eyes and ears reached out into the darkness. After a few minutes of walking Donald raised his hand, motioning the other two to stop. He quietly stole into a tent and in a few moments emerged with a handful of clothes. They continued their trek for another few minutes until again, he held up his hand. He moved close to the other two men and spoke in a hushed tone that would not have been audible from more than five feet away.

"Take the horses and move around the side of this tent on the left. Proceed forward another six tents. The sixth tent will be the one where your friend is being held. Tie the horses behind the fifth tent and proceed behind the sixth tent. One of you will slide along the near side of the tent toward the front of it and the other will do the same on the far side of the tent. Wait until I am addressing the guards. That way their attention will be diverted, and they will be less likely to hear you. Wait there until I emerge from the tent. When you hear my signal knock-out the guard closest to you. We will then drag them into the tent and bind and gag them. We should be able to at least get out of the camp before they wake or are missed."

"Would it not be simpler and less risky to slide a blade across their throats?" Louis asked.

"These men may be your enemies, but they are not mine. I will not murder nor tolerate murder. You will render them unconscious and that is all. Is that clear?"

"I hear you," Louis replied, his tone clearly indicating that he preferred his suggested method of silencing the guards.

"And if we hear you say something other than your signal?" Lawrence asked, redirecting the conversation.

"Then I would recommend you jump on the horses and ride as fast as you can. If you are fortunate, you just may make it out of camp," Donald replied. "Enough conversation. Let us get on with it."

"We will need more than a little good fortune to pull this off," Louis grumbled as he and Lawrence led the two horses behind the tent to their left.

Donald continued down the aisle of tents until he was almost to the one where the two guards were stationed. Without appearing obvious, he scanned the surroundings. He checked to see if anybody else was awake and could witness the upcoming exchange. He also checked his escape routes just in case the plan went sour and he had no choice but to flee. The night sky had become cloudy which would work to his advantage. He took a controlled deep breath. The next few minutes could throw his life into an entirely new direction. He almost started questioning his actions, but this was no time to be unsure of oneself. He put all doubts out of his mind and proceeded with his plan. When but a few feet from the tent's entrance he stopped and addressed the guards, trying to keep his voice a bit quieter than normal.

"I will speak with the prisoner," Donald informed the guards. It was not a question but a statement that one in authority would make.

"That is not permitted. Our orders are that only upon the express word of King Gallard is anyone granted access to the prisoner," the guard on the left answered, not moving.

"It is upon the king's order that I am here," Donald replied.

"Our supervisor gave us the order to not allow anyone in to see the prisoner. The king so directed him himself. Only upon orders from our supervisor or the king himself will we allow anyone into this tent."

"Do you know who I am?" Donald replied with more authority, struggling to keep his voice down. "I am Donald MacLean, Security Consul for King Gallard. I am responsible for all security measures in and around this camp. I am the one who gave your supervisor the order to bar anyone from entering the tent except on the king's direct order. Now step aside so that I may speak with the prisoner, as per the king's request."

"The king has ordered that you interrogate the prisoner in the middle of the night?" the guard replied. "That I doubt very seriously."

"Only King Gallard is higher than me when it comes to the security of this camp," Donald replied more tersely. "I do not care whether or not you find it reasonable that the king wishes the prisoner to be interrogated in the middle of the night or not. That is why I am here. Now step aside."

"Only upon direct order of our supervisor or the king himself will you enter this tent," the guard responded, his body tensing. "Now, it is my suggestion that you get a good night's sleep and come back in the morrow. However, if you cannot do so, then choose which man you will awaken this evening. I would advise against waking the king."

Donald took a moment and looked around as if he were in deep thought. The rest of the camp was quiet and still. His plan was not working as he had hoped. If he turned and left, he could not be certain of what actions Lawrence and Louis would make on their own. He suspected that they would dispatch of the guards, grab the prisoner, and flee. It would not be likely that they would retreat and meet with him again to formulate an alternate plan. He would have to flee himself since he had revealed his identity to the guards. If he stayed, he would most certainly be accused of aiding the enemy. At best he would be questioned regarding his desire to interrogate the prisoner in the middle of the night, and he did not know if he would be able to talk his way out of that one. The only way to protect his identity would be to kill the guards, but he would not allow that to happen. His hastily formulated plan had now painted him into a corner. He did not have time to re-think the plan or produce a new one. He took the only realistic option left open.

"So be it," he replied with a sigh. "I am satisfied."

In less than a heartbeat Lawrence and Louis both struck the guards at the nape of their necks, knocking them unconscious with hardly a sound. Quickly and quietly they pulled the guards into the tent where they bound and gagged them. Donald looked around hurriedly, afraid of the chance that their actions had been observed. But there was no other movement in the area, and he slipped into the tent.

For a moment Donald felt completely vulnerable. In fact, he was. Lawrence and Louis now controlled the situation. They could quickly and easily subdue him and take the prisoner with them. Their chances of escaping camp without being seen were not unreasonable. Why would they need to wait for Donald to question Marie in order to substantiate Andrew's story? They had no loyalty to him. He was their enemy. They could kill him or at best leave him as they were leaving the guards. If they did that, he would have much to answer for the following morning. Lawrence moved close to Donald.

"You have five minutes to question Marie," he informed

Donald quietly. "You have acted on good faith, therefore we shall as well. But five minutes is all you will be granted. After that, we take the lady." He motioned to Louis and the two of them exited the tent, taking the positions of the now unconscious guards. Donald moved over to Marie who unbelievably had not been roused by their activity. She was on her left side, facing away from him. He knelt and nudged her on the shoulder.

"My lady," he said, hopefully loud enough to wake her but not have his voice carry out of the tent. "You must awake."

Marie, startled, rolled over quickly to face Donald. She could not see his face in the dark although she could make out his form.

"We must be quiet," Donald warned before Marie was able to speak. "I do not have much time. I must ask you some important questions and you must answer me perfectly honestly. Your freedom, if not your life, hangs in the balance."

"Who are you?" Marie asked as she sat up. "Why do you steal into my tent in the middle of the night?"

"Allow me the secret of my identity for a bit longer," Donald replied. "We have a mutual friend and that is all I will say at this time. For now, you must allow me to ask the questions. I have the power to set you free this very night or to keep you here for the king to interrogate in the morning. Believe me, his interrogation in the morrow will be unlike anything you have ever experienced and not in a pleasant way I assure you."

"I am prisoner of a king who obviously is searching for something he values greatly," Marie stated. "He believes I have information to aid him in this search and has all but promised physical harm should I not answer his questions to his liking. You sneak into this tent in the middle of the night and ask that I place the least bit of trust in you? What a fool you must take me for!"

"You are no fool, but to assuage as best I can your justified doubts ..." Donald said as he stood and pointed to the corner of the tent. "Though there is little light to see by, you should be able to make out the forms of two men there on the ground. Those are the two men who were guarding your tent. I have risked much to speak with you this evening and my time is quickly running out. There are things I must learn from you that may very well change the course of both of our lives."

"Then ask your questions so that I either may leave this place or go back to sleep," Marie replied impatiently, yet with a glimmer of hope riding her voice.

"I know for a fact that you are close friends with Andrew MacLean. Do not ask how I know, that is not important. You must tell me how long you have known him. What I ask is not only for your sake but for his as well."

Marie could not help but wonder what this mystery man meant by that. Perhaps it had something to do with Andrew being held in her father's dungeon. Did this man truly know Andrew, or was he simply using Andrew's name as part of his interrogation technique? She decided to answer his questions, but cautiously.

"I have known him for six months," she replied. "He came to our village six months ago."

"He was on a quest," Donald continued. "A quest that by chance or by fate brought him to you. What did he tell you was the purpose of his quest?"

"He mentioned nothing of a quest," Marie lied. "He simply said that he was a man looking for a home and he found one in our land."

"Lady Talbot, you are justified in your caution and suspicions. You are a strong woman and from what I have heard, highly intelligent. I tell you again, I am not here to bring you any harm. In fact, I wish to save you from possible harm. However, I need for you to be completely honest. Without your honesty I cannot help you. Now please, what did Andrew tell you his quest was?"

"Very well," Marie replied, giving in a bit. "He said that he was searching for a man, or at least a descendant of a man. He had spent five years searching for this person, ever since the day he left Gallard's service. Or rather, the day he was run out of Gallard's service."

"And the name of that man, or at least his descendant, might be DuFay?" Donald asked.

"That might be wise a guess," Marie replied.

"You said he was run out of Gallard's service. What do you mean by that?"

"Andrew said that during a battle he acquired a certain object. The king demanded that Andrew relinquish possession of the object. Andrew refused, the king's men attacked Andrew, and he escaped."

"Would that object happen to be a sword?" Donald pushed. "A very special sword?"

"What is it with you men and your swords?" Marie asked. "I do believe that men are obsessed with their swords. Every last one of you should seek counsel. Yes, it was supposedly a unique and special sword but as to how special it was, I cannot attest. I know little about such weapons." She was not going to give Andrew's secret away. It was not surprising that someone in Gallard's service would know about the unsavory circumstances upon which Andrew left Gallard and the fact that the parting of ways was due to a sword. Gallard himself had mentioned the weapon as being the reason for Andrew leaving his service. But she was not going to reveal anything more about the DuFay sword.

"You and Andrew explored the lower levels of your father's castle, yes?" Donald continued, getting off the subject of the sword.

"Yes," Marie said cautiously, wondering how Donald knew of their expedition.

"You found a hidden room. What was in the room?"

"How do you know about the room?" she asked dumbfounded. While she suspected that her and Andrew's secret foray into the lower levels of the castle was no longer a secret, she could not even begin to guess how this man knew about the hidden room.

"Please, time is running out. Just answer the question."

"The room was full of antiquated items. Books, armament,

furniture, decorations, anything of which you could think. All of it hundreds of years old."

"There was something else in the room," Donald pushed. "Andrew found something else. He found that for which he was searching. Correct?"

Marie's curiosity was driving her mad. How could this man know all these things? Only she and Andrew knew of what they had found. Had her father tortured Andrew to the point that he revealed everything? Though she could not believe that, even if it had happened, who was this man and how would he know?

"Yes," Marie finally answered. "Yes, he found that for which he sought."

Donald stepped outside and retrieved one of the small torches outside of the tent. He ignored the inquisitive looks of Lawrence and Louis and stepped back inside. He walked back over to Marie. She was relieved that she could now see his face. Donald set the torch down for a moment and rolled up the sleeve on his right arm. He then picked up the torch and illuminated his arm.

"Is this what Andrew found?" he asked, showing Marie the scar on his forearm. Marie's eyes widened in astonishment and her mouth dropped open. She leaned closer to Donald and inspected the scar.

"I ... I cannot believe this," she said as she looked up at Donald. "This is not possible. Andrew told me that he was the only person alive who had that brand burned into his arm."

"Until this evening Andrew did indeed believe that he was the only person alive who bore this branding," Donald replied. "Fortunately for me, he was mistaken in what he thought he saw five years ago."

"Donald?" Marie asked skeptically.

"Aye," he replied. "I am Donald MacLean, Andrew's brother."

"How?" she asked bewildered. "He said that you were killed."

"And so he believed, though for that I do not blame him."

"But how do you know everything about Andrew's quest and

how did you know about our discovery in my father's castle?" Marie's question was answered by a voice from the front of the tent.

"There is no more time for explanations. MacLean, have you learned what you needed to learn? Time is short. We must leave."

"Lawrence!" Marie exclaimed with a relieved smile on her face. "I cannot believe you are here! How did you find me?"

"Later," Lawrence answered. "Your questions shall be answered later. We cannot wait any longer. We must leave now!"

"Leave we shall," Donald replied. "Lady Talbot, you must change clothes. We cannot leave with you wearing that dress. This uniform belongs to one of the younger men," he said as Lawrence handed him the clothes. "It should fit you well enough for us to sneak out of camp. Change quickly."

"What about them?" she asked, nodding toward the guards on the ground.

"They are bound and gagged. They should not awaken for some time but there are others who could very easily spot us and raise the alarm. Please hurry." Donald and Lawrence walked out of the tent. Donald nervously looked around the area He knew there was not much time until the camp started to awaken for the day. There was no turning back for him now. The guards knew his name and when they told their story Gallard would want him nearly as bad as he wanted Andrew. Lawrence and Louis retrieved the three horses as Donald waited for Marie. It seemed like an eternity to them for Marie to emerge from the tent. When she did, she was not recognizable as a woman. The clothes were a bit too large for her and there was no way to completely conceal her feminine facial features, but the dimness of the night would help hide her identity.

"Now what?" Lawrence asked as he also scouted their surroundings. He, too, knew that dawn was not far away and soon the camp would buzz with activity. They probably had only minutes to make their escape without being noticed.

"We shall walk out just as we walked in," Donald answered calmly. "If we keep our heads down and walk with a purpose, we should not raise any concerns if someone sees us."

"I am afraid we cannot allow that to happen," a voice called out from the darkness. Half a dozen men appeared out of the shadows and surrounded the foursome, fully armed and ready for business. The man who spoke approached Donald. Donald recognized the man as the guard who had questioned them at the road post.

"It appears you have good instincts," Donald said as he surveyed those surrounding them. "What gave us away?"

"Instincts," the man snorted. "I did not need instincts to tell me that you were not what you confessed to be. I know the name of Donald MacLean, though I had never met him before this evening. I could only take you at your word that you were who you said you were. I also had never met Marcus Fordham and therefore had no reason to doubt he was indeed Marcus Fordham," the man said, nodding toward Lawrence. "However, what you could not have known is that Sean Lancaster just two nights ago won a very nice dagger from me in a game of chance." He looked at Louis. "And you, my friend, bear as much resemblance to Lancaster as you do a toad."

"And THAT is an insult to toads around the world," Lawrence joked, showing not the least bit of fear or intimidation.

"I doubt you will feel much like joking come morning," the man said knowingly. "I am certain the two men you knocked unconscious will be more than happy to return the favor, and then some. Lay down your weapons and you will not be harmed … for now. I am certain the king will have many questions to ask you and he will desire you to be very alert."

"Six against three?" Louis asked. "I believe the numbers are not quite fair."

"How about five thousand against three?" the man replied sarcastically. "The entire camp will be awake in a matter of minutes.

It would be grave foolishness for you to attempt to fight your way free. Within seconds of the sound of swords clashing, a hundred men will encircle you. Again, I say, drop your weapons."

Lawrence turned his head and looked at Louis with a determined glare. Not ones to surrender, both men knew there was no way they were going to get out of there without a fight. The odds of them escaping were virtually none, especially with Marie in tow. Louis saw the resolve in Lawrence's eyes and answered in kind. Donald saw the men look at each other and knew what was about to happen. He knew they would not allow themselves to be captured and tortured by Gallard. Now he had an even bigger decision to make than before. Did he stay as well and fight alongside Lawrence and Louis, or did he attempt to flee with Marie? Did he and Marie even have the slightest chance of escaping? The man was right, at the first sound of conflict the entire camp would awaken. He knew that he, Lawrence and Louis would not be spared but he knew that Marie would not be harmed.

"Lay down your weapons!" the guard growled more forcefully.

"It appears you give us no choice," Lawrence replied as he lowered his sword. He turned his head to his right and behind him a bit and looked at Donald. Donald was standing close to Louis, on the left side of the horse Louis was leading. Lawrence gave a nearly imperceptible nod toward the horse. Donald furrowed his eyebrows a bit, not sure of Lawrence's meaning. Lawrence then turned his eyes toward Marie, who was almost directly behind him, and gave the same slight nod toward the horse he was leading. At this, Donald grasped Lawrence's intentions. Lawrence and Louis would engage the guards in combat while Donald and Marie jumped on the horses and made a break for freedom. It was a very risky plan since they were outnumbered, and the camp was already starting to waken. Donald knew the chances of him and Marie getting through the camp and into the open were very slim. However, he had no choice. He could not talk his way out of this situation. His position as Security

Consul for Gallard was now meaningless. For him, it was either escape or die trying. He returned Lawrence's gaze and gave one short nod of understanding. Lawrence looked back at Louis. "The man has left us with no choice." Louis nodded in understanding.

Donald looked at Marie who appeared nervous and confused. Donald could not tell whether she understood the non-verbal plan. She looked at him inquisitively, knowing something was going to happen but not what. He shifted his eyes from her to the horse by her side and gently motioned toward the horse with his head. She quickly understood that they were going to make a run for it. She shifted her weight so that she would be ready to jump onto the horse when the time came. Her wait was short.

"We shall simply have to kill you and your five thousand comrades," Lawrence said calmly as he looked into the eyes of the guard in front of him. Then suddenly, without warning, a cry of rage and force burst from Lawrence and in the blink of an eye he leaped forward and swung his sword at the guard who had been doing all the talking. The guard had been prepared for an attack and successfully defended against Lawrence's first blow but with lightning speed Lawrence re-directed his deflected sword toward the guard's midsection and delivered a fatal blow. At the same moment of Lawrence's attack, Louis also pounced forward and engaged the guard closest to him. There were several exchanges before Louis broke through his opponent's defense and skewered the man. Lawrence was already attacking a second guard.

At the very moment of Lawrence's first move, Donald grabbed the horse's reins and leaped onto the back of the beast. Seeing Donald make his move Marie did likewise. She quickly grabbed the reins and scrambled onto the horse Lawrence had been leading. By the time they oriented themselves on the horses, Lawrence and Louis had disposed of the first two guards, opening the path for the riders. Donald violently kicked his horse in its ribs and the stallion reared up momentarily, then bolted forward. Marie did the same and her horse chased after Donald's. As they dashed through the encampment, they could see men pouring out of their tents at the sound of fighting. The just-awakening men were too groggy to fully comprehend what was happening as the horses and riders bolted by at a full gallop. Several men had to leap out of the way to avoid being run down. The riders cleared the last tent and headed up the road, thundering across the wooden bridge.

In the growing light of dawn Donald could see that the guard who had confronted them at the post and then in the camp had evidently stationed additional sentries at the outer post due to his suspicions. There were now nearly a dozen men stationed along the road. As Donald and Marie approached within a hundred yards of the post, several men stepped out into the road with swords drawn as if to block their passage. Donald glanced to his left as Marie brought her horse even with his. He was surprised at her skill and comfort in handling the horse. She obviously had plenty of riding experience. Seeing the sentries, Marie stole a glance at Donald. He did not try to say anything over the thunder of the running horses. He simply leaned forward to make as small of a target as he could. Marie did likewise.

The sentries began waving their arms and hollering for the riders to stop. Donald and Marie ignored them and urged their horses on faster if that were even possible. Donald could see that the men along the sides of the road had retrieved their bows and were readying arrows. The situation looked grim. Despite the speed at which they would pass the post, Donald knew it would be nearly impossible to pass through the hail of arrows unscathed. He inched his horse closer to Marie's.

"Upon my signal," he yelled to her, "break to the outside of the road! If we can throw the arches off-balance, we might have a chance of making it through them!"

Marie nodded in understanding. She, too, saw the guards standing along the left and rights sides of the road. As they neared within fifty yards, they heard several arrows whistle by uncomfortably close. If either of the horses took an arrow it would mean disaster. When they were thirty yards from the archers, Donald yelled.

"NOW!!!"

Both riders tugged on their horse's reins, Marie to the left and Donald to the right. The horses, trained for battle, immediately responded without missing a stride. They broke for the sides of the road as planned. The archers, caught by surprise, jumped backward and several of them fell. The two horses charged by the post. Just when he thought they had made it through unscathed, Donald felt a sharp pain in his left thigh followed by one in his left shoulder. He cringed in pain but did not cry out. He glanced to his left and was relieved to see Marie keeping up with him. He stole a peek back toward the post and saw several guards heading for their horses. That was not good. He looked forward again. They would rendezvous with Andrew in about sixty seconds with nearly a dozen veterans of battle less than sixty seconds behind them. Andrew would not be happy.

Chapter 8

Even before he could see them, Andrew heard the thundering horses as they approached a bend in the road. It was obvious that whoever was approaching was either chasing someone or being chased. Since not a soul had ventured along the road since Donald, Lawrence and Louis had left, Andrew could only surmise that those who approached were the pursued. He drifted back into the thick foliage where the three horses, along with Sean and Marcus, were hidden from view. Despite his experience telling him that there were only two, maybe three horses approaching, he knew it was best to be cautious until the identity of the riders was certain. If they were not his friends, the thick, shadowy foliage would hide him well enough.

The horses burst around the bend in the road and the growing light of dawn revealed only that the two riders were men. Andrew maintained his silent position. The horses were reined to a stop in the road just thirty feet from Andrew.

"Andrew!" Donald called out as his adrenaline-charged horse pranced about.

"Here!" Andrew answered, making his way through the trees and onto the road.

"Andrew?!" Marie called out from behind Donald, sliding off her horse. "Andrew, what are you doing here? I was told you had been imprisoned."

"Where are Lawrence and Louis?" Andrew asked with great concern as he spotted the two arrows protruding from Donald's body.

"There is no time for explanations!" Donald interrupted, wincing in pain. "Andrew, there are a dozen of Gallard's men sixty seconds behind us at the most and I would venture many more behind them. We cannot outrun them."

"We cannot fight them, either," Andrew replied, "especially with those two arrows sticking out of your body."

"Take Marie and hide in the trees," Donald instructed. "I will ride on and draw Gallard's men away. Once they pass, ride back up the road a couple of hundred yards. There is a small game trail that leads west and down toward the river. Take the trail and stay hidden as much as possible. You should be able to follow the river away from Gallard's army. That will be your best chance of evading capture."

"You will not get far," Andrew argued.

"I will get far enough to at least give you two a chance of escape," Donald replied.

"No," Andrew replied, stepping over to Donald's horse and grabbing its reins. "I will not allow you to sacrifice your life. You have a destiny to fulfill. I will draw Gallard's men away while you and Marie escape. She can help with your wounds and escort you safely to her homeland."

"Andrew ..." Donald started to argue.

"No arguments," Andrew cut him off. "Get down or I will pull you to the ground. NOW!"

Knowing there was no time to argue, and that Andrew was right, Donald lowered himself to the ground and in a split second, Andrew hoisted himself onto the horse's back.

"Marie, take Donald back to your home and tend to his wounds. His safety I leave in your hands. I will evade Gallard's men and make my way back to Durinburg. I will find a way to contact you and by then you will have hopefully cleared my name with your father. Tell him that Gallard's army is ready to strike. Do not tell him of the sword or anything regarding the legend, at least not now. We must present that to him with much caution."

"Give us four days to make the journey," Marie replied. "I fear Donald's wounds will slow us down. We must tend to them and give him a day at least to rest."

"Four days it is," Andrew agreed although to him that seemed excessive. However, he did not have time to argue. "Give me your horse's reins. Take the other horses with you. Be careful." Andrew took the reins for the horse Marie had ridden and tied them with a rope to the saddle horn of the horse he sat upon. With a shout, he kicked his horse in its ribs. The horse leapt forward and with the second horse in tow, galloped down the road.

Donald and Marie darted into the woods as quickly as Donald's injured thigh allowed. Hardly ten seconds later, the dozen men which they had passed at the guard post galloped past them at full speed. Within another ten seconds the thunder of the horses' hooves faded away. The duo quickly walked deeper into the woods until they came to the hidden horses and Donald's former companions. As Donald's adrenaline began to subside, the pain from the arrows in his shoulder and thigh became more intense. He half-way collapsed on the ground beside Marcus, who was bound and gagged. Marcus' eyes did not hold much sympathy for his fellow countryman.

"Before we can go anywhere, we need to remove these arrows," Donald informed Marie. "I would enlist the aid of my two colleagues here but after what happened this morning, I fear they would prefer to increase my pain as opposed to alleviating it."

"Tell me what to do," Marie responded, kneeling beside him.

"First, search the horses and see if you can find some rope and any extra cloth. When the arrows are removed, we will need to fasten a patch over the wounds to slow the bleeding until we can properly cauterize and dress them later."

Marie hurried over to the horses. Knowing Andrew to be a resourceful person, she went to Annon first. She searched the saddlebags and was relieved to find a piece of rope about ten feet long and a quarter inch or so in diameter. She also found what appeared to be a clean shirt. She hurried back over to Donald.

"Thankfully, the arrows have reasonably small heads and did not penetrate deeply," Donald said as Marie knelt back by him. "You should be able to pull them out and not have to drive them through. First, you will take my knife and cut a small one inch slit in my skin where the arrows entered. You will need to grasp the arrows as firmly as possible and as close to the points of entry as possible. When you have a firm grip, you will then yank the arrow out quickly, as straight as possible, and with all your strength. Do not hold back, do not be afraid of causing me pain. If you are not able to pull the arrow out on the first, try I fear the pain from repeated attempts will be too great and I may fall unconscious. We must do this quickly." Donald reached to his belt and pulled out a razor-sharp six-inch dagger which he handed to Marie.

Marie took the dagger in-hand and moved around to Donald's back.

"What about your clothing?" she asked. "I cannot see your skin."

"Cut the clothing," Donald grimaced as the pain continued to increase. "Use the knife and cut the clothing."

Marie pulled the outer shirt away from Donald's body a couple of inches and cut a long slit in it. She then did the same to the blood-soaked under shirt. Now she could see Donald's skin and where the arrow had penetrated his shoulder. She moved the knife close to his skin and paused. The thought of intentionally cutting his shoulder was almost nauseating. She knew how painful it would be, although the arrow itself certainly had to be causing him more pain. She hesitated and tried to work up her courage.

"We do not have much time," Donald said, sensing Marie's hesitancy. "Do not think, just do what needs to be done."

"Okay, okay," Marie replied nervously. "This is not easy. I have never done anything like this before."

"Then today you will learn something new. Now do it before Gallard's guards come back and find us."

"Just give me a moment to steady my hand," Marie retorted, trying to buy herself a little more time to work up her nerves.

"We do not have a moment!" Donald replied impatiently. "Quit being such a woman, show a little courage, and pull the blasted arrows out!"

"Such a WOMAN?!" Marie replied angrily. "I should leave the arrows in you for that rude comment."

"Andrew was right," Donald said, taunting Marie. "You act tough but, on the inside, you are as tough as a new-born lamb. Your courage is hardly more than skin deep."

"Skin deep?!" Marie repeated. "Andrew said that?"

"Among other things," Donald answered, "and not all of them overly complimentary. There was head-strong, opinionated, assertive, stubborn, arrogant, vain ..."

"I am NOT arrogant and vain!" Marie retorted.

"So, you are admitting to being head-strong, opinionated and assertive?"

"I will show you assertive," Marie replied as she gritted her teeth and pressed the knife against Donald's shoulder. She cut a one inch slit at the point of entry as directed. Donald grunted in pain under his breath. The shaft of the arrow had some blood on it, making it slick. Marie cut a long strip of cloth from the shirt. She wrapped one end around the base of the arrow and the other end around her right hand as best she could in order to give herself the firmest grip possible. She stood bent-over and leveraged herself, then silently counted to three. "How is THIS for assertive?" she growled as she reached three and yanked as hard as she could. The arrow came out quickly and easily. Donald stifled a cry of pain as Marie stumbled backward. She quickly regained her balance and darted back over to Donald. Using the knife, she cut a large patch of cloth from the shirt and then she cut a length off the rope long enough to wrap around Donald's chest twice. She bunched the cloth together and pressed it over the wound. She held the cloth with one hand and wrapped the rope around

Donald's torso and under his arms with the other to hold the cloth in place. The rope went around Donald twice and Marie tied it as tightly as she could as Donald grimaced in pain. It was not a quality job, but it would hopefully slow the blood loss for a few hours.

"Well done," Donald finally managed to say as the stars of pain floating before his eyes started to disappear. "Now for the one in my thigh. Quickly."

Marie moved to Donald's right side and cut his blood-soaked trousers where the arrow had penetrated. With only a slight hesitation she proceeded to cut a small incision in his skin. She tossed the knife aside, stood, and while bending over grasped the protruding arrow as close to his leg as possible. She paused and looked into Donald's eyes. He met her eyes and with a nod of approval, indicated he was ready. Marie looked back at his bleeding leg, shifted her balance, and yanked on the arrow. This one, too, came out quickly and Donald was less able to resist a cry of pain. He fell back to the ground, his eyes shut tightly in deep pain. Marie quickly dropped to the ground beside Donald and covered the wound with another small piece of cloth cut from Andrew's shirt. She ripped a long strip from the remainder of the shirt and proceeded to wrap it tightly around the Donald's thigh. She tied it into a knot as tightly as she could, and a suppressed groan escaped Donald's firmly closed mouth.

"Good," Donald managed to say as his thigh pulsed wildly with pain. "That should do until we can properly care for the wounds later. Now we must move quickly from here and head back to Durinburg and report to your father."

"What of them?" Marie asked, looking toward Marcus and Sean. "Do we just leave them here?"

"We have no choice," Donald replied as he struggled to stand. "We cannot take them with us for they would only slow us down. We cannot release them else they try to stop us."

"But we cannot leave them bound and gagged in the woods like this," Marie countered. "There is no telling how long it would take someone to find them, if at all. They are well hidden from the road."

"You are right," Donald replied, mulling the situation over. "They are my fellow countrymen if not my friends. I cannot take the chance of them remaining here undiscovered for several days." He picked up the dagger Marie had dropped and hopped over to Marcus. He dropped the dagger in Marcus' lap. "I believe you should be able to eventually cut yourselves free," he said, looking at Marcus. "Though we part ways, I do not hold against you the animosity you now hold against me. Despite many questions and things to be explained, I feel Andrew's tale is true and should be farther investigated. I would that we had the time to convince you of this, but our time is less than short. I must return the lady to her father. Remember, you suffered no ill will on my part." He turned from the icy glares of Marcus and Sean and hobbled over to the horses where Marie was preparing them for departure.

"Perhaps you should ride Andrew's horse," Marie suggested, gesturing toward Annon. "He is the strongest and fastest of the three. I will ride one of the other horses and lead the third."

Donald limped over to Annon. He reached up and grabbed the saddle horn. After carefully shifting his weight to his injured leg, he lifted his right foot and placed it in the stirrup. With as much strength as he could muster, he lifted himself into the saddle. The process was quite painful, and he had to shut his eyes tightly from the pain. His thigh and shoulder throbbed mercilessly. Marie climbed up on the horse that belonged to Lawrence. She bent over and grabbed the reins of Louis's horse. With Donald in the lead they headed back up to the road. They stopped briefly before completely exposing themselves, listening for the sounds of approaching horses. They heard nothing. Donald moved into the middle of the road.

"Making it back to Durinburg is not going to be easy," he said. "There are a dozen of Gallard's men between us and the town, plus there certainly have been more men dispatched by now to find us and take us back to Gallard. We must avoid the road as much as possible."

"We are not going back to Durinburg," Marie stated firmly.

"We are not?" Donald asked, surprised. "Then pray tell, where do you suggest we go?"

"We must head to Habersham," she answered.

"Habersham," Donald repeated. "Why Habersham? Does your father have a safe house there, friends there, some type of protection for you?"

"None of which I am aware," Marie replied.

"Then why travel to Habersham?"

"There remains a mystery to be solved and I believe we can find the answer in Habersham."

"I thought Andrew had solved the mystery," Donald replied. "He was looking for the descendant of DuFay and he found him. He found me."

"That is part of the mystery," Marie acknowledged. "But there is another part that must be solved for the veil to be completely removed. It is something that is not completely known to Andrew."

"My lady," Donald replied, "It was left in my charge to deliver you safely to your homeland and your father. My brother entrusted your safety to me, and I will not break that trust. We cannot afford the time or danger involved in running off on some mystery-solving escapade to Habersham, especially since Habersham is for all intents and purposes opposite the direction of your home. Now let us forget this idea and return to your home."

"Andrew was right concerning one thing about me," Marie answered, determination in her eyes. "I can be very stubborn. If returning to my homeland is what you desire then by all means, proceed. However, if to look after my safety is what you desire then I suggest you head up this road, take the game trail to the river, follow the river northwest, cross the bridge at Dunnesboro, and proceed to Habersham for that is where I will be." With that final word Marie turned her horse and began to head up the road.

"I should not have allowed Andrew to talk me into this," Donald muttered under his breath as he followed Marie. "I have a feeling he chose the easier of two tasks."

Andrew pushed the horse furiously. Having the second horse in tow slowed him down, and he knew that he could not afford to lose any speed as he fought to elude his pursuers. His plan was to release the second horse well-away from Donald and Marie's position and trust that at least some of Gallard's men would find the horse and pause to investigate. It might only buy him a minute or so, but in a chase such as this every second he could put between himself and those chasing after him increased his chances of escape. He stole a glance backward and was relieved that no riders were in sight within the two hundred yards of road visible to him. He did not know how far behind him they were, but he was quite convinced that they were gaining on him. Just up ahead there was a strong curve to the right in the road. He decided that was where he would release the second horse. As he rounded the curve, he released the reins of the second horse. His horse picked up some speed and the horse he had released continued running but started slowing down. After about ten seconds, the second horse came to a stop and stood at the side of the road. Hopefully, that would give Gallard's men reason to pause if even only for a few seconds. Andrew intended on riding for several more minutes before implementing the second part of his plan. He bent low in the saddle in order to squeeze every bit of speed out of their flight as possible.

Four minutes later the horse started slowing on its own. Andrew knew the beast was exhausted and could not continue at this pace much longer. He began scouting the road for the ideal spot to complete his scheme. The surrounding tree-covered terrain had become hilly with the ground sloping up on his left and down on his right. Periodically a small stream cut across the road. Spotting what he was looking for, Andrew slowed the horse and finally reined it to a full stop near where the ground sloped off to the right more severely than it had thus far. A four-foot-wide bed of small and medium-sized rocks evidenced a storm water run-off to the right. Andrew quickly dismounted and grabbed his sword. He swung the sword and struck the horse sharply on its hindquarters and the beast took off running. Andrew strode over to where the ground dropped off to the right. He scuffed his feet around the area and overturned several of the rocks, making it appear as though he had taken flight down the dried-up streambed. He then bolted up the right side of the road for about twenty yards and crossed to the left side of the road. Here, the hillside was not very steep. Andrew pulled himself up the embankment using exposed roots and trees, trying to leave as little evidence of his passage as possible. He had stepped about ten feet beyond the tree line when he heard the thunder of approaching horses. Quickly, Andrew dropped down behind the trunk of a large tree that had fallen many years ago. Within seconds Gallard's men raced by. Andrew peered over the tree and counted ten horses and men. He could not know for sure if they were all the pursuers or if there were more coming up the road. Donald had said there were a dozen men after them, but he could have been estimating, and Andrew had no way of knowing whether any of Gallard's men had fallen for his decoy. This was the unknown factor that could mark the success or failure of his plan.

Andrew waited until the sounds of the galloping horses faded away. He cautiously rose up to better see the road. All was silent and still. He stood up and waited about fifteen seconds but heard nothing more. His horse likely only galloped a couple of hundred yards at the most before stopping so he did not have much time before Gallard's men started backtracking and looking for signs of where he may have dismounted. Andrew proceeded up the hillside, no longer concerned about how much evidence of his passing he left. Anyone who found his tracks and wished to follow him would have to do so on foot. The brush was much too thick for a horse. After about twenty minutes of walking, the hillside started to flatten and the woods thinned out a bit. Figuring he had ventured far enough from the road, Andrew altered his direction and started heading south, hoping to parallel the main road, avoid detection, and reach Durinburg. Since he was now on foot it was highly likely that Marie and Donald would reach the township before he did. That would at least give Marie time to convince her father that Andrew was not a spy and clear his name. Perhaps then he would be able to retrieve the DuFay sword, which he hoped remained hidden. What would happen after that, though, he could not begin to imagine.

Chapter 9

The sunlight was quickly fading as Marie looked for a place to camp for the night. The pain and loss of blood had rendered Donald into a semi-conscious state. He rode not far behind her, but he was doing all he could to remain seated on his horse. It would be up to Marie to find a place to camp, light a fire, and tend to Donald's wounds in a more proper manner. They had been following the river all day long as best as they could, occasionally having to sidetrack to get around changes in the terrain that were impassable. They were now passing close to the river in an area where large boulders had been strewn about by some historic flood or avalanche from the mountain to their left. Marie found a small clearing between several of the largest boulders and stopped. The area would provide enough room for the two humans and three horses as well as hide the light from the campfire should anyone be looking for them. There was no way she could be certain whether they were being followed or not. Nobody had any reason to believe that she and Donald were heading toward any other destination than her home, but there was always that sliver of doubt, that uncertainty that kept a person's guard up.

Marie led the horses into the small clearing and dismounted. She moved over to Donald and helped him down as best as she could. Donald managed to slide off his horse without collapsing to the ground and Marie helped him sit down. She quickly embarked on the task of gathering wood for a fire. Within ten minutes she had a nice pile of small and medium-sized branches. She stacked the pieces of wood to form a small teepee and stuffed a couple of handfuls of dried grass under the teepee. She then moved over to Andrew's horse and started going through the bags and pouches. After a couple of minutes, she was relieved to find what she was looking for: two fist-sized stones. She moved back over to the stack of wood and knelt on her knees. Leaning close to the base of the stack, Marie held the rock in her left hand still and with her right hand struck the second rock across the first in a sweeping motion. After several attempts she saw a few sparks fly from the rocks. Encouraged, she piled more dry grass and leaves beside the stack and began to strike the rocks together more aggressively. Sparks started flying with every strike. Faster and faster Marie worked the rocks until she started sweating. Suddenly, a few blades of the dried grass glowed orange briefly before dying out. Marie continued her efforts until she felt her arms were going to fall off. Finally, one of the dried leaves began to smolder and Marie gently blew on it. A small line of smoke rose from the debris. The leaf began to glow more and more and suddenly a small flame burst from it. Marie tossed some of the dead grass onto the leaf and the grass caught fire. As the flames grew, she used a stick and pushed the grass underneath the pile of sticks. Second by second the flames grew larger. Reveling in her success, Marie sat back for a moment. Satisfied that she had enough wood to keep the fire going for a while, she turned her attention to Donald.

Donald's eyes were closed, and he appeared to be sleeping. Marie moved over to him and stroked his hair away from his sweaty forehead. He stirred and opened his eyes about half-way.

"Need I ask how you feel?" Marie asked.

"It would be the polite thing to do," Donald answered groggily.

"What do we need to do next?" she asked. "How do I tend your wounds?"

"You need to cauterize them to stop the flow of blood and prevent them from becoming infected. If we do not, the wounds will fester, my flesh will rot, and I will die."

"Well, we cannot allow that to happen, can we?" Marie replied. "Tell me what to do."

"Remove the bandages and clean as much dried blood away from the wounds as possible. You will need to be able to see the wounds in order to treat them. Check the horses for a long knife. You will set the blade of the knife in the fire and leave it there until it gets as hot as possible. When it is ready, you will have to take the tip of the blade and first insert it into the wound about half an inch or so, and then you will have to press the blade against the outside of the wound. This should stop the bleeding and prevent infection as much as possible. There is still a chance that an infection has started and is beyond our treatment. If that has happened, there is nothing we can do about it."

"There are doctors in Habersham. They could treat you," Marie replied.

"I fear it would be too late," Donald answered. "The infection could spread very quickly and be beyond treatment by the time we get there. But no matter. That is beyond our control. We can only do that which we can do. Now we must get to it. Find the knife."

Marie stood up and walked over to the horses. She found a long dagger in one of Louis's saddlebags. Knowing his penchant for throwing daggers she was not surprised. This one had a blade eight inches long. She laid the knife next to the fire with the blade in the flames. She had also found a piece of cloth in one of Louis's saddlebags along with a metal cup. She walked down to the edge of the river and filled the cup with the chilly water. She also dipped the cloth into the river. Marie returned to Donald's side and knelt on her knees. She unwrapped the binding on his thigh. The dried blood made the binding and part of the patch stiff. She poured some of the water onto his thigh and used the cloth to wipe away as much dried blood as she could. She repeated this a couple of times until his thigh was as clean as she could get it. The wound was no longer bleeding but the skin around the wound was reddening deeply. This concerned Marie and she looked up at Donald. He returned her gaze.

"We can only do that which we can do," he said with a gentle smile. "Now retrieve the knife and do what must be done."

Marie complied and retrieved the knife from the fire, holding the hilt with the wet cloth. She remembered how, in her childhood, she had grabbed a metal pot that had been hanging over a fire and had burned her hand. To this day she could almost feel the pain if she thought about it enough. She knew that pain was nothing compared to what Donald was about to endure. She positioned the knife over the wound.

"Insert the tip of the blade into the wound for a couple of seconds, and then press it on top of the wound for a few more seconds," Donald instructed. "I will try to hold my leg still, but do not be offended if I suddenly kick you in the head."

"That you say to a woman standing over you with a hot knife," Marie replied. "If I were you, I would do a little more than try." She looked in his eyes one more time and he gave her a nod of approval. She looked down at his thigh, moved the knife as close to the wound as possible, and after a short pause, inserted the tip of the blade a half inch into the wound.

Donald shut his eyes and gritted his teeth, but it was not enough to prevent a loud cry of pain from escaping his lips. His body arched but somehow, he kept his leg still. Marie removed the blade and pressed the flat part of the blade against the outside of the wound. Donald cried in pain again. The complete process took maybe three seconds but to Donald it seemed an eternity. Marie moved away from him and placed the blade of the knife into the fire once again. She took the cup of water and gave Donald a long drink. He thankfully swallowed the cold liquid and leaned back against the large rock behind him.

"See?" he said, half panting. "That was not so bad, now, was it?"

"Being that I did not get kicked in the head I would say the operation was quite the success," Marie answered.

"One down, one to go," he said. "One down, one to go," Marie agreed. "I need to get more water. I will return in a moment." She took the cup and the cloth back to the river. She rinsed out the cloth several times and filled the cup with water. She returned to find Donald sitting up and slouching forward a bit.

"What took you so long?" he asked jokingly.

"I went for a swim," Marie replied in kind. "The water is quite refreshing. You should try it."

"In the morning," Donald answered, sounding as if he were about to fall asleep. "I shall take a swim in the morning."

Marie moved around to Donald's back and removed the binding and bandage. She repeated the process of cleaning the wound. Just as with Donald's thigh, the area around the wound was a dark red color. She did not know much about medicine, but this did not look good. She figured that even with what they were doing Donald would need attention from a real doctor as soon as possible. Having finished the cleaning part, she moved to the difficult part of the task. She retrieved the knife from the fire and returned to face Donald's back. Marie bent over and held the knife a couple of inches from his bare back.

"Unlike your thigh, I believe this might hurt a bit," she tried to joke but knew it was not a very funny thing to say. Donald did not reply but simply kept his head hung down on his chest, preparing himself as best he could for the pain. Marie proceeded with the grisly task and inserted the tip of the knife into the wound, then pulled it out and pressed the flat end of the blade against the wound. There was no cry from Donald this time, just a deep groan of pain. He began to slump over to the side and Marie quickly caught him. The exhaustion and pain had finally taken their toll and Donald had dropped into unconsciousness. She gently laid him on the ground, then walked over to the horses and again went through the saddlebags. She found a blanket in one of the pouches on Annon and draped it over Donald. Thankfully, the weather had been warm as of late and the temperature that evening would not dip below sixty degrees. Still, Marie knew that in Donald's weakened state he would need to be kept much warmer than usual. She spent the next thirty minutes gathering more firewood until the last light of the day faded away. Next, she lit a second small fire about five feet from the first one, closer to Donald's feet. The two fires together, if she could keep them burning through the night, should provide more than enough heat for Donald.

Marie sat down, quite tired from the long, chaotic day. Her stomach reminded her that she had not eaten in close to 24 hours. In her rummaging through the saddlebags and pouches on the horses she had not discovered anything to eat. While there were certainly fish in the river, she had never tried to catch fish and her lack of experience, along with the darkness, would make such an effort a waste of energy. She settled back against one of the boulders, wondering if she would get any sleep at all or if the excitement of the day, and the trepidation of spending the night outside while possibly being tracked, would keep her awake. For a couple of lonely hours Marie was able to stay awake as she contemplated all that had happened in the past few days. It was all a whirlwind starting with her and Andrew's discovery, her being kidnapped by Gallard's men, the interrogation, the rescue, and the escape. She desperately wanted to return to the safety of her home, but she knew that this was her one chance to solve the mystery of the foreign phrases she had found in her mother's books. Marie reached into a pocket of her vest and pulled out the carefully folded piece of paper. Ever since finding the hidden papers in her mother's study, Marie had carried a sample of the writings around on a daily basis. She had studied the foreign symbols time and time again until she could picture them in her sleep and write them from memory. However, they held as little meaning today as they did the first day she found them. It just happened that the day she was kidnapped she had the paper hidden in a pocket in her skirt. When she had changed clothes in the tent, she remembered to retrieve the paper. She gazed at the writing, vainly hoping that some meaning would come to her. But it was no use. She had looked at the paper a hundred times, often long enough to get a headache, yet the meaning of the writing remained foreign to her. Her eyelids began to grow heavy after a few minutes and she folded the paper and placed it back in the pocket. She no longer fought sleep and welcomed it like an old friend.

It seemed the dream began as soon as she closed her eyes. She saw herself on the outskirts of the enemy encampment, sitting in a field by a pond, the late afternoon sun dipping low in the sky. For some reason she had the feeling that she had been there with her friends Elizabeth and Heather, but now she was alone. She had to get to a safe place but in order to do that she had to make her way through the encampment. She knew that while there was daylight, she was okay. The enemy would not bother her. But as soon as the light faded and darkness overtook the land, her life would be in grave danger. If she were captured, there would be no interrogation, no imprisonment. There would be torture, and worse. Darkness was approaching, and she had little time left. She jumped to her feet and started walking quickly toward the camp. The closer she got to the camp the quicker the sun's light faded. She started to run. She finally reached the first of the camp's hundreds upon hundreds of tents, all evenly spaced in columns and rows. Daylight had all but disappeared. Marie had to choose a row to run down that would hopefully carry her to a safe haven on the other side of the camp while remaining undetected. All at once an enormous wave of déjà vu engulfed her. She suddenly had the overwhelming feeling she had been there before. She remembered having gotten lost in the maze of tents and having been confronted by one enemy soldier after another. In that memory she had barely escaped with her life. Now, fear started to overwhelm her as she darted down one of the foreboding rows of tents. It was completely dark with no moon and little light coming from the faint stars. She could barely see her way. As she neared a tent on her right, she sensed that someone had stepped out of it. On her left, she detected a shadowy figure emerging from another tent. Her panicked heart began to pound in her chest. She turned down a row to her left and more shadowy figures appeared in the darkness. It did not take long to realize that this time, there was no escaping the enemy. This time, unspeakable things would be done to her, and her life would be ripped from her. More and more men appeared outside of the tents and now her way was fully blocked. She could not go back, and she could not go forward. Her knees became weak as the terror took full grip on her. Out of the crowd of the faceless enemy, one man stepped forward. She could hear him speaking to the other men, but it sounded like he was speaking in no more than a whisper and she could not hear clearly what he was saying. The other men began to back away ever so slowly. The man approached her, speaking directly to her, but she could still not understand what he was saying. The man stopped directly in front of her and reached out, touching her on the shoulder. This time, she heard him clearly: "Marie." He said her name again, and again, as if calling to her. The voice became louder and louder. Suddenly, in the dream, she realized she was dreaming and with a start, woke up … and abruptly screamed as her eyes opened to the face of a man no more than a foot from her own. Her reflexes took over and without even a thought to it she leaped to her feet with the dagger in her hand. The fires had nearly burned out and she could not make out the face of the man. She took a defensive posture, the foreboding feeling from her dream no longer being just a dream. The voice from her dream spoke.

"Marie," the voice said, "it is okay. You are safe." It was a familiar voice, and Marie started to let down her guard.

"Lawrence?" she asked, almost wondering if she was still dreaming. "Lawrence, is that you?"

"Aye, it is me," he replied calmly.

"I cannot believe you are here!" she exclaimed excitedly, rushing forward and embracing him. His damp, wet clothes brought a chill to her, but she did not care. She was no longer alone with an injured man who was all but a stranger to her. She now had a long-time friend, someone she trusted and who made her feel safe. After several seconds she released him.

"I was certain you had been captured or killed. I cannot believe you escaped. What happened?" She looked around the small camp but did not see Louis. "Where is Louis?"

"Louis …" Lawrence started, then paused as if searching for the right words. "Louis did not make it," he finally said, a slight crack to his voice.

"Oh no!" Marie exclaimed, her heart feeling as though it skipped a beat. "What happened?"

"After you and Donald fled, we knew we had no chance of fighting five thousand men. The enemy began pouring from the tents like hornets from a nest. In no more than fifteen seconds after you left there were a hundred men confronting us. We saw a small opening between two tents and ran for it. It seemed that just as we would come up on a tent, half a dozen men would spill out and nearly block our escape. Fortunately, they were all still groggy and were not sure what was happening. We had to change directions several times and for all intents and purposes were lost, not knowing where to go. We were about to make a stand when I heard the roar of the river not far from where we were standing. I grabbed Louis and we ran for the river.

"It was probably a hundred yards to the river. We dashed across the field and heard a hail of arrows soar over our heads. As we approached the river, we could see that the embankment was fifteen or twenty feet high. We never hesitated. At a full run we leaped into the water, hoping that it would carry us away from certain death. I cannot tell you how long we were carried by the water. We fought desperately to keep our heads above the churning water and more times than I can count I swallowed a river. We slowly began drifting farther and farther apart and after several minutes I could no longer see Louis. The icy water and the constant fighting to stay afloat quickly sapped my strength. I must have hit my head on a rock for I blacked out at some point. I awoke to find myself lying on a sandbar, half out of the water. I looked around but did not see Louis. I walked back up the river half a mile but did not see him. I continued down river and finally, around dusk, I spotted him. He was still in the water, near the opposite side of the river, caught up in a small logjam. I waded across the river to him but knew before I reached him that there was little if any hope. I could see the broken shafts of two arrows sticking out of his back. I pulled his body out of the water …" Lawrence's voice cracked again. He had to look away and bite his trembling lip. Marie could see tears starting to form in Lawrence's eyes. She could not hold back her own tears and soon they were running down her cheeks. "I pulled his body out of the water and buried him along the riverbank in a little grove. After sitting there for I do not know how long I got up and continued downriver, hoping to find a town. Instead, I found you. And I am glad I found you instead."

"Oh, Louis," Marie sobbed, looking away and into the night. "Louis. You risked your life to save mine and you paid the greatest of costs. I would that I had died, and you had lived." She sat back down, not trusting her legs to keep her standing. "Why did he have to die? He was a good man, an incredibly good man."

"Indeed he was," Lawrence agreed, his voice shaky. "He was a good man and a great friend. He gladly risked his life to save yours and I would say he would not have regretted capture, torture, or death itself if it meant saving your life." Lawrence turned to Donald, desiring to change the subject.

"What happened to him? Is he okay?"

"He, too, felt the enemy's arrows. One in his shoulder, one in his thigh. I was able to remove the arrows and cauterized the wounds, but I do not know whether an infection will grow or he will be okay. The wounds looked as though infections may have started but with little experience in such areas I could not know for certain."

Lawrence walked over to Donald and bent over. He lifted the blanket to reveal Donald's injured thigh. He inspected the wound.

"An infection has indeed started," he said solemnly. "It does not appear to be that bad but without treatment it could very easily grow worse and take his life." Lawrence marched over to his horse and reached into one of the saddlebags. He retrieved two pouches and returned to Donald's side. "I am no physician, but this should help. It is something Ian gave me one time to help treat minor wounds." Lawrence opened one of the pouches and dusted Donald's wounds with a fine, white powder. From the second pouch he poured another, darker powder into a cup of water. He mixed it around a bit then leaned over and lifted Donald's head. He placed the cup at Donald's lips and tilted it up enough so that a little of the liquid poured out. Donald briefly opened his eyes, but Marie could tell that he was not totally conscious. He reflexively swallowed some of the liquid, then closed his eyes again.

"Perhaps that will help keep the infection from festering," Lawrence said as he gently lowered Donald's head to the ground. "However, I would feel much better if he were to receive attention from a true physician."

"Dunnesboro is the closest town," Marie said. "I do not know how much farther it is. Perhaps just a few hours ride, perhaps half-a-day."

"We cannot travel in the dark," Lawrence said. "The terrain is too challenging. We will have to wait until first light to move on. Until then, let us keep the fires burning and keep our fingers crossed that what we have done for Donald will be enough." Lawrence moved off to search for more firewood and Marie could only sit with her knees pulled up to her chest, rocking back and forth ever so slightly, dwelling on the fondest of memories of the life and fellowship of her friend Louis.

Chapter 10

Instead of a terror-fraught nightmare it was a most delicious aroma that brought Marie out of her slumber. Knowing that Lawrence was there and that she was safe, she had been able to sleep soundly despite being outside and sleeping on the ground. She opened her eyes and sat up. One of the fires had died out but the second still had a small flame flickering. Three long sticks were stuck in the ground, leaning out over the fire. On the end of each stick was a medium-sized fish, baking in the heat of the fire. Her stomach immediately rumbled and reminded her just how hungry she really was.

"Breakfast is served," Lawrence said as he stepped into the camping area from the direction of the river.

"Lawrence, you are amazing. I am famished," Marie said as she scooted over to the fire. She looked around the camping area. "Where is Donald?" she asked concerned, not seeing her patient where he had lain the night before.

"Do not worry," Lawrence replied. "He is okay. He is down by the river washing up a bit."

"How are his wounds?" Marie asked.

"They do not appear to be any worse than last night," Lawrence replied. "He seems to be recovering. The fish should be ready. Help yourself."

Marie reached over and pulled one of the sticks out of the ground. Lawrence had cut off the heads and tails of the fish and cleaned them. She gently plucked a small portion of meat off the fish and slowly placed it in her mouth. It was not too hot, and the taste was particularly good.

"My compliments to the chef," she said as she chewed the morsel. "It even tastes as though it were seasoned."

"I would not have a princess eat a bland piece of fish," Lawrence replied, smiling. "But do not ask the recipe for it is an ancient family secret."

"I see," Marie smiled back. "You are certainly full of surprises."

"As you are," Lawrence answered, his smile fading away.

"Now what would motivate you to such a conclusion?" she asked with a puzzled look on her face.

"If I am not mistaken, I believe home is that way," he said, pointing to his left. "However, it seems that you are heading that way," he finished, pointing to his right. "A rational person might find that curious."

"It only seemed reasonable to head for the closest town considering Donald's injuries," Marie replied.

"What would seem reasonable is for the king's kidnapped daughter to return to her most worried father as hastily as possible," Lawrence countered.

"We could not take a direct route back," Marie argued. "Gallard's men were chasing Andrew in that direction."

"Speaking of which, what happened after you and Donald bolted from the camp?" Lawrence asked. "Obviously, you made it back to Andrew. How did you end up split from him?"

"There were several of Gallard's men at the post along the road," Marie explained. "As Donald and I passed they gave chase. That was when Donald was struck by the arrows. We reached Andrew's hiding place with Gallard's men mere seconds behind us. Being injured, Donald would not have been able to ride long enough to evade capture. Knowing this, Andrew insisted that he trade places with Donald and lead Gallard's men away while Donald and I hid in the brush. Andrew took off and after Gallard's men passed us, Donald and I took a game trail toward the river, out of sight of Gallard's camp. We had intended to turn back south and head home, but I was afraid that Donald's wounds would threaten his life if we did not find him a physician as quickly as possible. It seemed that the quickest, and safest, route to medical attention would be the route to Dunnesboro or Habersham. Gallard would certainly have dispatched a hundred men to comb the road and lands south to find Donald and me. We would have been captured before the sun had set."

"Indeed, that does sound reasonable," Lawrence admitted, nodding his head. "Very reasonable. Now, why do you not tell me the real reason you are traveling to Habersham?"

"But I just told you," Marie replied innocently, taking another bite of the fish. "Our direction is dictated by Donald's injuries and Gallard's forces."

"Yes, that is what you told me," Lawrence replied, again nodding his head. "However, that is not what Donald told me hardly a half-hour ago. He is under the impression that you are heading to Habersham as part of some mystery, not as an effort to seek him medical attention. Now how would such an idea be impressed upon him?"

"His injuries have made him a bit delusional?" Marie offered half-heartedly.

"Nice try," Lawrence replied, not buying Marie's explanation. "Could this side trip have something to do with the DuFay Armor?"

Marie stopped chewing and a look of total surprise overtook her face. How could Lawrence know about the DuFay Armor? Andrew must have told him. The next logical question was, just how much did Andrew tell Lawrence? First Donald, now Lawrence. It appeared that Andrew could not keep a secret.

"The DuFay Armor?" Marie asked in reply. "What do you know about the DuFay Armor?"

"Andrew told us the story," Lawrence confessed. "He told us of his quest to find the descendant of Reginald DuFay, which turned out to be his very own brother. Well, his adopted brother. He told us of your discoveries in the dark, deserted passageways and hidden rooms in your father's castle. He told us that Gallard is most likely on a mission to take from your father the shield and now that he knows where Andrew is, the sword as well."

"My father has the shield?" Marie asked, perplexed. "What leads Andrew to believe that my father possesses the DuFay shield?"

Lawrence immediately regretted his careless slip. For whatever his reasons, Andrew had not wanted Marie to know that her father possessed the shield. Perhaps he was afraid that she would confront her father about the shield and her father would persuade her to reveal her own knowledge of the shield. That could possibly lead to her confessing Andrew's true purpose and place his life in danger. Lawrence knew that the point was now moot.

"Andrew spoke with someone in your village who had first-hand knowledge of your father's possession of the shield. He also believes that Gallard possesses the breastplate. Now that Gallard is here, I would say that at least three pieces of the DuFay Armor may very well be reunited."

"With whom did Andrew speak?" Marie asked, curiosity prompting her question. "Who could possibly know something like that?"

"Carl Bergman," Lawrence said, diverting his eyes from Marie. "Apparently he somehow knew that your father has the shield."

"Bergman?" Marie asked. "What could Mr. Bergman possibly know about what my father may or may not possess?"

"Bergman was one of the elders of the village when your father first came to Durinburg," Lawrence replied. "Apparently, the elders knew of the DuFay Armor and had been searching for clues. They actually found the shield." At this point Lawrence paused. He did not want to tell Marie that Andrew suspected her father of murdering the village elders. He chose his words carefully. "Somehow, the shield ended up in your father's possession, at least according to Bergman."

"I wonder if it was Mr. Bergman that Andrew was interested in spending time with instead of Heather," Marie mused. "They should have quite a bit to talk about now."

"Marie," Lawrence said, looking at her with soft eyes, not quite knowing how to say what he had to say. "There was an accident. It must have happened after you were kidnapped. Carl Bergman is dead."

"Dead?" Marie repeated, stunned. "Mr. Bergman is dead?"

"I am sorry to have to tell you. It was an accident in his shop. There was a fire. Nobody was around to help him. The rest of his family is fine, though," Lawrence quickly added. "Heather, Steven, and Ms. Bergman are fine."

"How awful," Marie said hardly above a whisper as Carl Bergman's face crossed her memory and a tear slid down her cheek. "Mr. Bergman was such a nice man. I spent many days and nights in his home over the years. He was a second father to me. What a tragedy."

"A most sorrowful misfortune," Lawrence agreed grimly.

"You said that Mr. Bergman was an elder of the village?" Marie asked. "I did not know that. Who are the others? If they know of the DuFay Armor perhaps they can assist us in determining the truthfulness of the legend. We should speak with them."

"I would that speaking with them were possible," Lawrence replied. "However, they have all passed away. Mr. Bergman was the last."

"All of them?" Marie asked, surprised. "How many were there and how did they die?"

"There were originally four," Lawrence said, not entirely comfortable with where he thought the conversation was going. "One drowned in the lake. Another was trampled by a horse. And just as Mr. Bergman died in an accidental fire so did the fourth elder. The first three died many years ago. I would say, in fact, that they died within a year of the discovery of the shield."

"So, the four elders who found the shield and were

knowledgeable of the DuFay legend all met with accidents and died," Mary mused aloud. "The first three died within a year of discovering the shield, and now Mr. Bergman. It sounds to me as though the shield were a curse, not part of a promise."

"It would seem so," Lawrence agreed, though not whole-heartedly.

"And now my father has the shield," Marie continued. "I wonder how my father came into possession of it. Would the elders have given it to him? That would seem unlikely. Certainly, he would not have taken it from them by force. My father would not do something like that."

"I do not have the answer to that question," Lawrence said. "All I know is the little bit that Andrew told me about the shield and a few conversations he had engaged in with Mr. Bergman."

"I cannot believe Andrew did not confide in me his knowledge that my father possesses the shield," Marie said, her feelings hurt. "After all that we shared, after all that we went through together, he did not tell me. I can only wonder what other secrets he has kept from me."

"Is your venture to Habersham a secret of your own?" Lawrence asked, prodding for information and trying to change the subject. "Why do you go there? The mystery has been solved and the descendant has been found. What need is there to journey to Habersham when instead you should be returning to your father where you would be safe?"

"Only part of the mystery has been solved," Marie answered. "Did Andrew tell you of the inscription on the sword?"

"Inscription? He must have conveniently forgotten that little piece of information," Lawrence replied sourly.

"There is an inscription on the sword. It is in a language completely foreign to us. I had a copy of the inscription taken to a scholar in Habersham who translated it for us. Part of the inscription was a phrase, 'Sword of the spirit.' The second part was what appeared to be some semblance of an alphanumeric code. We could not determine what the code meant. The translator had failed to provide additional information. My journey to Habersham is to obtain additional translation."

"Just how much importance could some ancient writing on a sword possess?" Lawrence inquired.

"I do not know," Marie confessed, "but I feel there must be some importance to it. Andrew and I discovered a painting while in the hidden room. In this painting were the six pieces of armor. Each piece had an inscription on it. I cannot chase away the suspicion that these inscriptions, and what they represent, are vital to the DuFay legend."

"Were the inscriptions the same on all six objects?" Lawrence inquired, his interest having been pricked.

"I could not tell with utmost certainty," she replied. "The writing was too small. However, my impression was that the writings were different."

"It is too bad that you do not have all six inscriptions to be translated. If you did, perhaps together they would hold more meaning than when standing alone."

In answer, Marie simply smiled as he reached into a pocket and retrieved the piece of paper. She handed it to Lawrence.

"Where did you obtain this?" he asked as he studied the strange symbols. "Did you find it in the same room in which the painting was located?"

"No," Marie replied. "My discovery was made in my mother's personal library. A few weeks ago I found several books in her private collection that contained loose, hidden pages. Within those pages I discovered not only the symbols engraved on the sword but also six additional sets of symbols in what appeared to be the same language. Five of the sets were of similar length to the first but the sixth was much longer. I cannot discard the suspicion that these symbols together are the key to the mystery revolving around the DuFay legend. I must know what they mean."

"And that is why you must travel to Habersham," Lawrence

logically concluded. "You are hoping that the man who interpreted the sword inscription will be able to interpret these other writings."

"Yes," Marie answered, looking at Lawrence hopefully. "That is why I must travel to Habersham. It is neither for myself nor for Andrew that I pursue this course. It is for my homeland. It is for our homeland. The meaning of these words could very well avert a bloody war which I fear is threatening home."

Lawrence stared into Marie's eyes for several long seconds. What was his primary duty here? Did he allow Marie to continue her investigation? If she continued to Habersham there was no guarantee that she would be able to obtain a translation of the writings and even if she were successful, there was no guarantee that the writings held any meaning that could potentially avert a war. Her life would continue to be in danger, and it would be very possible for Gallard's men to kidnap her a second time. On the other hand, he could force her to return to her home and her father, which would ordinarily be the wisest course of action. However, it would not be the most pleasant of trips for he knew that when Marie was in a foul mood, she could make life miserable for anyone near her.

"To say that it would be unwise to allow you to continue to Habersham without the appropriate escort would be an extreme understatement," Lawrence finally said. "You would need three or four of your father's men to secure your safety. It would be best to return to your father, now, without farther delay."

"But we must know the meaning of these symbols," Marie urged.

"Then as you did before, you can send an aide to Habersham with the piece of paper to obtain the translation," Lawrence suggested.

"We do not have time for that," Marie countered firmly. "Gallard's army appears poised to attack at any time. In fact, considering my escape, I would be greatly surprised if they have not already struck camp and commenced their march toward Durinburg. If we ride hard, it would be possible for us to reach Habersham late tonight. In the morning we could visit the linguist and obtain the translation of the phrases, then immediately start back to Durinburg. Normally it would be a three-day ride back home, but I believe we could cut the time to two-and-a-half days if we push ourselves and limit our rest stops. We could be home in less than four days from now."

"If Gallard's army is indeed on the move, it will take them at least five days to march to Durinburg," Lawrence stated. "That is too close for comfort. Your father needs to be warned as quickly as possible so he can make proper preparations." Lawrence paused for a moment. "What about Andrew? He will certainly reach home before we do. Would he not warn your father?"

"And take the chance of being killed on the spot? Andrew is brave but not stupid," Marie answered. "Nothing less than my testimony will convince my father that Andrew had nothing to do with my kidnapping. Until then, my father will consider Andrew a spy and if he has the opportunity, he will kill him."

"Then who will warn your father?" Lawrence asked. "A report, in person, by you or me would be the only report your father would believe. If we leave now, we would be able to reach Durinburg in two-and-a-half days if we travel quickly."

"Then you must leave now and warn my father," Marie said matter-of-factly. "I will continue to Habersham as planned and obtain the translation of the phrases. Three days and an evening from now Donald and I will return home."

"Marie, I hesitated to tell you this before but as you have insisted on proceeding with your journey to Habersham I cannot in good conscience keep this to myself." Lawrence paused for a moment and looked intently at Marie, hoping she would understand the seriousness of what he was about to say. "Andrew believes that Carl Bergman's death was no accident. Andrew believes that Mr. Bergman was murdered."

"Murdered?" Marie asked incredulously. "Why would someone murder Mr. Bergman?"

"Because he knew of the sword and the shield. Andrew also has a theory that my father and the other two village elders who knew of the shield were murdered as well."

"Who could have done such a thing?" she asked.

"Someone who wished to keep the DuFay legend a secret. Someone who was searching for the Armor and felt the need to remove all obstacles. Marie, men have died simply because they knew of this legend. You know more than most people. You are in great danger. You know I cannot allow you to proceed without an escort. The risk is too great."

"What of the risk to my father and his kingdom? What of the risk to your home and friends? Are those risks not much greater than what I take? Much must be risked for much is at risk," Marie countered. "Besides, who is going to mistake me for a princess in these clothes?"

"You have a point," Lawrence admitted. "There is little chance anyone would even guess your true gender under those rags." Lawrence mused the situation over for a few seconds, but he knew what needed to be done.

"Very well," he conceded, "you and Donald continue to Habersham, and I will return to Durinburg and warn your father. I expect to see you in less than four days. If you fail to show up, well, do not expect me to risk my life on another rescue attempt. I have a policy that I only rescue kidnapped maidens once per year and I have already filled my quota for this year."

"Thank you," Marie said with a smile. As they finished their conversation Donald came limping back into camp. He was moving quite well for someone who had been shot in the leg twenty-four hours earlier.

"There is nothing quite like a cold-water river bath to wake one up in the morning," he said cheerfully. "Ah, I see breakfast is served." He walked over to the fire and retrieved one of the wellroasted fish. "A bit on the done side, I would have to say."

"You should not have taken half the morning to bathe," Lawrence countered. "The fish were very tasty fifteen minutes ago."

"So, what is the verdict?" Donald asked as he chewed a large bite of the fish. "Do we continue to Habersham as the princess has deemed necessary, or do we return the princess to her home as the faithful friend has deemed necessary?"

"You and I will continue to Habersham," Marie answered.

"What a surprise," Donald replied sarcastically.

"Lawrence will return to our homeland and warn my father of Gallard's approaching army. We will rendezvous with him in three-and-a-half days."

"It is settled then," Lawrence announced as he walked over to his horse. "It would be best that I leave immediately. There is no time to spare. You father needs as much forewarning as possible." He grabbed his horse's reins and walked the animal to the outskirts of the camp before climbing into the saddle. As he sat on the horse's back, he turned and looked squarely at Donald. "Her life is entirely in your hands. Return her home safe and without injury. There will be much gratitude."

"I shall do my best to not disappoint anyone," Donald replied casually. "And do not worry, I will strive to keep myself safe and free from injury as well."

Lawrence managed a weak smile as he kicked his horse in the ribs, and they galloped back up-river.

"We should be moving as soon as possible ourselves," Marie stated as she kicked dirt onto the fire to extinguish it. "If we can reach Habersham early enough this evening, we may be able to catch the linguist before he returns home for the night. Otherwise we will have to wait until morning and waste this evening. How are your wounds? Are you able to ride?"

"They are rather painful as you can imagine but yes, I am certainly able to ride." Donald hobbled over to Annon and hoisted himself onto the massive horse's back. "Lead the way, Princess."

Without another word Marie climbed onto the back of the second horse and guided it out of camp, heading downstream and hopefully toward the answer to the mystery of the DuFay Armor.

Chapter 11

The overcast sky did its best to hide dawn's first light as Marie and Donald made their way toward Habersham. The duo had ridden well into the night and after only a few hours' rest, resumed their journey. They had not passed a single soul on the road and the trip had thus far been uneventful. For most of their ride conversation had been sparse. Donald was still mystified by the revelation of his history and his possible destiny. Both were a far cry from anything he could have ever imagined. His life, as well as that of his family, could be set on a path that might very well be quite difficult to traverse. He still felt that he needed more proof, more convincing of Andrew's story before he could begin to accept it as reality. And even if it were true, he did not know if he could be persuaded to accept the responsibility that came with it.

Marie, meanwhile, was pre-occupied with many different thoughts. She was still stunned at the news of the deaths of Louis and Carl Bergman. She had known both men very well and the sting of their passing would not soon pass. Not a little troubling to her was the news that her father quite possibly possessed the DuFay Shield. Pulling from deep within her memory, there were numerous events that made the prospect plausible. She was also discomforted by the notion that her father could be seeking to obtain the Armor for his own gain. And then, as she found happening quite often, her thoughts turned to Andrew. She could not help but wonder where he was and if he had escaped his pursuers. Feeling the need for conversation, she broke the long silence.

"I cannot help but wonder if Andrew was successful in eluding Gallard's men," she said, hoping Donald was in the mood to converse.

"You need not worry about Andrew," Donald replied, himself thankful for the broken silence. "He was always quite adept at eluding detection and capture."

"I am not surprised. He does appear to be well-skilled in many areas. As a matter of fact, it was not long ago that he was victorious in our annual Skills Contest," Marie replied.

"Skills Contest?" Donald repeated inquisitively.

"It is a series of challenges designed to test the skills of the competitors in various situations with various weapons, highlighted by the last event which is test of endurance over a long and difficult obstacle course. The contest is held over a two-day period."

"And Andrew won this contest?" Donald asked.

"By a very large margin," Marie replied. "He even set a new record for points acquired across all events."

"I am not surprised," Donald stated. "Andrew always was one of if not the best fighter in the kingdom. He has quite a talent for wielding weaponry. That is why Gallard elevated him to such a high status."

"A high status?" Marie asked, intrigued. "And what status might that have been?"

"Andrew was commander of Gallard's army," Donald replied. "Only the king himself and his three highest personal advisors held more power than Andrew."

"Commander?" Marie repeated, surprised. "Andrew was commander of the army?"

"Aye, for nearly five years before his sudden and mysterious departure," Donald affirmed. "He led our army to overwhelming victories in several campaigns. There were whispers that Gallard planned to take Andrew into his innermost circle at the conclusion of the last campaign. That was when I was nearly killed, and Andrew disappeared."

"I knew there was more to him than he was telling me," Marie said with vindication. "He always professed to have no desire to be in a position of authority or leadership, yet it did not take a person of great intuition to see that he was a person of authority and leadership. Is he truly as modest as he pretends to be?"

"For the most part, he is. However, there are times when he appears just a tad impressed with his skills. I would not say that he exhibits arrogance, but he does exhibit a certain degree of self-confidence that at times borders on arrogance. He most often lets his skills speak for himself and when they do, they speak very loudly."

"He must have been rather popular with the women considering his position, skills, and for the most part, charming personality," Marie said, fishing for information.

"That is an understatement," Donald replied. "He was easily the most popular bachelor in the entire kingdom though he would never admit to it. He could never be convinced that so many of the young ladies fancied him."

"That sounds precisely like the Andrew I know," Marie chuckled. "Did he ever pursue or court any of these young ladies?"

"Only one that I know of," Donald replied.

"And what happened?" Marie asked, her curiosity pricked.

"I married her," Donald answered with a sly grin.

"That must have settled well with him," she said sarcastically. "This is not something Andrew ever mentioned to me. You must tell me the whole story, or my curiosity will drive me insane."

"There was a young maiden in the village," Donald said, reaching far back into his memory, "a genuinely nice, wholesome, and beautiful girl. Her name was Cynthia. We were quite young then, hardly twenty years old. Andrew and I would challenge each other to approach her and speak with her though neither of us had much courage back then. It was not a large village, our home, so it was often that we saw this young lady. Gradually, we both had numerous opportunities to speak with her individually and we did so. Over time we both became very taken with her. She never treated either of us differently than the other and it was obvious that she had feelings for both of us. Though we were brothers, hostility arose between Andrew and me on account of Cynthia. I finally confessed to him that I was going to propose to her, and he did not take the news well. He said that he was intending on proposing to her. We argued as you can imagine, and the verbal battle soon transformed into a physical battle. It was quite the fight. Eventually, we both lay on the ground, exhausted, bleeding, and bruised. Nothing had been resolved other than the fact that neither of us could physically defeat the other. In the days following, Cynthia appeared to become more amicable toward me and a bit more distant toward Andrew. We never knew her reasons, but it was obvious that she had made her choice. It was not long after Andrew and I fought that I proposed to Cynthia. She accepted, and Andrew and I went back to being the closest of brothers."

"So, Cynthia chose you over Andrew and neither of you ever learned her reason?" Marie asked.

"To this day she has refused to confess to her reasons," Donald affirmed.

"And after that Andrew never pursued another woman?"

"None of whom I was ever aware," Donald replied.

"How intriguing," Marie mused. "How very intriguing."

Their conversation ended as the duo approached the outer buildings of the town of Habersham. The morning was in full swing and there were numerous people milling around, going about their daily business. The gray stone buildings looked cold and dreary as the sky continued to be shrouded by a heavy bank of clouds. There were two dozen buildings of various sizes and shapes spread out along several horse-trodden dirt streets. Hardly more than a passing glance was offered to Donald and Marie as they led their horses into the heart of town. The people seemed as cold as the buildings around them.

"A friendly town, I see," Marie observed facetiously as her eyes swept across the sober pedestrians along the street.

"That it is," Donald agreed in kind. "I have seen more joy in many a cemetery than I see in the faces of these people. I am grateful our time here will be short. Let us find this linguist you seek and be on our way."

"Pardon me, ma'am," Marie called out as an older woman passed close to their horses. "We are looking for Professor Mechem. Do you know where we might find him?"

The woman paused and looked up at Marie. Her expression was questioning and suspicious, but underneath she looked weary and sad. She looked into Marie's eyes for a few seconds, then wordlessly pointed up the street with a gnarled, bony finger. She slowly lowered her arm and continued with her morning business, never uttering a sound.

"That was extremely helpful," Donald said to Marie as he watched the woman shuffle down the street.

"Come on. We will find someone with a little less indifference toward visitors up the street," Marie said as she nudged her horse in the ribs. They passed two more buildings and several more people before they stopped again and inquired of a passerby as to the location of Professor Mechem's residence. Like the old woman down the street, the man did not speak a word but pointed toward a two-story building across the street. Marie and Donald lowered themselves to the ground and walked their horses over to the indicated building. A wooden sign hung next to the door had "Mechem" crudely painted on it. With a glance at Donald, Marie rapped on the door several times. Thirty seconds later the door opened, and a sad looking young man of sixteen years opened the door.

"Good morning," Marie said. "We are looking for Professor Mechem."

"He is not here," the young man said, hanging his head and looking at the ground.

"Would you know where we might find him, or when he might be returning?" Marie continued, her senses telling her that something was not right. "It is very important that we speak with him."

"He is not here," the young man repeated as he prepared to close the door. Donald reached out and held the door open.

"Young man, we apologize for our early-morning visit and any inconvenience it has caused you," he said softly. "However, we have traveled several days to speak with the professor regarding an issue of significant importance. If you will tell us when the professor is expected to return, we shall withdraw and return at such a time and inconvenience you no more." The boy looked up at Marie and Donald, meeting their eyes.

"The professor will not be returning," he finally said. "He had an accident yesterday morning. He is dead."

"Dead?" Marie repeated, stunned. "The professor is dead?" She looked at Donald but directed her question to the boy. "How did he die?"

"He fell from a ladder he had climbed to reach some books. His neck was broken."

"How tragic," Marie said with genuine sorrow. "Did you know him well?"

"I am his grandson," the boy replied solemnly.

"I am so sorry," Marie offered, not knowing what else to say. "My mother died when I was but a young girl. I know the pain you are feeling."

"Thank you," the boy responded automatically, without much feeling.

"What is your name?" Marie asked.

"Reinard," the boy replied.

"Reinard, we shall not impede upon your grieving much longer, but I must ask for your help," Marie said, hoping the boy would not shut them out. "Several weeks ago, I sent to the professor some documents and requested his aide in translating them.

They were especially important documents of a personal nature. I would like to retrieve them if you can find them."

The boy hesitated a moment and looked as if he were going to deny her request and shut the door. After a moment of decision-making, he slowly opened the door and allowed them to enter the house. He closed the door behind them.

"Please, sit," the boy instructed, pointing to a couple of crude looking chairs along one side of the small room. "I will retrieve the documents." As Marie and Donald carefully sat in the not-too-sturdy looking chairs, the boy disappeared up a set of stairs. After several minutes he returned with a small stack of papers.

"Are these your documents?" he inquired.

Marie took the papers from his hand and leafed through them. She let out a sigh of relief as she confirmed that they were hers. "Yes, these are my documents."

"The professor finished the translation several days ago," Reinard informed her, pointing to some of the papers she was holding. "Your papers must be very important."

"Why do you say that?" Donald asked.

"The professor is … I mean, was, not very excitable in general. He always went about his business in a stoic manner. However, during his work on your documents he became quite excited. I could hear him at all hours of the night digging through mounds of books, muttering to himself, and acting as if he were solving some long-lost mystery. He even started having me hide your papers whenever he left the house or was not working on them."

"How very interesting," Marie said, looking at the papers in her hand. "Have you read the papers? Did the professor tell you anything about them?"

"It was not my business to read them," Reinard replied defensively. "I never read the professor's work. He was very protective of his work, and he never mentioned to me anything about your pages. I swear this to you."

"I believe you," Marie replied. "Do not worry, I believe you." She looked over at Donald briefly before asking her next question.

"Reinard, what exactly happened to the professor? Were you here when he fell?" she asked innocently. The boy shook his head slowly.

"If I had been here, he would still be alive. I had left to retrieve some eggs for breakfast as I do every morning," he replied. "When I returned, I found him on the floor where he had fallen. It appeared that he had climbed the ladder looking for something, lost his balance or footing, and fell. He must have fallen onto one of the tables for one was broken into several pieces around him. He knew better than to climb the ladder. He should never have been up on the ladder."

"Why is that?" Donald asked.

"My grandfather was an old man, frail and weak. Three years ago, he nearly fell to his death while reaching for a book on an upper shelf. From that time on he never climbed the ladder but had me climb and retrieve books for him. He should not have been up there. He knew that he was not strong enough. I cannot imagine what he deemed so important that he could not wait just a few more minutes for me to return."

"That is very disturbing, indeed," Marie mused. "You could not tell from his documents the project on which he was working? Was he working on mine?"

"No," Reinard replied, "he was not working on your documents. As a matter of fact, it did not appear that he was working on anything. His tables were clear of any books or documents. He was highly organized. If he had been working on something, he would have had other reference books and documents on his table. Also, he rarely ever worked that early in the morning. He always claimed it took him breakfast plus an early morning walk to get his brain working." The boy looked to the ground, his eyes beginning to well up as the death of his grandfather once again worked on his emotions. "I used to walk with him."

"Reinard, you have been extremely helpful, and we cannot fully express our gratitude and sympathy," Marie said soothingly, feeling that it was time for her and Donald to leave. "I would that there was something we could do to help you in this most difficult time."

"Thank you," he said graciously.

"We will bother you no longer and be on our way. If you ever have need of friends or anything at all, please, come to Durinburg. Come to the castle and ask for Marie."

"Thank you," the boy repeated, still not looking up.

Marie and Donald exchanged a final glance at each other, then stood and left the home.

"It is no wonder the mood in the town is so sour," Donald said as they hefted themselves onto their horses and headed back the way they had come. "No doubt the professor was a popular and beloved man."

"I feel great sorrow for the boy," Marie said. "I did not even ask him if he had family or how he would survive without his grandfather."

"I am sure the boy has friends, if not close relatives, to help him during his grieving and after," Donald answered. "He is young, but he is no child. He will be okay."

"I hope so," Marie replied.

"Now, let us address those papers of yours," Donald said, giving in to his curiosity. "I was under the impression that you were taking something to the professor to be translated. I did not realize that you were traveling to the professor to retrieve that which he had already translated."

"Nobody knows of these papers," Marie answered. "That is, nobody other than you, me, and that young man back there."

"What is the nature of the papers?" Donald asked. "Why are you so secretive with them?"

"They were personal papers of my mother," Marie replied. "I found them a number of weeks ago while in her personal library, which is my personal library now. They were written in a language that I did not understand."

"Why did you feel it was important to have them translated?" Donald continued.

"On several of the pages I found writings that were nearly identical to those etched on the DuFay Sword. In fact, one set of symbols matched exactly those on the sword. I deduced that her writings, or at least part of her writings, must have been related to the DuFay legend. How my mother would know about that I do not know. I now believe the other similar writings are from the other five pieces of armor. These personal notes of hers may enlighten the shroud of darkness that envelopes this legend."

"Perhaps that is why the professor appeared excited and intrigued by your papers," Donald theorized. "Perhaps he, too, knew of the DuFay legend."

"That is a reasonable deduction," Marie agreed. "It is our bad fortune that he met with such a terrible accident. Who knows what information he may have been able to share with us?"

"I am not convinced that the professor's death was an accident," Donald said.

"In truth, neither am I," Marie concurred. "I did not want to say anything to Reinard, though."

"The pieces do not fit together. He was old and weak and had not climbed a ladder in three years. Why would he do so specifically while his grandson was out of the house?"

"Perhaps he was keeping a secret from Reinard," Marie replied. "The reality of the matter could be that he had a project so secret that he did not wish Reinard to know anything about it, or even that it existed. Who knows for how long he could have been secretly working on this project after sending his grandson out for eggs? Perhaps this time, he truly slipped and fell."

"You put forth a sound argument for someone who believes this to have been a malicious act," Donald said.

"I am only looking at both possibilities," Marie replied.

"Reinard said that it did not appear that his grandfather had been working on anything," Donald countered. "Why would someone wish to kill an old man, a harmless old professor, and make it appear to be an accident? How many enemies could an old man such as himself have?"

Instead of responding, Marie looked at the papers in her hand. A sudden revelation hit her, one that was entirely too obvious to have not been considered before.

"Perhaps it was not an enemy of his that killed him," she said in deep thought. "Perhaps it was someone else's enemy."

"That makes little sense," Donald responded. "Why would someone else's enemy wish to kill him?"

"Information," Marie answered. "Information. In his line of work, he was most certainly privy to much information, and I would wager some of it secretive in nature. Either he had information that someone wished to know, and he refused to tell them, or he had information that someone deemed was too sensitive for him to know."

"What kind of information would be of such a secretive nature?" Donald asked. "What is worth a man's life?"

"The DuFay Armor," Marie answered, still looking through the papers in her hands. "A king kidnapped another king's daughter in order to wring from her information about this legend. Men have fought over and killed each other because of this legend. Could it be that my secret dispatch to the professor was not so secret after all? Could it be that the professor was murdered on account of these papers?"

"How could someone have known about the papers?" Donald asked. "You admitted that you did not tell anyone about them."

"I do not know," Marie answered, her mind whirling.

"Besides, we do not even know if there is anything in the papers worth a man's life. They may contain no information of any value whatsoever."

Marie did not respond. She was reading the professor's translated pages, trying to determine if they did indeed carry any information of value. After reading several pages it was obvious that her mother had known about the DuFay legend. She had known a great deal about the legend. When Marie reached the bottom of the fifth page, her eyes widened, and her heart felt as though it skipped two beats. She reined her horse to a stop and read the page again. Her hands began to shake ever so slightly. She read the page for a third time, not believing what she was reading. Having noticed that Marie had stopped, Donald turned around and rode back to her. He could tell that she was very anxious and upset.

"What is it?" he asked, concerned. When she failed to reply, he asked again. "Marie, what is wrong?"

Marie finally looked up from the paper, her eyes full of confusion and disbelief. She looked around her surroundings as though she were caught in a dream. She finally looked back at Donald.

"I think…" she started, then stammered. "No, I cannot believe it!"

"What is it?" Donald asked a third time.

"I think … I think my father may have killed my mother!"

Chapter 12

Lawrence fought off the waves of exhaustion that sought to overwhelm him as daylight broke over the mountains to the east. He had not slept but a few hours in the past four days and seemingly every muscle and bone in his body cried out for rest. With such a dire mission at hand, sleep was a luxury he could ill afford to embrace. Every second of warning he could provide to King Talbot was a second more the king could prepare for war. Ever since leaving Marie and Donald, Lawrence had questioned his decision. However, despite his friendship and concern for Marie, deep down he knew he had made the correct decision. The king had to be warned and preparations made for a defense of the kingdom.

A cool morning mist hovered over the moat surrounding the castle as Lawrence approached. Without a soul in sight, the appearance created was one of abandonment and loneliness. It was an eerie feeling to say the least and Lawrence could only hope that the feeling was not a premonition of things to come. The drawbridge began a slow descent as Lawrence urged his weary horse on. The timing was perfect, as the bridge touched ground and the horse stepped upon it without hesitation. Within another two minutes Lawrence had left his fatigued steed in the hands of the stable boy and entered the castle. He located one of the castle's sentries and informed him that he had extremely urgent news for the king. The sentry instructed Lawrence to wait and disappeared into the castle. With all his might, Lawrence resisted the urge to sit on a nearby bench. He knew that if he were to sit, he would fall asleep in a matter of seconds. After ten minutes, the sentry reappeared and led Lawrence through several corridors to the king's personal chamber. Without delay, the door was opened by another sentry and Lawrence was ushered into the room. King Talbot, wrapped in a plush burgundy robe with gold trim, sat at a writing table. He beckoned Lawrence over to him.

"What is this urgent news you bring to me that interrupts what was a very sound slumber?" Talbot asked, obviously displeased with being awoken so early in the morning.

"Two pieces of news, my lord," Lawrence replied. "The first is with regard to the king's daughter."

"My daughter?" Talbot asked, standing up and approaching Lawrence. "What of Marie?"

"She was rescued three days ago, your majesty," Lawrence informed the king. "She was unharmed and should be returning to you within two days."

"How do you know this?" Talbot asked.

"I assisted in her rescue," Lawrence replied humbly.

"Then why is she not with you?" the king inquired. "Why is she not here?" Talbot moved closer to Lawrence, his face but a few inches from Lawrence's. "Where is my daughter?" he demanded firmly.

"After her rescue, Marie insisted that she had urgent business in Habersham," Lawrence replied, not intimidated by the king's proximity. "I heartily urged her to return home with me, as I knew your majesty was immensely concerned over her safety and would want her home as quickly as possible. However, she was quite insistent of her need to visit Habersham and there was no turning her mind."

"What urgent business could she possibly have in Habersham?" Talbot asked, confused. He turned and took a contemplative step away from Lawrence, his eyebrows furrowed as he tried to produce some reasonable explanation for his daughter's behavior. "She has no relations there and I do not believe she has been there but possibly once in her entire life."

"As to the nature of her business, my lord, I could not testify," Lawrence lied. "Whatever it was, she evidently felt it was worth the risk to her life."

"If her life was at risk, then why did you not accompany her and provide for her safety?" the king asked accusingly as he turned briskly to face Lawrence again. "Do not tell me that you allowed her to proceed without an escort."

"No, sire, she did not proceed alone. I would never have allowed that."

"Then who rides with her?" Talbot inquired.

Lawrence hesitated a moment. The story was unbelievably complicated, and there was really no short-cut to telling the tale. Her kidnapping and rescue, Donald MacLean, her trip to Habersham, every aspect of the situation was intimately entwined with the others and there was no separating them.

"I ask again, Morecraft, who rides with my daughter?"

"Your majesty, she rides with Donald MacLean, Andrew MacLean's brother," Lawrence answered, bracing for the king's reaction.

"MacLean's brother?" Talbot repeated in disbelief. "Andrew MacLean's brother? Andrew MacLean is a spy and kidnapper, and you trusted the life and safety of my daughter, the daughter of a king, to that man's brother? Are you bereft of any sense at all?"

"My lord, Andrew MacLean is no spy and most certainly had nothing to do with the abduction of your daughter. In truth, it was Andrew who led the rescue effort and were it not for his intellect and daring, your daughter would still be in captivity. He has saved your daughter's life for a second time."

The king offered a look of disbelief to Lawrence, then returned to his seat and slowly lowered himself into it. He remained silent for a few moments, contemplating the implications of Lawrence's words. Talbot had quite successfully convinced himself that Andrew was an untrustworthy soul, a liar, kidnapper and spy, and to hear Lawrence's words was a knife through his conscience. He looked up at Lawrence.

"Someone facilitated MacLean's escape from my prison, Morecraft. Obviously, someone who was a friend of his, someone who was close to him, and someone who trusted him. He had but few close friends during his tenure here and you were perhaps the closest. Tell me, Lawrence, by your honor, did you aid in MacLean's escape from my prison?"

"My lord, by my honor and that of my long-passed father," Lawrence replied, pausing only momentarily to see if the king had any reaction to the mentioning of the deceased village elder, "I had no hand in the escape of Andrew MacLean from your prison."

"If not you then who?" Talbot inquired, not flinching. "Other than you his closest companions were the Bergman family. I know he spent much time in the presence of the blacksmith and formed a bond of friendship with the man, but Bergman died well before Andrew's escape and therefore could not have had a hand in it."

"Yes," Lawrence replied, doing his best to soften the accusation in his tone, "I heard of Mr. Bergman's most unfortunate accident. It was such a shame for him to die in something as simple as a fire, as my father did so many years ago."

Talbot's eyes peered into Lawrence's eyes and for the briefest of moments, Lawrence could sense a confession in the king's gaze. It quickly passed, but the king's penetrating glare did not.

"I agree, it was a shame that both men met with such deadly accidents. They both were great losses to our kingdom," Talbot said measuredly. After a moment of silence, he continued.

"Perhaps that other friend of yours, Louis Connor, had a hand in the matter. The three of you have been thick as thieves for some time now."

"While Louis did enjoy friendship with Andrew, he never fully trusted him," Lawrence replied. "I would be hard-pressed to believe that Louis participated in any way in the escape of Andrew from your prison. His allegiance was always with you, my lord."

"I shall summon Connor to my presence just the same and have him vouch for his own allegiance, if you do not mind."

"That will not be possible," Lawrence replied sadly, his eyes slightly diverted from the king.

"And why might that be?" Talbot inquired.

"Louis Connor is dead, my lord," Lawrence replied.

"Dead?" Talbot repeated, a look of concern crossing his face. "How did this happen?"

"He took part in the rescue of your daughter. He and I engaged her captors while she fled with Donald MacLean. We were able to fight our way through to an escape, or so I thought. Two arrows in the back were his demise."

"You will tell me everything that has happened," Talbot instructed Lawrence. "I will know who kidnapped my daughter, what his purpose was, how she was rescued, how you came to meet this brother of Andrew MacLean, where MacLean is now, and why you returned here while entrusting my daughter's life to a complete stranger."

Lawrence took a few moments to gather his thoughts then launched into a tale of cunning heroism and devastating sorrow, though carefully leaving out any direct reference to the DuFay Sword. The king sat back in his chair, his mind devouring the captivating story. He did not interrupt Lawrence but let him finish speaking. When Lawrence fell silent, having completed the story, Talbot stood and paced thoughtfully across the room.

"Why does this king march upon my land?" Talbot asked, though it was more of a rhetorical question than a question directed at Lawrence.

"Of that, I cannot be certain," Lawrence lied.

"To march such a large army such a long distance this king must be highly motivated to some particular end."

"It would stand to reason," Lawrence agreed.

"And then to kidnap my daughter? Was it his intention to use her to force me to relinquish my throne?"

"It would not be out of the question, my lord," Lawrence replied. He felt as though he were caught in the middle of a tug-of-war between Talbot and Andrew. On the one hand, he had a loyalty to Talbot that he was not ready to throw away despite having heard Andrew's theories and accusations regarding Talbot. On the other hand, he knew Andrew to be an honest man and his theories and explanations did make sense. Lawrence knew that it was not his place to share Andrew's theories with Talbot and therefore he was trying to be careful in what information he passed on to Talbot. That was why he was trying to refrain from mentioning anything about DuFay and Andrew's prior history with Gallard.

"What purpose is there to this man's actions?" Talbot asked again, more to himself than to Lawrence. "We are not a nation of wealth. We are not an important center of commerce and trade. Durinburg has little if any significance ..." Talbot's voice trailed off as a realization struck him. His eyes widened ever so slightly as he silently explored this thought. After several moments of silence, he turned to Lawrence.

"You have done well, Lawrence Morecraft, and I can see that you are exhausted from your adventure. Rest for a time. Then I would have you gather some men, locate my daughter, and escort her to me immediately. I do not care what she says, I do not care how strenuously she may protest. You will bring her to me without farther delay, even if you have to tie her to a horse. Am I clear in this matter?"

"Yes, your majesty, you are perfectly clear," Lawrence replied. "By your leave," he said, and left the room.

Chapter 13

The chattering of the nocturnal light life, though normally soothing, provided Andrew little peace on this cool autumn evening. The leaves that littered the forest floor crunched with nerve-wrecking loudness as he attempted to move as soundlessly as possible amongst the trees. It had been four days since he had ridden hard and fast from Marie and Donald but in his mind, and body, it seemed twice that long. He had been forced to make his way back to Durinburg on foot after abandoning his horse. Thankfully, he had not encountered any of Gallard's men nor any other unfavorable situations. Since setting out on foot Andrew had slept little, knowing that he needed to reach Durinburg as quickly as possible. He knew he would not be able to approach King Talbot on his own without risking being executed on the spot, therefore he would have to wait for Marie to warn her father. Andrew had no way of knowing if Marie and Donald had made it back safely to her father. His only play was to covertly approach someone he knew well, someone he trusted and who trusted him, who could locate Marie if she were indeed back home and inform her of Andrew's presence. That is why he now carefully approached the Bergman home.

Andrew continued to be convinced that the death of Carl Bergman had been no accident, therefore it would mean that Talbot had become suspicious of him. Andrew staunchly believed that Talbot was well informed of the time he had spent with the Bergmans and that Talbot suspected the two of them had colluded on Andrew's escapade into the depths of the castle. It was also not of out the question that somehow Heather's assistance in his escape had been discovered or at least was suspected. In that event, it was almost a foregone conclusion that her house and her every move would be watched in the event Andrew attempted to contact her. Therefore, Andrew had quietly taken up position where he could see the Bergman's home and the area immediately surrounding it. For an hour he had sat as still as the rocks surrounding him, continually sweeping the area with his eyes, looking for any suspicious movement. He had seen the three remaining members of the Bergman family several times since he had begun his surveillance but there had been no other activity to raise his guard. Cold, tired and hungry, Andrew finally decided to approach the home and hoped that there were no concealed eyes watching his movements.

He approached the house from the rear. As quietly as possible he inched his way around the side of the house and toward the front. The sky was mostly cloudy which dramatically cut down the glow from the half-full moon and stars and helped keep his movements clandestine. When he reached the front corner of the house Andrew paused, then slowly slid around the corner and made his way along the front of the structure. Reaching a window, Andrew peeked inside. He could see Mrs. Bergman, Steven and Heather seated at the dinner table, partaking of their evening meal. Nobody else was visible. Andrew dropped low so he could pass beneath the window and not allow his form to be silhouetted by the interior light filtering through the window. He made his way the final few feet to the front door and while standing to the side, gently rapped on the solid wood. He heard a chair being scooted across the floor as one of the inhabitants rose to answer the knock. As the door opened, Andrew did not wait for an invitation. He darted inside, nearly knocking Mrs. Bergman over, and quickly shut the door behind him.

"Andrew!" Heather called out, her eyes wide open with surprise as she jumped to her feet.

"Please forgive my rude intrusion," Andrew said to Mrs. Bergman, who was still in a bit of shock at his sudden appearance and uninvited entry. "I could not risk waiting for an invitation lest there be unfriendly eyes in the forest."

"Unfriendly eyes?" Mrs. Bergman asked, her senses returning to her. "Whatever do you mean?"

"Andrew, what are you doing here?" Heather asked, slowly approaching him.

"I missed dinner this evening and remembering how wonderful a cook your mother is, I could not resist stopping in," Andrew replied with a grin. "In truth, I have missed dinner the past four evenings as well as a few breakfasts and lunches."

"What is this about unfriendly eyes?" Mrs. Bergman asked, still a bit confused. "Andrew, what is going on? I heard you had been arrested for espionage. Is this true?"

"Did you find Marie?" Heather asked anxiously, not letting Andrew answer her mother's question.

"Yes, we found her. She is okay. Well, at least the last time I saw her she was okay," Andrew replied.

"When was that?" Heather asked.

"Four days ago," he answered.

"Heather, please," her mother said with a bit of reproof, breaking into the conversation. "Andrew, six days ago King Talbot himself came to our home and asked us many questions concerning you. It was an unsettling conversation to say the least. I must know what is happening, for there is much talk about the village as to your loyalty and intentions, and if they be foul to the king and the kingdom you will find no welcome in this house."

"Mother!" Heather cried.

"No, that is fair," Andrew replied, holding his hand up to Heather. "Your mother is right. She must know. If you will close the shutters on the windows, I will be happy to tell you everything."

For a moment, Mrs. Bergman did not move. She eyed Andrew

carefully, trying to read his expression and body language. Her curiosity was great but her instincts to protect her family were greater. She could not afford to make the wrong decision. After a few moments, she addressed her son.

"Steven, close the shutters," she instructed. "Andrew, come and sit at our table. You may fill your stomach with dinner as you fill our ears with your tale." After closing the sturdy wooden shutters, Steven joined his mother, sister and Andrew at the table. After taking a few bites of meat and bread to quiet his rumbling stomach Andrew launched into the yarn of mystery, adventure, and intrigue that had formed the past five and a half years of his life. No detail was spared. As he finished off the last bite of his dinner, he described his arrival outside of their home that very evening. Then, he sat back and waited for Mrs. Bergman's reaction.

"So that is what Carl was doing when he disappeared for hours on end," she said, the mystery finally being solved. "He was searching for clues to the DuFay Armor mystery."

"It appears so," Andrew agreed.

"You truly suspect King Talbot killed my husband?" she asked in disbelief.

"It is but a suspicion at this point in time," Andrew answered, "for there is no proof. But it would make sense if Talbot had any thoughts whatsoever that your husband knew of the DuFay legend and was investigating it himself, or in the least helping me. Talbot does not desire that the legend be resurrected until he is ready to raise the dead himself. He would not do so until he possessed the DuFay Armor."

"But the king has shown nothing but kindness and generosity to the people of this country since his arrival over fifteen years ago," Mrs. Bergman argued.

"A wolf in sheep's clothing," Andrew replied. "He needs the people of this country to trust him and love him in order for them to support his claim to the DuFay lineage."

"But he is already king," Mrs. Bergman countered. "What more is there?"

"A man's lust for power can know no bounds," Andrew answered. "There are many more towns and villages for him to rule. Talbot wants them all. There have been any number of men in the past who have wanted to rule the entire world. They have destroyed nation after nation in pursuit of such ultimate power. They have set themselves up to be gods, to be bowed down to, and to be worshipped. In the end they are themselves destroyed or conquered, but the chaos and death they bring in their endeavors last long after they have turned to dust."

"You have the sword, and you believe Talbot has the shield," Mrs. Bergman mused. "Who has the breastplate and the other pieces?"

"As to that, I cannot be one hundred percent certain," Andrew admitted. "I suspect that my former king, Gallard, has the breastplate. He most certainly knows of the legend. I believe that is why he has marched so from home and ultimately, to this land. He must know that this land was once the realm of DuFay and has come here in hopes of laying claim to the line. He at least knows that I am here and that I possess the sword. He could very well also know that Talbot has the shield. I do not know for sure about the other armor pieces."

"So, the DuFay Armor is coming home," Mrs. Bergman said thoughtfully.

"It would appear so," Andrew agreed, "and it could very well be a most violent homecoming."

"What are you going to do next?" Heather asked, thankful for an opportunity to get back into the conversation.

"The king has to be warned of Gallard's approach," Andrew replied. "However, I cannot do that without Marie. Talbot will never believe that I am not a spy without the testimony of his daughter. At the same time, Talbot cannot know that I have the sword. I hesitate to consider the lengths he would go to in order to obtain the sword," he said, looking at Heather. "Also, I must find a way to retrieve the sword from my room in the castle. However, I fear that I will not be permitted to return, at least not unattended."

"Surely Talbot will search your room if he has the least bit of suspicion that you possess the sword or anything else related to DuFay," Mrs. Bergman said thoughtfully. "Will he not find the sword?"

"It would be possible, I cannot deny that. However, I hid the sword in the chimney above the fireplace. It would not be easy to discover."

"I could get it!" Steven cried out excitedly.

"No, it would be too dangerous," Andrew replied, shaking his head.

"Please, I know I could get it!" Steven argued. "I could do it without anybody seeing me!"

"You heard Andrew, it is too dangerous," the boy's mother said firmly. "You are not to get involved in this."

"But I want to help!" Steven pleaded.

"I know you wish to help, and I am certain that somewhere down the line your help will be most welcome," Andrew replied, trying to calm the boy down. "There will be a time. However, there would be great danger to you if you should attempt to retrieve the sword and I will not allow you to be placed in harm's way. It will be best for someone whose presence in the castle would not be suspicious to retrieve the sword. Marie shall bear the task of recovering the sword from my room."

"Regardless of the degree of truth to this DuFay legend," Mrs. Bergman said, "The king will not relinquish his throne. Are you so sure … ?" Before she could complete her question, a loud knock sounded on the door. All four people in the house looked at one another with anxious concern.

"Andrew, quick, the back room!" Mrs. Bergman instructed quietly. "Heather, show him where to hide and come back out quickly." The knocking repeated, this time followed by a deep voice.

"In the name of the king, open the door!"

"One moment!" Mrs. Bergman called out, trying to buy a few seconds. Heather led Andrew to the back room as her mother moved slowly to the front door. The impatient knocking became anxious pounding.

"I say, in the name of King Talbot, open this door!" the voice called again. As Heather returned to the main room, her mother motioned for the children to sit at the table and pretend to be eating dinner. She reached out and unlatched the bolt that held the door in place. After taking a deep breath, she opened the door.

"What is the meaning of this late-evening visit?" Mrs. Bergman boldly demanded. Without waiting for an invitation, three of Talbot's elite castle guards pushed their way past her and entered the home.

"We are here to escort Andrew MacLean to King Talbot," the lead guard informed her. "MacLean is guilty of espionage and is an escaped prisoner. He was spotted earlier this evening entering this home. Where is he?"

"He was here," Mrs. Bergman confessed, "but only for a brief time. He left after dinner."

"It would appear to me that dinner is not yet over," the guard replied, eyeing Heather and Steven at the table littered with food. "MacLean is a spy, and it is treason to harbor a spy. If you do not cooperate with us, you will be charged with treason and arrested. Your son and daughter will also be arrested, and I promise you, prison cells in the dungeon are none too pleasant. Now I ask you again, where is MacLean?"

"Here," Andrew called out as he stepped from the back room. "I am here. These people are innocent of any wrongdoing. Leave them out of this."

The two guards that had to this point remained silent drew their swords. The lead guard placed his right hand on the hilt of his sword, ready to pull it should Andrew show any aggression.

"Andrew MacLean, you are under arrest for espionage and escape from prison," the lead guard stated with authority. "This very evening you shall be taken before the king at which time he will pronounce your sentence. Should you resist, we have been granted authority to execute you immediately. For the sake of your life and the lives of these three souls, I highly recommend that you not resist."

"I look forward to appearing before the king," Andrew replied boldly, stepping to within an arm's length of the guard. "I have urgent news for him."

"Turn away and place your hands behind your back," the guard ordered as he pulled a length of rope from his belt Andrew complied, and the guard quickly bound his hands tightly. Not desiring to take any chances, the guard wrapped another longer piece of rope around Andrew's torso to farther bind his arms against his body and secured it. "Exhale," the guard instructed, and Andrew did so. The rope was pulled tight and firmly fastened. Satisfied that Andrew was adequately restrained, the guard turned him around and with no little gentleness pushed Andrew out the doorway. He then turned to the Bergmans.

"It will be reported to King Talbot that you gave refuge to a spy," he informed them without compassion. "Pray that his dealings with this man will assuage his anger and he shall take no action against you." With those words the guard exited the house. Speechless, Mrs. Bergman shut the door.

"How many men does it take to escort a lone man to the king?" Andrew asked as he spotted a dozen more guards outside of the house. "In truth, I am flattered that the king believes me important enough to spare no less than a dozen of his finest men to be my escorts."

"I have never harbored the least thought of fondness for you, MacLean," said the guard who was leading the group. "In fact, I have resented your presence in our village from the day you first arrived. You strut around as though you are royalty, expecting all who see you to stand in awe and admiration. You are here but two months and somehow weasel your way close to the king's ear while there are dozens of men who have served him faithfully with all their hearts for many years, yet not offered such an honor. It does my spirits good to see you fall from grace and be revealed for the scoundrel you truly are. And when you are presented before the very people whom you have befriended in your time here and they are shown what type of man you are, I will get much joy from it."

"It saddens my heart to hear you say that," Andrew replied sarcastically. "I had so desired to have your friendship."

"If you receive anything from me it shall be the tip of my sword in your heart," the guard replied gruffly. "A lot can happen between here and the king's court."

"If you have any fondness for the king's daughter and desire to see her returned safely and unharmed, then you best keep your sword in its scabbard and your tongue still," Andrew replied undaunted. His retort was answered by a sharp blow to his kidneys.

"Speak again, and it will not be my fist in your back," the guard answered.

Tired of the banter, Andrew chose to remain silent. The remaining thirty minutes of walking went by wordlessly. The group soon passed across the bridge and into the castle grounds. There was virtually no activity in the communal area at this time of the night. Andrew was led into the castle and after several more minutes of walking, they arrived at the large double doors leading to Talbot's court. The two guards at the doors opened them immediately, and Andrew was pushed inside none too lightly. He was directed to stand on a small platform in the middle of the large but plainly decorated room. The platform had rails on its front and two sides, but the back side was open. Andrew complied and stood on the platform, waiting for whatever his fate was to be. After a minute of total silence, a door to his left opened and in walked King Talbot along with Angus, Malcolm, and three other men Andrew had seen around on several occasions but had never met personally. They appeared to be men of the law by virtue of the books and papers they were carrying. The six men walked over to a twenty-foot-long table that sat fifteen feet in front of the platform on which Andrew patiently stood. After the king had taken his seat in the middle, the other five men took their seats. Talbot then addressed Andrew.

"In retrospect, your escape from the dungeon was not such a surprise," the king said, looking at the prisoner. "A man as resourceful as yourself would be difficult to keep imprisoned for any respectable length of time. Especially a man who has close friends. Need I bother asking which friend chose to be the facilitator of your liberation?" Andrew remained silent.

"Morecraft, perhaps?" the king continued, pondering his own question. "Then there is Morecraft's friend Connor, but I do not believe Connor held you in high enough regard to assist in freeing you. Indeed, after his devious behavior in the Skills Contest, I would expect he would just as soon see you spend no small amount of time in the lonely darkness of the dungeon. Dare I venture as far as to theorize that your fellow conspirator may have been a certain young lady with shiny golden hair?" Andrew continued looking at Talbot without expression, without response.

"We shall come back to that point in a moment," the king continued, waving his hand. "What is surprising to me, though, is that a week and a day after your escape you chose to return. You could have disappeared, never to be seen nor heard from again, yet you came back, risking capture and execution. What could have been so valuable as to motivate you to gamble so? What lure did you find completely irresistible?"

"If I were to hazard a conjecture, I would say it was a golden-haired lure," Angus offered.

"That would be a reasonable presumption," Talbot replied, not taking his eyes off Andrew. "She is very lovely to be sure. Very alluring. However, I cannot help but feel that there was something else drawing Andrew back to our homeland. Something perhaps more valuable than a beautiful young woman. Something that sparkles and shines much brighter than her long, golden locks. Am I right, Andrew?" Still, Andrew did not reply.

"Do you have anything to say, MacLean?" Talbot asked with a bit of irritation at Andrew's silence.

"Your majesty appears quite content at the sound of his own voice," Andrew replied. "I would not presume to rob you of such pleasure."

"My pleasure will best be served when you tell me where the DuFay Sword is," the king retorted.

"Whose sword?" Andrew asked innocently.

"Do not take me for a fool," Talbot replied sternly. "You know of the DuFay legend, of that much I am certain. Your escapade into the depths of the castle was spurned by more than simple curiosity. The countless hours you spent in our libraries studying the history of this land and the endless questions you presented to the people of this territory were not born from boredom. And though you spent many evenings at the Bergmans on the pretense of Bergman's daughter, you spent no little of that time in the company of her father instead of his daughter. Bergman is, or should I say was, quite the renowned historian of this land. It was his key that granted you passage beyond the gate and into the bowels of this fortress."

"And that is why you had him killed? For simply providing me with a key?" Andrew asked.

"Bergman's death was an accident," Talbot replied innocently.

"Just like the deaths of the other three village elders?" Andrew shot back.

"All unfortunate accidents," the king answered as if with regret. "Those were truly honorable men, worthy of profound respect. It was a shame they all met with untimely deaths." Talbot's eyes took on a threatening look. "One never knows when or where another accident will happen. No person is immune from accidents. Not even beautiful young ladies."

"Leave her out of this," Andrew growled. "She has nothing to do with whatever it is you want from me."

"To the contrary, she has a great deal to do with what I want from you," the king countered. "Aiding in the escape of a prisoner is a high crime. She could either be imprisoned or executed, whichever I decide."

"What makes you believe she had anything to do with my escape?" Andrew asked.

"MacLean, do you believe anything at all happens in my own home without my knowledge?" Talbot answered. "Heather was spotted leading your horse down the street the very evening of your escape. A young woman such as herself being followed by a horse such as yours does rather stand out from the ordinary."

"You have yet to tell me why you believe I possess this sword to which you have referred," Andrew said, trying to change the subject. "Even if I admit to knowing of the DuFay legend, it would not of necessity mean that I possess his sword."

"True," Talbot replied. "But you have it, nonetheless. The curiosity of young men is astounding, is it not? One of the stable boys confessed to having pried around your horse a bit when you first arrived. He admitted to having seen a magnificent sword, a weapon of beauty beyond description. Understandably, he was reluctant to reveal his intrusion into your privacy, but we can be very motivating when circumstances so require. I have the shield and you have the sword. Quite the interesting scenario, is it not?"

"Yes, quite interesting," Andrew replied sarcastically. "Though I must admit, it is not quite as interesting a scenario as that of thousands of men marching toward your walls."

"Ah, yes, the approach of Gallard's army," Talbot replied knowingly.

"So, you are indeed aware of the impending attack," Andrew stated.

"Lawrence Morecraft reported to me early this morning," Talbot answered. "He saw the army with his own eyes as he helped rescue Marie."

"Then you must know that I had nothing to do with her kidnapping," Andrew surmised, surprised and joyful to hear that his friend had escaped almost certain death.

"I know that you led the effort to rescue her," Talbot responded. "And it would so reason that you had nothing to do with her abduction. However, only my daughter's own words will convince me beyond all doubt."

"Where is Lawrence now?" Andrew asked.

"He is leading a group of my men to meet with Marie and your brother and escort them back here safely," Talbot answered. "How ironic it is that two MacLeans participated in a second rescue of my daughter."

"Marie and Donald should have been back long before I arrived," Andrew stated, perplexed. "They were mounted, yet I was on foot. I take it Lawrence knows where they are?"

"Evidently my daughter had an errand to tend to that she deemed more important than returning directly to her worried father," the king replied somewhat bitterly. Knowing the danger of the situation in which he had left Marie and Donald, Andrew could not fathom them having done anything but return home as quickly as possible. Puzzled, he changed the subject.

"As Lawrence has made report to you, you therefore know how large the army is that approaches and the danger your kingdom faces," Andrew said.

"Angus?" the king said, addressing his military advisor and bidding him to respond to Andrew's statement.

"According to Morecraft, the army of Gallard numbers around five thousand men," Angus replied. "We have perhaps a thousand men here, ready for battle on a moment's notice. We have an additional three thousand men spread out within a half-day's ride of the castle. Gallard's men will be tired from their journey.

Though we will be outnumbered, there resides in my mind no doubt that through cunning strategy and better physical condition we can thwart a direct attack."

"It is quite a foolish strategy to underestimate the strength and resolve of an army that is poised to invade your land," Andrew warned.

"What would you know about war strategy?" Angus taunted. "What army have you ever led into battle?"

"Enough!" Talbot shouted, tiring of the conversation and eager to hold the prized weapon in his hands. "I believe it is time that you relinquished the DuFay Sword."

"Another man once tried to take the sword from me," Andrew replied, a warning tone riding his voice. "Two of his trusted advisors forfeited their lives for their efforts."

"MacLean, I will have that sword," Talbot responded sternly. "I have spent my entire life pursuing the DuFay Armor and I will not be denied my destiny."

"Your destiny? Whatever destiny you have, it does not include sitting upon the throne of DuFay," Andrew countered. "You are not heir to the DuFay line, and you are not a man worthy of the honor. Pursuit of the armor will only bring you destruction, not glory."

"That line has long died out," Talbot stated knowingly. "There is no blood heir to the DuFay throne. The heir to the DuFay throne is the man who is wise enough and strong enough to obtain the armor. That is the man who is worthy of the honor, glory and power of ruling a thousand valleys and ten thousand mountains."

"You are wrong, your majesty," Andrew replied. "The DuFay line endures, and that man is the only one worthy of possessing the armor."

"And who might that be?" Talbot asked. "Do you suppose that you are the man worthy of wielding the DuFay Armor? Do you have dreams and aspirations of ruling the world? That is why you came to our land, is it not? You are looking to claim the DuFay throne for yourself."

"I have no desire for power or to rule over people," Andrew replied. "I have not the ego to do so. No, I desire nothing more than to ensure that the wrong man does not lay claim to the throne of DuFay and lead the world into darkness. You are the wrong man, Talbot, and the heir of DuFay is closer than you could ever imagine."

"Enough!" the king shouted, slamming his hand on the table. "The DuFay line has melted into history. A new line will be established, and it will be MY line! You will deliver the sword to me, now! If you refuse, I swear to you, those you hold dearest to you will suffer more than your imagination can conjure. Aiding in the escape of a prisoner is a high crime and those who are guilty are punished mightily!"

"Do not drag her into this!" Andrew responded angrily. "Leave Heather and her family alone!"

"She aided in your rescue," Talbot replied with a smug grin on his face. "Morecraft was kind enough to reveal that tidbit of information to us. Her family gave you refuge while knowing that you were an escaped prisoner, condemned for espionage. They are all guilty and shall be sentenced and punished accordingly.

"However," the king said, lightening his tone. "Were you to cooperate, we would see fit to drop all charges against them."

"You are a cruel man," Andrew stated, not the least bit afraid of insulting Talbot. "You would destroy them just to steal a legend?"

"No, you would destroy them to keep a legend," Talbot answered. "The choice is yours. You may keep the sword and destroy your friends, or you may save their lives by relinquishing the sword. What is your decision?"

Andrew knew that he was backed into a corner. He also knew that Talbot was quite serious when he threatened harm to the Bergman family. A man guilty of murder would not give a second thought to torture and inhumane treatment. The choice was a simple one. He would have to relinquish the sword, at least for now.

"It seems you have made the decision for me," Andrew replied in defeat. "I will hold you to your word, Talbot. I will deliver the sword to you, and you will not harm the Bergmans."

"So let it be ordained," Talbot agreed.

"Unbind me and I will lead you to the sword. It is in my room."

The king nodded to one of the guards who stepped forward and cut the bindings from Andrew. After having been tied up so long, Andrew's arms and hands were nearly numb. He rubbed his hands and arms in order to restore circulation as he led the procession of men out of the courtroom. It took several minutes for them to reach his room. As Andrew opened the door, he was not entirely surprised to see that the room had been thoroughly searched. The drawers to all the dressers were open, his clothes had been thrown about, the bed was in total disarray, and every piece of furniture had been scattered about.

"It seems the chamber maid has not visited my room in some time," Andrew joked. "Someone should do something about that."

"The sword?" Talbot urged Andrew, ignoring his comment.

Andrew walked over to the fireplace, bent low, and stepped inside the cavity. He then straightened up and his upper body disappeared. He rummaged around a bit, then stepped onto a protruding block in order to reach a bit higher. Talbot and his men began to grow impatient as Andrew appeared to stall for time.

"The hour is late, and we do not wish to spend the entire evening in your room," Angus growled. "Retrieve the sword and let us be on our way."

Andrew did not respond but appeared to continue his search. After another ten seconds, he stepped down and exited the fireplace. His hands and clothes were layered with black soot. More importantly, his hands were empty.

"Well?" Talbot asked impatiently. "Where is the sword?"

"It would appear, your majesty, that my hiding place was not as secure as I thought," Andrew answered, wiping his hands on his already dirty clothes. "The sword has been stolen."

Chapter 14

The trek back to Talbot's court was quiet but tense. While Talbot fumed at what he was certain were lies coming from Andrew, Andrew was trying to envision what had happened to the sword.

"You truly must take me for a grand fool," Talbot said to Andrew as they reconvened in Talbot's court. "Am I to believe that you would be so careless as to allow the sword to be stolen? Come now, Andrew, surely you do not believe me to be so naïve."

"My lord, I swear to you, the last time I touched the sword was to return it to its place of concealment above the fire pit," Andrew replied. "I would not think it unreasonable that the men you dispatched to search my room discovered it and elected to keep it for themselves."

"I choose my men carefully, MacLean, and none would turn against me," Talbot countered. "If they had found the sword we would not be standing here now."

"For many men, loyalty has a price," Andrew answered.

"Who else, pray tell, knew of the existence of the sword and that it was in your possession?" Talbot inquired. "If you wish us to believe that it was stolen you will have to offer credible evidence."

Andrew could think of three people who had definitive knowledge of the sword and he hesitated to reveal their identities to the king. The first was the king's own daughter. She was truly the only one who had seen the sword in his room and knew of its hiding place. However, he could not bring himself to consider her a suspect. They had built a strong mutual trust over time and in his mind, there was no chance that she would steal the sword. The second person was Carl Bergman. Though Carl had neither seen the sword nor had an awareness of its hiding place, he knew that Andrew possessed it. Again, Andrew could not bring himself to believe that Carl would have had the opportunity or intention of stealing the sword. The third was Heather. Andrew had told her about the sword and asked her to retrieve it the night she freed him. The sword had not been with Annon and therefore Andrew had surmised that Heather had either not been able to locate the sword, or she had not been able to get to his room unobserved. As he was preparing a response, the door to the room suddenly opened and Marie, Donald and Lawrence strolled into the room.

"What is the meaning of this intrusion?" Talbot demanded, not immediately recognizing Marie. She was still wearing the clothes Donald stole for her and her hair was bunched up under a leather helmet. Marie reached up and removed the helmet, allowing her thick, dark hair to flow down beyond her shoulders.

"Marie!" Talbot exclaimed, jumping from his seat. He ran over to her and embraced her tightly, tears of joy flowing from his eyes. "My prayers have been answered! You have returned safely! The joy of my heart has returned home!" He continued to hold her tightly, as though he was afraid to let go lest she disappear from in front of his eyes. He finally released her and gently held her face in his hands. "My daughter has been returned to me. My heart can finally rest easy. My precious daughter." He leaned forward and kissed her on her forehead.

"You are okay? Have you been injured in any way?" Talbot asked, his eyes searching her.

"I am not injured, Father," she replied with a forced grin. "I am okay."

"I must hear of your ordeal, every detail," he said anxiously. "When you are finished, I will destroy those who abducted you and they will regret the first breath that brought them into this world."

"It appears I have interrupted business of yours, Father," Marie said with a coolness she had never used in addressing her father. "Perhaps I should come back later when your dealings here are finished."

"Nonsense," Talbot said. "You have been missing for over a week. No other business is as important as my daughter is to me. I will send for food and drink and if you are not too weary, I wish to know everything that has happened to you."

"Very well," she said. "I will return to my chambers and change clothes then return to you here."

"Lawrence," the king said, turning his attention from Marie. "You have seen to the safe return of my daughter. I cannot express the depths of my gratitude. You shall be well rewarded."

"No reward is necessary, my lord," Lawrence replied humbly. "In truth, it is not I who should receive the bulk of your gratitude. Donald MacLean deserves the accolades. He had the courage to believe the implausible. He had the fortitude to overcome the formidable. He had the cunning to consummate the rescue of your daughter. He discarded his allegiance to a king and was nearly robbed of his life. It is not I whom you should thank. It is this man," Lawrence said, nodding his head in Donald's direction.

"It seems not that long ago that a MacLean entered this castle a hero, having saved the life of my daughter," Talbot said, stepping over to face Donald and grasping his shoulders tightly. "Ironically, it is a different MacLean who now enters this castle yet still a hero for saving the life of my daughter. You have presented me with a debt I could never repay."

"Your majesty, I only did that which had to be done," Donald replied, "that which any decent man would have done. I truly regret that the king I chose to serve my entire life, a man I thought to be decent and upright, kidnapped your daughter and threatened her life. I am greatly comforted that she has been returned to you unharmed."

"You shall be rewarded for your bravery," Talbot stated. "Indeed, you shall be well rewarded."

"No reward is necessary," Donald replied, shaking his head. "However, if it would not be too much trouble, I would be most gracious for a place to rest this evening and perhaps a change of clothes."

"Modesty is most certainly a family trait, that much is clear," Talbot said, looking from Donald to Andrew. "It is the least we can do. Andrew, you may return to your room this evening with your brother. There you will be able to refresh yourselves. Food and clothes will be brought to you."

"And to think I was looking so forward to spending another evening in that very lovely, dark, dank, lonely cell," Andrew replied sarcastically.

Talbot shot Andrew a contemptuous glare. "Do not test my tolerance. Another visit to your former cell can certainly be arranged with but a word."

"Father," Marie said with reproof. "Despite what suspicions and ill feelings you may have regarding Andrew, if it were not for him, I would not be standing in front of you. Perhaps a little less contempt and a little more courtesy is in order."

"I stand corrected," Talbot said, forcing an emotionless smile. "Gentlemen, you will all be well-cared for, and we shall shower you with our gratitude. However, for now, I will spend a bit of time with my daughter. In the morning we shall gather for continued conversation. I bid you all a good evening." He turned to his advisors and nodded to them.

With brief bows of courtesy, Andrew, Donald and Lawrence left the king's courtroom. Angus, Malcom and the other three men likewise left, though through a different door near the back of the room.

"I shall return in a few minutes, my lord," Marie said as she quickly excused herself and followed in the direction of Andrew, Donald and Lawrence. She caught up with the trio a dozen steps down the hallway.

"Andrew," she called out, causing the men to pause. All three turned to her. Marie looked behind her to ensure that nobody was within earshot.

"I have figured it out!" she exclaimed quietly. "I have figured out the mystery of the DuFay Armor!"

"When? How?" Andrew asked, dumbfounded.

"I cannot go into details right now," she replied, looking back down the hall, "we do not have the time. I will say for now that I was able to obtain more translations, and everything fits into place. I will tell you everything tomorrow."

"You expect me to sleep tonight after this revelation?" Andrew asked in disbelief. "I would rather you have not said anything and simply came to me tomorrow."

"I thought you could use something to dream about other than Heather," Marie replied with a devilish grin as she turned and headed back down the hallway. Andrew simply shook his head.

"And exactly who is this Heather person?" Donald asked with teasing curiosity.

"Ah, allow me to educate you," Lawrence said as he placed his arm around Donald's shoulder and led the man down the hall.

It took Marie thirty minutes to clean herself, don fresh clothing, and rendezvous with her father in his study. The hour was late, and she was exhausted to a degree that she had never known, but there were questions that needed to be answered. The journey from Habersham to her home seemed to take an eternity as she read and re-read page after page of her mother's notes. While one exciting mystery had been solved another had presented itself, and it was a very troubling one at that. She would not sleep until this new mystery was solved and she was afraid she would not be able to sleep after it was solved.

King Talbot waited patiently for his daughter to return. A steward had brought to the king's study wine, water, and portions of various meats and breads along with a few pieces of fruit. Talbot sipped on a hearty, dry red wine as recent events raced through his ever-restless mind, not the least of which was the apparent theft of the DuFay Sword. While he held little trust in Andrew, he could not fully dismiss the possibility that the sword had indeed been stolen just as MacLean claimed. That would present a new problem in that there was obviously someone else who knew of the DuFay legend, and this person could end up being an incredibly significant stumbling block to his plans. In the morning he would order intense interrogations of everybody who worked and lived in the castle and if that proved fruitless, he would expand the interrogations to any person he suspected in the least of knowing anything about the DuFay legend. He would most certainly interrogate Andrew again and this time, he would get honest answers.

Marie strode into her father's study, breaking his deep thoughts. The royal ruler stood and beckoned her over to the table set with food and drink.

"My dear, you look lovely and refreshed. How you can accomplish that in so little time after what you have been through is amazing to me. Come, have something to drink and a bit to eat. You must be near starving."

Though Marie did not wish to waste any time, she was indeed famished. She smiled at her father and walked over to the table of food where she filled a plate with assorted items. She ate in silence, her father completely content to let his daughter regain her strength before having her recount her harrowing experience. The silence lasted nearly ten minutes and as his daughter finished her meal, Talbot beckoned her to one of two cushioned chairs close to the fireplace and the warmth it offered the room.

"I realize you must be exhausted and desire nothing more than a night of sound sleep," the king said to his daughter. "I must confess, I have slept little myself since you were abducted. However, considering the magnitude of the events of the past several days and the report of an army which, for all intents and purposes, is at our doorstep, it is quite vital that you tell me everything that happened to you. Let us start with how you were kidnapped."

"I believe it was the morning after you imprisoned Andrew," Marie started, with a touch of accusation in her voice. "In truth, I did not know of his incarceration until several days later. Oddly enough it was during the time I was being interrogated that I was informed of his imprisonment. I found it rather odd, how he was so quietly spirited away. I also found it quite odd that this man knew about it before I did." The king did not respond but merely sat still, his penetrating eyes not leaving those of his daughter.

"I was on my way to visit Heather Bergman," Marie continued. "Someone stole up behind me and placed a cloth over my face. In but a few seconds I lost consciousness. I do not know how much time passed but when I awoke, I was bound and gagged with a sackcloth over my head, lying on a cart being pulled by what I determined to be a single horse and rider. Finally, after more than two days, we reached our destination. I was cast into a tent. There, the sackcloth and gag were removed."

"How frightened you must have been," the king responded, his heart wrenched at the thought of what evil could have befallen his daughter. My instincts told me to have a guard with or around you at all times, but my heart told me you needed your privacy. I made the wrong choice, and you could very well have paid for it with your life. My conscience shall never allow me to forgive myself for placing you in danger."

"Do not blame yourself, father," Marie replied. "Had you ordered anyone to keep watch over me, I would have simply eluded him with no great difficulty."

"True," Talbot answered, nodding his head with a knowing smile. "What happened next?"

"For nearly two full days I was kept in solitude. Little food or water was given to me. Finally, I was taken from my tent to a royal tent for interrogation. The king of the army himself questioned me."

"Gallard," Talbot stated knowingly.

"Yes, King Edwin Gallard," Marie confirmed.

"What did he ask of you?" Talbot inquired. "What information did he seek to draw from you? Our strengths? Our weaknesses? How many warriors we have?"

"Surprisingly enough, he did not inquire at all of those things," Marie answered. "He was for the most part solely curious as to Andrew."

"Andrew?" Talbot repeated in puzzlement, sitting up a little straighter in his chair. "What interest did this man have in MacLean?"

"Apparently, they knew each other some years back," Marie replied, carefully choosing her words. "At some point they had a very serious disagreement which created a great rift between them."

"Did Gallard describe the nature of the disagreement?" the king asked.

"He made reference, though in general nature only, to a personal belonging of Andrew's," Marie replied. "Apparently this king greatly desired this object and felt Andrew should have given it to him out of loyalty and obedience. Andrew did not feel the same way and was forced to flee. It must have been an exceptionally heated disagreement, for this king has been searching for Andrew for over five years now. He knew of Andrew's presence in our village, and he knew that Andrew had become a rather highly visible figure here. He was using me in hopes of convincing you to turn Andrew over to him."

"This does not make sense," Talbot mused, sitting back in his chair. "What object could have been of such excellent value that it would motivate this king to muster his army to capture one lone man? Why would he kidnap you instead of simply taking MacLean in the first place? This king surely knew that kidnapping you would place him and his army in great danger. He could have avoided all confrontation by simply abducting MacLean instead of you. I cannot understand what would have persuaded him to believe that MacLean was so important to me."

"Nor I," Marie agreed.

Talbot sat back in his chair, his eyebrows pulled together in puzzlement and concentration. It had to be the sword. Gallard must have known that Andrew possessed the DuFay Sword and demanded that it be given to him. What else could it have been? Surely not jewels or gold or silver. Though valuable they were, in and of themselves they would not warrant a king leading his army who knows how many hundreds of miles to retrieve them. And having come to know Andrew over the past several months, Talbot was thoroughly convinced that Andrew was not a man who sought material possessions. Jewels, gold and silver would hold no sway over MacLean, unless they were imbedded in the DuFay Sword. If Gallard knew of the sword, then he knew of the DuFay legend. If he knew of the DuFay legend, then he could very well know of the history of Durinburg. And if that were the case, then his journey was most certainly not predicated on retrieval of the sword alone but on capturing the DuFay Armor. And therein was hidden the purpose of Marie's abduction. Gallard would have used her to not only demand that Talbot deliver MacLean to him, sword in hand, but to also force Talbot to relinquish the DuFay Shield. To make such a bold move, Gallard must have in his possession at least one of the pieces of the DuFay Armor. The excitement was intoxicating. The DuFay Sword had come to him and now at least one of the other pieces of armor was coming to him. Ignoring the mountainous task of actually obtaining the sword and whichever piece or pieces Gallard possessed, Talbot could not help but picture himself wearing the breastplate and holding the shield in one hand and the sword in the other, with a magnificent crown on his head, and the belt around his waist, and the boots on his feet. Nations would bow to him. The world would pay homage to him. Supreme power would be his.

"Father?" Marie said, breaking the silence and the dream. She had seen her father's face take on a strangely dreamy look, and it was very confusing. "Are you all right, Father?" she asked.

"Hm? Oh, yes, I am fine," Talbot replied as though being awoken from a dream. "I am fine. I was just considering your encounter. It is all quite intriguing. I can see the sleep in your eyes, my dear. Perhaps it is time for you to retire to your boudoir," he suggested.

"How did Mother die?" Marie inquired suddenly, taking her father by surprise.

"How did your mother die?" Talbot repeated, not certain he had heard his daughter correctly.

"Yes, how did she die?" Marie asked again.

"Where on earth did that come from?" the king asked, befuddled. "How did we get from you being kidnapped to your mother's death?"

"Something of late reminded me of her," Marie answered.

"Marie, how could you have forgotten?" her father asked. "You took care of her yourself for several weeks once she took ill. You were by her side when she breathed her last. Surely you have not forgotten."

"I do recall Mother becoming ill," Marie answered, deep in thought. "It was what, five or six years after we arrived here, was it not?"

"That is correct," Talbot confirmed, wondering what could have possibly brought on this topic of conversation.

"I had always seen her as strong and healthy," Marie said thoughtfully. "I do not recall ever seeing her sick, or weary, or even hearing her complain of any ailments before that time."

"Indeed, she was a strong woman," Talbot agreed. "Alas, we are all but human, frail in flesh. Sickness can take the strong just as it takes the weak. It was her great misfortune and our great loss that such a merciless malady took hold of her and refused to release her."

Marie pondered for a moment, wondering how to say that which weighed heavily on her heart without appearing to offer accusation.

"I do not recall anyone suffering an illness such as hers since that time," she finally stated thoughtfully.

"There may have been others outside of the castle," Talbot responded as he became a little suspicious of Marie's train of thought. "We cannot keep track of every illness and every death in our kingdom. Why has this become such a great concern of yours so many years later?" he asked. "I would think these to be memories best left in the past."

"Is it possible," Marie continued, not directly answering her father, "that Mother's illness was not entirely of chance but was possibly imposed upon her?"

"What are you saying, Marie?" her father asked, his wariness becoming more intense. "What would lead you to even suggest such a thing?"

"Our libraries contain a number of books on medicine and illnesses, and I have read many of them over the years," she replied evasively. "I became intrigued with the science and study of the human body, and I spent hours and hours with Ian, pestering him with question after question. I must have nearly driven him to madness."

"I have yet to understand what this has to do with your mother," Talbot stated impatiently.

"Do you remember back during the Skills Contest, when Andrew's horse was poisoned?" Marie asked.

"Of course I remember," her father replied.

"Something about how his horse was lying in the stall, how helpless it looked, how it looked to be in pain, reminded me of mother's last day."

"That was some time ago, my dear," Talbot reminded her. "How is it that such thoughts bother you now?"

"I do not know," Marie lied. "Perhaps something I saw or heard during my recent ordeal brought these remembrances to my mind."

"When you spoke with Ian, did you speak of this suspicion concerning your mother?" the king inquired.

"Not specifically, to the best of my recollection," Marie replied. "We only spoke in broad generalities."

"Are you certain of this? Have you ever voiced these thoughts to anyone else?"

"I am reasonably certain," Marie answered. "It was so long ago, though, it is difficult to be positive beyond doubt. I do know that it has never been a topic of conversation with anyone else."

"Perhaps I shall speak with Ian tomorrow, myself, and see if his memory matches yours," Talbot said thoughtfully. "I would ask that you not speak of this to anyone else, at least for now. We will most likely be facing war in a few short days and it would not be advantageous for people's minds to be preoccupied with things of the past."

"I understand, Father," Marie replied. "If I may have your leave, I would like to retire for the evening."

"Of course, of course," the king said. "I apologize for keeping you so late into the evening. Please, go and sleep well. And I assure you, if it ever becomes revealed to me that your mother was indeed poisoned and by whom, the murderer shall taste the same death," he stated with much conviction. Marie did not respond, but simply left the room and closed the door behind her.

Chapter 15

It was nearly mid-day when Marie finally awoke from a long but virtually restless sleep. Her dreams had been many in number and vivid in nature. She dreamed of her father's kingdom being attacked. She dreamed of being kidnapped all over again. And she dreamed of her mother and the two of them spending time reading together. She had woken several times during the night with a pounding heart due to the nature and reality of the dreams, only to fall asleep and dream more. But now she was awake and eager to share what she had learned from her mother's journal. She dispatched a handmaiden with instructions to deliver a message to Andrew, asking him and Donald to meet her in her private study, the one that used to belong to her mother. Marie dressed and quickly consumed the light breakfast that had been left for her by one of the servants. She was gathering the sheets of paper she had found in her mother's journals, along with the papers she had been given in Habersham, when a knock sounded at her door. She was initially startled, as though she was about to be caught doing something improper. Hesitating for only a moment, she called out.

"Who is it?"

"It is Ian," a man's voice replied.

"Just a moment," Marie responded. She quickly hid the papers under her bed. She stepped back to make sure they were hidden. Satisfied, she walked over and opened the door.

"To what do I owe the pleasure of your visit?" she asked sweetly.

"Your father was concerned about your condition, considering your ordeal over the past several days. He requested that I pay you a visit and ensure your good health."

"That is typical of my father," Marie smiled. "I assured him last night that I was not injured nor felt any ill-effects from my abduction and escape. Other than a sore seat from riding a horse for several days straight, I mean," she added playfully.

"That is good to hear," the physician replied with a smile. "Nothing more serious than a bump or bruise then?"

"Nothing at all."

"If you do not mind, in order to fulfill my duty, may I proceed with a quick examination?" Ian asked.

"It is quite unnecessary," Marie responded, anxious to meet with Andrew and Donald.

"I am sure it is," Ian said, "but you know your father. He will want to know that I performed an examination, however brief it may be. It will only take a few minutes."

"Very well," Marie acquiesced. She stepped back and allowed Ian to step into the room.

"You may sit," he instructed, waving to a chair. Marie complied. The physician began his examination, which to Marie seemed quite trite. He looked over her arms, then around her neck, then looked into her eyes and ears, all done rather quickly. As he stood in front of her and felt her shoulders and neck, he nonchalantly asked the question she had been expecting.

"So, what is this theory that fills your mind of your mother's death having been from poison?" he asked.

"I believe the true purpose of your visit has finally been revealed," Marie said slightly accusingly. "We could easily have skipped this token examination and proceeded directly to the point."

"Now, now," Ian said with a bit of reproof in his tone "Your father did ask me to pay you a visit and ensure that you felt well today. That was his first request. He then asked me of my recollection of your mother's illness and if I had ever suspected that she had been poisoned. I inquired as to what had brought such thoughts to his mind and he confessed that you had entertained such a notion."

"And what is your recollection?" Marie asked before Ian could continue.

"I recall that your mother fell ill and over a period of two or so weeks her health gradually worsened. I recall that none of my remedies were effective in relieving her of this illness. Whether that is a testimony to my failed skills as a healer or the nature of her malady I do not know."

"So, you had never before seen an illness such as hers?"

"Nor since," Ian admitted.

"What did you tell my father?" Marie inquired.

"I told the king that while I was greatly puzzled at the nature of you mother's illness and my inability to cure her, I do not recall at the time considering poison as the culprit."

"At the time," Marie repeated. "And now? Has your opinion been moved one way or another at all over the years?"

"I cannot say that it has," Ian replied. He stepped back and gave Marie an inquiring look. "Might I ask what, after all of these years, has caused you to think upon the nature of your mother's death and form this rather bold theory?"

"You know me and my love of books," Marie answered with a sheepish grin. "I have ready many, including books on the human form and nature. During my readings I have encountered topics addressing illnesses, diseases, poisons, and other maladies. It is most likely that during my studies, I read descriptions of some of the symptoms my mother displayed during her illness."

"I see," Ian said thoughtfully. "Perhaps you read some of these books while you were held in captivity and that is why the topic is fresh on your mind?"

"That is, of course, ludicrous," Marie replied, becoming anxious to end the conversation. "The truth of the matter is that while

I was being held prisoner, I saw a man who was very ill and it was he who reminded me of my mother's illness," she lied. "I think it would an issue of significance if my mother was indeed poisoned, do you not agree?"

"The past is best left in the past, my dear," Ian said soothingly. "No good can come from dredging up painful memories and giving them new life. Your mother's death was tragic indeed, but it was a part of life and a path we must all take in one form or another. In dreadful times such as these we should concentrate on life and its preservation. We need not look for conspiracies in the past. We have plenty in the present."

"Any you care to share with me?" Marie asked, half-jokingly.

"I am sure you have your own and need not the irrational speculations of an old man," he replied with a knowing smile. "My exam is complete. I shall report to your father that you are in good health and appear to have not suffered any injuries from your ordeal. Except, that is, for a sore backside." The physician turned for the door. "Have a pleasant day," he said over his shoulder.

Marie sat unmoving for several minutes, contemplating not just what Ian had said but what he had not said. Having been around for so long there was likely not much that went on in the castle of which he was not aware. The words and tones he had chosen told Marie much more than what he had voiced. She finally stood and retrieved the papers from under her bed. She hid them in her dress and headed for her study.

Andrew and Donald arrived at Marie's study nearly fifteen minutes after she had entered. She begged them to come in and close the door, then invited them to sit at the table with her. The secretive papers were spread out on the table. Her mother's original writings were laid out separately from the translator's papers.

"What is all of this?" Andrew asked as he looked over the sheets of paper.

"The papers on this side of the table were found in journals my mother had kept over the years," Marie said excitedly. "I found them a number of weeks ago."

"What language is this?" Donald asked, examining one of the pieces of paper. "I have never seen writings such as this."

"My mother wrote her journals mostly in ancient Greek, or so Joseph our librarian believes," Marie answered. "Some of the writings, though, were in a different language which he confessed to be unknown to him. I was able to have her writings translated. The papers on the other end of the table are from the man who translated her writings."

"The reason for your trip to Habersham," Andrew correctly deduced.

"Now you understand why I had to go," Marie replied.

"That, I understand. What I do not understand is why you kept this to yourself."

"I was not sure that they held any information of significance," Marie answered. "I did not wish to make an issue of my mother's writings if they held nothing of importance. Besides, there was neither the time nor opportunity for us to discuss them."

"So, what do your mother's journals have to do with the DuFay legend?" Andrew asked, foregoing the argument.

"Look at this piece of paper," Marie responded, handing one of the sheets from her mother's journal to Andrew. "Do you see anything familiar?"

Andrew scanned the paper and Marie could see the look of recognition on his face.

"It is the writing from the sword," he answered, somewhat mystified. "The symbols are the same."

"Yes!" Marie confirmed, not able to contain her excitement. "The writing is precisely the same! My mother knew about the DuFay Armor!"

"This does not prove that she knew of the legend," Andrew countered. "She could have seen these symbols in a book or somewhere in the castle and not knowing what they were, wrote them down for farther study."

"Take a look at these other pieces of paper," Marie continued, handing Andrew two more of the sheets. Andrew looked over the papers, this time with more puzzlement than recognition.

"They have some similarity to the sword writings, but they are not the same. It is obvious that they are the same language, though."

"Do you not remember the painting we saw in the room below the castle?" Marie asked. "Do you not recall the writings on the shield and breastplate?"

"I recall that the writings were so small as to be unintelligible," Andrew answered.

"Yes, yes," Marie responded quickly, "but these are the writings on the shield and breastplate."

"How can you be certain?" Donald asked.

"Because of the translation! Look, the translation of the writing on the sword was, 'The sword of the Spirit.' The translation of this second phrase is, 'Above all, taking the shield of faith.' And the translation of the third phrase is, 'Having on the breastplate of righteousness.' Is it not obvious? Sword, shield, and breastplate! And there is more! 'Stand firm with the belt of truth buckled around your waist' and 'feet fitted with the readiness that comes from the Gospel of peace!' 'The helmet of salvation!' It is all here, Andrew!"

"It would seem to make sense," Andrew surmised, looking from the sheets of translation to the original writings of Marie's mother.

"It does not seem to make sense," Marie argued, "it does make sense. Perfect sense."

"What, then, are the meanings of these phrases and what is their origin?" Donald asked, puzzled.

"They come from the Holy Scriptures," Andrew said knowingly. "They are phrases from the Bible."

"Yes!" Marie exclaimed. "That is what my mother thought as well. How did you know this?"

"Perhaps a long-lost memory from my childhood," Andrew replied, deep in thought. "The phrases, they are familiar to me."

"I do not recall reading the Holy Scriptures while we were growing up," Donald said.

"The memory is before then," Andrew answered, trying his best to clear the fog of amnesia and over twenty years of time. "I have a memory of reading the Scriptures. There are others with me, though I cannot see their faces."

"Your family?" Marie asked curiously.

"Perhaps. I do not know. It is but a shadow of a memory. What of the rest of your mother's writings?" Andrew asked, getting back to the task at hand. "Does she mention DuFay by name? Does she mention the legend and how DuFay's blacksmith supposedly instilled spirits within the armor?"

"She does mention the name DuFay several times and she does recite the legend," Marie answered. "She also expands on the phrases."

"What did she say about the phrases?" Andrew asked.

"It appears that all six are included in one section of Scripture. Here is what she wrote:

'Wherefore take unto you the whole armour of God, that ye may be able to withstand in the evil day, and having done all, to stand. Stand therefore, having your loins girt about with truth, and having on the breastplate of righteousness; and your feet shod with the preparation of the gospel of peace; Above all, taking the shield of faith, wherewith ye shall be able to quench all the fiery darts of the wicked. And take the helmet of salvation, and the sword of the Spirit, which is the word of God: Praying always with all prayer and supplication in the Spirit, and watching thereunto with all perseverance and supplication for all saints.'"

"What does all of that mean?" Donald asked.

"It means that at least the part of the legend about the blacksmith putting spirits in these items is not true," Andrew answered matter-of-factly.

"How can you know that?" Marie asked.

"It is right here," Andrew replied, pointing to the paper from which Marie had just read. "The blacksmith was obviously deeply knowledgeable about the Holy Scriptures and paid them much respect. He would certainly have not been a sorcerer and would not have believed in the practice of such evil. Therefore, he would not, and could not, place any kind of 'spirit' into an inanimate object."

"It would stand to reason, then, that unless Talbot or Gallard already has the helmet or crown, and the belt, and the boots in addition to the shield and breastplate, this impending battle is a waste of time and life," Donald said. "Unless all six pieces are brought together, individually they have little if any power."

"Do you not see?" Andrew asked, looking at his companions. "The helmet, boots and belt are virtually meaningless and certainly powerless as are the sword, the shield and the breastplate."

"Meaningless?" Marie asked incredulously. "How can you say that? After all you have been through, after all we have been through, how can you say that they are meaningless?"

"These things in and of themselves are powerless," Andrew replied matter-of-factly. "There is no spirit of power in the sword. There is no spirit of knowledge in the shield. And there is no spirit of perfection in the breastplate. And there certainly is no spirit of DuFay that will be awakened when three, or four, or even all six pieces of armor are brought together."

"What about the legend?" Marie asked, not wishing to give up that which she had come to believe over the past several months.

"I would say that the legend we know today bears some, but little, resemblance to the truth from hundreds of years ago. All legends have some origin in truth but over decades and centuries the truth is replaced by exaggeration and embellishment."

"Then what is the truth?" Donald asked.

"I would venture that DuFay was a man of God who ruled his kingdom as such," Andrew explained. "His blacksmith forged these items in his honor and being a man who believed in God himself, he placed these inscriptions on them. Perhaps to remind

DuFay of the true reason for his success, perhaps to remind future generations of the reason for DuFay's success. Who knows? That is likely the truth from which the legend was born. Over the years the truth became skewed as the story was told over and over, handed down from generation to generation. Perhaps the generations after DuFay did not honor God as he did and deviant elements from other cultures began to influence DuFay's descendants. When people recited the legend, they threw into the mix stories of the spirits as being entities instead of qualities. Somewhere along the line, DuFay's own spirit was inserted into the legend. The result is the legend that we have been told. Little truth, much fantasy."

"What about the part of the legend regarding DuFay's descendant?" Marie asked. "If you are correct in your assertions, then what is Donald's place in all of this? The legend states that when the three, or six now, pieces of armor are brought together with the heir of DuFay, peace and prosperity will be brought to the land."

"Do you still not see?" Andrew asked, looking back and forth between Marie and Donald. "No matter who you are, heir of DuFay or not, possession of these items is not the key to peace and prosperity. The key to peace and prosperity lies in what these items represent. Look back at the writings of your mother. 'Truth.' 'Righteousness.' 'Gospel.' 'Faith.' 'Word of God.' 'Prayer.' Those things are the keys to peace and prosperity. Reginald DuFay evidently lived and ruled by these qualities and therefore his kingdom flourished. You do not need beautifully crafted armor and a fanciful legend to bring order to chaos and peace to conflict or to create a harmonious society. Look, read this section of writing from your mother:

'Finally, my brethren, be strong in the Lord, and in the power of His might. Put on the whole armor of God, that ye may be able to stand against the wiles of the devil. For we wrestle not against flesh and blood, but against principalities, against powers, against

the rulers of the darkness of this world, against spiritual wicked-
ness in high places.'

"If the fight is not against flesh and blood, then physical
swords and shields and breastplates and helmets are useless. It is
what they represent that matters. So even if Donald, as heir to
DuFay, possessed all six items and stood on the highest hill and
all peoples bowed down to him, if he did not govern and rule
according to these standards, he would be a failure. His kingdom
would be a failure and the society around him would be a failure."

"Andrew, I have never heard you speak of such things," Marie
stated, looking at Andrew in a new light.

"Nor I," Donald echoed, though not as impressed as Marie
appeared to be. "You must have experienced some rather potent
preaching during your five years of travel. I did not realize you
were so persuadable."

"It has nothing to do with being persuaded, nor anything I
have seen or heard during the past five years." Andrew replied.

"Whatever the case," Donald responded, "People want a
leader who can lead them into battle, who can wield a sword and
conquer their enemies."

"That is exactly the point of these writings," Andrew said.
"The only difference is that the battle is not physical. It is spiritual.
Spiritual battles are for more important, and far more deadly, than
physical battles."

"My brother, we have spent countless hours and countless
days training for the types of battles we are about to face from
Gallard and his army," Donald argued. "We have spilled much
blood and suffered many bruises learning how to defend ourselves and defeat our enemies. We have trained all our lives to
engage in, and survive, these physical battles, not your so-called
spiritual and supernatural battles."

"Perhaps if we had spent more time training for spiritual
battles, we would have little if any need to train for physical
battles," Andrew countered.

"Boys," Marie interjected, not wanting the battle of wills to continue. "We can debate these philosophical speculations at another time. Right now, we must decide what to do with this information. A war is about to be waged and we must determine if there is a way to stop it."

"Gallard will stop at nothing," Donald said, turning his attention to Marie. "He is intent on obtaining the shield and the sword. His army is well-trained and very experienced and unless your father has thousands of soldiers hidden under the rocks and behind the trees outside of the castle, I would say Gallard has quite the advantage in numbers. He will destroy this place and everyone he finds here if he believes it will lead him to the sword and shield."

"I believe your father is quite obsessed with obtaining the DuFay armor as well," Andrew said, looking at Marie. "Will he fight a battle when he has such small odds of winning?"

"I do not know," Marie replied, looking worried. "He has never spoken with me about these things. He is an incredibly determined man, I do know that much. And he is very stubborn."

"So that is where you got that trait," Andrew jested, trying to lighten the mood.

"And a few others," she shot back with a look Andrew had seen on Talbot's face several times. "He must be told the truth."

"He will not care about the truth," Andrew responded. "I fear he cares only about obtaining the DuFay armor and, like Gallard, there is little that will stop him from pursuing his goal."

"We must try," Marie answered. "We must tell him everything we know."

"He will not listen to me," Andrew said knowingly. "And he will not take well to learning that DuFay's true heir is sleeping in his own home. Our presence would only incite him."

"Then I shall tell him myself," Marie said thoughtfully. "Come tomorrow, I will tell him."

Chapter 16

Talbot's war room bristled with activity as two dozen of the king's highest-level advisors worked on strategies to defend the kingdom. Some of the discussions were conducted via calm conversations while others became nervous arguments. All ideas were being entertained to produce the best means of protecting the king and the peoples of the kingdom. It was a daunting and ominous task before them, and they knew that survival was not likely considering the numbers of the enemy. And time was short.

"You have seen Gallard's army?" Talbot asked Angus, who stood before the king in full battle dress.

"I have, my lord," Angus replied. He pointed to a spot on the map spread out on the large table around which six men stood, including Malcolm. "They are here, a day's march out. Perhaps a day and a half."

"That close," Talbot mused, looking at the map.

"We have destroyed the bridge at Lincolnshire Crossing," Angus informed the king. "That should slow them down. There is not another bridge for ten miles in either direction. The water is hardly waist-deep at that location and the river is close to seventy-five feet wide. However, there are many large boulders and much debris scattered up and down the river for several hundred yards. It will be neither an easy nor quick task moving their men and horses across the river. They will have to leave their wagons and most of their supplies on the other side unless they choose to construct another bridge. Should they choose to do so, such an undertaking would easily encompass at least one if not two days."

"We could place archers on this side of the river," the king said. "Cover would be minimal, however, we would not need many men. A few dozen armed with a supply of arrows would farther slow the enemy's advance."

"It is an idea worthy of consideration," Angus replied although he was not sold on the idea entirely. "Gallard could easily have two separate divisions break off from the main body and cross up-river and down-river, out of the range of the archers. They could then flank our men and box them in. We would lose every one of them."

"Not if we have our men pull back before Gallard's men complete their crossing," Talbot countered. "Station three dozen men along this section of river, spread out as you deem to be most effective for our intent. Make the most of the natural cover. Where natural cover is lacking, fashion shields and barriers for the men. When Gallard does as you suspect and sends men to cross the river out of the range of our archers, have our men retreat and reform within our walls."

"It will be done, your majesty," Angus acquiesced.

"Malcolm, what is the status of food and supplies?" the king asked, turning to his Minister of Agriculture.

"We have enough food and water to sustain up to three hundred people for two weeks at most," Malcolm replied. The king turned to Angus with a questioning look.

"I fear the battle will be well over in two weeks' time," Angus replied honestly. "We shall certainly make a dent in their armor before they come within sight of these walls. These walls are strong, my lord, and we shall sweat and bleed to protect all within. However, I fear by their number alone they will not take long to breach our defenses."

"You are my military advisor," Talbot said sternly, looking Angus in the eyes. "You have earned your position through strength and intelligence. You will find a way to repel the enemy and keep them outside of these walls. Our walls are built on the foundations of ancient ramparts that thwarted countless attacks hundreds of years ago. They guarded and kept safe the DuFay Armor for over a hundred years. We have yet to complete the task upon which we embarked over twenty years ago. You know what is at stake Our defenses must stand. See to it."

"Yes, my lord," Angus replied without argument. "By your leave, I will continue our preparations."

"You have my leave," Talbot replied. Angus walked quickly and purposefully out of the room.

"He is right, my lord," Malcolm addressed the king as he watched Angus leave. "The outcome is inevitable. By all reports we are outnumbered two to one, perhaps three to one. Angus is indeed wise in the ways of war and shall set forth the greatest defense possible, but he is no sorcerer and cannot conjure up another two or three thousand men to match the enemy."

"And I do not expect him to," Talbot replied, returning his attention to the map on the table. "However, he must put forth the greatest effort possible in order to maintain the enemy's attention. When the enemy figures out a way to breach our defenses, and they most certainly will, we will have to make our escape. Their full focus must be on the castle. When the time comes, we will make our way through the underground passageways and exit far from the castle and fighting."

"What about the DuFay Armor?" Malcolm asked. "What about all for which we have worked? Will you abandon everything?"

"Certainly not," Talbot replied. "What is left here for us? We know MacLean has the sword. We have the shield. Gallard has the breastplate, of that there is little doubt. Though we have not determined the identity of the DuFay heir, in all truth, what does it matter? We may not be able to defeat Gallard's army today and lay hold of the breastplate, but I believe that it will not be long until we possess the sword. And then we will raise another army, an army larger than anything Gallard could ever imagine, and crash upon him as a tempest-driven wave crashes upon the shore."

"Raise another army?" Malcolm asked skeptically. "How would you accomplish that?"

"We resurrect the DuFay legend," Talbot replied confidently. "First, there must be chaos. There must be raids. The lands must become fruitless and even poisonous, killing crops and livestock. Rifts will be created between neighboring kingdoms. Wars and rumors of wars shall fill the land. Then, when the people are in despair and the harvest is ripe, we plant whispers in dark corners that the spirit of Reginald DuFay is stirring in the land. Then there will be heard rumors that the heir of DuFay has surfaced and is searching for his ancestor's holy armor. We shall create a history for ourselves. In town after town, in village after village, stories will be told of how we have overcome evil in far-away lands and brought light to the darkest corners of civilization. People will witness us repelling savage, barbaric raids, and they will witness us restoring bountiful crops to lands that had suddenly become unproductive and even deadly. They will embrace our leadership and hail us as their saviors."

"Yes, they will," Malcolm agreed with a smile. "Just as these people did twenty years ago."

"Just as these people did twenty years ago," Talbot said, though he was not smiling. "But we will have the sword and the shield this time. We will convince the people that the absence of the remaining pieces of armor is the only thing standing between them and ultimate peace and prosperity and joy. They shall be consumed by their desires, and they shall without pause stand behind the sword and the shield, ready to embark upon a campaign to reclaim the other pieces and finally inaugurate their true king. They will follow me by the thousands, and the tens of thousands. No army on earth will be able to withstand my onslaught. Gallard will fall. The breastplate will be mine. We will find the other pieces of armor. The world will be mine." Talbot looked at Malcolm. "And there will be great reward for those who stand with me."

"You are my king," Malcolm replied obediently. "I have followed you for over twenty years and will follow you till I draw my last breath."

"Go now and make the necessary preparations for our escape. You know what to do."

"Yes, your majesty," Malcolm said with a bow of the head. He then turned and left the room.

"I would have some time alone," Talbot called out to the remaining men in the room. "You may continue your discussions and preparations elsewhere."

With respectful bows, the men turned and left the room. As the last man left, but before the door to the room could close, Marie entered quietly. Talbot did not notice her entrance as his attention was focused on the map. Her silent steps did not betray her presence as she crossed the room and approached her father. Suddenly realizing that he was not alone, Talbot looked up with a start. He quickly calmed as he recognized his daughter.

"Marie! You gave me quite a fright. I thought I was alone."

"I must speak with you, father," Marie said with an air of uncertainty. She did not know exactly how to say what she needed to say. She had to tell her father all at once that she knew of the legend of DuFay and that the legend he so desperately sought was hardly more than a fairy tale. Where to begin? How to begin? For the first time in her life she stood before her father, shaking with nervousness. Seeing her hesitation and reading the look on her face, Talbot moved around the table and stood before her. He gave her a look of paternal concern.

"What is it, my daughter? Your countenance is disturbingly dark."

"There is much I must tell you, yet I do not know where or how to begin. I fear you will take no great delight in what I have to say."

"Speak what is on your mind, Marie. I am your father, you do not need to fear me."

Marie hesitated a little longer, still unsure of how to begin.

Looking into her father's eyes she felt as though she was five years old again, a little girl standing before her strong, bold father. She started to speak but fumbled over her words. She looked to the floor, took a deep breath, and began again.

"I know why the army of Gallard is marching upon our kingdom," she confessed.

"What do you believe to be his purpose?" her father inquired.

"His purpose for coming here is the same as was your purpose in coming here so many years ago," Marie answered nervously.

"Oh? And just what purpose do you believe this to be?" her father asked, his brow furrowing a bit.

"He seeks the DuFay Armor."

"What is the DuFay Armor?" the king asked innocently, not giving anything away.

"I know of the legend of Reginald DuFay," Marie answered. "I know of the sword, the shield and the breastplate, the helmet, the belt and the boots. I know of the tale that when the heir of DuFay rises from the land and possesses these items, Reginald DuFay's spirit will be resurrected and through his descendant he will bring peace and prosperity to the world. I know that Reginald DuFay once lived and ruled from the ruins upon which you built our home. I know that Andrew possesses the sword," and then she took a long shot, "and I know that you possess the shield."

"You appear to know quite a bit," Talbot answered, taking a step back and resting on the edge of the table. "What else do you believe that you know?"

"I know it is all a lie," Marie answered, then corrected herself. "Well, most of it is a lie. There was indeed a great king who lived hundreds of years ago by the name of Reginald DuFay. He did have a prosperous, peaceful, and joyful land. And, in his honor, a sword, shield and breastplate of great beauty and symbolism were fabricated, along with a crown and belt and boots. But there are no mysterious powers within these man-made items and bringing them together in the hand of the true descendant of

Reginald DuFay will no more bring peace to the world than cause swine to speak."

"I see," her father said thoughtfully, as if a revelation had just been made. He peered into her eyes. "This is quite interesting. Please, continue."

"Our journey to this land was not incidental, was it? You knew of the legend and the history of this region. You brought us here in hopes of discovering the DuFay Armor and possessing it. Once in your hands, the armor would enable you to spread your rule across land after land and peoples after peoples. You came looking for the DuFay Armor, yet it is power that you seek."

Wordlessly, Talbot walked to the opposite side of the table and sat in his oversized chair. He folded his hands across his midsection and gazed at his daughter. When he failed to speak, Marie continued.

"Do you deny these things?" Marie asked, confused that her father had not come right out and objected to all she had said.

"No, you are correct my dear, though I must set you straight on a few points," the king replied. "First, I knew nothing of the DuFay legend before we arrived here. I chose this spot to construct the castle because of the natural defenses that the location provides against attack. A quality, mind you, that shall come in quite handy in very shortly. During construction we discovered artifacts detailing the rule and legend of Reginald DuFay. It was an exciting time, and we most anxiously embarked on a mission to determine if the items comprising the DuFay ..." Talbot paused for a brief moment, as if weighing his next words, "... armor were still here. Yes, we did find the shield. However, we never found the sword or breastplate or the other items you have mentioned. And secondly, our motivations were not power and prestige. Far from it. History was our motivation," the king said, leaning forward in his chair, then standing. "Learning of the past was our motivation. Look around you, my dear. Hundreds of years before my grandfather's grandfather was born a great castle stood right here where we now stand." Talbot began to slowly walk around the room. "We have walked in the footsteps of a great man who came before us. During his time there were made great works of art, great works of literature, and great advances in science. We have seen some of these things around the castle. What a wonderful time it must have been to live and breathe and enjoy life! Imagine the banquets! Imagine the festivals! Men of great wisdom walked these halls. I look not for power, my dear, but for the wisdom and knowledge of these men who came before me and in whose footsteps I am not worthy to walk."

"That would seem inconsistent with your order to burn books that were found in the castle upon our arrival," Marie said slightly accusingly. "Surely those books presented great opportunities for learning."

Talbot's enthusiastic expression turned to cautious curiosity. "Where did you hear such a thing?" he asked.

"Several weeks after our arrival here I went to ask Joseph a question about a book," Marie replied, creating a lie so as not to cause Joseph any grief. "He did not see me enter his research room. He was busy throwing book after book into the fireplace. I stood there for who knows how long before he caught me out of the corner of his eye. He was startled to see me and appeared rather anxious. I asked what he was doing, and he said he was getting rid of some old, tattered books that were beyond repair. I saw the books and they did not appear to be worn and tattered to me. I said so. He replied that you had determined that some of the books were evil and had to be destroyed. He then ushered me out of the room and shut the door."

"You remember a lot to have been so young at the time," Talbot stated in a tone that reflected anything but a compliment.

"There is something I do not remember, though," Marie continued. "I do not remember seeing any objects of art or literature in the castle that reflect the name of DuFay. You said that you discovered such artifacts during your excavations. Where are they?"

"They are in safe keeping," Talbot replied warily. "They are of great value and need not be displayed where they could become damaged or stolen."

"I would certainly value the opportunity to see them some time," Marie said, fishing.

"I would that war was not upon us, else I would enjoy providing you such an opportunity," Talbot countered. He moved to where he was facing his daughter, less than half-a-dozen feet in front of her. He looked at her as though he was trying to peer inside her mind, and indeed he was greatly curious as to what was prompting these questions from her. "It would appear that we have moved from an offering of information to a course of questioning," he said, looking deeply into her eyes. "In fact, there is a growing air of accusation in this discourse which sits none too well with me. My time is precious with war at our door, and it is better spent devising strategies for defending my daughter and this kingdom than defending myself against spurious suppositions. Is there anything else you wish to ask me before I give you leave?"

Marie knew that she was pushing hard, perhaps too hard, with her father. So much of her wanted to politely bow and leave the room in silence. She did not want to be disrespectful to her father, and not being able to be one hundred percent certain of her suspicions, she felt guilty for questioning his motives. But there were things that she had to know, and things she had to tell her father.

"You said that you found the shield during the excavations and construction of the castle," she said.

"That is correct," Talbot replied. "As I said, we found many artifacts."

"So, it was not in the possession of the elders of the village?"

"How could it have been in their possession if we found it in the castle ruins?" her father replied somewhere sternly. His daughter was half-a-breath away from accusing him of lying, and his anger was close to surfacing.

"It is just that I had heard that the elders of the village had actually found the shield before our arrival," she replied.

"I have no doubt that they did indeed find a shield," Talbot answered, seeing a way around his daughter's unspoken suspicions. "I have no doubt that they found many shields, and many swords, and many other objects over the years as they dug in and around the ruins. Who knows what all they retrieved that had been buried by time? I am certain that they found much, as we found much. Perhaps they, too, found a fabulously exquisite shield and convinced themselves that it was the shield of Reginald DuFay himself. I assure you, my daughter, that whatever it was they found, it was not the shield of DuFay. I have the shield of DuFay, and it was my workers who discovered it during their excavations."

A rap on the door from the hallway to the room interrupted the conversation. Talbot bid the person to enter, and the door opened. One of the elite Castle Guard approached the king and whispered something into his ear. A look of surprise and excitement crossed Talbot's face.

"You are certain of this?" he asked the guard, who nodded in affirmation. The look of surprise was replaced by a smile of satisfaction. "Good. Very good."

"What is it, Father?" Marie asked, her curiosity aroused.

"Good news," he answered. "Come, you will want to see this," he said as he walked briskly across the room and into the hallway, not even pausing to see if his daughter was following him.

Chapter 17

T he delicious aroma of a freshly cooked meal hung in the air outside of the Bergman home, an occurrence that was common each day. Anyone passing by the house would have felt a rumble in their stomach, though they may have just finished a grand meal elsewhere. Anyone inside the house would have their stomachs trembling as though they had not eaten in days. The food's flavor filled the entire house and was so strong that the occupants could taste the meal before they had taken the first bite. Donald and Andrew, along with Heather, sat at the table inside the modest home, waiting with as much patience as possible for the meal to be served. Mrs. Bergman removed a medium-sized kettle from over the fire and carried it to the table. There, she took a ladle and scooped the steaming soup into each person's bowl. A loaf of freshly baked bread was quickly divided into five sections and the table's occupants wasted no time delving into the gourmet cuisine.

"This is fabulous," Donald commented as he savored the flavor of the thick mixture of meats, bullion and seasoning. "I have never tasted anything like it. What is it?"

"I am not certain of the proper pronunciation," Andrew said as he watched his brother's enjoyment of the meal, "but I believe this particular dish is a combination of boiled horse and goat intestines. Am I not correct, Mrs. Bergman?"

"Intestines?" Donald asked as he stopped a helping of the hash half-way to his mouth, and a look of surprise and border-line disgust crossed his face. "This is horse and goat intestines?"

"Tasty, no?" Andrew asked with a smile he could not hide.

"Do not let Andrew spoil your mid-day meal," Heather said with a feigned look of disapproval thrown at Andrew. "It is nothing of the sort. It is a simple soup made of lamb's meat, aged and seasoned for flavor."

Donald looked back and forth between Andrew and Heather, not entirely sure who to believe. With a look of helplessness, his eyes beckoned to Heather's mother.

"Your brother is simply being a brother," Mrs. Bergman said with a smile. "He probably gave you honey-coated bugs when you were children and told you they were pieces of candy."

"If only that were the worst thing he did," Donald replied sourly as he deposited the contents of the spoon into his mouth.

"I would venture, though, that Mrs. Bergman could make even the most revolting horse and goat bowels into a fabulously tasting meal," Andrew said as he continued with his own meal.

"May we turn the conversation in another direction?" Heather asked as she paused in her own eating. "Or would you prefer to continue discussing such disgusting things?"

"What is our next move?" Donald asked Andrew. "Gallard's army is nearly here and when it arrives our escape will for all purposes be blocked."

"There are ways away from here other than the front gate," Andrew replied, stealing a glance at Heather. "But I agree, we should not tarry much longer. I must discover what happened to the sword, though. I cannot leave here not knowing."

"But you said the sword is meaningless, as are the other pieces of armor. What purpose would be accomplished in finding the sword?"

"Talbot, or Gallard, could still use it to fulfill their malicious intentions," Andrew replied. "I cannot allow that to happen. Though I do not believe that the heir of DuFay will, by his simple existence and possession of the Armor, bring upon us a land flowing with milk and honey, I do believe that men such as Talbot and

Gallard can do fantastic harm to the land. Their desires for ultimate power will result in a terrible tyranny and the people will suffer. People always suffer under a tyrant. Plus, I made a vow to deliver the sword to the rightful descendant of DuFay and that vow will not be fulfilled until the sword is placed into his hands."

As if in response to Andrew's words, the door to the home opened and Steven walked in, dragging what appeared to be a large bundle of firewood behind him. He quickly turned and closed the door after checking to see if anyone was outside.

"It is about time you came home," Mrs. Bergman addressed her son. "You have nearly missed the meal. Come, sit and have something to eat."

"Horse and goat bowels," Heather said with a sly grin aimed at Andrew.

Steven did not answer but went about his business of pulling apart the bundle of firewood. He appeared to be in a bit of a rush as the wood fell from the bundle and scattered on the floor. Everyone at the table stopped and turned their attention to the boy, curious to see what he was up to. After nearly half a minute, Steven reached down and pulled something from the pile that was not a piece of wood for the fire. It was bundled up tightly and black soot stained the garment. He stood and slowly turned to the group at the table. He looked at Andrew, almost afraid of the reaction that was surely to follow. With a bit of hesitancy, he walked over to Andrew and offered the bundle to him. Andrew reached out and took the offering. He wasted no time in removing the thin pieces of leather wrapped around the bundle that were holding the garment in place to protect the contents. The subdued lighting in the house could not hold back the glimmer from the DuFay Sword as Andrew peeled away the protecting fabric. Everyone was speechless and looked at the magnificent weapon with complete awe. Finally, Andrew spoke.

"Where did you find this?" Andrew asked Steven, who was still nervous and looking guilty.

"I found it where you said it would be," Steven answered, afraid to look Andrew in the eye. "Above the fireplace in your room."

"But I looked for it two days ago and it was not there," Andrew countered, looking at Steven with a little suspicion.

"I took it before you looked," Steven confessed.

"Steven Bergman, I told you in no uncertain terms that you were not to get involved," the boy's mother said sternly. "I forbade you from trying to retrieve the sword. You disobeyed me and put your life at risk. How could you do such a thing?"

"I am sorry, Mother, but I had to," Steven replied, his eyes pleading for forgiveness. "Andrew said that the king killed my father. I had to do something, anything, to keep him from getting the sword."

"How did you retrieve the sword without being caught?" Andrew asked, intrigued.

"After the king's men took you away the other night I ran to the castle and convinced two of my friends to help me steal it. They work in the castle, so they were able to go to Andrew's room without the least bit of suspicion. They hoisted me up from outside using the rope and bucket that is used for bringing bath water to the room. Jonathan crouched down in the fireplace, and I stepped onto his back. I was just able to reach the sword. They then lowered me back to the water. I hid the sword where I knew it would not be found. When I saw you and your brother arrive here a while ago, I went and retrieved the sword because I knew you would want it."

"That was a remarkably brave thing to do," Andrew said as he looked at the young boy with admiration, "and smart."

"It was a foolish thing to do," Mrs. Bergman corrected Andrew, shooting looks of disapproval at her son. "Very, very foolish. You could have been caught, or worse. Did you not pause to think about such things?"

"Yes, Mother, I knew it was dangerous," Steven replied with a tear in his eye. "But I did it for Father."

Mrs. Bergman stood in silence, looking at her son with both pride and concern. Deep down she was proud of what he had done and the risk he had taken to honor his father, but she was still a mother and the thought of what could have happened to her only son overwhelmed all other emotions. She did not know what else could be said about the incident, so she changed the subject.

"Sit and have something to eat," she finally said, turning and filling his plate. Steven looked at Andrew, who gave him a nod and smile of approval. Feeling better, Steven went over and sat by his sister and began eating.

"So now that you have the sword, we can leave?" Donald asked.

"Leave?!" Steven asked, shocked. "You cannot leave! You have to stay!"

"There is a war coming between two men motivated by greed and power," Andrew replied to the boy. "There is no winning of this war, and everyone caught up in it will be destroyed. We must leave if we are to escape destruction."

"Mother, are we leaving too?" Steven asked, looking anxiously at his mother.

"This is our home," she answered. "We do not have anywhere else to go. We have no relatives with whom we could stay. We have no choice but to stay and hope for the best."

"You are known to be friends of mine," Andrew said. "Talbot already suspects that Heather aided in my escape from the dungeon and there is little doubt in my mind that sooner or later, he will discover Steven's actions in recovering the sword. If you stay and if Talbot succeeds in holding off Gallard's army, things may become very unpleasant if not outright dangerous for your family."

"You are a man of the road, Andrew," Mrs. Bergman replied. "You have traveled many years from one town to the next, but always on your own. We have never traveled farther than a few days from our home. We would not know where to go or what to do. I would not know how to provide for my children. How long would we last? Everything we know is here. We have crops and herds to feed us. Steven is nearly old enough to assume his father's craft. Heather and I can make dresses and clothes in order to help provide for our needs. We have much here. We will have nothing if we leave."

"You would have a future," Andrew argued. "You and Heather can make dresses and clothes wherever you go. Steven, if he so chooses, can follow in his father's footsteps in nearly any town in which you decide to live. Crops will grow in other lands. There is nothing here so precious to you that you cannot leave it. In fact, you will be taking with you the one thing that is most precious to you, and that is your memory."

"This is the only home we have known," Mrs. Bergman continued her argument. "I have lived here all my life. Heather and Steven were born in this very house. We have many friends here, some so close they are like family. I just do not know if we can give up our history, our home."

"I realize it is a frightening prospect, leaving your home of so many years," Andrew answered. "I was forced to do so myself. But it will be better than staying here and facing an uncertain future at the hands of King Talbot. Your children will be able to form lives and memories elsewhere, and you will be able to forge friendships elsewhere. We will find for you a good village. We will help you build a home and become established."

"Andrew," Donald said, finally speaking up. "After we leave here, I will have to return home without delay. I have my family to protect. For all I know Gallard has already sent word back of my betrayal and taken my family into custody. I must return to them with all speed. As it is, I have delayed my return too long. I cannot assist you in this endeavor."

"I understand," Andrew replied. "I would not hold it against you."

"But Donald is the heir of DuFay!" Heather exclaimed. "He cannot leave!"

"Being of the DuFay bloodline grants me no royalty," Donald replied, shaking his head. "Gallard and Talbot would kill me on the spot if they knew my heritage. There is nothing they would desire less than another challenger to their claims, especially the very descendant of DuFay And in truth, I have no desire to become such a powerful man. No, there is nothing but certain death for me if I stay here. I must leave as well."

"Annette," Andrew said, using Mrs. Bergman's first name. "Though it is not an easy decision, you do not have much time to contemplate the alternatives. In fact, it would be best that we leave as soon as possible, this very evening in fact. Gallard's army is close, and it is certain that he has advance scouts keeping their eyes on the region. It will be difficult to slip away at night but nearly impossible to do so during the day. Every hour we delay, Gallard's army is an hour closer."

"Mother," Heather pleaded. "We must leave with Andrew We will be okay I am sure of it."

"Very well," Mrs. Bergman gave in, still uncertain of her decision. "If it will mean protecting you and your brother, then we will go. We will start packing immediately."

"Only bare essentials," Andrew instructed. "And by that, I mean primarily clothes. We cannot be slowed by having to carry large loads. Pack only what you can carry. Everything else must be left behind."

Suddenly, a heavy pounding on the front door startled everyone. The pounding was followed by a loud, commanding voice.

"In the name of King Richard Talbot, open this door!"

Everyone in the room looked at each other, panic shooting from their eyes. The DuFay Sword lay on the table, uncovered. Andrew moved to cover it but before he could the front door burst open, and the king's guards rushed into the room. Andrew and Donald were immediately confronted with the sharp points of a dozen spears. Heather, Steven and their mother were roughly pushed back away from the table.

After several seconds of silence, King Talbot calmly and casually walked into the home. Half a dozen steps behind him, Marie entered with a look of total confusion on her face. Having watched her father break down the door to the home of her best friend and practically surrogate family disturbed her greatly. Talbot walked over to the table, opposite the side where Donald and Andrew sat not with looks of fear but looks of total contempt. Moving his eyes to the table, Talbot spotted the sword, half-covered by its shroud. He reached over and gently pulled the garment aside, revealing the sword from tip to hilt. A smile of triumph crossed his face.

"The DuFay Sword," he murmured in delight. "I see you have found that which you claimed to have lost only two days ago," he said, looking at Andrew. "How convenient. Do you wish to continue your lie of not knowing how it disappeared from your room?"

"At this stage I would say it is a moot point," Andrew replied. "But to satisfy your curiosity, I removed and hid the sword before you arrested me. It had not been in my room for quite some time. I thought it safe to retrieve it, but obviously my thinking was in error."

"As it still is," Talbot replied, grasping the sword and holding it upright. "You must think me such the fool. No, you did not hide the sword before your arrest. I would venture that you somehow convinced this young man over here to retrieve the sword should you be taken into custody a second time, which would ordinarily mean your execution. When you were brought to me the other night, from this very home mind you, the lad carried out his instructions and retrieved the sword."

"Steven would do no such thing," Andrew lied. "In fact, his mother specifically forbade him from getting involved though he desperately wished to give me aid."

"There were two boys who assisted Steven in procuring the

sword," Talbot shot back. "They were witnessed entering your room while we were engaged in our discourse. After our visit to your room and the discovery that the sword was missing, we questioned the boys. They were most cooperative. Little to his knowledge, the boy here has been under scrutiny since yesterday morning. I knew it would be nothing more than a matter of a few days before he fetched the sword and returned it to you."

"The sword is not yours," Andrew said firmly. "It shall never be yours. You are not the heir to the DuFay line and have no right to possess it."

"The DuFay line died out many, many years ago," Talbot answered. "There is no descendant, no heir to come back and bring paradise to the land. The sword belongs to whoever is strong enough to obtain it and hold on to it. And as you can see, I have obtained it and am holding on to it."

"And now that you have it in your hands, shall our fates be the same as the fates of Justin Morecraft, Patrick Bergen, Connor O'Banion, and Carl Bergman?" Andrew boldly asked.

Talbot gave Andrew a look of utter contempt.

"What do you mean by that?" he challenged.

"Did not Morecraft, Bergen and O'Banion meet with untimely accidents soon after you obtained the DuFay Shield?" Andrew asked, not backing down. "And the only reason that Bergman did not meet a similar accident is that you did not know of his involvement with the other three?"

"Are you accusing me of murder?" Talbot asked incredulously. "Here I stand with a sword in my hand and there you sit with half a dozen spears inches from your throat, and you wish to accuse me of murder?"

"You deny any involvement with their deaths?" Andrew asked.

"I do not need to deny anything," Talbot responded in anger. "I am the king of this land, and I will not be the subject of your insulting accusations."

"Then you do not deny involvement in their deaths?" Andrew pushed.

"Accidents happen every day," Talbot retorted. "A man who reads by candlelight dies when his house burns down. A man who works with horses is trampled to death. Another man drowns while swimming in the lake. A fourth man, a blacksmith, dies when his workshop catches on fire. You wish to insinuate that I had something to do with these deaths? A young man fell out of a tree and broke his neck a week ago. Do you wish to accuse me of his death as well?"

"Did he have any knowledge of the DuFay legend?" Andrew asked sarcastically. "It seems that those people who are close to the legend have a habit of dying in strange accidents. There were four elders of the village, all with intimate knowledge of the DuFay legend. Three died within weeks of discovering the shield and somehow the shield ends up in your possession. They had to die, else they might dispute your claim to the DuFay throne when the day came that you made such a claim. You could not afford to allow to remain alive anyone who knew the truth and could challenge you. I dare say our fates are sealed."

"Your fate was sealed the day you came into possession of this sword," Talbot responded. He looked around the room, his mind contemplating the situation.

"I have been considering what I should do with you and your brother," the king said to Andrew. "You are not exactly guilty of any crime, at least none of which I am aware. Granted, you did escape from prison, but you did so in order to save my daughter. As it turns out you were not guilty of the crime for which you were imprisoned anyway. I have long been suspicious of your motivations for coming to our land, and in truth, I have never fully trusted you. For the sake of my daughter I allowed you to stay and even offered you a position in my administration. When I learned for certain your knowledge of the DuFay legend and your possession of the sword, your intentions became quite clear. You would usurp me and claim the throne of DuFay for yourself.

Your words here this afternoon have shown beyond the shadow of a doubt that you have set yourself against me. Therefore, I have decided that your visit to Durinburg must come to an end. You will leave our village by nightfall, you and your brother, never to return. The day your face is seen within a hundred miles of here will be the last your eyes shall see."

"What of my land?" Andrew asked, though he knew the answer.

"Your land is forfeit," Talbot replied. "It shall be given to someone more worthy, someone loyal to me. Now, as for this young lady and her brother," he said, turning to face the Bergmans. "They shall be imprisoned in the depths of the castle until I decide on their fates."

"NO!" Mrs. Bergman cried, stepping in front of her children in a vain attempt to protect them. "They have done no wrong!"

"They are criminals!" Talbot shouted. "Your daughter aided in the escape of a prisoner of the king. When your son entered Andrew's room without permission, he became guilty of trespassing. When he took the sword, he became guilty of theft. He will be punished accordingly."

"Father, no!" Marie said, stepping forward. "You cannot do this!"

"Stay out of this, Marie," Talbot answered, holding his hand up to hold her back. "They have broken the law and they must be punished."

"But Andrew was wrongly jailed! How can you hold Heather guilty of helping him escape when he was wrongly imprisoned, by you, in the first place?"

"Andrew's guilt has nothing to do with it," he replied. "She does not determine who is guilty and who is innocent. That is the job of the king. That is my job. I am the law, and I determine when the law is trespassed, and I determine the penalty."

"What about mercy?" she pleaded, desperately wanting to save her friends. "Is mercy not also the responsibility of the king?"

"Those who break the law must be punished under the law,"

Talbot replied, not wavering. "If there is no law, there is no order. Without law is chaos. I will not have chaos in my kingdom."

"Well then I have some bad news for you, your majesty," Andrew said. "Because a maelstrom of chaos is about to land on your front doorstep and there is nothing you can do about it."

"I do not need to do anything about it," Talbot replied with a smirk, which remark caught Andrew by surprise. He then turned to the guard in charge.

"Take the girl and the boy down to the prison. I want two guards outside their cells at all times and if any guard is found asleep or away from his post he will be executed on the spot. Do I make myself clear?"

"Yes, your majesty," the guard responded. "It will be done."

"Father, you cannot do this," Marie pleaded as the guards carried out their orders. Heather and Steven were no less than shoved out of the house while another guard held back their crying mother. "This is not right."

"I decide what is right and what is wrong," he responded firmly.

"Spoken like a true tyrant," Andrew stated.

"But earlier you said that power and prestige were not your goal," Marie reminded her father, "and that all you wanted was to learn about the past. You said that all you wanted was the wisdom and knowledge of the men who walked this land before you."

"And I will have the wisdom and knowledge of the men who walked before me," Talbot answered. "I will have the wisdom and knowledge of Reginald DuFay, one of the greatest rulers this land has ever known, when I obtain the final piece of the DuFay Armor."

"Father, how can you do this?" she asked as tears started rolling down her cheek. "How can you allow yourself to become so corrupted?"

"Corrupted?" Talbot repeated in surprise. "My dear, I am far from being corrupted. The world needs strong leaders, wise leaders, skilled leaders. What I am doing I do not do for myself. I do it for the people. They need something, someone, to believe in. I will provide that and more."

"Who are you?" she asked in disbelief. "What have you become?"

"I am your father," he replied sternly. "You will respect me and honor me. In time you will see that what has been done in the past, and what is being done today, is for the best. It is for your well-being and to secure you the best future possible."

"I hope my well-being and future are much better than what my mother experienced," Marie said with no little accusation in her tone. She did not bother waiting on a reaction from her father. She immediately turned and nearly ran out the door. Talbot watched her leave. He then turned to Andrew, Donald, and Annette.

"Mrs. Bergman, I regret that your daughter and your son committed their crimes and therefore must be punished. I shall strive to be fair and not heavy-handed. As for you two," he said, addressing Andrew and Donald, "I suggest you begin packing. The sun shall be setting in a few hours." With a smug smile, Talbot exited the house leaving Andrew, Donald and Mrs. Bergman alone.

"I cannot believe this is happening," Mrs. Bergman said, collapsing into the closest chair and covering her sobs with her hands. "My children are now prisoners. What am I going to do? I cannot leave them. I … I do not know what to do."

"Do not worry," Andrew said as he laid a hand of comfort on her shoulder. "I know what to do." His offer of comfort and determined tone did little to ease her worries.

"I take it your plan does not involve heeding the king's rather explicit instructions?" Donald asked, fearing he knew the answer.

"Our business with Talbot is not finished," Andrew replied, a plan forming in his mind. "We shall be visiting Durinburg Castle one more time."

Chapter 18

K ing Talbot sat alone in a small dining room that was set aside for his use only. He was half-way through his breakfast, mulling over the future of his kingdom. The reports he had received thus far of the size of the enemy did not bode well for his future. He looked up inquisitively at the guard who had just entered the dining room.

"My lord, a messenger approaches," the guard reported.

"A messenger?" he asked.

"Yes, sire. A lone man on horseback, carrying a white banner. Shall we lower the bridge?"

"Do so," the king replied. "Take him to my court and have him wait. Inform my advisors, especially Angus and Malcolm, that they are to convene in the court immediately. I will be there as soon as I finish my morning meal."

"Yes, my lord, it will be done," the guard said as he bowed his head and left the room.

"So, it begins," Talbot said to himself as he finished his breakfast.

The messenger stood at the podium, looking about nervously. At least a dozen men stood around a long table speaking to each other in muted tones and periodically glancing at the stranger in their midst. He was only there to deliver a message from his king, yet he felt as though he were on trial. He knew that it was not uncommon for the reply to be sent via the messenger's head in a basket. He felt little comfort in the knowledge that he was there to present nothing more than in invitation. After nearly twenty anxious minutes, a door in the back of the room finally opened and all heads turned to see who it was. With boldness and authority King Richard Talbot strode into the room. The men around the table respectfully bowed their heads in silence as the king made his way to the large, ornate throne that dominated the room. Without hesitation, Talbot lowered himself onto the throne and as if on cue, his advisors took their seats at the table. After everyone was settled Talbot spoke, addressing the messenger.

"I assume you have been sent by the king who has intruded upon this sovereign land," Talbot said accusingly.

"I have been dispatched by King Edwin Gallard," the messenger replied, mustering as much courage as he possibly could.

"Are you here to negotiate and present terms?" Talbot asked, getting straight to the point.

"No, my lord. Those are matters well above me."

"Then why have you been sent to me?"

"My lord the king Edwin Gallard wishes to speak with you in person. He is willing to meet with you outside of your walls in a location of your choosing. Just the two of you with neither guards nor advisors," the messenger replied.

"Outside of my walls?" Talbot repeated. "Does your king believe me to be so foolish as to leave my protection while he has nearly five thousand men at my doorstep? I think not. I will meet with your king, but he must come to me."

"You will understand if my king is hesitant to step within your walls lest he not be permitted to leave of his own accord," the messenger answered.

"Are you questioning my integrity?" Talbot asked, anger riding his voice.

"Not at all, your majesty," the messenger quickly responded. "But as you are wary to step outside of your walls, my king is wary to step inside your walls."

"Then unless your king has a loud voice, I do not see a meeting taking place," Talbot said.

"Your castle is built on the shores of a large lake," the messenger said. "Perhaps you would be willing to meet with King Gallard on the lake, where neither you nor he would be concerned of an ambush or being taken prisoner."

Talbot did not respond immediately but looked questioningly at Angus. After a moment of consideration, Angus nodded his head once in agreement. Talbot turned his attention back to the messenger.

"Very well, it is agreeable. I will meet your king on the water. We will both be allowed a single rower and nobody else. We shall meet three hundred yards offshore, out of the range of even the strongest of bowmen. There is a small rock outcropping by which we shall meet. It is not large enough for a man to hide on, should your king ponder the use of it to his advantage. Those are my terms, and they are not negotiable."

"Very well," the messenger replied. "It is agreed. Two hours from now?"

"Two hours from now," Talbot confirmed. He nodded to one of the guards standing by the podium who proceeded to escort the messenger out of the room.

"The rest of you may leave us. Your services are no longer needed here," Talbot said to his advisors. With gentle murmuring, the men left the room. When the door had closed, Malcolm addressed the king.

"What do you believe to be the purpose of this meeting?" he asked. "Is Gallard looking to offer terms?"

"Undoubtedly so," Talbot replied. "He will make demand for MacLean and the sword in the very least. If he suspects that I have the shield, he will make demand for it as well. He will indicate that if we deliver upon his requests, he will withdraw his army from this land. But we all know that is a half-truth. He may withdraw today but he will be back tomorrow demanding our allegiance to him as 'the heir of DuFay.'"

"Then what course of action do we take?" Angus asked. "If we tell him we possess neither the sword nor the shield he will not believe us and will tear this place apart, killing everyone who stands in his way."

"We could stall," Malcolm, not known for his military prowess, offered. "We could deny any and all knowledge of the DuFay legend."

"Gallard will not accept that, not for a second," Talbot countered. "It is a foregone conclusion that he does indeed have a spy in our midst. How much he knows at this time we cannot know. However, he has acquired enough intelligence to have marched his army hundreds of miles to get here. That is the sign of much determination."

"Why do we not turn the sword and shield over to Gallard?" Angus said, an idea creeping into his mind.

"Have you gone mad?" Talbot asked incredulously.

"Do we not have other majestic swords and shields in our possession?" Angus continued. "We found quite a few during our excavations. Can we be certain that Gallard would know what the true sword and shield of Dufay would look like?"

"He knows what the DuFay Sword looks like," Talbot informed his advisors. "He has seen it, if not even held it in his own hands. I fear there would be no fooling him on that matter."

"You have possessed the sword for less than twenty-four hours," Angus said. "As far as Gallard is concerned MacLean still has it."

"Unless Gallard has captured MacLean and discovered that the sword is now in my hands," Talbot countered. "There might be the possibility that we could pass another shield off as the DuFay Shield but there is no way of us knowing if Gallard has an exact description of the shield and would spot a fake. We cannot possibly know what information Gallard truly possesses and how much he simply presumes. This meeting will tell us what we need to know."

"I believe it would be prudent if you were to permit me to accompany you to this meeting," Angus said.

"Are you ready to trade your sword for an oar?" the king asked.

"The terms of the meeting did not forbid weapons," Angus answered with a smug smile.

"Then let us go make preparations for our little excursion on the lake," Talbot said and led the way out of the room.

The two hours passed quickly. Two dozen well-armed soldiers had escorted the king and his military advisor to the shore of the lake, which had been accessed through a single door at the rear of the castle. The morning mist had yet to fully dissipate from the lake's surface and visibility was limited to about a hundred feet. Angus gently propelled the canoe across the lake, his warrior's instincts giving him much caution. He took a full ten minutes to cover the three hundred yards to the point of meeting. Slowly, the shape of the rock outcropping came into view. Also coming into view, to the right of the outcropping, was another canoe with two men seated in it. Instead of rowing directly toward the other canoe Angus directed his canoe to the right of it and slowly paddled around it and the outcropping in a reconnaissance maneuver. Satisfied that there was no apparent ambush danger, he stopped the canoe ten yards from the other one. There were several moments of silence as the two pair of men assessed each other.

"A fine morning, is it not?" Gallard said as he took in a deep breath, breaking the silence.

"That remains to be seen," Talbot replied.

"I see that you opted to have your military advisor serve as your rower," Gallard said, hoping to impress Talbot with his knowledge. "A rather wise precaution, though unwarranted in this case."

"Let us not waste time. What is your purpose in marching upon this sovereign land?" Talbot asked, getting to the point.

"A direct man," Gallard said, nodding his head. "I respect that I shall return the courtesy. My purpose is the same that brought you here many years ago. I am in pursuit of Reginald DuFay. Or rather, I am in pursuit of the history, and future, of DuFay."

"Reginald DuFay? Who is Reginald DuFay?" Talbot asked innocently.

"As I respect a direct man, I loathe a stupid man," Gallard replied. "Do not feign ignorance, Talbot. We can make this quite easy, or we can make it unnecessarily difficult. I am aware of your knowledge of Reginald DuFay. We both know that Durinburg Castle was once the home of Reginald DuFay many, many years ago. We both know of the legend of DuFay, and we both know of the DuFay Armor."

"Very well," Talbot said. "I am aware of the legend of Reginald DuFay, and I am aware that he once called this land home. What I am not aware of, still, is your purpose in invading my land."

"I would not call it an invasion," Gallard answered thoughtfully. "I would call it more of a coming home."

"What do you mean by that?" Talbot asked, his eyebrows furrowing slightly in confusion.

"Well, I do not know exactly how to say this," Gallard replied almost apologetically. "Surely in the twenty years you have dwelled in this castle you have discovered many artifacts of the DuFay family. Correct?"

"You may assume what you will," Talbot answered, still unsure of where Gallard was going.

"It is hardly an assumption," Gallard replied. "You would be very surprised in learning just how much I know of you and your time here in Durinburg."

"My patience has its limits, Gallard, and you are testing those limits," Talbot said impatiently. "Either state your purpose or withdraw."

"Very well," Gallard responded. "You know the DuFay family crest." It was a statement of fact and not a question to which Talbot offered no response. "I believe you should recognize this," Gallard said as he pulled up the sleeves of the overcoat and shirt on his right arm. There, burnt into his right forearm, was the crest of the DuFay family. Talbot's eyes widened only slightly at this revelation. "This family crest was emblazoned upon the right forearm of the eldest son in the line of Reginald DuFay from his day until this day. It has been in my family line since the tradition began. My grandfathers bore the mark as did my father, as do I, as does my eldest son. I have come to claim my inheritance, to claim my destiny. I have come to protect and care for the land as my ancestor Reginald DuFay did hundreds of years ago."

"That is quite a story," Talbot said casually. "In truth, it is a very amusing story."

"It is no story, it is the truth," Gallard replied confidently.

"So, you expect me to simply hand over the keys of Durinburg Castle to you based solely upon this outrageous claim of yours? You expect me to open the doors and just walk away, leaving everything behind?"

"It does not have to be that way," Gallard answered. "You are a man of knowledge and intellect. You have proven your leadership abilities. Once the DuFay Armor is reunited with the heir of DuFay, there will be a great land that will need great leaders and lords. I would not think it unreasonable that you could remain a man of much power and influence in my administration. You would have lands and people to shepherd, much as you do now."

"But under your ultimate leadership," Talbot surmised.

"Of course," Gallard admitted. "After all, I am the heir of Reginald DuFay and the rightful ruler of the land. As the legend says there will be great peace and prosperity once I am returned to the throne of the land. All I need to do is obtain all six pieces of the DuFay Armor. Your kingdom appears to be doing very well but could you imagine it prospering even more?"

"Oh yes, I certainly can envision greater prosperity," Talbot replied. "I have envisioned it for a long time. You see, you are correct," he said casually. "I do know the DuFay family crest. And I do recognize the brand on your arm. In fact, I see it daily. It bears a striking, if not exact, resemblance to this." Talbot reached out and rolled the sleeves up on his right arm. There, to Gallard's amazement, on Talbot's forearm was the same design as on his own forearm. Gallard was speechless.

"The rightful heir of Reginald DuFay already occupies Durinburg Castle," Talbot informed Gallard. "You are nothing more than an imposter, obsessed with power and prestige, looking to take that to which you have no rights. As the descendant of Reginald DuFay, I will rule this land as he did. The DuFay Armor will be mine."

"No, Talbot, you are the imposter," Gallard stated, finally getting his thoughts together. "I am providing you with an opportunity to save yourself, your daughter, and your people. Simply hand over the DuFay Shield, which I know to be in your possession, and we can avoid the shedding of blood. I am afraid that if you do not relinquish possession of it, I will be required to take it by force."

"What of the sword?" Talbot asked. "You have no claim without it, and I can assure you that it is nowhere within the walls of Durinburg."

"Ah, yes, MacLean," Gallard said. "It was quite fortuitous that he stumbled upon this place and elected to remain. I had been searching for him for several years even as I was watching you. Imagine my surprise and delight when I learned that he and the DuFay Sword were here with the DuFay Shield."

"Then you will be disappointed to learn that he is no longer in Durinburg," Talbot responded. "I banished him from the kingdom and he, along with the DuFay Sword, is well away from here by now."

"He may not be as far away as you believe," Gallard said smugly. "He and that traitorous brother of his were spotted by my scouts early this morning. A dozen men were dispatched to follow them and obtain the sword by every means necessary. I would not think it out of the question that the sword has been retrieved by now. I expect it shall be in my hands by this evening."

"Oh, I seriously doubt that," Talbot said, then quickly realized that if he were not careful, he was going to reveal the truth of the location of the sword. "As you know, MacLean is a man of much cunning. Sending a dozen men after him will be a vain effort. Even if, by some chance, your men are successful in capturing him he will likely have hidden the sword. You will not find it with him."

"You underestimate my men," Gallard countered. "We have remarkably effective ways of extracting information from people. Your daughter was but a few hours away from experiencing our methods of persuasion before she escaped."

"Kidnapping her was a mistake," Talbot growled. "It is fortunate for you that no harm befell her. Otherwise you would have a steel blade in your heart this very moment."

"I shall grant you one final opportunity to relinquish the DuFay Shield to me and save the lives of you, your daughter, and your people," Gallard warned. "If you do not, your castle shall be over-run by this time tomorrow and all you know, all you love, will be dead. You are vastly outnumbered, and your men have little if any battle experience. Nearly all my men are veterans of war and there is not a single shred of fear in any of them. Your walls shall not hold them back."

"These 'negotiations' are over," Talbot announced. "You may crash upon my walls as the storm-driven waves crash upon the shore, but you shall not breach the walls of Durinburg Castle. And when you turn to leave this land, if by some chance your life is spared, I promise you shall do so without the DuFay Breastplate."

"So be it," Gallard replied, undaunted. He turned and nodded to his rower, who dipped his paddle in the water and pulled the boat away. Talbot waited to speak until they were out of sight and even then, he spoke in a soft tone.

"Are we prepared?" he asked.

"Yes, my lord, preparations are complete. The men are waiting for my word to move into their final positions."

"Gallard is quite confident in his ability to breach our walls. Is it possible that there is a weakness we have overlooked?" the king inquired.

"No, my lord, we have been thorough in our preparations. This lake wraps around most of the castle. If the enemy attempts to approach by the water, they will be easy targets. Even if they make shore, they will have the moat to cross. It is thirty feet wide and ten feet deep. Any man who tries to cross it will again be easy prey. The drawbridge will be pulled closed and there is a foot-thick wooden gate behind it. We have the ability to reinforce the gate should they somehow manufacture access to it. I am confident we will be safe behind the castle's walls."

"There is always the unknown," Talbot warned. "We shall not underestimate the determination and ingenuity of greed. Let us return to shore and prepare for the onslaught."

"As you wish, my lord," Angus said, and turned the boat back to shore.

Chapter 19

Donald and Andrew cautiously made their way through the dark yet peaceful forest. While there were no indications of anybody else being in the area, they did not want to draw attention to themselves.

"Tell me again why I am assisting you in this mad endeavor?" Donald asked as he surveyed their surroundings.

"Because you are an honorable man and you will not suffer a young woman and her brother to suffer such a miserable destiny," Andrew replied. "If that is not enough, you now have a reputation and being a MacLean, you must live up to it."

"And what reputation might that be?" Donald asked.

"Why, you are a hero, my brother," Andrew replied. "As a hero you have no choice but to rescue damsels in distress along with their younger brothers."

"This hero business is much over-rated," Donald responded glumly. "There is too much danger involved."

"Ah, but the rewards can make the risk very worthwhile," Andrew countered.

"You are the only one to benefit from this rescue," Donald said. "You get the beautiful girl in the end, and I get ... would you please remind me once again what I get out of it?"

"You get the satisfaction of knowing that you did the right thing," Andrew answered, "Plus, you get to spend time with your charming brother."

"Tell me when he shows up," Donald replied sarcastically. "How much farther is it?"

"We are near," Andrew answered.

After having been commanded to leave Durinburg, Donald and Andrew had given the appearance that they were complying with Talbot's directions. Andrew's belongings from the castle had been unceremoniously dumped outside of the castle's main entrance and a young boy was waiting by the pile of clothes, holding the reins of Andrew's horse and Donald's horse. With a word of gratitude to the boy, Andrew and Donald packed up the miscellaneous belongings and departed Durinburg Castle. They had ridden well into the night and even camped for the evening to ensure that anyone following them would be satisfied that they had indeed left as ordered. In the morning, convinced that spying eyes were no longer upon them, the brothers changed direction and headed back toward Durinburg though not by the same route. Not only did they desire to avoid Talbot's long-reaching eyes, but they also desired to get a look at Gallard's army. From a distance, Andrew and Donald had seen Gallard's army marching toward Durinburg. The brothers spent several hours shadowing the army, hoping to get some idea of Gallard's plan of attack, before breaking off and continuing their own heading. Andrew had led Donald to the camouflaged cave where he and Carl Bergman had engaged in that mysterious conversation seemingly a lifetime ago. There they hid the horses and rested for most of the evening before striking out on foot. An hour had passed since that break and now the sun's rising rays were beginning to bathe the eastern horizon in a pinkish hue.

Andrew's scheme had the appearance of simplicity though fraught with much danger. The two brothers would enter the castle's bowels through the secret passageway by which Heather had led Andrew to his freedom not that many days ago. They would subdue the guards keeping vigil over Heather and Steven and then lead the brother and sister to freedom through the same secret passage. They would return to the Bergman's home, again hopefully avoiding detection by either Talbot or Gallard, gather

Mrs. Bergman and the belongings she was packing, and lead the Bergman's to a new life in another land. It sounded simple enough, except the part about avoiding detection and getting executed.

Andrew paused for a moment, peering intently into the dark woods, looking for any familiar landmark that would indicate the proximity of the passage. He continued through the woods wordlessly until he came to a rocky outcropping to his right at the base of a small bluff. He studied the outcropping in the waning light of the pre-dawn moon, not entirely sure if this was his intended destination. He approached the rocks and poked through some thick bushes growing at the base of the outcropping. Taking a step forward he seemingly disappeared into thin air. Left by himself, Donald nervously looked around, half-expecting an ambush for some reason. Nothing other than the usual nocturnal sounds filled his ears. As suddenly as he had disappeared, Andrew reappeared.

"This is it," he announced. "This passage will lead us into the dungeon."

"Not to insinuate that I have doubts regarding your little plan here," Donald said, still looking around, "but I am getting a bad feeling about this. I feel that despite our best clandestine efforts our journey has not gone unnoticed."

"You believe we have been followed?" Andrew inquired, looking around.

"I do not know," Donald answered. "Perhaps it is just a bout of paranoia. Nevertheless, I believe we should move quickly and get away from here as soon as possible."

"You will receive no argument from me," Andrew agreed. He reached into a pack he had been carrying and pulled out two small lanterns like the ones he and Marie had used during their explorations of the castle's lower levels. Using a couple of flint stones, he was able to ignite some dry grass and leaves. Using this fire, he lit the candles in the lanterns then quickly extinguished the fire. He handed one of the lanterns to Donald. "Come see what lurks in the dark of the earth," Andrew said menacingly as if to frighten his brother.

"That did not frighten me when we were children and it does not frighten me now," Donald replied. "Besides, you are leading the way. All I have to do is run faster than you."

Without another word Andrew turned and brushed by the bushes that concealed the secret passage. Donald did not pause but boldly followed his brother's footsteps.

Andrew did not hesitate or move with much caution. He knew that there was no time to spare. They had to rescue Heather and Steven as quickly as possible and escape to a place far from Talbot's grasp. The passageway narrowed considerably in several places and the men had to turn sideways on a couple of occasions. Twice they had to bend slightly in order to avoid the low-hanging ceiling. The constant echoing of dripping water accompanied every step the men took and on more than one occasion they splashed through shallow puddles on the floor. The air was not entirely dank due to a slight draft, but neither was it fresh. It still had the smell of ages to it. The men continued through the passageway for fifteen minutes when Andrew finally slowed and held up his hand. Donald slowed, too, trying to be as quiet as possible. After another minute of their slowed approach Andrew stopped. He moved close to Donald and spoke in a whisper.

"This passageway ends in about another thirty yards. We will exit into a small room. The exit is barely more than a crack and it is just large enough for us to squeeze through. We will have to be extremely careful and extremely quiet so as not to alert the guards. Hopefully, there are only two of them. If there are more, well, this might not be quite as easy as I had planned."

"That is an understatement," Donald replied smartly. "Lead the way, brother."

Andrew proceeded down the corridor even slower than before, wary of kicking a rock or making a noise that would alert the guards to their approach. After several minutes, the corridor narrowed to an unbelievably small width and Donald questioned whether they would indeed be able to fit through the opening. A sudden thought ran through his mind, and he tugged on Andrew's shirt.

"What of our lights?" he asked in a barely audible voice. "Will the guards not be able to see them?"

"We will leave them here," Andrew answered. "We will be in total darkness once we enter the main corridor, but we can feel our way along. There should not be anything in our way and the passage is mostly straight with only a couple of minor bends. The guards will undoubtedly have lanterns of their own so the advantage of darkness will be ours for only a brief time. They will not be anticipating anybody approaching them from this portion of the corridor. If we remain close to one side of the corridor and move ever so slowly, we should be able to avoid detection until we are nearly upon them. I would prefer to subdue them without killing them but that may not be possible. If there are more than two it will not likely be possible and our success will depend on our swords."

"My sword is sharp and ready," Donald replied, anxious to get this insane endeavor over-with so he could return to his own family and ensure their safety. The brothers set the lanterns on the floor of the passageway and as silently and gently as possible, squeezed their 6-foot plus frames through the impossibly small opening.

True to Andrew's word, complete darkness greeted them as they slipped into the main corridor Donald reached out and grasped the tail of Andrews cloak so as not to bump into his brother or totally lose him in the inky blackness. Keeping his right hand on the wall to his right, Andrew proceeded forward slowly. It took them nearly ten minutes to navigate the passageways leading to the prison cells. Finally, Andrew stopped. He could see a glow barely illuminating the corridor about twenty more yards ahead, past a slight bend in the passage. He could also hear voices, though how many different ones he could not determine. With a pace that would challenge a snail for last place in a race, Andrew moved forward, inch by inch. The glow ahead of them grew little by little as the corridor straightened out and they got closer to their target. Finally, Andrew could see the guards. To his relief only two guards were visible. He could only hope that there were no others stationed just out of his sight and that it was nowhere near time for a shift change. Both guards were seated, one on either side of a prison cell door. The guard closest to Andrew and Donald was slightly turned so that his chair and body faced the other guard rather than straight ahead. That was good. His peripheral vision would not catch Andrew and Donald's movements until it was too late. Andrew turned and grasped Donald's hand, turning the palm up. With his index finger, Andrew drew two imaginary lines on Donald's palm to indicate that there were two guards. Donald in turn patted Andrew's hand to indicate he understood the message. Andrew turned back to face the guards and prepare for his assault.

The attack would have to be swift, like the strike of lightning, and it would have to be as quiet as possible. Ordinarily Andrew would have let out an intimidating battle cry as he rushed forward but that would not be a good strategy in this case. If there were any other guards between the prison and the iron-gate they would undoubtedly hear his war shout and rush to join the melee. No, he would have to suppress the urge to verbally knock the sentries off their guard. He would have to rely on the shock of seeing someone appear from the darkness to give them pause, and hopefully that would provide him and Donald the edge they needed to take care of the guards with as little noise as possible. Andrew gently removed his short, two-foot sword from its sheath and sensing the movement, Donald did likewise. After two deep breaths, Andrew was ready.

With unbelievable quickness Andrew sprung from the darkness. The first guard did not know what hit him. The butt of

Andrew's sword crashed into the base of the guard's skull, knocking him unconscious with a single blow. The second guard barely had time to recover from the shock of seeing a man appear from the lower end of the corridor before Andrew was upon him. The guard managed to grasp his sword and send a feeble strike at Andrew, but Andrew easily parried the weak blow and sent his forearm into the side of the guard's head. The guard was knocked backward against the wall of the corridor but was only momentarily stunned. He grasped Andrew's tunic and with a mighty effort slammed Andrew into the opposite wall. The impact with the wall sent stars swirling in Andrew's head but he quickly shook it off and brought a knee up into the guard's gut. The man grunted as the breath was momentarily knocked out of him. It was all the advantage Andrew needed. He sent a strong right hook into the guard's chin which knocked the man back. He was about to deliver a second blow when Donald stepped forward and, mimicking Andrew's first move, sent the butt of his sword into the back of the guard's skull. The guard wobbled for a second, then crumpled to the floor.

"I presume you expect an expression of gratitude for your intrusion?" Andrew asked Donald as he rubbed the back of his skull. "I had him, you know."

"I could not allow you to take credit for subduing two guards," Donald replied. "Your ego is already so immense I did not think you would be able to squeeze it back through the crevice. Being your brother, I could not allow you to be forced to remain here for the rest of your life."

"Kind as always," Andrew answered as he searched the unconscious guards for the cell key. Finding it, he quickly moved to the cell door and unlocked it. Grasping the guards' lantern, Andrew peered into the cell. It was slightly larger than the one in which he had been imprisoned but not by much. This one was about twelve-feet by twelve-feet and the ceiling was barely high enough for him to stand. Scattered about the floor were strands of straw, such as one would find in a stable for horses. There were no pieces of furniture in the cell, not even a cot for sleeping. In one corner of the cell was a small puddle that was formed by a steady dripping of water from a crack in the ceiling. Andrew could make out two forms huddled together on the floor under a single, tattered blanket. He slowly moved forward and with slight trepidation, pulled the blanket back. Heather's golden locks seemed to shine even in such a miserable place. She was laying on her right side and cuddling her brother who was in front of her. Both appeared to be asleep. Andrew reached out and gently brushed Heather's hair back revealing her peaceful, sleeping face. He almost regretted having to waken them. But he had no time to spare, and they needed to leave as quickly as possible. Andrew gently nudged Heather's shoulder. At first, she did not respond but upon a second, firmer nudge, she opened her eyes. Thinking Andrew was one of the guards she became startled and gasped, her arms tightening around her brother.

"Heather, it is me, Andrew," he said gently, reassuringly. "Look at me."

It took a few moments for Heather's eyes to focus on Andrew's face in the dull light of the small lantern. When she finally recognized him, she sat up and threw her arms around his neck.

"I knew you would come!" she said as tears rolled down her cheeks. "Steven knew, too! We knew you would not leave us down here!"

"Andrew!" Steven said, abruptly sitting up as he came awake. "I told Heather you would come for us! I told her!"

"I see you were given the upgraded accommodations," Andrew said jovially as he released Heather. "You should have seen mine."

"I did," Heather reminded him. "I guess freeing the man who kidnapped the king's daughter is not as great a trespass as actually kidnapping the king's daughter."

"We must leave quickly and quietly," Andrew said, returning

to the business at hand. "There is no telling whether or not our altercation with the guards was heard by others. Come, we must leave by the secret passage. Can you walk? Are you injured?"

"They did not harm us," Heather said as she stood up and brushed the straw from her hair and dress. "We are okay. Is Mother okay?"

"She is packing some things and will be ready to leave as soon as we can reach her. It will not be easy, as Gallard's army is all about Talbot's land. However, I am certain we can make it to her without being spotted. In a few hours you, your brother, and your mother will be on your way to a new life in a new land."

"What of the guards?" Donald asked, anxious to make their escape.

"We will bind them, gag them, and leave them in the very prison cell they were charged to guard. We must hurry."

Within five minutes the two guards had been immobilized and unceremoniously dumped in the prison cell. Andrew closed the door and locked it but left the key in the lock. He was not so insensitive that he desired the guards to remain locked away for eternity. Quickly, the group made its way down the corridor to the secret passageway. Andrew went first, followed by Heather, her brother, and then Donald.

The group had not taken but a few steps when Andrew stopped dead in his tracks. He lifted his hand and motioned for the others to be quiet. He shaded his lantern as much as possible. After a few seconds, his worries were confirmed. He heard voices coming from the escape route and he could barely make out the glow of a torch. He turned and ushered his followers back down the corridor and out the narrow crevice.

"What is it?" Donald asked. "Why are we back here?"

"Apparently, you were not being paranoid," Andrew replied. "We were followed. Someone is coming down the passageway."

"What are we going to do?" Heather asked, her voice full of fear.

"We need to somehow block this crevice," Andrew replied.

"We need to make it so they cannot get through." He examined the ceiling above the crevice. "Solid rock. Any hopes of bringing the ceiling down can be forgotten."

"Can we pile stuff up against the opening?" Heather asked. "There are some chairs and other pieces of furniture in some of these rooms."

"Anything we can stack up they can knock down," Andrew replied glumly. "We have to leave them no choice but to turn back."

"And that leaves us just exactly what escape route?" Donald asked.

"The front door," Andrew replied, though with no excitement.

"We had better do something quickly," Donald advised. "They will be here any minute."

"I am thinking, I am thinking," Andrew said tersely, his mind racing. He was about to give up and recommend that they run as fast as they could for the gate when his eyes came to rest on one of the lanterns. The flickering flame gave him an idea. He took the candle out of the metal box and held it up to the crevice. The flame danced and bent toward the crevice. He moved the candle away from the opening, and it settled down. He again moved it in front of the crevice and again it bent toward the opening.

"That is it!" Andrew cried excitedly.

"What is it?" Heather asked.

"They can break down a barrier of wood, but they cannot break down a barrier of smoke!"

"Of course!" Donald said. "We set a fire at the entrance of the crevice and the draft will take the smoke into their passageway! They will either turn back or suffocate!"

"Go back to the cells and grasp as much straw and wood as you can!" Andrew instructed Heather and Steven. They headed back down the corridor and returned a few moments later with their hands full. Andrew instructed them to drop the straw and pieces of wood onto the ground at the base of the crevice. They did so, then turned around to find more. Andrew wasted no time in setting the kindling ablaze. The dry, ancient wood and straw burst into flames almost immediately. Just as planned, the smoke was caught in the draft and carried into the crevice with little remaining in the main corridor. Heather and Steven dropped a second load of flammables onto the pile and the fire grew.

"That should be enough," Andrew said as the brother and sister were about to run for a third load. "If it does not make them turn back it will at least give us enough time to make our escape through the main gate."

"But what of Talbot?" Donald asked as Andrew turned and led the group toward the main exit. "Are we not going to pop up in the middle of his castle? He is not going to just allow us to waltz out of his castle with a 'Fare thee well.' "

"I suspect that by now Talbot's attention is firmly on Gallard's onslaught. Steven, would you be able to find us a way out of the castle, a way where we can avoid being spotted?"

"I think so," Steven said, though a bit unsure.

"Do your best," Andrew said, laying a hand on his shoulder. "That is all one man can ask of another."

The group turned back down the passageway but to everyone's surprise Andrew stopped at the cell confining the two guards. After verifying that the guards were still unconscious, he reached out and unlocked the door.

"Having an attack of your conscience?" Donald asked.

"An attack of self-preservation is more like it," Andrew replied. "Since we are going to have to escape through the castle and will be in plain view, we need all the help we can get. The tunics and helmets of these two guards may help us avoid immediate detection."

"I fear we are going to need more help than this," Donald replied as he bent over to untie one of the guards in order to remove his tunic. Within two minutes both guards had been stripped of their uniforms and once again were bound hand and foot.

Andrew and Donald donned the garments which, although not a perfect fit, would not draw attention. After picking up the iron helmets that were on the floor by the chairs, Andrew led the way down the hallway without shutting and locking the cell door.

"Did you forget something?" Donald asked. "Perhaps locking the cell door?"

"Call it an attack of the conscience," Andrew smiled. "I know what it feels like to be locked away in the dark. I would not do that to another person. We should be well-away from here by the time those two men regain consciousness and slip their bindings. Keeping them locked away would serve no purpose."

"You have become soft in your old age," Donald replied, and the group fell silent as they headed for their freedom.

Chapter 20

T he still waters of Durinburg Lake lay enshrouded by a thick, white veil of morning mist. Though the blanket of fog ended at the shores of the lake, the stillness seemed to creep into the neighboring woods. Usually even at this early hour of the day the forest's feathered inhabitants would be busily chirping their good mornings and setting about hunting for breakfast. On any other day squirrels would be seen scurrying along the ground and up and down various trees, searching for nuts and berries. If this day had been like the day before it, the woods would have been filled with a symphony of chirps and squawks and calls from creatures of all types. However, this morning was different from all others. The inhabitants of the woods and fields sensed something ominous in the air, something that had last been felt several hundred years earlier. Their instincts could not be ignored. The animals took to hiding, and it was well that they did.

The shadows came forth from the darkness, first one by one, then by the dozens, then by the hundreds. They moved through the forest with disciplined silence and order. A lone deer walking along the single-lane road that cut through the forest lifted its head in alarm and then bolted into the trees as three columns of horses and men appeared around a bend in the road. The column seemed to have no end. Three hundred large horses in full battle array were followed by dozens of horses drawing carts of varied sizes, and behind the carts were thousands of men, most of them veterans of war. The parade marched toward its destination without pausing and without change in cadence.

The sun's first rays had just broken over the mountain when the army passed the forest's boundary and stepped into open ground. Small huts and structures along the road were ignored, meaningless at this time to the horde. It continued forward, step by step, breath by breath. As the target came into view there came a change in the advancement. Even as the foot soldiers to either side of the road continued forward, the battle-dressed horses veered off to the side and allowed the horses drawing the carts to proceed. The army met no resistance as it approached its destination. The area was devoid of movement. The inhabitants of the land had either fled or taken refuge behind the perceived safety of the castle's high, thick stone walls. At two hundred yards from the castle the soldiers stopped in perfect unison. The horses drawing the carts also came to a halt. There was a flurry of activity as dozens of men stepped forward and commenced unloading the contents of the carts, which included mainly various pieces of wood and rope and tools. With practiced efficiency they laid the contents on the ground in an orderly, pre-determined manner.

High atop the ramparts of the castle, Talbot and Angus curiously watched the early-morning activity.

"What are they doing?" Talbot asked, looking intently at the enemy.

"I cannot be certain, but it looks as though they are constructing some kind of structure or device," Angus replied.

"Something they will use in an effort to scale our walls?" Talbot asked.

"It is possible, but doubtful," Angus answered. "The structure will not likely be large enough but for a few men at a time. We would pick them off easily. It would make more sense for them to construct a bridge of some sort that would allow them to cross the moat."

"That drawbridge is a foot thick if not more and the gate behind it is a foot thick, with reinforcement. There is a portcullis as well. They could batter against it for a month and it would not weaken," Talbot said. "Gallard's spy would have noted that and reported it to him."

"Then a catapult?" Angus suggested.

"That would be my guess," Talbot agreed. "But they are much too far away for it to be more than minimally effective. And even if they moved closer, what do they believe they could throw over the walls that would harm us?"

"Rocks would truly do us no harm," Angus mused. "The only other thing I could think of would be fire balls of some sort. Yet again, they would not represent much of a threat to us. Other than the stables there is not much outside of the castle that would be in danger of burning. Whatever they toss over the walls will fall harmlessly to the ground."

"Then we shall wait and see what they have planned," Talbot said. "Are they out of range of our archers?"

"Unfortunately, they are. I have lined the walls with the strongest and best bowmen but even their arrows would not be able to reach the enemy's front line."

"Do we have lookouts stationed so as to keep an eye out for an assault via the lake?" Talbot inquired. "It would not be out of the question for Gallard to attempt to divert our attention from the true point of attack."

"Yes, my lord. We have eyes where they need to be. We shall not be surprised."

"Very well. I shall be in my war room. I expect an immediate update if anything changes." Talbot turned and headed inside the castle.

The black gate materialized out of the shadows as the glow from Andrew's lantern chased away the darkness. He slowly approached the gate, wary that Talbot may have posted extra guards to prevent anyone from passing by the bars of iron. To his relief there was nobody in sight. He reached out and pushed on the gate, though he was certain it was locked. He was right. The gate did not budge.

"Lovely," Donald said, exasperated. "Just lovely. Why did I believe for an instant that this would be easy?"

"Oh ye of little faith," Andrew smiled as he reached into his tunic. "An intelligent man always has the key to get out of a sticky situation." He pulled the gate's key out of a pocket and inserted it into the lock. He tried to turn it, but the key would not turn. He exerted more effort, but still the cylinder in the lock would not budge. Andrew removed the key, inspected it, then once again inserted it into the keyhole and attempted to unlock the gate. To his dismay it did not work. The gate remained locked.

"An intelligent man would have brought the right key," Donald muttered.

"This is the right key," Andrew replied. "It is the same key I used to unlock the gate previously."

"What is the problem?" Heather asked, moving forward to see for herself.

"It would appear that Talbot felt you and your brother to be such dangerous criminals that he changed the lock on the gate," Andrew answered.

"Or he knew that you would try to rescue us," Heather suggested.

"Whatever the case, the gate is locked," Andrew said as he grasped the bars with both hands and tried to shake them. "Your father's construction is strong and solid. We will not be able to break the gate down. We will have to find another way out."

"I do not know of another way out, other than the one secret passage," Heather said, becoming worried. "We could search these corridors for months and not find another way out, even if one exists."

Andrew pondered their situation for a few moments, feeling the same sense of dread that the others were feeling. Heather was probably right. Even if there was another way out it could take them forever to find it. And while there was still the secret passage they had originally planned to use, it was certain that their pursuers would eventually pass through the smoke and enter the dungeon. Somehow, they had to find a way to open the gate.

"Steven," Andrew said, turning to the young lad. "You helped your father on many projects, correct?"

"Yes," Steven acknowledged.

"Can you think of any way that we can get around this locked gate? Is there any weakness in the gate and bars that might enable us to break through?"

"I did not help my father with this gate," Steven said. "I helped him mainly in the making of tools and a few weapons. I only assisted him a few times with gates and doors."

"Then you are our expert," Andrew smiled, "for none of the rest of us has even the smallest knowledge of metal working. You shall be our salvation."

"I do not understand," Steven said. "I do not know how I can help."

"Do you see this lock?" Andrew asked.

"Yes," the boy answered.

"You are going to pick it and open the gate."

"Pick the lock?" Steven questioned.

"Surely you are not a stranger to locks. A young boy is full of curiosity. I would wager that you, the son of a blacksmith, have had some experience in getting past locks."

"I do not know what you are talking about," Steven said defensively. He looked nervously at his sister. "Why would I do something like that?"

"Now that I think about it, there were several times Father thought someone had broken into his locked cabinets," Heather said thoughtfully. "That was where he stored certain artifacts he found around the castle and outlying areas. He never seemed angry, only puzzled that the items were not exactly as he had left them."

"I am not a thief!" Steven cried. "I have never stolen anything!"

"Steven, I know you are not a thief," Heather said soothingly.

"I do not care whether or not you have ever done anything like this before. But if you have, you are our only hope. This is your chance to become a hero."

"A hero?" he repeated questioningly.

"Yes, a hero," Andrew said, laying a hand on the boy's shoulder. "We came to rescue you. Now it is your turn to rescue us. Will you give it a try?"

Steven looked at the faces staring at him, their expressions pleading for his help. He did not know if he could do what they asked. It was true that he had picked some of his father's locks before, but they were simple locks. This one looked to be more complicated. He had never tried to pick a lock like this one. But the chance of impressing the man he had come to look up to, the man he so much wanted to be like, was irresistible. He had no choice but to try.

"I will need the key and I will need a couple of pieces of long, thin wood or iron. They will need to be able to fit into the lock," Steven said, looking at the lock. He had not even started working on the lock and already a bead of perspiration formed on his forehead.

Lawrence Morecraft closely watched the enemy, his mind striving to deduce the battle plan of Gallard. It had been nearly two hours since the army had arrived and commenced their construction projects. Three catapults had been constructed with impressive speed. Along with the catapults was a long wooden platform about sixty feet long by fifteen feet wide. The platform could be nothing other than a makeshift bridge to carry the enemy soldiers over the moat. This puzzled Lawrence. There was a buffer of land between the bottom of the castle's protective walls and the moat which was about ten feet wide. Even if the enemy were able to maneuver the bridge to span the water it would do them no good. Other than the main gate, which was well protected, there was only one other doorway in the castle's walls. This was at the rear of the castle. There were more than a dozen soldiers stationed by this door and on the walls above the door to thwart any attack from that direction. So, even if Gallard was able to cross the moat, it would do him no good. His men would not be able to scale the stone walls and they would not be able to breach the main gate. As far as Lawrence could figure, Gallard's plan must be to try to bridge the moat at the main gate and somehow batter down the drawbridge and the gate behind it. But that would be nearly impossible due to the thickness and strength of the drawbridge and gate. As he stood baffled, Lawrence watched the catapults slowly creep forward as dozens of men pushed them from behind. When they were about 150 yards out, they stopped. About half the men returned to the carts and started unloading what looked like clay jars from the carts. The start of the battle was imminent. Lawrence wasted no more time. He quickly found Angus, who was not far away, watching the same scene.

"Have you determined their battle plan?" Lawrence asked Talbot's military advisor.

"Not entirely," Angus admitted. "I do not know what they believe they can throw at us that will have any significant impact."

"Whatever they have planned I would say it is only moments before they commence their attack."

"But their infantry has not moved a muscle," Angus countered. "How could they commence their attack with their infantry so far away?"

"Evidently the first phase of their attack does not involve the infantry, only the catapults," Lawrence guessed. "Those catapults are on the verge of being in range of our archers. We should pre-empt their attack with one of our own. Give the order for the archers to commence firing. Let us see if we can at least put the enemy off-balance."

"Very well," Angus said, agreeing with Lawrence's suggestion. "Give the command. Commence attack."

Lawrence nodded and ran over to a small group of men standing nearly fifty yards away. One of the men stood by several different colored flags attached to ten-foot poles. Another man stood with a horn in-hand. Another stood by these two, apparently their superior. Lawrence approached this man.

"The command is given," he said. "Archers are to commence firing."

The man to whom Lawrence spoke did not reply but turned to the other two men.

"Archers, loose!" he commanded. The man with the horn took a deep breath and let out a long, loud blast on the instrument. The man by the flags lifted a pole with a green flag that was embroidered with the likeness of an arrow. An eerie silence followed the blast from the horn. There was no shouting from Talbot's men, no battle cries, nothing. The men stationed along the rampart walls silently lifted their bows, loaded them with arrows, and commenced firing.

There was a soft whistling in the air as the projectiles flew over the castle's walls and toward the enemy combatants. Most of the arrows fell just short of the catapults. Every now and then a couple of arrows would strike their targets and embed themselves in the wooden structures. However, no damage was done. The catapults remained in their places and their operators temporarily took refuge behind them. When it was evident that the arrows presented little danger to them, Gallard's men continued with their preparations.

"A rather pathetic effort if I do say so myself," Gallard's military advisor said to his king as he watched hundreds of arrows fall short of their targets.

"Do not underestimate them, Walter," Gallard advised. "Even the weakest of animals, when backed into a corner, can become quite vicious and deadly. You can count on them having a surprise or two in store for us. We must be on our guard."

"It does concern me a bit that we have yet to meet any ground forces other than that brief encounter down by the river," Walter said. "Surely that was not the extent of their defenses. Your spy indicated that Talbot's troops numbered perhaps two thousand men. I cannot believe that all of them are stationed behind those walls."

"Have our scouts reported any signs of Talbot's troops outside the castle walls?"

"No, my lord, they have not," Walter replied. "But I take no comfort in such reports. This is Talbot's land. I am certain he could hide men wherever he desires."

"Any word from the men dispatched to apprehend the MacLean brothers?" Gallard asked.

"None as of yet," Walter answered. "I had expected news by now."

"You know how elusive Andrew can be," Gallard said. "I should have sent an entire company after him instead of a mere dozen men."

"You should have sent me," Walter said as he lifted his right hand and gently traced the scar on the left side of his face. "We would have the sword by now and MacLean would be dead. Both would be dead."

"You will have your chance at vengeance," Gallard assured his advisor, "of this I am certain. We have not seen the last of Andrew MacLean. There was no way I could send you after him, though. You are my military advisor and as such your presence is required with the army. Now, go check the status of preparations. It is time to commence the attack."

"With pleasure," Walter smiled menacingly as he left the king's side.

Chapter 21

For a full five minutes Angus watched volley after volley of arrows soar through the air only to fall harmlessly to the ground. By normal standards five minutes was not much time at all but in this case, it was long enough for Angus to realize that the effort was a waste of resources reluctantly, he called for a cease-fire. The trumpeter let loose with two long blasts of the horn and the man holding the green flag lowered it out of sight. Within but a few seconds the salvo ceased, and the archers stood at ease. Lawrence re-joined Angus at the edge of the wall and peered out at the enemy.

"That was not exactly effective," Lawrence said, looking at the hundreds of wasted arrows protruding from the ground in front of the enemy's front line. "We did hardly more than provide them with arrows to shoot back at us."

"Not a single injury or casualty," Angus said, shaking his head. "They are just too far away."

"What of the ground assault?" Lawrence asked.

"It is not time," Angus replied. "We have to make sure their full attention is on the castle before we signal for the ground assault to begin. We must maintain the element of surprise."

"The longer we wait the greater the chance we are discovered," Lawrence countered.

"It is a chance we shall have to take," Angus responded. "Only if our defenses are breached will we send them in. Our only chance is to attack Gallard's army from the front and the rear. If we send in the men now, they will be vastly outnumbered and will be slaughtered. There would be nothing to keep Gallard from over-running us if he should somehow get past the gate. Messenger!" Angus called to a young boy standing close by. "Inform the king that the enemy is preparing to attack. Go!"

The young boy took off running. Angus and Lawrence turned their attention back to the enemy. All three catapults were being loaded with numerous clay jars although it was impossible to tell what exactly the jars contained. The jars were just large enough to hold about a gallon's worth of contents, whether liquid or solid. About six jars fit into the basket of each catapult. When the catapults were fully loaded there was a moment of silence and stillness. Then, after two minutes, a loud trumpet blast from the enemy chased away the silence. In an instant the three catapults were launched. The eighteen clay jars were hurled over one hundred feet into the air and seemed to float toward the castle in slow motion. Twelve of the jars fell into the moat and disappeared beneath the water's surface. Three of the jars struck the ground at the base of the castle's wall and shattered. Three other jars struck the castle's wall about ten feet to the right of the drawbridge. As the jars disintegrated upon impact, a thick black liquid burst forth and smeared the stone wall and the ground.

"What is that?" Lawrence asked, peering over the wall and seeing the black liquid on the ground.

For a moment Angus did not answer but simply followed Lawrence's gaze over the wall. He looked at the black liquid then looked at the catapults that were being repositioned and reloaded. Suddenly, realization hit him, and his eyes widened.

"They are going to burn down the drawbridge!" he said anxiously.

"How?" Lawrence asked, still confused.

"Do you not see?" Angus responded, suddenly worried. "Those jars are filled with pitch or some similar compound, something that is highly flammable. Since they cannot approach the drawbridge, they are using the catapults to cover it with the pitch. When they have succeeded in doing that, they will undoubtedly set the drawbridge on fire. They can simply wait for it to burn completely and reveal the gate. They will then repeat the procedure in order to burn the gate. They do not need to knock the gate down, they will burn it down!"

"What is happening?" Talbot asked as he rushed to Angus' side. "What is this business about burning the gate down?"

"My lord, the purpose of the catapults has become clear," Angus replied. "Gallard is using them to launch jars full of pitch at the drawbridge. Once the drawbridge is covered, he will set it afire. Then he will repeat the process and burn the gate. Therein lies the purpose of the long wooden platform they have constructed. After the drawbridge and gate have burned away, Gallard's men will somehow move the platform to span the moat. They will be able to rush us."

"Can we not return the favor and burn their makeshift bridge?" Talbot asked.

"No," Angus replied, shaking his head. "While we could certainly shoot flaming arrows at it, the wood will not catch fire and burn without something to accelerate the flames. We do not have pitch or any other substance that would catch fire such as they do. The most we could accomplish would be some minor smoldering and perhaps a small fire or two but nothing that would slow them down or result in considerable damage to their bridge."

"If they succeed in catching the drawbridge on fire, is there anything we can do to douse the flames?" Talbot asked.

"No, my lord," Angus replied, shaking his head. "The best we could do would be to send some men with buckets out of the back doorway and have them work their way along the foot of the walls to the front of the castle. They could scoop water out of the moat and attempt to control the fire. However, the ground around the drawbridge will undoubtedly be totally engulfed in flames as well. The men would not be able to get close enough to the drawbridge to have any impact on the flames. You could be certain that Gallard would have his archers ready for just such a reaction on our part. Even as our men attempted to fight the fire, arrows from Gallard's archers would rain upon them like a driving tempest. We would not be able to provide adequate cover for them. They would be cut down within but minutes."

"Can we get the men out there before the fire is started?" Talbot asked desperately. "Perhaps if we were able to coat the door with water first it would lessen the damage by the flames or even prevent them altogether."

"I fear we do not have enough time," Angus replied. "Even now the catapults are ready to launch a second volley. They have adjusted their aim and range based on the first volley. It is not likely that the second will miss. I would venture that three volleys will be all they need before setting the fire. We have perhaps ten minutes and that is all. It is not enough time to get men out there."

"We must try!" Talbot shouted. "We will not allow our enemy to breach these walls so easily! Morecraft, you will find two dozen men and send them out the back gate with buckets and shields. Twelve men will circle the castle to the left and twelve will circle the castle to the right. Six on each side will carry buckets and commence dousing the ground and drawbridge with water. The other six on each side will take the largest shields they can find and provide as much cover as possible for the bucket men. Gallard will have to move his archers forward in order to reach our men. Our arches will hold them at bay. That should provide the protection our men need. Now, see to it!"

Without question or response Lawrence ran as fast as he could along the rampart and down the closest set of stairs. Even before he reached the bottom, Gallard's catapults released their second volley. The clay jars smashed violently against the drawbridge, spewing their contents wildly. Lawrence heard the thunderous crashes but did not pause. When he finally reached the open commons area, he grabbed the first twenty-four men he saw, explained the plan, and set about to find shields and buckets for them.

The candles in the lanterns burned ever so closer to their ends and their flames were slowly diminishing. Andrew, Donald and Heather stood back from the gate, giving Steven plenty of room to work. Frustration had caused the young boy to nearly give up on several occasions but encouragement from his sister and Andrew had motivated him enough to continue his efforts to open the gate. But now, after striving for nearly two hours without any success, he was near tears. He was about to give up once again when he felt the lock give a little. Excitement at his near success caused him to make a sudden move which resulted in the lock re-engaging.

"I almost had it!" he called to the others.

"Keep trying!" Heather cried out as she and the MacLean brothers moved closer to the gate.

"I am!" Steven replied, re-energized and working harder than ever. "This lock is much more complicated than any I have ever seen."

"Talbot had much to hide," Andrew said, peering down the corridor.

"Andrew," Donald said, a bit of concern riding his voice. "We cannot have much longer. Surely the men following us have entered the dungeon and are making their way toward us this very moment. Without a retreat …"

"I know," Andrew said, nodding his head, "I know. We will have to deal with that situation when it arises."

"Hurry, Steven," Heather urged, hearing Andrew and Donald's conversation. "We must get out of here!"

"I know!" Steven answered, his hands and fingers cramping from the effort. "I am doing the best I can!"

"Andrew," Donald said, looking down the hallway, "perhaps you and I should return down the corridor. If we stay here and our pursuers catch up with us there is no telling what they will do with the boy and the girl. We cannot be certain who the people following us are or if they are even aware of Heather and Steven's presence. If we meet these men down there, away from here, we just might be able to prevent them from finding these two. It will give them the chance to avoid capture and continue efforts to open the gate. If nothing else, at least Talbot's men will return at some point, and they would no longer be trapped."

"No longer be trapped?" Heather asked, astonished. "They would most certainly return us to our cell, if not worse. How do you consider that anything less than being trapped?"

"Andrew?" Donald asked, ignoring Heather.

Andrew was about to agree with Donald's plan when he held his hand up for silence. He took a few steps down the corridor, cocking his head to the side and listening intently. After a few seconds he quickly returned to the others.

"I am afraid we have run out of time," he said matter-of-factly.

"They are coming?" Steven asked, turning his attention from his task.

"Someone is coming," Andrew confirmed. "We have but a few minutes more before we are discovered. Steven, you have toyed around long enough. We need you to open the lock, and right now."

"I have been trying!" he protested. "I cannot do it!"

"You can, and you will," Andrew said sternly. "You said you almost had it a moment ago. You can do it."

"But my fingers are cramped. I can barely move them!"

Andrew reached out and gently took Steven's hands into his own. With a light touch he began massaging the boy's fingers which were dwarfed in Andrew's large, muscular hands. He spoke gently to the boy, trying to ease his nerves.

"Steven, you can accomplish anything to which you put your mind. Remember when you could not hit the target with your bow and arrow? You were frustrated but you would not allow early failure to thwart your determination. You practiced, and practiced, and practiced. Before you knew it, you were hitting the target every time. But that was not good enough for you. You wanted to hit the center circle. So, you practiced more and soon you were hitting the center of the target. And remember your determination to save my sword? You showed great bravery and skill in doing so. This task is no different. You know how to do this. Now, take your tools and lead us to freedom."

As Andrew released his hands, confidence and energy crept back into Steven. Nobody had ever believed in him, not as Andrew was now believing in him. He had always been treated as a little boy, expected to fail. But now he was being treated as a man. They believed in him, and they were relying on him. He turned back to the lock. It was no longer an insurmountable obstacle in his mind. It was a simple toy. He knew he could unlock the gate. He closed his eyes and remembered what he had done to cause the lock to move earlier. Deftly, he moved his fingers around, working the small instruments in the lock.

"Andrew ..." Donald said nervously as the corridor behind them started to glow from the light of an approaching torch.

"I know, I know," Andrew replied, pulling his sword from its sheath.

"You can do it!" Heather said, encouraging her brother. "I know you can do it! Make Father proud!"

As the glow from the torches brightened, voices could be heard echoing against the stone walls. Andrew and Donald assumed positions to protect Heather and Steven. It was only a matter of seconds now before they were seen.

"Almost have it!" Steven said, his fingers moving slowly but with purpose. "I almost have it!"

"There they are!" a voice called from behind the torch. "We have them!" The corridor erupted with the sound of men running.

"Got it!" Steven cried as the lock gave and the gate swung open.

"Move!" Andrew commanded as he pushed Heather and

Steven none-too-gently past the iron bars. Donald was barely past the bars himself when Andrew slammed the gate shut. The lock re-engaged immediately, which was fortunate for no sooner had the gate closed than the pursuers slammed against the bars, pushing with all their might and cursing.

"MacLean!" one of the men yelled in frustration.

"Sorry," Andrew said, feigning sincerity, "but strangers are not allowed in the castle. I believe you know the way out."

"You will not elude King Gallard much longer," the man sneered. "Your years on the run are coming to an end."

"To that, I cannot disagree," Andrew replied. "I will welcome the end of my journey. But for now, I believe I will continue my journey this way, toward daylight."

"And into Gallard's hands," the man responded smugly. "There is no escape for you that way. By now Gallard is well on his way to breaching the castle's defenses. Enjoy the last few moments of your freedom … and your life."

"I shall. And I wish you much enjoyment of your return trip through the dungeon," Andrew replied and led his small group to daylight.

Chapter 22

Angus and Talbot watched helplessly as the third salvo from the catapults soared through the air and crashed into and around the raised drawbridge. Gallard's men had moved the catapults several yards closer in order to reach the top of the drawbridge with the projectiles. Nearly the entire drawbridge was now covered with pitch as well as the walls to either side. It was only a matter of minutes before Gallard's arches moved in with their fiery arrows to set the wooden bridge ablaze. Looking down from the top of the wall, Angus could see Talbot's men cautiously moving along the base of the castle with their buckets already full of water. He called out to the signalmen.

"Archers to the ready!"

The trumpeter made two quick blows on the horn and the flagman raised the green flag again. The archers around the tops of the castle's walls stood and readied their bows. They had been restocked with arrows after their initial volleys at the enemy and therefore had plenty of ammunition.

Down below, the men had commenced throwing buckets of water on the drawbridge, attempting to wash off the pitch. However, the water had a negligible effect. The pitch appeared to be resistant to the water and stuck to the wood of the drawbridge. The men kept losing their footing on the slick, black substance that covered the ground. Two men fell into the moat. Angus turned his attention from his men to Gallard's men. Two dozen of Gallard's archers, armed with arrows that were already flaming on their ends, slowly drew closer to the castle. Accompanying each archer was another man who was carrying an over-sized shield as protection for the archers.

"My lord, I fear our efforts to wash off the pitch are proving to be in vain," Angus said to Talbot as both men peered over the edge of the wall. "We should draw the men back."

"Not yet," Talbot said firmly. "I will not give up the draw-bridge so easily. They will continue to throw water on it even should Gallard's men be successful in setting it on fire. We must prevent the drawbridge from being burned down! Give the order for the archers to commence firing. We need to keep Gallard's men far enough back that their arrows cannot reach the castle."

"Archers, attack!" Angus called, not hesitating. Another single, long blast erupted from the trumpet and hundreds of arrows once again filled the air. Gallard's archers were now within range of Talbot's bowmen and the deadly projectiles from the top of Durinburg Castle's walls showered down on the approaching enemy. The protective shields being carried by Gallard's men were quickly turned into wooden pincushions as dozens of arrows imbedded themselves into each shield. The onslaught of the missiles succeeded in slowing the approach of the enemy, but only for a few seconds. he shields were proving immensely effective. None of Gallard's men suffered any injuries and they continued moving forward.

"We must drive them back!" Talbot shouted. "You are my military advisor! Is this the best you can do?"

"We can lower the drawbridge," Angus said, desperate for a plan of action.

"Are you mad?" Talbot asked in astonishment. "Lower the drawbridge?"

"We could lower it half-way," Angus suggested. "That would create an angle to protect the underside of the drawbridge, where the pitch is. The archers would not be able to reach it with their arrows from a long distance. They would have to approach much closer. Our archers would attack from two directions: from the top of the wall and from ground level. Those shields would not be able to protect them in both directions."

"Then do it!" Talbot commanded, seeing no other option.

Angus rushed over to the side of the rampart facing the castle's compound and yelled to the men charged with operating the drawbridge and the gate.

"Lower the drawbridge half-way!" he yelled as loud as he could. "Do it!"

Without hesitation two men stationed by a large wooden wheel at the base of the gate slowly turned the wheel, allowing the iron chain wrapped around it to play out. Through a system of pulleys, the end of the chain was attached to the top of the drawbridge. Slowly, the drawbridge began to descend. While this was happening, Angus rushed over to the closest group of archers.

"You men take the rear door and make your way to the front of the castle. As soon as you are in position commence firing at the enemy. They are intent on burning our drawbridge and gate and if that happens, they will storm the castle and kill us all. Only you can prevent them from doing so. Now go! There is little time!"

The men immediately abandoned their stations and rushed to the closest stairs, nearly falling as they descended the steps as quickly as possible. Angus returned to Talbot's side.

"There is not enough time," Angus said as he watched Gallard's archers approach to within fifty yards. "They are close enough."

No sooner had he uttered those words than Gallard's archers stopped their forward advancement. In unison they lifted their bows and took aim. For them to fire, the shield-bearers had to move the shields to the side just a fraction to provide clearance. Nine of the archers released their arrows in unison. Three never had the chance, as arrows from Talbot's archers cut them down. Three of the arrows missed the drawbridge entirely, striking the castle's stone wall where black stains marked the impact of several pitch jars. Flames erupted as the pitch immediately caught fire. Other than being an ominous sight, the flames were harmless. Two arrows sailed over the descending drawbridge, imbedding in the now-exposed gate. The ancient wooden gate was tough and refused the tiny flames on the ends of the arrows. The arrows soon burned out, leaving only some minor smoldering. Four of the archers' arrows, however, flew true to their marks and struck the exposed, pitch-covered underside of the drawbridge. From their viewpoint Talbot and Angus could not immediately see if the arrows had indeed struck the underside of the drawbridge. They anxiously waited, holding their breath, hoping that the arrows had missed and fallen harmlessly into the moat. Within a minute black smoke began curling out from the sides of the drawbridge, giving proof that the attack was successful. Talbot slammed his hand on top of the stone wall, shouting in frustration.

"No!" he yelled, realizing that it was now only a matter of hours before Gallard's army would be able to storm the castle. He turned to Angus. "You should have foreseen this and planned a proper defense!"

"I apologize for failing you, your majesty," Angus replied through gritted teeth.

"They are already preparing to launch more pitch," Talbot said as he watched the catapults being loaded. "No doubt as a result of the drawbridge being partially lowered. Instead of having to wait until the drawbridge burns away in order to commence their attack on the gate, they can do so immediately."

"I would recommend pulling the drawbridge back up, though not all the way," Angus suggested. "That should at least partially protect the gate. We could also open the gate, thereby protecting it from the burning drawbridge and provide little if any target to Gallard's catapults."

"And when the drawbridge is reduced to ashes Gallard will move his bridge forward and extend it over the moat. We will have to shut the gate eventually," Talbot replied.

"But we will have bought more time to prepare a more adequate defense against Gallard," Angus responded. "We can also commence the ground attack which will slow him down."

Talbot glared out over the wall at Gallard's forces. He could continue to stall but unless he was able to miraculously create an ingenious plan to resist Gallard's advances, the result was all but clear.

"We have seen all we need to see for now. Order the drawbridge to be raised to three-quarters and order that the gate be partially opened for now. Have the men outside return to within the walls. They can be of no effect where they are. Order the ground strike to commence immediately. And figure out a way of destroying those catapults before they destroy us!"

"It will be done, my lord," Angus said respectfully, though not entirely sincerely.

"I will be in my war room," Talbot said as he turned to leave. "Send me word when our men commence the ground assault. I hope for our sakes that part of your plan of defense proves effective."

"It will be done," Angus repeated, this time not even bothering to feign sincerity.

Andrew peered from around the corner of the corridor's end and cautiously looked around the great foyer. The noisy room was crowded with hundreds of Durinburg's inhabitants. Fathers were reassuring mothers of their safety and mothers were trying to reassure their children that all was going to be well. Most of the older villagers sat in silence while many of the younger children could not help but cry in fear. Although the room's occupants spoke to each other in hushed tones, the combination of all the voices and the poor acoustics of the room resulted in a gentle roar. Donald, Heather and Steven all moved forward to see what was causing the commotion.

"So much for a clandestine escape," Donald said, looking around the room.

"No, this is good," Andrew countered, "this is exceptionally good for us. We should be able to move about without drawing much attention, if any. This room is full of villagers. I do not see any of Talbot's men. Obviously, we cannot leave by the front door and out the main gate. We will need to work our way to another exit, then work our way to the rear of the castle where there is a door in the exterior wall."

"Will Talbot not be watching all of the ways in and out of the castle?" Donald asked.

"That is a good point," Andrew reluctantly conceded, looking around the room. "And undoubtedly Gallard will have all visible exits under watch as well. Steven, you are the most familiar with the castle. Do you know of any other hidden exits from the castle, any place we could escape that is not likely to be watched?"

"I am not aware of any others," Steven replied dejectedly.

"Heather?" Andrew asked hopefully.

"I do not know of any other secret exits, either," Heather answered. "I know of the main gate and two other exits, but they are not hidden. Talbot would surely have his eyes on them."

"This is not exactly going according to plan," Andrew mused as he surveyed the room. "I had hoped Gallard's attack would have been delayed a bit longer, enabling us to possibly sneak out the main gate."

"What now?" Donald asked.

"You and I will need to find another way out," Andrew replied. "Heather and Steven will have to find a place to hide so Talbot does not discover their escape. When we have figured a way out of here, we will gather them and make our departure."

"Andrew, the longer we wait the more danger Mother will be in," Heather said as she gently grasped his arm. "For all we know Gallard's men could already have found our house and …" her voice trailed off, not wanting to voice her deepest concerns.

"I know, I know," Andrew replied, placing his hand over hers in a gesture of comfort. "We will find a way out of here, I promise, and we will find her. Then I will take you and your family far away from here to a place where you will be safe. Right now, I need you and your brother to find a place to hide. Do you know of a place where you and he can remain hidden for a while?"

"The main library has a hidden chamber behind one of the walls. Marie and I used to play hide and seek when we were children, and we found this room by accident. We could hide in there."

"It is my guess that most of the rooms in the castle are fully occupied by the villagers," Andrew mused. "The library is likely full of people. You would not be able to pass unnoticed. Can you think of any place else, a place out of the way where people are not likely to be roaming?"

"I know of a place!" Steven exclaimed, excited at the chance to help yet again. "There is a loft in the stable building, far in the back. It has not been used in many years. It would be easy for us to sneak into the building and into the loft without being seen."

"I hate that you would have to leave the main structure and enter the common area," Andrew responded. "There is much danger out there."

"There is a door near the rear of the castle. It is not far from the stable," Steven replied. "With everyone's attention diverted to the front of the castle we should be able to make our way to the stable without being seen."

"We do not have time to continue this debate," Donald said, anxious to be on the move again. "I say follow the boy's suggestion."

"Very well," Andrew agreed, not thrilled with the plan but knowing that they did not have time to conjure a safer course of action. "You must make every effort to keep from being spotted, especially by Talbot's men," Andrew said, looking at Heather. "Your hair would be difficult to miss. Find cloaks for yourselves, something you can pull over your heads and hide as much of your faces as possible. Make your way to the loft and remain there until Donald and I come for you. Now go."

"Do not make us wait long," Heather said as she lifted a hand to Andrew's cheek. "We will not leave our mother alone and unprotected." Andrew covered her hand with his and gave her a reassuring smile. She returned the smile and after a few tender moments, reluctantly turned to her brother. "Okay, little brother, lead the way."

As Heather and Steven disappeared into the crowd, Donald looked at Andrew.

"And in which direction shall we proceed ourselves?" he asked.

"Do you smell that?" Andrew asked, sniffing the air.

"Aye, smoke," Donald replied.

"Where there is smoke, there is fire. Let us see if we can find its source." Without another word Andrew stepped out of the shadows and into the crowded room.

Alone in his war room, King Talbot anxiously paced back and forth as he considered the situation. His grand scheme for ultimate power had not included a war, especially a war that he was almost assured of losing. He knew the numbers and the nearly inevitable outcome. Once Gallard had successfully burned the drawbridge and the gate the battle would be over. Unless a miracle appeared on the near horizon, his kingdom was lost. His only hope would be to escape with the sword and shield through one of the secret passageways under the castle. He may not acquire the DuFay Breastplate this day, but he would make sure that nobody else did, either. For over twenty years he had been hunting the DuFay legend and even though he was about to be driven from the land, he took comfort in the great progress he had made while there. He had garnished a great depth of knowledge and understanding about Reginald DuFay and his legend from the secrets held deep within the castle's bowels. He had obtained the DuFay Shield and the DuFay Sword. And he now knew where the DuFay Breastplate was. His daughter's revelation about the crown, belt and boots made his plan more difficult now. He could be a little more patient in his ultimate quest. Somehow, he would create the perfect plan to take the breastplate from Gallard and then find the three newly revealed pieces. All he needed was a little more time.

A sudden, loud knock on the door stirred Talbot from his musings. He circled to the back side of his large oak desk and poised himself as though he were studying some papers on the desk, then he commanded the visitor to enter. Angus strode boldly into the room.

"Your majesty, our forces have arrived at the flank of Gallard's army and have engaged the enemy," he informed the king.

"Very well," Talbot said, not looking up from the papers scattered on the desk.

"Do you not wish to view the battle?" Angus asked, a bit confused by the king's rather casual response.

"I have a more important matter to tend to at the moment," Talbot replied, surprising Angus.

"A matter more important than the defense of your kingdom against an invading army?" Angus asked, not trying the least bit to be polite. "Pray tell, what might this matter be?"

"Preservation of the future and our ultimate goal," Talbot replied coolly.

"And does your majesty wish to inform his military advisor of this plan for preservation?"

"In due time," Talbot responded.

"In due time?" Angus repeated, none too pleased with the king's refusal to reveal his plans. "Your majesty, your men, my men, are fighting and dying for you on the battlefield this very moment. None of them have the slightest idea of what this war is truly about. Is it your intention to abandon your loyal subjects at the time they need you most? They need to see their king standing behind them, directing the battle. They need the inspiration that only your crown can provide. If we are to have any chance of defending this castle and defending our lives, we need for you to come out of hiding so the men can see you and continue to fight for you."

"Hiding?" Talbot said defensively. "You believe I am hiding from battle?"

"There is that appearance," Angus responded honestly.

"Do not forget your place," Talbot warned Angus. "I will not have any subject of mine accusing me of being a coward and hiding from battle. It is only because of my bravery and my intellect that we are even standing here today, closer to obtaining the DuFay Armor than any of us ever truly imagined. It is my responsibility to ensure that all the years we have spent here, learning what we have learned and obtaining what we have obtained, do not go to waste. I cannot do that babysitting our men. That is your job as their military leader. Do not forget your place."

"Yes, your majesty," Angus replied through gritted teeth.

"If my recollection is correct, we set aside fifty men outside our walls with orders to not engage in the battle, correct?" Talbot asked.

"That is correct," Angus answered.

"Send them to Edward Finley's farm. There is a small shack in the woods behind Finley's cottage. Have them wait there. They must not be seen, do you understand?"

"What importance could there be of a shack in the woods on the Finley farm?" Angus asked.

"Our future," Talbot replied with a knowing smile on his face. "You will also order another fifty men from within the castle's walls to stand ready at the royal dock."

"Your majesty, fifty men? I need every able man ready to repel Gallard's army when he broaches the gate!" Angus argued in disbelief. "I cannot afford to send a single man away from the front gate."

"You will do as I have ordered you to do," Talbot countered sternly.

"We are outnumbered so heavily yet you desire to remove one

hundred men from battle?" Angus asked. "How do you expect me to adequately protect you when you compromise my resources?"

"There is no time for me to explain my actions to you, nor as king am I required to do so," Talbot responded. "You will carry out my instructions without question and without delay. If you are unable to do so I will find someone who can and will. Do I make myself clear?"

"Yes, your majesty," Angus said, giving in though with much disconcertment.

"Good. Now see to it. We do not have time to waste. Find Martin. Have him gather a dozen of his best men and come to me in my study."

"As you wish," Angus said, confused but not desiring to push the king any farther. He turned quickly and exited the room.

"Guard!" Talbot called out. One of the two sentries guarding Talbot's war room immediately appeared in the doorway.

"Locate my minister of agriculture and have him meet me in my study. Find my daughter, also, and escort her to my study as well. Do not allow her to tarry and do not be put off by questions. If she will not follow you without pause you have my permission to carry her. If it comes to that, though, I advise that you protect yourself well from her fingernails."

"Yes, your majesty," the guard replied and left to fulfill his orders.

"For the preservation of our future," Talbot muttered to himself as he left the room.

"This does not bode well for Talbot's future," Donald said as he and Andrew peered out the window of one of the towers in the castle's outer wall. The brothers had passed through the castle without being recognized and had made their way into one of the watchtowers. From there they were able to see the action outside of the castle's walls as well as the activity inside the main gate. Even as plumes of black smoke stretched into the sky from the burning drawbridge, Gallard's men continued their assault on the main gate. Every few minutes the catapults launched more of their malevolent missiles at the castle's gate. Andrew and Donald could see the battle being waged along Gallard's flank where Talbot's men fought bravely but in vain. They were no match for Gallard's well-trained army.

"Not at all," Andrew answered. "It does not bode well for any of our futures."

"How long?" Donald asked.

"Three hours at most," Andrew replied. "The drawbridge will soon collapse from the fire. Gallard will then fully attack the main gate and burn it as well. Talbot's archers will be able to slow the advance but not by much. His men who are now on the ground fighting will last a couple of more hours at most. They cannot stand against Gallard's men. Their training has been very weak over the years. They were not prepared for a real war. They have heart, but their skills are lacking."

"Well, my brother, you are the brains of the family. How do you plan to get us out of this mess?" Donald asked.

"I am not sure," Andrew answered, distracted momentarily by some activity in the courtyard.

"What is it?" Donald asked.

"Angus," Andrew replied. "He is speaking with Martin, Talbot's captain of the guard." Donald turned and looked down into the courtyard.

"That man with whom Angus is speaking is Talbot's captain of the guard?" Donald asked, sounding a bit confused.

"Yes. Why"

"I have seen that man before," Donald replied.

"Here?" Andrew asked.

"No, not here," Donald answered, squinting his eyes a bit and holding his hand up to shade his eyes from the bright sky. "I do not recall his name and I never met him formally, but I definitely remember him. He was one of Gallard's men. We would not see him very often, perhaps three times during the span of a year, nor for any more than a couple of days at a time. He always remained close to Gallard. I thought it strange that I started seeing him more often as we approached this land."

"Of course you saw him more often," Andrew said confidently. "He was reporting to Gallard on Talbot's defenses and who knows what else. This confirms that he is a spy for Gallard."

"If that is the case, why is he still here?" Donald asked. "Now that the attack has begun would he not return to Gallard, his job being done?"

"Perhaps his job is not done," Andrew said, concern riding his voice as he saw Martin hurriedly depart from Angus, gather several men and head back into the castle. "I do not like the looks of this. We need to get down there and see what is going on." Without another word, Andrew and Donald ran down the six flights of stairs in the watchtower and made a beeline toward Angus, who was now barking directions at various people.

"Are you mad?" Donald asked as they approached Angus. "Remember the king's orders? We will be executed on sight!"

"We have no choice but to chance it," Andrew replied. "I am going to bet that Angus and Talbot are too busy to conduct an execution. But I hope to convince him that Martin is on his way to conduct an execution of his own."

Angus had his back turned to Andrew and Donald and was caught off-guard as the brothers rushed up to him. Instinctively his hand went to the hilt of his sword, and he stopped just short of drawing it.

"MacLean! What are you doing here? You were banished under penalty of death!"

"Where is Martin going?" Andrew asked, not answering Angus' question.

"Martin? What business is it of yours? I should have you killed here and now!"

"I have no time to argue with you!" Andrew said angrily.

"Martin is a spy for Gallard! He could be on his way this moment to execute Talbot!"

"It is true," Donald added. "I have seen that man in Gallard's castle and in his camp many times."

"Martin, a spy?" Angus asked, not immediately convinced. "I do not believe it. He has served Talbot faithfully for many years."

"Believe it or not, it is the truth!" Andrew argued. "We do not have the time to debate the matter. Considering your general disposition toward me in the first place I have my doubts as to my ability to confidently convince you. Martin was responsible for Marie having been kidnapped, of this I am certain. And now he could very well be on his way to murder Talbot and likely Marie and steal the sword and shield! Where is the king and his daughter?"

Angus paused for a moment, torn between Andrew's convincing argument and the carnage that was going on outside the castle's gate. He was responsible for directing the battle for Talbot and leaving his post went against every instinct in his warrior's body. On the other hand, if there was the slightest chance that Martin was a spy and that Talbot was in danger, he could not ignore it. Despite his dislike of Andrew, he knew Andrew well enough to respect him and recognize that Andrew was no fool and no liar. He made his decision.

"Talbot is in his study. He ordered me to have Martin and twelve of his best guardsmen report to him there. As for Marie, I do not know where she is. I suspect Talbot is preparing for an escape."

"If that is the case then he will have the sword and the shield with him," Andrew surmised. "It is of little doubt that he has sent for Marie to join him. Martin will have the perfect set-up to execute Talbot and Marie. With the two of them out of the way, Gallard will eventually claim the throne of Durinburg as his own. He will have three pieces of the DuFay Armor, and I would not be surprised if he knows where the other pieces are. You can count on him not wanting any influential people in Talbot's administration to remain alive. It will be your death sentence."

"Morecraft!" Angus shouted as Lawrence Morecraft rushed by.

"The attack on Gallard's flank is failing!" Lawrence paused and reported, not immediately recognizing the MacLean brothers who were still in the uniforms of the prison guards. "I must prepare the men inside the walls for a full-frontal attack!"

"Forget the attack," Angus said, waving off a look of confusion on Lawrence's face. "The king may be in danger. I need for you to go and ensure his safety."

"I just spoke with Martin. He has twelve men and is on his way to the king's study to do just that," Lawrence argued. "I am needed out here."

"Martin could very well be the danger!" Angus retorted, short on patience. "Go with the MacLean brothers and see that the king is safe! I will take care of what needs to be done out here, then I will follow."

For the first time, Lawrence took a closer look at the two men with Angus. A look of complete surprise sprung on his face.

"Andrew? Donald? What are you two doing here?" he asked.

"It is a long story," Andrew replied impatiently. "There is no time for an explanation. We must get to Talbot's study. I fear Martin is on his way to assassinate Talbot and Marie!"

"Then let us waste no more time," Lawrence said and led the way into the castle.

Chapter 23

Marie did not need any extra prodding to join her father in his study. She had been in one of the libraries, helping keep a group of children distracted from Gallard's onslaught by leading them in songs and entertaining them with stories she had read in the books lining the library's walls. As soon as the guard informed her of Talbot's instructions, she excused herself and followed the guard back to her father's study. The guard opened the door to the study for her and she entered the room, immediately spotting Malcolm and her father standing around a large table upon which the DuFay Sword and DuFay Shield rested. It was obvious that the two items were being prepared for travel, as several blankets lay stacked beside them. The two men glanced up as Marie entered and Malcolm gave Talbot a quick glance of concern. Talbot returned the look with a slight nod, indicating everything was okay.

Wordlessly, Marie approached the table, not able to take her eyes off the sword and the shield. Individually they were beautiful, but together they were breathtaking. She could not begin to imagine what a sight it would have been for all three, no, six items of the legendary DuFay Armor to be together. Glorious was the only word that came to her mind but even at that, it seemed trite. Having seen the sword, she focused her attention on the shield. She reached out and ran her hand along its edges, mesmerized by the finely polished gold and the dozens and dozens of sparkling precious gems. She could identify the rubies, emeralds, and sapphires quite easily, but there were several stones she did not recognize right off. The engraving on the shield was flawless. Calling it a work of art did not do it justice. It was difficult to believe that a mere man was capable of creating something so stunning.

"Magnificent, are they not?" Talbot asked his daughter as her face was illuminated by the shield's reflection of the candles on the table and walls.

"That word does not even begin to describe them," she replied in awe. "Why have you summoned me?" she asked, finally looking up from the table and into her father's eyes.

"It is time for us to leave," he replied bluntly.

"You are leaving in the middle of the battle?" Marie asked incredulously.

"We must leave in order to save our lives," Talbot replied. "There is no way we can hold off Gallard's army. They are too many. Once the main gate has been breached, they will flood through it like water through a broken dam and there is nothing we can do to stop the flood. We will be overrun in minutes. While the commoners might be spared, though it is doubtful, there is no doubt that Gallard will execute anyone and everyone of influence or royalty. We have no choice but to make our escape while we can."

"But what of your people?" Marie asked, thinking of the women and children she had just left. "You would abandon them so easily? Have you no affection at all for your loyal subjects?"

"I would that we had the time and ability to save every last one of them," the king sighed with false sincerity. "Alas, we do not. We can only pray that Gallard will exercise some degree of humanity and spare their lives. There is no question that he will not do so with us, and therefore it is imperative that we leave as soon as possible."

"I see that you have the time and ability to save your precious sword and shield," Marie noted sarcastically. "I suppose you will assure me that it is in the best interest of the people that you take these icons with you so that someday you can rule them along with a thousand other kingdoms."

"So that I can bring peace to them and a thousand other kingdoms," Talbot corrected her. "It is all in the quest for peace and harmony."

"Ah, yes, peace and harmony. Such as that which lies this very moment outside your walls? Is that the kind of peace and harmony for which you seek?"

"As one who loves the outdoors, I do not need to remind you that some of the most beautiful days are the ones that start out with the most ominous storms," Talbot responded. "What you see today is simply the storm before the calm. You must look beyond the ugliness of today in order to see the beauty of tomorrow."

"But there will always be ugliness," Marie countered. "There will always be someone else seeking the legend of DuFay, bringing armies against you to steal away the peace and harmony. The more powerful you become, the more enemies you will have. Do you believe you will rule a thousand kingdoms without having to fight and kill for them? Your life will be full of storms, and you will never be able to see the sun as it breaks free from the black clouds."

"My daughter, you simply do not understand," Talbot said condescendingly. "But in time, you will. One day, that which I rule shall be passed on to you and your offspring and their generations after them. This I promise you."

A loud knock on the room's main door interrupted the conversation. Malcolm and Talbot exchanged glances and quickly moved to finish bundling the sword and shield.

"Enter!" Talbot commanded as he and Malcolm turned from the table to face the front of the room. They maintained their positions to keep the sword and shield out of direct sight, despite the objects being completely wrapped in blankets. The door opened and Martin and his twelve men entered the room.

"You sent for us, your majesty?" Martin asked as his men took positions around the room.

"I did," Talbot said, watching Martin's men curiously as they moved around the room, almost as if to surround him. Marie did not miss the slightly odd behavior, and she suddenly felt very vulnerable.

"What is your bidding?" Martin asked almost derisively.

"It is time we make our escape," Talbot informed him. "There is a hidden passageway that will take us beyond the walls of the castle and away from the fighting. You and your men will provide our protection."

"Where exactly does this hidden passage end?" Martin inquired.

"As I said, beyond the castle walls and away from the fighting," Talbot replied cautiously. Martin's attitude had a rather disquieting nature to it.

"I will need to know more than that in order to provide the king with the protection he needs," Martin countered.

"You need to know only what I determine you need to know," Talbot responded. "It is not like you to question my intentions, Captain of the Guard. Now prepare your men for our departure. We will leave as soon as my military advisor returns."

Martin did not respond immediately but hesitated as he glared at Talbot with what could be nothing other than utter contempt. He nodded to the two guards closest to the room's main door. The men nodded and exited the room, closing the door behind them.

"I am afraid that you will not be leaving at all, your majesty," Martin said as he stepped closer to Talbot. The king furrowed his brow in momentary confusion, but the reality of the situation dawned upon him, and his eyes opened wide with concern.

"What is the meaning of this?" Talbot asked, taking a nervous step backward.

"Andrew was right," Marie said, answering her father's question. "Martin is a spy for Gallard."

"I never liked that man," Martin stated, his eyes never leaving Talbot. "He is too smart and too arrogant for his own good. No matter. He is either dead or Gallard's prisoner by now, though I do so hope for the former. I take it those are not your traveling clothes bundled on that table behind you."

Talbot took another step back as if to protect the sword and the shield. He knew it was of no use to play innocent and ignorant. He could see the knowing look in Martin's eyes. His only hope was to stall until Angus arrived, though as skilled and strong as Angus was, he could not take on eleven men by himself.

"Traitor," Talbot spat at Martin. "All these years I have been most kind and generous to you. I have entrusted the safety of myself and my family to you and this is how you show your gratitude?"

"Do not worry, my gratitude will be well displayed once I deliver the sword and shield to Gallard and he displays his gratitude toward me," Martin replied.

"I will offer you more," Talbot said hopefully.

"What do you take me for, a traitor?" Martin smiled. "Oh, wait, I believe you do take me for a traitor. Here is what I offer to you, your majesty: Relinquish the sword and the shield to me of your own accord and I will spare the life of your daughter. She will serve King Gallard at his pleasure, but at least she will be alive. Refuse to do so and I will take her life right before I take yours."

"Do not consider for a moment laying a hand on my daughter," Talbot growled. "You would pay dearly for doing so."

"I do not believe you to be in a position to threaten anyone," Martin responded calmly. "I certainly enjoyed humbling her and escorting her to King Gallard once before. I would relish the opportunity to do so again."

"So, it was you who kidnapped her," Talbot concluded. His voice took a malevolent tone. I promised my daughter that the day I discovered who abducted her I would take vengeance upon him."

"How sweet," Martin replied undaunted. "Unfortunately, it does not appear that you are quite in the position to take vengeance upon anyone or anything."

"I am a father who keeps his word," Talbot retorted resolutely. While engaging Martin in conversation, Talbot had slowly and imperceptibly reached to his side and grasped the handle of a six-inch dagger hidden in his belt, under his tunic. With a quickness that surprised everyone in the room, Talbot withdrew the dagger and lunged at Martin. Caught completely by surprise, it was only Martin's subconscious reflexes that saved his life. As Talbot lunged forward with the dagger pointing directly at Martin's heart, Martin turned away several inches. Though it missed his heart, the dagger still penetrated his torso nearly two inches. Martin cried out in surprise and pain as he threw Talbot to the floor. The king quickly got to his feet. Acting strictly on impulse, Martin yanked the dagger from his chest and without the slightest pause, stepped forward and plunged the dagger into Talbot's own chest. Martin stood there for a few seconds, staring into Talbot's unbelieving eyes, his own full of vile hatred and animalistic savagery. Only when he felt the warmth of Talbot's life dripping on his hand did he step away, leaving the dagger in place. Slowly, the king sunk to his knees, then toppled over.

"NO!" Marie cried as she rushed to her father's side. She sank to the floor next to him, cradling his head in her arms, the tears flowing freely from his eyes.

"Father," she sobbed, brushing the king's hair away from his eyes. "Oh Father, please do not die," she begged. "Do not leave me. Stay here with me."

"The choice is no longer mine," the king said weakly, reaching up and grasping her hand. "My daughter, my precious daughter. Do you know how proud I am of you? You have grown into a strong, wise woman, so much like your dear mother." The king paused for a moment, fighting for words. "I so wanted to see your children. How beautiful they will be. How smart they will be."

"Father," Marie whispered, barely able to control the sobbing that threatened to overtake her. "What will I do without you?"

"You will live," he replied just before the blood seeping into his lungs caused a coughing spasm that racked his body. "You will be stronger than I was. Look not to power, look not to prestige. Enjoy all the fine things this world has to offer, whether you have much or have little." Another coughing spasm overtook the king and a faint trail of blood seeped from the corner of his mouth. "It has taken the shadow of death to throw light on the vanity of my wasted life." His eyelids began to shut, but he fought to keep them open. "Escape," he murmured. "You must escape."

"How?" Marie asked, the tears flowing down her cheek. "The gates are guarded. There is no way out."

"Behind the kingdom," Talbot wheezed as his eyes briefly moved and focused on a tapestry on the far wall. "Finley's farm. Look behind the kingdom." He mustered enough strength to lift his hand and gently caressed her cheek. "My daughter, I see the black clouds of the tempest before me, and I fear there is no sun behind them." With those final words, the king breathed his last and his lifeless hand dropped from his daughter's cheek. No longer able to hold back her sobbing, Marie's body shook as she broke down and burst into tears. Though not known to be a man of much empathy, Malcolm nonetheless moved over to Marie's side and placed his hand on her shoulder.

Martin looked down at Marie and the king he had just killed, not the least bit of sympathy or regret abiding in his heart. His instructions had been clear. He was to obtain possession of the sword and shield and dispose of the king and his advisors. Gallard had left Marie's final fate to Martin's discretion. He looked at Malcolm, knowing what his next move must be. Martin reached to his side and withdrew his sword from its scabbard.

"You followed Talbot in life," Martin said menacingly. "Now, you must follow him in death." Just as Martin was about to step forward and plunge his sword into Malcom's chest, a commotion outside of the room caught his attention and gave him pause. The doors of the room suddenly burst open, and Andrew, Donald and Lawrence rushed into the room. It took only a second for them to comprehend what had happened and what was about to happen. Martin jumped back away from the doorway, his sword coming around to point at the newcomers.

"Marie, are you okay?" Andrew asked, keeping his eyes on Martin and the other men in the room.

"Father," she whimpered, "he killed my father."

"Are you harmed?" Andrew repeated, slowly kneeling beside her.

"He killed my father," she repeated, refusing to look up, able to do nothing but cradle his lifeless body in her arms. Andrew took a quick glance down at Marie and did not see any signs of injury. He had no time to bring her back to reality. The situation was dire to say the least. Although the two guards outside of the room had been disposed of, Martin and his men still outnumbered the newcomers by eight. For a moment Andrew considered Malcolm but it had been obvious for a long time that Malcolm was not a fighter, and it was questionable whether he had ever held a sword in his life. In a knock-down, drag-out fight, he would be more of a liability than an asset.

"There is no escape," Martin said emphatically. "You are outnumbered outside the gate, as you are in this room. Gallard has the castle surrounded. It is only a matter of time before his army pours through the main gate."

"You shall not live long enough to see that happen," Andrew said menacingly.

"Now that is not a nice thing to say to the man who all but saved your life," Martin replied sarcastically. "Or in the least delayed the inevitable."

"What do you mean?" Andrew asked, taking the bait in order to give himself time to formulate a plan of attack.

"Peterson would have tortured you beyond anything you could imagine, or in the end endure," Martin replied. "He would have pulled from you the location of the sword eventually, even if it meant torturing and killing your friends. Then he would have killed you. I could not let that happen."

"So it was you," Andrew replied, still working on a plan of attack. "Why kill him? You both are Gallard's men, seeking the same goal, which is to retrieve the sword."

"My ambitions are a little higher," Martin responded. "If I were to bring Gallard the shield, his gratitude would be great, as would be my reward. However, if I were to bring him both the sword and the shield, I would be elevated to a position of great power, nobility and wealth. I could not allow Peterson to get his hands on the sword."

"I shall never cease to be amazed at how many times a man's obsession with power and wealth leads to his doom," Andrew replied.

"Yet it is ironic how you shall meet your doom here, in this room, and I shall walk away a hero to my king," Martin countered.

"Marie," Andrew said firmly, touching her on the shoulder. "You need to leave the room." When she did not respond, he reached down to grasp her arm and lift her to her feet. "Did you hear me? You need to leave, now. Find Angus and inform him of what has happened. He will protect you."

"There is no protection for her," Martin stated. "She will be dead by the end of the day, though she will certainly live much longer than you and your two comrades."

"Marie!" Andrew said more urgently. "Did you not hear me? You can do nothing for your father. He is gone. You must leave the room, now!" None too gently Andrew pulled Marie to her feet. Marie reached out and grabbed the dagger that was still embedded in her father's chest. Just as she reached her feet and with surprising quickness, she lunged toward Martin, intent on ramming the blade into his chest and finishing the job her father had started. However, Andrew was quicker and was able to grasp her before she took two steps. She screamed in frustration and fought Andrew's grip, but to no avail. Andrew pulled her back and toward him, his hands firmly grasping her wrists.

"And just what did you believe you were going to do with that tiny little blade?" Martin sneered. "Avenge your father? If not for your friend your blood would be mixed with your father's blood on that blade."

"Let me go!" Marie screamed. "Let me go! I will kill him!"

"Yes, by all means, let her go," Martin said with a taunting smile on his face. "I am curious to see exactly what she plans to do with that dagger."

Andrew pulled Marie's arms down so they were out of Martin's line of vision. He looked intently into Marie's wild eyes as his right hand smoothly reached for the dagger. He gave her a nearly imperceptible nod as he squeezed her hand in a gesture of reassurance. Slowly, understanding began to creep into the hate-filled whirlwind that tore at Marie's mind. She loosened her grip on the dagger and Andrew grasped it by the blade. She returned his short nod in acknowledgment. As Andrew released Marie's hands, she whirled around, lunged in Martin's direction, and let out a yell as though she were attacking him. Martin pulled his sword back in preparation to run it through her. However, before she came into range of his sword, Marie quickly ducked to the ground. As Martin took a step toward her, he felt a sharp pain in his chest. He looked up at Andrew who stood with his right arm outstretched toward him. Martin slowly looked down and saw the hilt of the dagger protruding from his chest. The full length of the blade had penetrated his chest, fatally piercing his heart. He looked up at Andrew in disbelief.

"That was rather unexpected," Martin said in shock, his legs beginning to give out underneath him.

"That was the idea," Andrew replied, watching the captain of the guard crumple to his knees.

"Curiosity killed the cat," Marie said triumphantly as Martin's eyes rolled back and he fell to the floor, dead.

"Your leader is dead," Andrew announced to Martin's henchmen, "as is his plan for stealing the sword and shield. Throw down your weapons and your lives will be spared."

"There is no life for those who commit treason," the man closest to Andrew replied. "If we surrender, we will be executed. However, there is much reward for those who fulfill their missions. We shall deliver the sword and the shield to King Gallard, and we shall receive our reward."

"So be it," Andrew replied. With the speed of a striking cobra he took three steps forward and swung his sword at the man. His opponent was quick as well and successfully parried the blow. Marie, knowing a blood bath was on its way, quickly scampered out of the room. Within seconds all fourteen occupants of the room were engaged in a fierce hand-to-hand battle. The room was too small and too crowded for full-length swords to be used so the combatants were relegated to smaller knives and their bare hands. The size of the room and their positions near the exit worked in the favor of Andrew, Donald and Lawrence. Their backs were nearly against one of the walls of the room, therefore there was no way for any of their opponents to attack from the rear. The fighting became fierce and turned into an unrestrained brawl. Andrew and Donald had been well-trained in close-quarters, hand-to-hand combat and were holding their own. Lawrence, whose hand-to-hand fighting skills had been honed via many a tavern fight, was also able to hold off his attackers for the most part. Malcolm flailed about, never having engaged in a fight in his life. Just as they gave, though, the four men received as well. Lawrence felt a pain in his mid-section as one of the guards swiped at him with a dagger. Ignoring the pain, he thrust his right knee up into the man's midsection which rendered the attacker breathless. Without pausing, Lawrence grabbed the man and rammed him into the closest wall, head-first. The guard fell to the ground, either dead or unconscious. Lawrence did not care, as another guard was quickly upon him.

Twice Donald was struck in the face so hard he felt for sure he was going to black out. Somehow, he was able to maintain consciousness and continue the fight. He felt Andrew knocked into his side on more than one occasion. Within ten minutes four of the guards were knocked out of the fight, evening the odds a bit. But Andrew, Donald, Lawrence and Malcolm were quickly tiring. They were now fighting with their backs against the wall and nowhere to which they could fall back. Just as things looked to be turning for the worse, Angus burst into the room. Without pausing he quickly grasped the nearest guard and literally threw him across the room. The guard violently crashed into the table holding the sword and shield and fell to the ground, unconscious. Hardly missing a beat, Angus took his sword and ran it through the next closest guard. Rejuvenated by the reinforcement, Andrew landed several powerful blows on the chin of the guard who had momentarily been getting the best of him. The guard stepped back, stunned, his legs becoming wobbly. Andrew did not hesitate. He stepped forward and landed a punch that finished off the man. Not to be outdone by his brother, Donald slammed his fist into the solar plexus of the man with whom he was grappling. The man doubled over, the breath knocked out of him. Donald powerfully brought his knee up and firmly struck the man's chin. His eyelids fluttered for a moment and then the man fell backward, unconscious. The remaining two men, seeing nine of their comrades on the floor either unconscious or dead, pulled back from the fight and surrendered.

"What took you so long?" Andrew asked Angus as he gasped for air.

"Lest you forget, there is a battle being waged outside of this room as well," Angus replied.

"Where is Marie?" Lawrence asked, looking around. "Did you see her in the hallway?"

"She is in her study, just on the other side of this wall," Angus answered. "She told me what was happening. I instructed her to hide in her study until the fighting was over." As he finished speaking, Marie walked into the room.

"Marie, you should have waited for me to come and get you,"

Angus chided her. "For all you knew we could have been the ones lying on the ground instead of these traitors."

"I saw the fight," Marie said absentmindedly as she moved back over to her father's side.

"How?" Angus asked. "You were in your study."

"Through there," she said, pointing to the common wall between her study and that of her father's. Hidden in the shadows was a small opening in the wall, a void where one of the stone blocks was missing. Angus walked over to the wall and inspected the opening. Peering through it he could make out a portion of Marie's private study.

"You could see what was happening through this hole?" he asked. "You could hear everything that was going on in here?"

"Everything," Marie confirmed, kneeling by her father.

"That used to be your mother's study, did it not?" Angus inquired, looking at Marie quizzically.

"A long time ago," Marie acknowledged, her hand gently brushing the hair from her father's lifeless cheek.

"So that is how she knew," Angus said, turning his attention back to the hole. "She heard everything."

"What do you mean?" Marie asked, her attention suddenly captured by Angus' careless words. "Who heard everything?"

"It is nothing," Angus said, trying to dismiss the subject. He turned from the wall. "We must find a way to get you out of here."

"You are talking about my mother, are you not?" Marie asked, standing up and facing Angus. "Who else could you possibly be speaking of? What do you mean she heard everything? She heard everything about what?"

Realizing that he was cornered, Angus gave in.

"Yes, your mother," he admitted reluctantly. "Your father long suspected that she knew about the DuFay legend and his search for the armor, though he tried desperately to hide his intentions from her. He was afraid that if she found out she would hinder his efforts."

"And just what did he do about it?" Marie asked accusingly. "It seems that everyone who knew about the legend, outside of my father and his 'trusted' advisors, met with fatal accidents. My mother's illness, in retrospect, seems less of chance and more of intention."

"Your father did not do anything about it," Angus replied. "He would not allow a hair on your mother's head to be harmed."

"But he had no problem with harming the hairs on the heads of other people who knew about the legend," Lawrence concluded. "Are you saying that my father's death was no accident?"

"I had nothing to do with your father's death, nor the deaths of the other elders," Angus said defensively. "The king ordered that anybody who could pose a threat to his plan be warned off and if they did not listen, they were to be scared away. I warned your father as well as the other elders to cease their searches for the DuFay legend and to keep what they learned to themselves. That was the extent of my involvement. After their deaths I learned that Malcolm had, on his own accord, arranged for the men to meet with their accidents."

"Did he poison my mother as well?" Marie asked.

"Ask him yourself," Angus answered.

"I am afraid you will get no answer from him," Donald said, bending over Malcolm's lifeless body. The front of his tunic was saturated with blood and a large gash yawned down his torso. "Whatever secrets he had, he has taken them to his grave."

"It is convenient to place blame on a dead man," Lawrence said, not convinced of Angus' answers. "I wonder what his response would be to such accusations."

"Believe what you want, it is of no matter now," Angus replied. "Our time is short. The main gate is burning as we speak and will collapse within the hour. There is nothing that can stop Gallard's forces. We must find a way out."

"Talbot had a plan to escape," Andrew said, looking around the room. "He had the sword and shield with him as well as Marie. He ordered you to have Martin meet him here."

"He also ordered me to have fifty men gather near a shack in the woods on the Finley's farm and another fifty gather by the pier where Talbot's private barge is docked," Angus added.

"What did he have in mind?" Donald asked. "He obviously could not be in two places at once."

"Perhaps he had planned to split up the sword and the shield," Lawrence suggested. "One would somehow be taken to Finley's farm and the other would be spirited away on his barge. That would eliminate the possibility of Gallard obtaining both at the same time."

"Though not impossible, I would not think that a likely scenario," Andrew countered. "Talbot spent much time and effort, and even spilled blood, to possess both the sword and the shield. It would be extremely unlikely that he would tolerate either one of them being taken from his immediate possession. No, I think it more likely that one of the escape routes was to function as a diversion."

"Before my father died, he said I must escape and then said something about the Finley's farm," Marie volunteered. "He said to look behind the kingdom for Finley's farm."

"That does not make sense," Lawrence said. "How can the Finley's farm be behind the kingdom?"

"Could he have meant behind the castle?" Donald asked.

"No, he specifically said behind the kingdom," Marie replied.

"Angus, what was the king's plan for escape?" Andrew asked.

"Unfortunately, he did not see fit to reveal his plan to me," Angus answered bitterly. "Perhaps his trust was in Malcolm instead. He merely instructed me to find Martin and then report back to this room."

"His escape route would have been close by," Andrew surmised as he looked around the room. "Perhaps it is located in this very room itself." The walls of the room were lined mostly with bookcases. Andrew walked over to the closest one which was along the wall on the right side of the room. He ran his hands along the edge of the bookshelf where it met the wall. There was about an inch of space between the bookcase and the wall. He jammed his fingers into the gap as far as they would go and then pulled. Nothing happened. With a second, stronger effort, the bookcase began to move. With a final exertion of strength Andrew toppled the bookcase to the floor. Instead of a secret passage, as he had hoped would be revealed, there was nothing but the block wall. He walked over to the next bookcase and repeated the procedure. Again, there was nothing but the block wall. Undaunted, Andrew continued this process until the floor of the room was nearly covered with books and broken bookcases. He stepped back and looked around the room once again, refusing to believe that the room did not contain a secret passageway. His eyes fell on a tapestry hanging on the wall at the rear of the room. He had skipped over the tapestry initially since it did not extend all the way to the floor, and he could see the block wall extending from the floor up at the bottom of the fabric. He approached the tapestry and looked at it more closely. It appeared to be a depiction of a region of land, almost like a map. It showed mountains and rivers as well as a large lake. On one shore of the lake was a castle.

"Behind the kingdom," Andrew murmured to himself. He reached out, grabbed the fabric, and ripped it off the wall. To everyone's amazement, hidden by the tapestry, was a boarded-up opening in the block wall.

"If I were to venture a guess, I would say that this passageway finds its exit somewhere around Finley's farm," Andrew said matter-of-factly.

"I never knew," Marie said, staring at the secret doorway. "In all my years here and all the time I spent in here with my father I never knew there was a secret passage in here."

"Now the question is what do we do?" Lawrence asked. "Do we take the secret passage, or do we take a boat ride?"

"Both," Andrew said with a smug smile. "But first, you have an errand to run. Heather and Steven are hiding in the loft in the stable. If you would be so kind, please find them and bring them here. In the meantime, we will draw up our plan for escape."

"I cannot wait to see what you come up with this time," Lawrence grumbled as he turned and left the room.

Chapter 24

G allard watched with much delight the black smoke from the burning gate rise high into the nearly cloudless blue sky. His invasion plan was moving along quite nicely. He looked at his military advisor.

"Has there been any word on MacLean?"

"The MacLean brothers were followed into an underground passage that led into the castle," Walter replied. "Unfortunately, our men were not able to apprehend the brothers or the sword before being blocked by a locked gate. They have been trying to break the gate down, but it is holding solid."

"At least we know where they are," Gallard said. "Are all of the exits being watched?"

"Yes, my lord. There is not a door in the castle's walls that does not have our eyes upon it."

"Truthfully, I am more concerned with the doors that cannot be seen," Gallard said. "If there is one secret passageway you can rest assured that there are more."

"With the castle sitting on the shore of the lake, that at least eliminates one direction in which they can escape," Walter surmised.

"I wonder about that," Gallard said, more to himself than his subject.

"Do you wish to send out patrols to look for possible underground exits?" Walter asked.

"It would be prudent to do so," Gallard agreed. "I will not

come this far only to have the sword and shield spirited out from under my nose."

"I will make the arrangements," Walter said.

"How is the battle proceeding on our flank?" the king asked.

"Very much in our favor," Walter answered. "Most of the enemy are either dead or have fled. I would say there are only a few hundred still fighting. We have taken our share of casualties to be sure, though. We should be thankful that their training was so weak."

"I would take heart over training any day of the week in any battle," Gallard countered. "Start moving the main body of our army to the front line. I do not desire to waste any time once the gate is fully destroyed. I want men prepared to move the bridge in place the moment the way is clear, and I want plenty of protection for them. Move the catapults forward so the projectiles can reach the top of the wall. That will help keep Talbot's archers occupied so they are not able to engage against our men."

"Yes, my lord," Walter said. He wheeled his horse around and went about carrying out the king's orders.

"You should have accepted my offer," Gallard mused aloud, looking at Durinburg Castle. "At least you would have lived. You should have accepted my offer."

Lawrence, Heather and Steven hurriedly strode into Talbot's study. Heather immediately ran to Marie and wrapped her arms around her friend.

"I am so sorry," she said, tears streaming down her cheeks. "I am so sorry about your father. He was a good man."

"Thank you," Marie said, wondering to herself just how good of a man her father had been. No matter what, though, she would always love him and remember him as a loving, kind and gracious father who would have done anything for her. Heather finally released Marie and looked anxiously about the room. She spotted Andrew standing with Donald and Angus by the table. It was obvious that Andrew and Donald had been in a vicious fight. Both had numerous bloodstains on their clothes and faces, though it was not readily determinable if the blood was theirs or that of the men they had fought. Several of the castle's guards were bound and sitting along one of the room's walls. Several more were lying on the ground and it was obvious that those men were no longer any threat to anyone. Heather wanted to run up and throw her arms around Andrew, but she refrained from doing so. It was neither the time nor the place. Out of the corner of her eye she saw two people whom she recognized as being from the village, but she did not know their names. One was a rather young and slender man, probably in his late teens or early twenties. The other was possibly his father.

"So, what grand scheme has your ever-conniving mind come up with this time?" Lawrence asked as he approached the three men at the table.

"It would seem apparent that Talbot's intention was to make his escape through the secret passageway and out to the Finley's farm. According to Marie, the farm is a reasonable distance from the castle and should be far away from the fighting. There is a river that flows along Finley's farm and away from the castle. It is possible that Talbot has some canoes or small boats moored and ready for his escape. It would be faster than trying to get away on foot or horseback."

"Sounds reasonable," Lawrence said, nodding his head. "What about the men stationed at the king's dock, behind the castle?"

"I can only surmise that they are part of a diversion plan," Andrew replied. "It is for certain that Gallard would see the boat leaving the dock and with fifty men fully armed lining its rails, it would give the appearance of Talbot trying to escape. With Gallard's attention focused on the boat and chasing it down, it would have given Talbot a bit more of a chance to escape in the other direction without being detected."

"Not a bad plan," Lawrence said. "If anything, Talbot was definitely a shrewd man. What of the man and boy?" he asked, nodding in the direction of the strangers.

"They have graciously volunteered to be part of the distraction," Andrew answered. "In order for Gallard to take the bait he must believe that Talbot and Marie are on that boat. Mr. Guston will pose as Talbot. His son, Timothy, will pose as Marie."

"No insult intended, but Timothy is not quite as pretty as Marie," Lawrence said, glancing at the king's daughter with a smile. "How is he going to pass for her?"

"By wearing this," Andrew replied, holding up a dress that belonged to Marie. "His head and face will be mostly covered by a hooded cloak. His father will wear a set of Talbot's clothes, along with a royal robe."

"That is it?" Lawrence asked. Do you honestly believe that Gallard will fall for the deception? It seems too simple."

"There is one more piece to the plan," Andrew said. "In order to fully sell it, Angus will have to board the boat with the imposters. Gallard would be hard pressed to believe that Talbot would allow his military advisor to be out of his sight at a time like this. He will believe that Talbot is trying to make his escape over the lake. Actually, it would not be a bad escape plan in and of itself."

"Then why not use the lake for an escape?" Lawrence asked.

"For one, Gallard could simply follow the shore of the lake and wait until Talbot landed to attack him again. At best, Talbot would have been able to get away with perhaps a full day head start between him and anyone who tried to follow him along land. That is not much time when being pursued by an obsessed maniac. Second, I cannot help but feel Talbot knew the secret passage was a better escape route. We will have to trust his instincts."

"We should hurry," Angus said, a little anxiously. "The sooner we get this plan underway the better."

"What about the dozens of people who are huddled inside the castle?" Marie asked. "Will Gallard spare their lives?"

"That we cannot know," Andrew responded a little apologetically. "There is nothing we can do for them."

"I do not believe that for an instant," Marie argued. "If the secret passage is good enough for our escape, then it is good enough for their escape."

"We do not have time to gather them together and lead them through the passage," Donald rebutted. "We will be doing well to get away with our own lives."

"Besides," Lawrence said, "we do not know what is truly on the other end of this tunnel. We could run into an entire company of Gallard's men."

"Oh, so the people would be better off staying here and facing Gallard's entire army?" Marie retorted. "Let me see, stay here and face almost certain death, or flee through the passageway and at least have a chance to live. Hmm, yes, that is such a tough decision."

"Marie, we do not have time to argue the point," Andrew said. "We need to leave now. I am sorry about the people, but they will have to take their chances by staying here."

"That is not acceptable," Marie said emphatically as she sat down in the closest chair. "I will not accept that answer. I will not run away and leave them to die. My father is dead. Therefore, I am the ruler of Durinburg. The people are my responsibility. I must protect them as best I can. If they do not leave, I do not leave."

"Heather, she is your closest friend," Lawrence said, turning to Heather. "Speak some sense into her. Convince her that if she stays here, she will die. Convince her to come with us."

"I cannot do that," Heather said, taking a chair next to Marie. "I have to agree with her."

"Women!" Lawrence cried out, throwing his hands up in the air. "Do they not have a hint of sense to them?"

"I am sure you know the answer to that question well," Andrew said, a slight smile on his face. "We have discussed it over many a pint."

"What are we going to do?" Donald asked.

"We shall do what we have to do," Andrew replied. "Lawrence, you are an authority figure to these people. They know who you are. Get them up and get them down here. I am sure you can find some of Talbot's sentries who are roaming around trying to find something to do. Enlist them in this effort. You have fifteen minutes to get the people moving. I want you back here as quickly as possible. You, Donald and I will lead the way through the tunnel and the people can follow us. Once we are through the tunnel, though, the people will be responsible for their own safety and what they do. Marie, is that agreeable with you?"

"It is a good start," she replied.

"A good start," Lawrence said, shaking his head as he headed for the doorway. "Is there any pleasing this woman? I swear, the more time I spend around women, the more I ..." His voice faded down the hallway. Andrew could not suppress a smile of amusement.

"Angus," Andrew continued, "we need to buy as much time as possible. It will take a good while for the people to make it the tunnel. Go pull the archers from the walls. Have them start blockading the gateway with anything and everything they can find. Carts, furniture, stone, wood, whatever is not permanently attached to something else gets thrown on the pile. I want the pile as high and thick as possible. When everyone else is inside the castle, if the pile is not already on fire due to the flames from the gate, have it set on fire. That should delay Gallard's men another hour or so. Have our men follow us into the tunnel. There would be no use for them to remain and face being slaughtered by Gallard."

Angus paused for a moment, not entirely certain he appreciated Andrew giving orders. However, Andrew was right in what needed to be done and he appeared quite ready to take the lead in the escape. Therefore, Angus held his tongue and ran out of the room.

"Marie, though I hate for you to be out of my sight, I believe you should locate the king's physician and have him join our party," Andrew instructed the king's daughter. "There is little doubt that somewhere along the way we are going to need his services. Hurry now. As soon as Lawrence and Angus return, we will be ready to leave."

"I always knew it pained you to be away from me," Marie said with a sly smile. "At least you have the courage to admit it."

"Women," Andrew said, shaking his head as Marie left the room.

Twenty minutes later Lawrence returned to Talbot's study. About a dozen women and children accompanied him, all looking scared and unsure. Marie had arrived with Ian just a few minutes earlier and Angus walked into the room on the heels of Lawrence.

"Surely they are not all you found," Marie said worriedly.

"No, there are more heading down the hallway," Lawrence replied. "I sent several of your father's sentries around the castle to corral everybody and bring them down here. Do you wish me to return and extend a personal invitation to every man, woman and child in the castle or will this do?"

"I will let you know," Marie replied, undaunted. Lawrence simply rolled his eyes in frustration and joined the other men at the king's table. The imposters were now fully dressed in their disguises and ready to depart. Andrew took the bundled-up shield off the table and handed it to Angus.

"What are you doing?" Donald asked. "Why are you giving him the shield?"

"It is best to separate the sword and the shield," Andrew replied. "We cannot chance being caught with both of them in our possession."

"How will we get the shield back?" Donald asked.

"Do not worry about that," Andrew answered. "They were apart for hundreds of years, it will not hurt for them to be apart a while longer."

"I guess I will not be getting my own kingdom to rule after all," Donald said somewhat dejectedly. "So much for being the heir of DuFay."

"You do have your own kingdom," Andrew replied. "It consists of your wife and your children. The qualities that made Reginald DuFay a great king and ruler are the same qualities that make any man a great husband and father. Wisdom, prudence, kindness, loyalty, dedication, honesty and above all, fear of the Lord. Though you do not possess the DuFay Armor, you can learn much from what it stands for. We all can."

By now, dozens and dozens of villagers were gathered in the hallway, nervously standing about, not knowing where they were going or what was going to happen. Marie exited the room and began speaking to the people, trying to calm them down and reassure them that everything was going to be all right.

"It is time," Andrew said to Angus. "Move quickly. Stay as close to the middle of the lake as possible and head for the southernmost end. Should Gallard's men somehow get ahead of you and it would not be possible to land without being confronted, drop the shield into the lake."

"Drop the shield into the lake?" Lawrence asked, perplexed. "Why should he do that?"

"It is far better that the shield be lost in the depths of the lake than be held in the hands of Gallard," Andrew replied.

"What if Gallard's men are waiting for us at the end of this tunnel?" Lawrence retorted. "There will be no lake into which we can toss the sword."

"Then let us pray that Gallard's men are not waiting for us," Andrew responded. "Angus, although there is no doubt that the dock is under the eyes of Gallard, be sure that there is no attempt to hide the king and his daughter as they board the boat. We want Gallard to be informed that Talbot and Marie have boarded the boat and are trying to escape. Let the bundled shield be seen as well as this sword that will stand in for the DuFay Sword. Take these two men and go, now."

"Protect her," Angus said, nodding toward Marie who had re-entered the room. "Lead these other people to safety. Someday our paths will cross again. You are an honorable man, MacLean. You have my respect." Angus stretched his hand out toward Andrew. Without pause, Andrew reached out and grasped Angus' hand and gave him a short nod of the head.

"You know what to do," Andrew said more than asked as he handed a parchment to Angus with his left hand.

"I hope you know what you are doing," Angus replied, taking the parchment and stuffing it under his outer shirt. The men released their grips and Angus headed out of the room with Guston and Timothy close behind him.

"Are the people coming?" Andrew asked Marie.

"They are coming," she acknowledged. "There are perhaps two hundred waiting for instructions."

Andrew walked out of the room and stood in the hall. As Marie had said, there were at least two hundred people, mostly women and children, waiting in the hallway. By the light cast off from dozens of torches Andrew could see the looks of fear and uncertainty on the people's faces. He understood their fear of not knowing what was ahead of them, mixed in with the fear of knowing what was behind them. Although he knew this was costing him precious time, he also knew that he could never have simply left them behind to face possible execution by Gallard.

"People of Durinburg, let me have your attention," Andrew called out and the hallway quickly grew silent. "I know you have much fear in you right now. I assure you, we all have a degree of fear within us. We cannot control what is behind us. Therefore, we should concentrate on what is ahead of us. We are going to travel through a tunnel that leads from this room to what we hope is an exit far away from here, a place where the enemy does not have its eyes focused. We do not know how long this journey will take nor do we know the condition of the tunnel. However, your king was confident that he could pass through it safely, and therefore we, too, are confident that we can pass through it safely. Follow us. Move quickly and quietly. Do not tarry, for you will have dozens of your friends and fellow countrymen behind you. It is imperative that everyone gets into the tunnel before the enemy breaks through the main gate and enters the castle's grounds. If they discover our avenue of escape our lives will certainly become forfeit. Once we are through the tunnel, you will be on your own. Flee in whatever direction seems best to you, though I would recommend a direction that leads away from the castle. I hope that someday you will be able to return to your homes and continue your lives in your homeland. But for now, it is time to leave." Andrew turned to the sentry standing outside of the study.

"Remain here until every man, woman and child has passed into the tunnel," he instructed the young man. "When there is nobody left in the hallway, enter the room yourself and lock the door. Barricade it as best as you can. We have re-hung the tapestry on the wall above the tunnel entrance. After you pass into the tunnel pull the tapestry down so that it covers the opening. Hopefully, should Gallard's men find this room, they will not realize that this passageway exists, and our escape route will remain a secret. Do you understand?"

"I understand," the sentry said, standing tall. "I will ensure nobody is left behind."

"Very well," Andrew said, reaching up and grasping the young man on the shoulder. He then re-entered the room.

"It is time to make our grand escape," he announced. "I will lead with Donald behind me. Marie, Heather and Steven will follow with Ian behind the boy and then Lawrence behind Ian. Donald, if you would, please carry the DuFay Sword. Is everybody ready? Marie?" Andrew asked, spotting her kneeling across the room.

Marie knelt by her father's lifeless form. Tears of sorrow once again rolled down her cheeks. She felt that all she had to do was shake him and call to him and his eyes would open, and he would be okay. The finality of death was difficult for her to grasp. Leaving him there on the cold stone floor was almost unbearable, but it was a necessity. She knew that they could not carry his body with them and there was no time for a burial. She placed her hand on his cheek once again, then bent over and lightly kissed his cheek.

"Goodbye, Father," she whispered. "I will always love you." She took one of his cloaks that had been hanging on a hook on a wall and gently covered his body. She paused ever so briefly before covering his head, then pulled the cloak over his face and stood.

"I am ready," she announced to Andrew. "Let us leave this place."

Andrew did not say a word but simply grabbed a torch and disappeared into the tunnel's entrance.

Chapter 25

G allard and Walter walked toward the front of the catapults to get a closer look at their handiwork. It would only be a matter of minutes before they could storm the castle.

"Do my eyes deceive me or are they piling up debris in the gateway?" Gallard asked as he peered at the front gate.

"Desperate times breed desperate measures," Walter replied. "They know they are defeated. They are simply trying to buy a few more minutes of life."

"A rather pathetic attempt," Gallard said. "A few small pieces of debris will pose little if any obstacle to us." As the two men were conversing, a lookout rode up to them at full speed and just pulled his horse to a stop in time to keep from ramming into the king's horse.

"Your majesty!" the man called out.

"What is it?" Gallard answered gruffly, irritated at nearly being run over.

"We have spotted a group of people boarding a large boat at the rear of the castle," the man said, so excited that he was nearly out of breath.

"Talbot?" Gallard asked.

"Yes," the man nodded, "the king and his daughter have boarded the boat along with fifty very well-armed men."

"Anybody else?" the king asked. "Anybody other than Talbot, his daughter, and the guards?"

"Yes, my lord," the lookout nodded. "There are several other people accompanying the king, including a very tall, very power-ful looking man who was carrying something bundled up."

"That would be Angus, Talbot's military advisor," Walter informed the king.

"I want your eyes on that boat," Gallard instructed Walter. "You have seen the king and his military advisor. You will be able to confirm if it is truly them."

"You believe a decoy is being attempted?" Walter inquired.

"Let us call it prudent skepticism," Gallard replied. "I want reasonable assurance that it is indeed Talbot on that boat before we give chase."

"I shall return as quickly as I can," Walter told the king as he wheeled his horse about and proceeded toward the castle at full speed.

The mustiness of the damp, dark tunnel was quite powerful. The constant dripping of water echoed throughout the darkness and the floor was covered with a thin film of algae, making foot-ing treacherous at times. So far, Andrew had been duly impressed with the construction of the tunnel. Instead of being a natural formation that had been converted into a secret passageway, the appearance of the tunnel was that it had been dug from one end to the other. The walls and ceiling were reinforced, though the ancient timbers gave Andrew no confidence in their ability to con-tinue holding back the uncountable tons of rock and earth pressing down on them. The floor of the tunnel was mostly flat with few if any steps or bumps. It was a most welcomed change from the tunnel that he had first made use of to escape from the dungeon beneath the castle. There had been little conversation during the trek that had already lasted nearly thirty minutes. Andrew main-tained a reasonably slow place, despite his instincts to the contrary, in order not to place too much distance between his group and the dozens of people following them. Plus, being in unfamiliar territory, he preferred caution over speed. He estimated that they had traveled nearly a mile thus far. He had no idea how much farther they would have to travel before once again seeing daylight. His main concern, however, continued to be the condition of the tunnel. It was quite possible that over the hundreds of years of its existence, the tunnel could have experienced a cave-in anywhere along its length. If that turned out to be the case, it would be their doom. Worse, a cave-in could occur while they were walking through the tunnel. He could only hope and pray that neither scenario became reality.

Andrew felt moisture in his boots and looked down to see that there was now standing water on the trail. He had certainly stepped in a few puddles along the way, which was not surprising for an underground tunnel. But now, they were no longer just puddles. The entire floor had about an inch of water on it and the water was getting deeper with every step he took. Suddenly he realized there was a third scenario which he had failed to consider. The tunnel could be flooded, which would almost certainly block their escape. He continued walking for another twenty yards and the water rose to the middle of his shins. Andrew came to a full stop and peered down the tunnel as far as he could see, hoping the floor of the tunnel would come into view. However, all he saw was the reflection of his torch on the surface of the water.

"What is it?" Marie asked, moving up to Andrew's side.

"It appears we may have a problem with excessive moisture," Andrew replied, indicating the water covering the floor of the tunnel ahead of them.

"How deep do you think it gets?" Marie inquired.

"I cannot know for sure," Andrew answered. "However, it does appear that there is less and less distance between the surface of the water and the ceiling of the tunnel. Either the ceiling is getting lower, or the water is getting deeper. Can you swim?" he asked, semi-jesting.

"I can, but I would prefer not to," she replied, crossing her arms over her chest as if a sudden chill swept across her.

"Hold the line. I am going to walk ahead a bit and see just how deep the water gets. As long as it does not fill the tunnel completely, we will at least have a chance to get through. Some of the women and children will be hard-pressed to make passage but they will have to do so. If the tunnel is indeed filled with water, well, we will not have to worry about what is waiting for us on the other end."

"Yes, we will only have to worry about what is waiting for us back in the castle," Marie responded worriedly.

"I shall be back in a moment," Andrew said. "Pass the word down the line that we are taking a short break. I would not want the people to get anxious by us stopping." He turned and continued his march down the tunnel. As he walked away Lawrence moved up to Marie's side.

"Just where does he think he is going?" Lawrence asked, watching the torchlight slowly fade away.

"I believe he is going for a swim," Marie replied, hugging her arms close to her body to ward off the chill of the cold, dreary stone surrounding her.

Walter's steed pounded the ground furiously as the fifteen-hundred-pound animal galloped toward King Gallard. Hearing the approaching horse, Gallard turned and faced his military advisor as Walter reigned the horse to a stop five feet from the king.

"Your report?" Gallard asked.

"From all appearances, it is Talbot," Walter reported. "I was not able to get close enough to identify him with one hundred percent certainty and he never looked completely in my direction. He only spent a few minutes on the deck before disappearing into the cabin. However, there was no mistaking Angus. He is definitely on the boat."

"And the sword and shield?" Gallard pushed.

"My lord, I could not say whether they are on the boat or not. Angus did have something he was carrying around that had the size of a shield, but it was completely enshrouded in blankets."

"Talbot would never allow himself to be separated from either one," Gallard mused, gazing out toward the lake and spotting the boat as it slowly came into view from around the back of the castle. "But would he make his escape so obvious?"

"As I said before, desperate times breed desperate measures," Walter responded. "He knows that by crossing the lake he could easily gain a half-day head start on us if not more. He does not have an army to tow behind him, therefore he could move much faster than we could."

"Unless we leave the army behind us," Gallard countered. "We would not need them since Talbot would be so weakly protected. We could take a hundred men and give chase and leave the main body of the army here to continue securing the castle."

"Our men and horses are exhausted, your majesty," Walter argued. "We have been pushing them hard for the past several months and most especially over the past few days. We would have to push them to the brink of breaking in order to catch up to Talbot."

"Then push them!" Gallard replied sternly. "Do you think such prizes come without sacrifice, without pushing man and beast to their breaking points and beyond? We are pursuing the greatest prize this world has ever known. No sacrifice is too large. We will spill whatever blood is necessary and leave man and beast dead on the trail behind us if that is what our quest requires. Go choose one hundred of our best men. Have them fully equipped and sup-plied for the ride. We will leave within the half-hour. Tell your commanders to continue the assault on the castle and secure it as soon as possible. Kill anyone who offers resistance but leave the rest alive. There may be much information yet to be gleaned from the commoners."

"Yes, your majesty," Walter replied, and turned to carry out his orders.

"He has been gone a little longer than my comfort level will tolerate," Lawrence said as he stared down the darkened tunnel. "That cannot bode very well for us."

"I shudder to think that we may have to turn around and head back to the castle," Marie replied.

"It is not the thought of returning to the castle that makes me shudder," Heather said, "it is standing in this freezing water surrounded by cold stone and earth that makes me shudder. I hope we do not have to stay here much longer."

"We may not have to," Lawrence said, looking down the tunnel. "I believe I see the glow of a torch."

The glow grew brighter as Andrew sloshed his way through the water toward his comrades. It took a full two minutes from the time Lawrence first saw the light of the torch until Andrew stood by their sides. His clothing was saturated from just above his waist to his feet.

"There is good news and there is bad news," he informed the others as they patiently waited for his report. "The maximum depth of the water is up to my waist. Other than the children, nobody should have any difficulty wading through it. That is the good news. The bad news is twofold. First, the maximum depth of the water extends for well over a hundred yards. Considering that wading through water, especially water up to your waist, can be rather difficult, it will present a formidable challenge for many of the women and children. The water is quite cold, as you already know, and spending that much time in water that cold will sap a lot of warmth from our bodies. There will be many people in danger of losing their strength and not being able to continue.

"The second part of the bad news is that there is a partial cave-in of the tunnel. It is just beyond the end of the standing water. The tunnel is partially blocked although not enough to keep us from continuing past it. What concerns me is the strength of the ceiling. With this many people passing by it and having to climb over some rocks and earth, there is no doubt that the effects of our passing will be felt by the ceiling. If it is as weak as it appears, it may not take much to cause another cave-in or even a complete collapse of the ceiling."

"Is there any way of reinforcing it?" Donald asked.

"If we had tools and timber I would say yes," Andrew replied. "However, we have neither. We certainly do not have time to return to the castle and search for the items we would need."

"What you are saying is that we will have to take our chances," Marie stated.

"I see no other option unless someone is willing to offer an alternative," Andrew answered. His companions remained silent. Andrew turned to Ian.

"Master Physician, what do you know about the effects of extended exposure to cold water?" he asked.

"It is quite elementary," Ian answered, "though the extent and severity of effects depend on just how cold the water is. The exposed person will commence shivering within a brief time of entering the water. The colder the water is, the more violent and uncontrollable the shivering will become. The person's blood will slowly cease flowing to the body's extremities as it concentrates on keeping the heart and other organs warm. First, fingers and toes will go numb. Then, entire arms and legs will lose feeling. Soon the person will cease shivering as his body temperature drops and he will begin to feel warm. He will slowly become very tired and eventually lose consciousness entirely. At that point it would be exceedingly difficult for the person to be kept alive."

"Let us hope the water is not cold enough to affect anyone that severely," Marie said worriedly.

"It is nothing we have any control over," Andrew stated matter-of-factly. "Therefore, we can only press ahead and do our best to overcome these obstacles. We should not waste any more time. The people are already chilled as it is. Pass the word down the line that we are ready to continue. Ian, you should stay here and inform the people of what they will be encountering farther down the tunnel and how they might be able to prepare themselves for it. Tell them how the water will affect them and that no matter how tired or cold they feel they must forge on. They will have to help each other. As you bring up the rear of the line you will be able to help anyone who falters."

"Understood," Ian said, and he moved to the side of the tunnel.

"Steven, the water will come close to your shoulders though it will not be deep enough to cover your head. If you need assistance, do not be afraid to ask for it. Understand?" Andrew asked.

"I understand," Steven replied. "I will be okay."

"Very well," Andrew said, "here we go."

Andrew turned and retraced his earlier steps down the tunnel and into the water. Andrew had not described to the others just how fast the water level rose, and sooner than they had expected the water was well over their knees. In another ten yards the water level approached their waists. In another twenty it was up past Andrew's waste. It was well over the waists of Marie and Heather and true to Andrew's word, Steven found the water nearly shoulder deep. It did not take long for Heather and Marie to start shivering a bit and Steven soon followed. Their progress slowed significantly as they struggled to walk through the bracing water and the extra exertion made their hearts speed up to pump the much-needed blood to their legs. Not a person spoke a word as they turned their full attention to the otherwise simple task of walking. After what seemed like an hour of walking but in reality, was less than ten minutes, the water level finally began to decrease. Soon, it dropped beneath their waists. After another five minutes of walking the water was down to their ankles. Their bodies had become accustomed to the chill of the water and being exposed once again to the cool air in the tunnel made them start to shiver.

"The partial collapse is just ahead," Andrew informed the others as he continued to lead them down the tunnel. After walking another thirty yards the deteriorated section of the tunnel came into view. Several large pieces of ancient timber lay broken and splintered on the tunnel's floor, most of them nearly covered by rock and dirt. The travelers would have to gently scurry over a three-foot-high pile of rubble while avoiding touching the walls or disturbing the debris. Any sudden moves, loud noises, or upsetting of the rocks and timbers could easily cause a catastrophe.

"We must proceed very carefully here," Andrew informed his followers. "I know everyone is anxious to taste fresh air and feel the sun on their faces, but unnecessary haste will spell ruin for many. Donald, once you are through, you will wait and assist the others in their passage. Ensure that they exercise great caution and pay close attention to the children, especially the boys. I fear the boys will be too aggressive by their young nature and youthful confidence. Make sure they proceed slowly."

"Aye," Donald replied. "I will see you on the other side."

Andrew slowly approached the ominous obstacle. He was not impervious to the same fear and apprehension that would grip each person who would soon be following in his footsteps. He lifted the torch and carefully inspected the damaged section of the tunnel from the bottom of the wall to the right, up across the compromised ceiling, and down the other wall. The walls themselves did not look to be anything but solid. The ceiling, however, was anything but solid. The exposed earth and rock looked as though they could come crashing down at any moment. The ceiling was only four feet off the floor, so the taller men would have to bend over significantly in order to make passage. Andrew examined the scattered rock and dirt on the floor of the tunnel. Fortunately, the damaged area was less than ten feet in length. However, the danger it represented made the distance seem much, much longer. Andrew took a deep breath and carefully climbed over the mound of rubble. The footing felt reasonably solid and there was little if any movement of the debris under his feet. As he finally stepped back onto solid ground, Andrew let out the breath he did not know he had been holding.

"Marie, your turn," he announced and after a brief hesitation, the princess commenced her scaling of the rocks. She proved to be quite agile and light-footed and was able to make passage rather quickly. Heather took no time in following and after she had passed, Steven did likewise. Lawrence was next and due to his size, he proceeded with much more caution than the two young women and the boy had displayed. Thankfully, there had been no evidence of any additional weakness in the ceiling. Finally, Donald made his way over the obstacle.

"Well done," Andrew said to the others. "It seems the tunnel should bear up to the passage of the others. Let us hope they exercise adequate caution. Donald, see to it, my brother."

"No worries," Donald replied. "I shall hold up the earth with my own shoulders if it comes to that."

"Let us hope it does not come to that," Andrew replied. "I have seen your scrawny shoulders." With a brotherly smile Andrew turned and continued into the darkness of the tunnel.

Chapter 26

A ndrew felt his strength being sapped away by the long trek through the cool, dank tunnel. The saturated clothes that covered over half of his body weighed him down and required more of a physical effort to walk than what would have otherwise been required. He could only imagine what the people behind him must have been feeling and how many of them would be near exhaustion. However, the struggle for survival often pushed people beyond their self-imposed limits and he could only hope that none would fall behind. Not a word had been spoken in the last twenty minutes between him and those who followed closest. Every ounce of energy was being required to simply put one foot in front of the other. No words were required as they were all thinking and feeling the same things.

The glow of the torch in Andrew's hand was gradually diminishing and this caused him no little concern. If the torches died before they reached the end of the tunnel it could very well mark a dark end to their journey. Without even the faintest bit of light they would not be able to see what lay before them. The tunnel could have caved in, and they would not see it until they literally ran into it. They could come upon another section of the tunnel that was completely flooded. Over the years a void could have opened in the tunnel's floor and without warning he could fall into it. Andrew shuddered at these ominous thoughts. He had to remain positive. They really had no choice but to move forward, even if the torches failed. He quickened his pace, hoping to out-race the dying torches.

Ten minutes later Andrew slowed. The ever-fading glow from his torch seemed to reveal what appeared to be the end of the tunnel not far ahead. He cautiously moved forward, confused at what he saw. He looked to either side of the tunnel but only saw what seemed to loom in front of him. A wall of rock. His heart sank and he wanted to cry out in frustration. It was a dead end. Their escape had come to a fatal end.

"What is it?" Marie asked, moving up to Andrew's side along with Heather and Lawrence. "Why are we stopping?"

"Unless you have the ability to walk through solid rock, I am afraid we have no choice but to stop," Andrew replied, pointing his torch at the wall.

"Oh no," Marie said anxiously, moving toward the wall. "This cannot be."

"The tunnel ends?" Heather asked, her voice trembling not only from the cold air that surrounded her but also from the fear of what appeared before them. "It just ends?"

"It appears so," Andrew replied.

"My father would not have planned an escape through a tunnel from which there was no escape," Marie said, reaching out to touch the wall. "This cannot be the end."

"Perhaps we missed a branch tunnel," Lawrence suggested. "I do not recall seeing a fork in the way but there may have been another way and we simply missed it."

"We did not miss anything," Andrew said, frustrated. "There were no other paths, no other openings. I was watching very carefully for any such thing. This is the only path."

"It cannot be," Lawrence replied. "We had to have missed it. One of us will have to retrace our steps and find the true exit."

"We did not miss anything!" Andrew nearly shouted in response. "I am telling you, this is the only path down here! If you desire to waste your time then please, go ahead and go back through the tunnel. You will find nothing."

"It would appear we have plenty of time on our hands to waste," Lawrence replied sarcastically.

"Wait!" Marie called out, her hands running up and down the wall that blocked the path. "This is not rock!"

"What?" Andrew asked, stepping forward and touching the wall himself.

"It is not rock! It feels more like wood!" Marie replied excitedly. "Look around the edges where it meets the sides of the tunnel. You can see the gaps. This is the end of the tunnel, only something is blocking it!"

"Lawrence, get up here," Andrew commanded, handing his torch to Marie. Lawrence stepped forward and handed his torch to Heather. "Let us see if we can move whatever this obstruction is."

The two men placed their hands on the wooden barricade and pushed. At first, nothing happened.

"Harder!" Andrew instructed and the two men leaned into the wall and pushed with more effort. The obstruction moved several inches then stopped.

"Again!" Andrew said, "Put everything you have into it!" The men pushed with all their might and the obstruction, no longer able to withstand the force behind it, toppled to the ground. Andrew reached behind him and grabbed his torch from Marie. Cautiously, he stepped through the opening in the tunnel and into what appeared to be a small room, no more than twelve feet wide by twelve feet long. The room was void of furniture except for a small wooden table and a cot that looked as though it had not been slept on for many, many years.

"What is it?" Marie called out, eager to exit the gloomy tunnel. "Are we out?"

"It appears we are," Andrew replied. "I do not know where we are, though. This seems to be a small shack. I can see faint traces of daylight around two windows and the front door."

"We must be there!" Marie exclaimed. "This must be the shack on Finley's farm! This is what my father meant." She quickly moved toward the front door. Andrew reached out and grabbed her by the arm, holding her back.

"Not so fast," he said, pulling her away from the door. "We do not know what is out there. Gallard could have half his army waiting outside, expecting your father to walk through that door any moment now."

"What choice do we have?" Marie asked. "How many of these people do you believe can make the journey back through the tunnel? We either face Gallard's army back in the castle or we face it here. I for one am not stepping foot back into that awful tunnel."

"At least let me take a look and see what is out there first," Andrew replied. Reluctantly, Marie agreed and stepped back. With a final look at his friends Andrew reached out and grabbed the handle on the door.

Gently, he lifted the wooden bar until it was free of the latch on the wall that held it in place. He pulled the door open just a crack and peered into the daylight. It took a few moments for his eyes to adjust to the light since he had spent nearly two hours in the darkness of the tunnel with only the small torch proving illumination. His field of vision was limited and all he could see were trees. He opened the door a bit more and still all he saw were trees of the forest. Finally, he opened the door wide enough to allow him to step through it and he did so. He looked left and right and then stepped back into the shack.

"Lawrence, I believe you should go first," he said, nodding to his friend.

"That dangerous, huh?" Lawrence said, stepping forward.

"Trust me, it will be better for you to walk out of here first than me," Andrew replied.

Without another word, Lawrence carefully peaked out the door and then stepped through it. He looked left and right. Something to the right caught his attention. He immediately walked to his right and the others inside the shack waited anxiously. They heard muffled voices and after a few moments Lawrence appeared back in the doorway.

"It is okay," he announced. "Everybody can come out now."

Without hesitation, Marie quickly stepped through the doorway followed by Heather and Steven. Andrew waited until Ian had passed, then walked out himself into the welcomed light and warmth of the late afternoon sun. He was followed by a long procession of villagers, shielding their eyes as they walked out of the shack and toward their freedom. To the right of the shack there were nearly one hundred of Talbot's men armed and ready for battle. Lawrence returned to the leader of the men and spoke briefly. He then walked back to Marie.

"They were here waiting for your father," Lawrence informed her. "However, they were not informed of where they were going to take him. They were only instructed to come here and wait for him. With your father gone I believe they are your men to command."

"My men to command?" Marie asked, unsure of what exactly to do. Lawrence was correct. Since her father was dead, the rule of the kingdom and people now fell upon her shoulders. It was not a responsibility that she had ever truly considered.

"How long have they been waiting?" Andrew asked.

"Two hours," Lawrence replied.

"Have they seen any of Gallard's men?"

"They saw what appeared to be a five-man scouting patrol across the field some time ago," Lawrence replied. "The men did not slow down nor give any indication that they had spotted Talbot's men."

"The people are in much need of a break," Andrew said as he watched the stream of villagers exiting the shack, many of them immediately finding a place to sit or lay on the ground. Though overjoyed at finally being in the open and out of the tunnel, they all had the appearance of being near exhaustion. "I would recommend that you send a couple of Talbot's men on reconnaissance to keep an eye out for Gallard's men. We would not want to be caught off-guard while we catch our breath."

"I will see to it," Lawrence replied, returning to the group of warriors. After a brief conversation with the captain of the men, three riders were dispatched with orders to keep watch for any of Gallard's men that might be approaching the refugees.

"What now?" Marie asked Andrew as they both found a sunny spot on the ground and sat down.

"Truthfully, I am not sure," Andrew replied, looking up into the sunny sky. "We are still in much danger, and we should not tarry long. By now it is almost certain that Gallard's men have breached the castle and found it to be deserted. He would immediately send out more scouting patrols in all directions, searching for your father. I do not know how far away from the castle we are right now, but it is not nearly far enough. These people must be on their way, and soon."

"To where?" Marie asked, looking around the woods at her fellow countrymen. "Where do they go? Their homes are lost, their land over-run. They have nothing but the clothes on their backs."

"They go wherever they can," Andrew replied, "as long as it is far from here. They have the same things that they used to build their lives here: Their inner strength, intelligence, and resolve. I know it is difficult, but they can build new lives in other lands. If they try to return to their own homes, who knows what Gallard might do to them. It is true, he might leave them alone, but I would not bet my life on it. If I were one of them, I would get away as far as I could, as fast as I could. Perhaps one day, many months or years from now, they can return to this place and continue their lives. But I would not bet on it."

"Where are you going?" Marie asked him point-blank.

"I made a promise to the Bergman family that I must keep," he replied. "I do not dare try to look beyond that promise right now."

"Mind if I tag along?" she asked, half-jesting. In truth she did not know where to go or what to do. Her father's kingdom no longer existed. There was nothing, and nobody, to rule over. She felt like an orphan of life.

"I do not know," Andrew replied mischievously. "I guess we could take a vote. I am sure you would get Heather's vote and most likely Ian's. But I am not sure about Lawrence. You do seem to vex him a bit from time to time."

"He is a big kitten, that one," Marie replied with a grin on her face. When it comes to fighting men, he has the heart of a lion. But when it comes to women, he is a kitten. He would not admit it, but I know he looks at me from time to time. Do not worry about Lawrence. His vote would not be in question."

"Then it seems I would be outvoted, and you would be allowed to join us," Andrew responded. "I guess there could be worse things in life to happen to a man."

"You would miss me," Marie replied playfully. "You know it."

"Women," Andrew sighed as he laid back and closed his eyes.

He felt as though he had just closed his eyes when Andrew heard his name shouted with unsettling urgency. He had been napping for nearly thirty minutes and although his mind felt sluggish and his body was a bit slow to respond, Andrew jumped to his feet. Lawrence was rushing over to him.

"A battalion of Gallard's men has been spotted approaching this way!" he reported.

"How many and how far?" Andrew asked.

"Our scout estimated five hundred at least, nearly half on horseback, little more than two miles away. We have perhaps thirty minutes before they get here, if that long."

"Are you certain they are coming for us?" Andrew asked.

"Of that I have no doubt," Lawrence replied. "They are fully armed and with that number of men and horses they are more than a simple scouting patrol."

Barely five minutes earlier, Donald had been the last person to exit the tunnel and he had just sat down to rest when he saw Lawrence and Andrew conversing. There was no mistaking the urgency of their discussion. He wasted no time in joining the two men.

"What is the matter?" he asked, stepping up to Andrew's side.

"I see the tunnel did not collapse on you after all," Andrew said with a sly smile. "This must be your lucky day."

"Gallard's men are approaching," Lawrence replied to Donald. "There are perhaps as many as five hundred if not more."

"How many men do we have here?" Donald asked, looking around.

"There are a hundred men on horse," Lawrence answered. "They are the ones who were expecting Talbot to emerge from the tunnel instead of us."

"How many archers followed us through the tunnel?" Andrew asked.

"I believe there are fifty," Lawrence replied. "There are another two hundred foot-soldiers who came with us as well."

"So, we have perhaps three hundred and fifty men to challenge five hundred of Gallard's men, all of whom are much better trained than Talbot's men," Andrew mused. "Those are not odds I care for."

"What can we do?" Lawrence asked desperately.

"We can fight," Andrew replied without pause. "We must fight. We live or die, here and now. We cannot outrun horses and there is no place to hide hundreds of unarmed men, women and children."

"What is your plan?" Donald asked. "You were always the better one at strategy."

"We need to draw Gallard's men into the forest, take away their advantage of being on horseback, and reduce their advantage in numbers," Andrew replied. "We should position ourselves to force the primary engagement to take place here, just in front of us. Our foot soldiers will be positioned just outside the tree line. I want them to be seen by Gallard's men. Ten yards into the forest, hidden behind trees as best they can, will be the archers. Fifty yards into the forest, the hundred horsemen will be positioned, half a hundred yards to the left and half a hundred yards to the right. Behind them will be stationed all able-bodied men from the commoners that escaped with us."

"And then?" Lawrence asked.

"When Gallard's men are within fifty yards of the forest, our men will turn as though to flee in fear. Gallard's men cannot know at this point in time that we have an extra two hundred men from the castle, nor can they know we have the archers, so they will be focused on the first group of men they see and will not consider there to be others. As Gallard's men approach the edge of the forest, intent on chasing down and slaughtering Talbot's men, the archers will commence firing. They should be able to release three volleys each before the enemy is upon them. That should not only reduce the enemy's number by several dozen it should slow them down as well. Twenty yards into the forest those first hundred men will stop and grab the ten-foot-long spears they are about to cut for themselves. Gallard's men will shake off the archers' attack and continue rushing headlong into the forest. As they penetrate the forest, their eyes will take a few moments to completely adjust from the bright afternoon sun, which will be in their eyes upon their approach, to the shadows of the forest. Our men will lift the spears and Gallard's men will impale themselves and their horses on the pikes, slowing if not stopping their mad onslaught. At the same time, our horsemen will rush in from both sides and engage the unsuspecting enemy. Then, the common men will attack with spears of their own."

"It sounds so simple," Donald said sarcastically. "Gallard's men should surrender right now and save their own lives."

"It will be anything but simple," Andrew replied. "In truth I do not expect many of us to survive this clash. It will be violent, and it will be bloody. We can only hope that Providence is on our side today and we somehow are able to stand against this vicious, brutal tide."

"I will get the men busy cutting the spears and get them in position," Lawrence said as he turned and rushed away.

Marie and Heather had been standing off to the side, listening to the conversation but not interfering. Now they approached Andrew and Donald.

"What can we do?" Marie asked. "Can we help?"

"You can retreat to the tunnel," Andrew responded. "We will replace the barricade and hopefully your presence will not be discovered. After the battle is over you should be able to make your escape."

"I will NOT step foot into that tunnel ever again!" Marie stated quite firmly.

"This is no time to exercise your stubborn streak!" Andrew replied, just as firmly. "If you stay out here your life will be forfeit. It is that simple. If you hide, you will have a chance to live."

"Live for what?" Marie countered. "What do I have to live for? My father is dead, I have no family, and I have no home! I will not cower in a dark corner, waiting for death to find me. I will fight with you, behind you, or in front of you, but I will fight! If my life is taken from me here, today, I will have no regrets. If I hide like a frightened child and survive this day while you and everyone else here dies, I will regret it for the rest of my life. I will not live like that."

Andrew could see that the argument was futile. There was no way he could force Marie and Heather to hide in the tunnel. The best he could do would be to get them as far away from the fighting as possible.

"Take the women and children and lead them as far from here as you can," he finally said, conceding the argument. "Their men and older boys will be fighting for their lives, and they will need a strong leader. They already look up to you. They will follow you. Do this, and perhaps you will be able to save their lives."

Marie paused for a moment, considering Andrew's instructions. She did not wish to run away, and she found herself reluctant to leave his side. They had been through much together over the past several months and a bond had formed between them. She was not sure exactly what her feelings were for him but the thought of turning her back on him, to leave him here to fight and die, was almost more than she could bear. He was right, though, and she knew it. She had to lead the people away. It was their only chance.

"Very well," she finally said, though with no little disappointment. She looked into his eyes more deeply than ever before and felt herself drawn to him in a way she had not previously experienced. She wanted to embrace him, and even kiss him, but instead she simply turned and headed toward the hundreds of refugees waiting for someone to tell them what to do. Heather did not pause, though. She stepped forward and embraced him tightly as tears fell from her eyes. She did not want to consider that this might be the last time she would ever see him, but the reality was not to be ignored. Andrew put his arms around her and returned the embrace. After a few moments Heather released him and took a step back, looking into his captivating eyes. No words were necessary. He gave her a knowing smile and with a reluctant smile of her own, Heather turned and followed Marie.

"And now for us?" Donald asked, looking after the women.

"If you wish to embrace me you will have to bathe first," Andrew jested. "You are too rank to hold that close even though you are my brother."

"As though you smell like a field of flowers yourself," Donald replied. "I meant, now that you have given directions to everyone else, what are you and I to do?"

"It would be a good time to pray," Andrew replied, not joking the least bit. The three men knelt on the ground and Andrew commenced with a prayer.

"Heavenly Father, we come before you, helpless, tired, and full of fear at those who now approach us. You have brought us to this place and time by design, as part of your plan for our lives and this kingdom. We do not know what lays before us. You have instructed us to put on the armor of God to fight the spiritual battles that confront us daily, but what we face is more than a spiritual battle. We have neither the skills nor weaponry nor numbers to fight off those who come to slaughter us. Our survival is dependent on you. We pray that it would please you to blind and confuse our enemy, to give us strength beyond that which we ever knew we could possess, in order that the enemy may be defeated, and the people saved. If it is pleasing to you to bring us into your presence this very day, then we pray that you will forgive us our sins and cleanse us from unrighteousness, that we may be presented to you as good and faithful servants. We pray this in the name of your Son, our Lord and Savior, Jesus Christ, amen."

"Amen," Donald and Lawrence repeated.

Chapter 27

The drumming of the horses' hooves vibrated the ground as Gallard's garrison approached the forest. When they were one hundred yards out, they stopped. Various commands were shouted to the ranks and a front line began forming. Nearly two hundred horsemen came together and stretched out in a line three hundred yards long. Behind them the infantry formed into two companies of a hundred and fifty men each. Talbot's men, as directed by Andrew, were positioned nearly thirty yards outside of the tree line. As always seems to be the case, an uncanny silence engulfed what was soon to be a bloody battlefield. There was no movement on either side. This was the time reserved for negotiations or surrender, when either side could send an envoy to meet the other side and perhaps avert a war. However, there were to be no negotiations on this day. There was to be no surrender. This was a battle that would be waged until one side was thoroughly destroyed. No quarter would be given this day.

When it was obvious that there was to be no talks, the commander of Gallard's forces gave the order and a trumpet sounded. Immediately the two hundred horsemen commenced their attack. Slowly at first but with increasing speed, the horses made their way across the field toward Talbot's men. Talbot's men held their ground until the approaching enemy was less than fifty yards away. Then, all at once, they turned and fled into the forest. Emboldened, the horsemen urged their steeds to a full gallop, intent on crashing into the forest and running down the fleeing cowards. However, instead of crashing into the forest, they crashed into a hail of arrows when they were hardly thirty yards from the tree line. Men and horses tumbled to the ground, but the charge continued. Gallard's infantry raced across the field behind the cavalry, their battle cries echoing across the valley. The horses and riders plunged into the forest only to be met by the death-dealing spears wielded by the fallaciously retreating foot soldiers. Caught by surprise, dozens and dozens of Gallard's men were thrown to the ground. Without hesitation Talbot's men vaulted upon the stunned horsemen and the ground was soon littered with wounded and lifeless bodies.

As Gallard's infantry followed the cavalry into the forest, Talbot's horsemen converged from both sides, charging into the throng of men and mowing down as many as they could before their progress was stopped and they were yanked from their horses. Still, they continued to fight bravely and furiously.

Despite the relative success of Andrew's plan, his forces were still vastly outnumbered, and Gallard's men pushed farther into the woods. The men of the village moved in and joined the battle, grabbing swords from the hands of the dead wherever they could. The archers continued using their bows and arrows as best they could but they, too, soon scavenged swords and joined the hand-to-hand battle. Andrew and Donald, with a final look and nod that only brothers can share, bolted forward and did what they were trained to do.

The battle seemed to rage for longer than either brother had ever known. No sooner would they dispatch with one foe than one or two more would step forward. Both brothers fought with a sword in each hand, one being used mainly to parry attacks and the other to rain massive, deathly blows upon the enemy. There was no way of telling how the battle was going, no time to pause and ascertain if their side was winning or losing. The only thing they could do was keep fighting, to keep pushing forward. The bodies were piling up everywhere and it was getting difficult to move around without tripping on an arm or leg, some still attached to their owners, some not. For the briefest of moments, Andrew found himself without an opponent confronting him. He was about to consider the oddity of the situation when his instincts cried out and he whirled around. Less than ten yards away a horse and rider were bearing down upon him at full speed. The rider had a sword raised high and a devilish grin on his face. There was no time to react. Andrew froze, awaiting the deathblow that was a heartbeat away. In less than a heartbeat, however, he felt someone crash into his side and propel him out of death's grasp. Out of control, Andrew collided into a tree. His breath was knocked out of him, and he was suddenly engulfed by an overwhelming since of déjà vu. He quickly regained his senses and took stock of the situation.

The horse and rider had galloped on nearly twenty yards before stopping and turning. On the ground, about ten feet from him, Andrew saw Donald lying face down. He could already see a small trail of blood seeping along the ground from underneath his brother and his worst fear began to seep into his heart. The horseman had begun to charge again, and this time Andrew was prepared. He positioned himself to let the horse pass him on his right side. However, at the very last moment, Andrew stepped to the right and swung his sword at the front legs of the charging beast. With a scream of pain, the horse crashed to the ground and the rider was thrown twenty feet through the air. His body glanced off a tree and he twisted around completely twice before slamming into the ground. Andrew wasted no time. He rushed over to the stunned man who lay on his back, trying to get his bearings. Instinctively, the man reached for the sword that lay on the ground to his right. Without pausing Andrew plunged his sword into the man's heart. He did not feel the sense of satisfaction he had yearned for years ago when he had desired to avenge what he thought was his brother's death. There was no relief, no sense of fulfillment. There was only the vexation of spirit that always followed taking a man's life. Andrew removed the sword and dashed back to his fallen brother.

He slowly and gently turned Donald onto his back. His brother was not dead but the brutal gash in his chest would soon rob him of his life. A wave of emotions crashed upon Andrew. There was grief, there was sorrow, there was regret, but there was mostly rage. He was enraged that his brother lay on the ground with his life flowing away when it should have been him. He was enraged that he had not better protected his brother. He was enraged at the events of his life that had led to this very moment. Andrew shouted his rage to the forest, unable to contain his emotions. He needed an outlet. He needed to release that which consumed him. He looked around his surroundings with fire in his eyes. One of Gallard's men approached him, his sword held high, poised to strike Andrew a fatal blow. Andrew leaped to his feet with inhuman quickness. Before the attacker could react, Andrew's own sword struck the man a fatal blow. Suddenly there was another man charging toward him. And another. And another. Without thinking, acting on pure instincts and reflexes, Andrew fought like a caged wildcat. His arms never quit moving as they swept from side to side, swords in both hands, cutting down opponents in single blows. The men kept coming and he kept fighting. Time stood still. The adrenaline surging through his veins gave him a strength which he had never experienced, and he did not tire. At some point, after nearly twenty bodies had piled up around him, some part of Andrew's brain recognized that he was alone and nobody else stood before him. Still fully energized, Andrew looked around, almost hoping there was another foe to battle. But there was none. He could see other men fighting but they were well-away from him. He finally began to calm down a bit and when he was certain there was no immediate threat, he returned to his brother's side. Andrew knelt to the ground and gently placed a hand on Donald's cheek. Streaks of blood gave what little color there was to Donald's face. His pale skin told of a life near its end. Slowly, Donald opened his eyes.

"As it seemed you had things in hand, I thought I would lie

down and rest a bit," Donald said weakly. "I believe the trek through the tunnel has weakened me more than I suspected."

"Yes, you should rest now," Andrew replied, trying his best to smile.

"The battle?" Donald asked, his eyes trying to look around to see what was happening.

"Do not worry," Andrew answered, "the battle is won."

"Good," Donald said, and a short coughing spell racked his body. His eyes started to droop closed, and Andrew reached down and grabbed Donald's limp hand.

"Look at me," Andrew commanded, his eyes beginning to tear up. "Stay with me, brother. It is not your time. It is not your time," he whispered pleadingly.

"I am afraid it is," Donald replied, his voice getting weaker. Every breath was becoming an almost impossible effort. "It does not hurt, though. I do not feel any pain."

"But I do," Andrew countered as a tear rolled off his cheek.

"No greater love hath a man than he lay down his life for another, right?" Donald said, doing his best to smile at his brother. "You are my brother. I would give my life a hundred times for yours."

"As would I," Andrew replied, gripping Donald's hand even tighter.

"I never told you this," Donald said, his voice now barely above a whisper. "When I was a boy, I begged my mother for a brother. I wanted a brother so we could play, and fight, and go on grand adventures. Year after year she would only say 'maybe.'" Another coughing spasm racked Donald's body and a thin film of blood seeped out of the corner of his mouth. "But then one day my father brought you to our home and I suddenly had the brother I had always wanted. And you have been more of a brother than any brother I could have imagined."

"And you have been more of a brother than any brother of my own flesh could have been," Andrew replied, the tears now flowing down his face and onto Donald's chest.

"My wife," Donald whispered, and Andrew moved closer so he could hear the words. "My wife," he repeated, unable to finish his thought.

"I shall tell her you fought bravely and that you saved many lives," Andrew promised.

"My family," Donald struggled. He reached up and grabbed Andrew's arm with strength that defied his dying body. "My son! Alexander will be in danger! If Gallard … if Gallard …" His breath began to fail him.

"I shall protect your family, and your son, as if they were my own," Andrew assured his brother. "They are my family."

"I fear there shall be no resurrection for me this time," Donald said, the life fading from his eyes.

"There will be," Andrew replied earnestly. "There will be the final resurrection. I will see you then, my brother. I will see you then."

"… will see you then," Donald managed as his last breath left his body.

Andrew closed his eyes and wept. He had thought he had lost his brother once before and the pain at the time was immense. But it was nothing compared to the pain and grief he felt now. Having lost a loved-one once was bad enough. Having lost that loved one a second time was excruciating. He finally opened his eyes. Gently, Andrew reached out and pulled Donald's eyelids completely closed.

"Now ends your journey," he said, brushing the sweat-encrusted hair from Donald's face. "Goodbye, my brother. May your soul rest peacefully in the arms of the Lord."

Chapter 28

The journey to meet Annette Bergman had become a funeral procession. Andrew led the way on a horse that had belonged to one of Talbot's men. Strapped to another horse behind him, led by a rope Andrew held tightly in his grasp, was Donald's body. Following him were Lawrence, Marie, Heather, Steven and Ian. The other refugees had dispersed in all different directions, eager to flee the bloodshed and start lives elsewhere until hopefully, someday, they could return to their homes. Not a word had been spoken since the group had left the war-torn forest.

Weary and worn, both emotionally and physically, Andrew fought to remain awake during the thirty-minute journey to the camouflaged cave. The sorrow he felt was much greater than that which he had felt nearly six years ago when he thought Donald had been killed. So much had happened since then and they had been through so much over the past several days. He had been overjoyed at being with his brother once again. Although he had formed some exceedingly close relationships since his arrival in Talbot's realm, nothing could compare to the bond between brothers. He had experienced the feeling of family once again. But now that feeling was gone. He felt as though a part of himself had been violently ripped away and he could never get it back.

The boulder-strewn valley finally came into view. It was easy to tell where the obscure cave entrance was as a horse and cart were stationed outside of it. Andrew guided the group to their destination, and they all dismounted. Without a word he entered the cave and within a minute Mrs. Bergman came running out. With a shout of joy, she rushed over to her children and embraced them as only a mother could. Tears rolled down her cheeks and she kissed both Heather and Steven repeatedly on the cheeks. Neither child could hold back tears of their own and the family reunion touched all who witnessed it. When Andrew failed to emerge from the cave, Marie silently walked over and, with a little residual trepidation, entered the darkness.

The far end of the chamber had a very faint glow thanks to the torches that Mrs. Bergman had lit. Marie passed by the two horses Andrew and Donald had left while they carried had executed their rescue plan. Mrs. Bergman had provided some grain and water for the horses which twitched and snorted as Marie passed them. She slowly made her way to the far end of the chamber. As she walked along, she gazed at the recessed cavities and the ages-old cadavers that occupied them. It was a rather morbid scene and gave her more of a chill than the coolness of the rock and earth that surrounded her. Finally, she reached the end of the corridor that opened into a large room. She could see more cavities cut into the walls of the room and more ancient bodies filling them. In the middle of the room two caskets sat atop a pedestal. Andrew stood next to the pedestal, facing away from her, both of his hands set on one of the caskets as though he were propping himself up. His head hung low, and he did not look up as she walked in. For the first time she could remember, she felt completely awkward in Andrew's presence. She did not know what to say or if she should even say anything when it was so obvious that he was in much pain. However, she felt they had a special friendship, a bond that required her to comfort him as best she could.

"Andrew?" she asked tentatively. He did not look up or acknowledge her presence right away. "Andrew, are you alright?"

It took another fifteen seconds before Andrew stirred and lifted his head. He did not turn to face her.

"Am I alright?" he said, repeating her question rhetorically. "No, I am not all right. Several days ago, I reached the point of total exhaustion and I do not know what has kept me on my feet since then. Nearly six years ago my life took a drastic, unexpected turn due to this wretched sword and now I feel as though those years have been completely wasted. Nearly six years ago I was forced to flee the only place I had ever called home. Today I have been forced to flee a place I was hoping would become home. I have lost my brother for the second time. And for what? What have I accomplished?"

"You have prevented great evil from overtaking the land," Marie replied encouragingly. "If it were not for you, Gallard would have obtained the sword many years ago and he would likely have the shield even as we speak. Who knows if he has found or is on the verge of finding the other three pieces of the DuFay Armor? He would be planning his conquest of every land from where the sun rises to where it sets. His would have been a reign of tyranny and the people and land would have suffered. What have you accomplished? Can you not see it for yourself?"

"There will always be tyrants and dictators," Andrew countered. "The future will see many Gallards and Talbots, men bent on obtaining and abusing power. I have not stopped anything. I have only delayed it."

"And the future will see many Andrew MacLeans as well, people who will stand up to the dictators and tyrants," Marie argued.

"If it were not for me, Donald would still be alive and your father would still be alive," Andrew said solemnly.

"You cannot know that Andrew," Marie countered. "You cannot know what tomorrow would have held for them had they lived beyond today. We all die, Andrew. Some of us will die today, some of us will die tomorrow. We cannot control that. It was my father's time to die, and it was your brother's time to die. We can only move on and continue to live our lives as best we can. Kingdoms and nations rise and fall. They have throughout history. It was my father's kingdom's time to die. It is fate. We do not make fate, we only experience it."

"For nearly six years, my life has been filled with a singular purpose, with a singular goal," Andrew said. "It consumed me as nothing ever has. All other thoughts, all other purposes, were set aside. Now that purpose, that goal, no longer exists. I feel lost."

"Then form a new purpose, a new goal," Marie urged. "Your journey did not define your life, it simply was a part of your life. That part is over and now you will move on to another part of your life. You have friends with you who care deeply for you. Lawrence is practically a brother to you. I have seen the two of you together many, many times and it is obvious you share a deep friendship. If that were not enough, you have a beautiful, sweet young lady standing just outside this cave who would not hesitate to spend the rest of her life with you if you only asked her. That could be your future, Andrew, you only have to choose it."

"I am no longer sure what future I desire," Andrew replied. "I do know that as long as I possess this sword, I will be a target of Gallard and will always have to have eyes in the back of my head. Yet I cannot simply toss the sword aside. It has become part of me."

"It is an emotional attachment, nothing more," Marie argued. "You must part with the sword if you are ever to have any peace in your heart and soul. You must leave it behind if you are to ever move ahead."

"I know," Andrew replied, "I know."

"I will leave you to your thoughts," Marie said as she turned to leave. "But remember this: The worth of your life is not determined by what you do for yourself. It is determined by what you do for others. Today, a chapter of your life has ended. Tomorrow, a new one starts. The choice is yours as to whether you wish to share it with your friends or continue with a lonely, purposeless life. Choose wisely." She paused for a moment, looking for a reaction from Andrew, but saw none. She left the troubled man alone, her heart going out to him.

"What is taking him so long?" Lawrence asked as Marie exited the cave. "I would feel much better if we were to get away from here as soon as possible."

"He has much to consider," Marie answered. "It is tough when an unwilling hero finds his task completed."

"Mrs. Bergman, are you ready to leave?" Lawrence asked.

"Everything is packed and ready to go," she acknowledged. "All we need is for someone to say the word."

Andrew finally appeared in the cave's entrance, leading Annon and the other horse. The last rays of the day had all but disappeared below the horizon as he stared out at his friends.

"What now, Andrew?" Lawrence asked. "Where shall we go?"

"I have one task left to complete," Andrew said as he walked over to the horse bearing his brother's body. "I must take my brother home so he can receive a proper family burial. I owe him that much, if not more."

"Andrew, your brother was a descendant of Reginald DuFay, the rightful heir to his kingdom," Marie offered. "What better place to bury him than with his ancestors?"

"You believe I should bury him here and not with his father and his father's father?" Andrew replied.

"These ARE his fathers," Marie countered. "This is where he belongs. I am sure his wife and family would understand."

Andrew thought deeply on the dilemma. The trek back to his homeland would be quite long and difficult, especially with a body in tow. Marie was right, this is where Donald should be laid to rest.

"We will bury him here," Andrew conceded, "in this very cavern where so many of his predecessors found their final resting places. There is an empty cavity near the rear of the tomb, as though it awaits the last of the DuFay line. We shall lay him there."

With little conversation, Donald's body was gently removed from the horse and carried into the cavern. With the others standing by, Andrew delicately placed his brother's body into the empty cavity.

"His soul rests in your arms, Heavenly Father," Andrew said. "We are reminded that one day we all shall pass from this earth. I pray that we all shall rest in your arms and be in your glory for all eternity. Guide us along the path of righteousness while we remain on this earth. Protect us from the evil one."

The group solemnly exited the dark tomb and entered the fading light of the day.

"There is one more thing I must do," Andrew said. "I must return to Donald's family and inform them of his passing. They must be told of who he was and that for which he died fighting. I cannot leave them not knowing. And I must see to their safety. I fear Gallard may seek revenge for Donald's treason."

"What about us?" Heather asked anxiously. "You promised to help us find a new home, a place where we could start our lives anew."

"Circumstances have changed," Andrew replied, feeling somewhat chastised. "I have to do this."

"Then let us come with you," Heather suggested quickly, fearing that she was going to lose him.

"That will not be possible," Andrew replied dourly. "It is certain that once Gallard realizes that Talbot is dead, he will renew his search for me and the sword. Whoever is with me will face much danger and I will not allow that to happen. I will not allow someone else I love, someone else I care for, to die on my account."

"But those who love you, who care for you, would most readily bear that burden if it meant lightening your burden," Heather argued. "Are we not to bear each other's burdens?"

"Not to the point of death," Andrew responded. "I will not allow that to happen."

"So, you find it that easy to walk away from us, to abandon us?" Heather asked, her heart dropping with every beat.

"It is the most difficult thing I have ever had to do," Andrew countered.

"It does not have to be like this, Andrew," Lawrence said. "You do not have to go off alone once again. We all have faced death. We are not afraid of Gallard."

"I appreciate your concern and will always appreciate your friendship, but this is something I must do," Andrew replied.

"No," Marie said sternly, stepping forward to face Andrew, shaking her head. "No."

"What do you mean, 'no'?" Andrew asked, confused.

"I mean that we will not allow you to turn into a nomad and roam aimlessly from country to country for five more years, or ten years, or even one year," Marie replied firmly. "That part of your life ended when you came to my father's land. It is time you had a new life, the kind of life you have preached to others time and time again. You said earlier that there will always be tyrants and dictators and I told you that there will always be men to stand up to them. Well, I have news for you. The type of man who stands up to tyrants does not grow on trees. He grows in homes headed by strong men and women. Those are your own words spoken over half a year ago. Your battle with tyrants is over. It is time you trained boys to become men who can face and defeat the tyrants in their days. Or do you not hold to your own words?"

Andrew looked sheepishly at Marie. He knew that she was right. He was using the sword and Gallard as excuses to avoid more responsibility. What did he fear so greatly that he would rather face more years of being alone and being chased by Gallard? He had professed many times to want nothing more than to settle down and have a family and now that the opportunity was presented to him, he hesitated. Were the responsibilities of being a father and a husband so intimidating that he would rather spend the rest of his life alone, wandering the world, running from the past?

"I stand with Marie," Heather said, stepping up to her friend's side. "We will not allow you to take another step alone. Where you go, we go."

"You cannot run faster than me," Steven said, stepping forward as well. "Besides, you promised to teach me how to fight with a sword and I will hold you to that promise."

"I am afraid you are outnumbered, Andrew MacLean," Mrs. Bergman said as she, too, stepped forward.

"It seems your friends are full of wisdom," Ian said, who up to this point had remained out of the conversation. "You should heed their words. They are very stubborn if you have not learned that in your time with us."

"I have never had a brother," Lawrence said, "until you came along. You lost one brother today. I will not allow you to lose another."

A wave of emotions crashed over Andrew. Even as he was mourning the death of his brother, love as he had never known was being showered upon him. In an instant his sorrow began to turn to joy. He did not feel worthy of the affection of those in front of him, the people who were quickly becoming as close as any family member he ever had. He was humbled deeply, and his eyes became misty.

"Marie," Andrew said finally, "what about your kingdom? Now that your father is gone it is yours. Do you not wish to return someday to claim that which is yours?"

"My father's kingdom is gone, Andrew," she replied. "Even if Gallard were to withdraw tomorrow, the people are gone. There would be nobody to rule. And in truth it is not a responsibility that I care to be burdened with. My life has become common, and I bear no regret."

"What is this?" Lawrence gasped in jest. "Marie Talbot is common? Does that mean you will get your hands dirty? Does that mean you will have to learn how to cook?"

"Among other things," she replied. "Perhaps even raise a

family if I can find a man worthy of my affection," she added slyly.

"Good luck with THAT," Lawrence replied rolling his eyes.

"Oh, I do not know," Marie responded with a mischievous grin, "one may be closer than you think."

Lawrence made as if to scan their surroundings, then replied jovially, "My eyesight must not be what it once was." He turned to Andrew. "What shall our heading be, captain?"

"As it seems I have no choice in the matter," Andrew replied, "we will head north, to my former homeland."

"Then let us waste no more time here," Lawrence said as he swung up on his horse. Marie smiled and mounted her horse. Heather joined her mother in their wagon, and Steven and Ian hoisted themselves onto their mounts.

Andrew turned and looked at his friends in the pale early-evening light. A man was fortunate to have one good family. This would be his third. He nudged his horse in the side and whispered in its ear.

"Home, Annon."

Chapter 29

He walked alone through the halls and rooms of the abandoned castle. It had been over two days since his onslaught had ended. He had been greatly perplexed to learn that not a soul had been found when the troops had finally breached the gate and stormed the castle. It was as if the hundreds of people who had been trapped within the walls had simply vanished. Other than the people who had boarded the royal barge, not a single person had been spotted leaving the castle. Most of the rooms were in disarray, indicating that they had been full at one time, and that the occupants must have left in haste. But to where was the question. He would unravel the mystery, of that he was confident. He was admiring the works of art lining the halls and hanging from the stone walls when one of his captains approached him.

"My lord, you will want to see this," he informed the king. "Earlier this afternoon we discovered several bodies in one of the rooms on a lower level. We left the room as it was found, waiting for your arrival."

"Very well," Gallard replied, giving a final glance at a beautiful tapestry. "Show me."

It had taken but a day for Gallard and his men to catch up to Talbot's royal barge. They had found it abandoned on a rocky section of the lake's shore many miles south of the castle. The barge was devoid of any contents, save two surprising items. On the deck they had found a royal robe along with a dress fit for the daughter of a king. The realization of the hoax was immediate. Talbot had used decoys to lure Gallard away and Gallard had taken the bait hook, line and sinker. He had become so furious that he was within a heartbeat of executing his military advisor, but at the last second his wits prevailed. The ride back to the castle had been long, silent and exhausting. Gallard was just planning to find a room in which he could catch up on some much-needed sleep when his captain had approached him. Hopefully, whatever his captain had found would justify the delay in his rest.

They traveled down a couple of staircases and hallways before the captain paused in front of a door that had been broken down. The smell of death was not quite as pungent as Gallard had expected. The coolness of the subterranean room had slowed the decomposition process. He stepped into the death chamber and surveyed it. He immediately recognized the dead body of his spy, Martin. Gallard considered it to be no great loss and gave Martin's cohorts hardly more than a passing glance.

"It appears that several died during a fight," the captain said, looking down at the bodies. "These over here apparently survived the fight and were tied up. Unfortunately, their injuries and lack of food and water must have proven too much for them and they died as well. But there is one body over here that is different than the others. The clothes are much, much different and he is separated from the other bodies. He was covered with this." The soldier handed Gallard an exceptionally fine robe, a robe fit for a king. Gallard took the robe and looked at it closely. He then bent down and looked at the man it had covered. There was no doubt as to the man's identity. Gallard at once recognized the face of Richard Talbot and with that recognition came a flood of questions. What had happened in this room? Obviously there had been a great fight but were Martin and his men not able to kill anyone other than the king? Such a thing was difficult to believe. And where did those who did the killing go? The room had been locked from the inside. Was it possible that one of the dead men had locked the door before his life had ended? What would the purpose have been?

"My lord, over here," another man called out, standing by a large wall map.

Gallard remained bent over the corpse of Talbot for several more seconds, his mind trying to picture exactly what had earlier transpired in that room before he stood and approached the officer who had called to him. Without a word the officer pulled the map down and revealed the entrance to the secret tunnel.

"Ah, the mystery is solved," Gallard said as he peered into the blackness. "At least we now know where the people went. Have you sent anyone into the tunnel?"

"Yes, my lord, we did," the man replied. "Five men. They came back and reported that the tunnel ends in a small shack in the woods, quite some distance from the castle. It is the same place where nearly five hundred of our men were killed in battle the day we took the castle. Only a handful, perhaps thirty, survived the slaughter. Nearly two hundred of the enemy fighters were slain as well."

"I take it that I would be foolishly optimistic to hope that one of the bodies belonged to Andrew MacLean," Gallard mused.

"I am afraid that there was no sign of either MacLean," the man replied.

"Were there any tracks leading away from the battle scene?" Gallard asked.

"Yes, my lord, there were. Hundreds as a matter of fact leading in all different directions."

"Well done, MacLean, well done," Gallard said as he took a final peek into the tunnel before leaving the room. He returned to the main level of the castle where his military advisor was waiting.

"Any sign of MacLean's body?" Walter asked though he felt sure he knew the answer. Gallard shook his head.

"We will not find his body," the king replied. "He is very resilient, that man. He has well over a two-day head start on us and could be close to a hundred miles from us. We do not even know in which direction he fled."

"It appears that the DuFay Breastplate shall not be reunited with the sword and shield after all," Walter said. "We do not even know if he still has the sword, nor if he has the shield as well."

"MacLean would never part with the sword," Gallard answered him. "He cannot. He would as soon cut off his hand than relinquish the sword to anyone. It is not over, Walter," Gallard said intently. "We will not surrender our dream so easily. I charge you to track down this renegade. Find him and kill him. Bring me the sword. I will continue the search for the shield. Kill anyone who is with him. Let nothing stand in your way. Your reward upon your victorious return will be greater than any you could ever imagine. But I warn you, do not return empty-handed. The next time you see me, if the sword of DuFay is not held in your hands or at the least the head of Andrew MacLean, I promise you it will be the last time you see the light of day. Do you understand me?"

"Perfectly, your majesty," Walter said contemptuously. Without another word he purposefully strode out of the room, already planning his search in his mind.

As Gallard stood alone, contemplating what to do next, another one of his guards entered the room.

"My lord," the man said and waited for a response.

"What is it?" Gallard replied impatiently, desperately wanting nothing more than to rest.

"Per your orders we have had patrols scouring the area for any sign of refugees. This afternoon a rather strange cavern was discovered in a valley not too far from here."

"What made this cavern so strange?" Gallard asked, his curiosity having been tweaked.

"First, the entrance was very well concealed. We only discovered it because we were following wagon tracks which lead to its entrance. Then we went inside. It is a burial tomb, my lord. There were a number of bodies, most of them appearing quite old, laid to rest in cavities along the walls."

"Most of them?" Gallard repeated, intrigued. "What do you mean most of them?"

"There was one body, all the way in the back of the tomb, which could not have been more than two days dead, three at the most," the man answered. "Ordinarily we would have not thought much about it, except this body was dressed in the uniform of a guard. One of our guards."

"Where is this body?" Gallard asked. "I must see it."

"It is outside. We took a cart out and retrieved it," the man replied. He led Gallard out of the castle and into the main courtyard. They walked over to a cart which was covered with a large burlap blanket. Gallard reached over and threw the blanket aside. He immediately recognized the face of the man on the cart and his lips pulled back with a trace of a grin.

"Donald MacLean," Gallard sneered. "A fitting end to a man who betrayed his king. I only regret that your brother's rotting corpse does not lie here beside you." As he was about to turn away something caught Gallard's eye. There was a rip in the sleeve of Donald's tunic which revealed his forearm. Gallard paused for a moment. "Step away," he instructed the man, who quickly obeyed and took several steps back from the cart. Gallard moved closer and pulled the ripped sleeve back. There, on Donald's forearm, was the unmistakable mark of DuFay. Gallard could not have been more surprised if Donald's corpse had come to life and sat up in the cart.

"This is impossible," Gallard said to himself, not able to take his eyes away from the scar. "This cannot be. All these years, right under my very nose, yet I saw nothing. How could I have not known? Three generations of MacLean have lived in my very own land, and I have visited their homes many times, yet I never saw this symbol nor heard any of them speak of it." His mind whirled as the implications of this discovery dawned upon him. "If Donald was given the mark, was Andrew given the mark as well? Would that be why Andrew refused to relinquish the sword so many years ago? But Andrew is not of the blood line. He was adopted. The mark could not have been passed on to him. It had to be kept in the blood line. It had to be kept in Donald's blood line …" Realization hit him like a blow to the head. He did not need to search for Andrew. He knew where Andrew was going. And he knew how to bring him back. Gallard turned to the man still waiting patiently off to the side.

"Go find my military advisor," he ordered the man. "Tell him I must speak with him immediately."

"Yes, my lord," the man said as he bowed slightly, then turned and hurried away. Several minutes later he returned with Walter.

"You asked for me, my king?" Walter said with a bit of irritation as he approached Gallard.

"Andrew MacLean is heading home, to Nordham," Gallard informed his military advisor matter-of-factly.

"Why would he do that?" Walter asked. "He is a traitor to his king and homeland, a wanted man. He would not risk going back home for fear of being recognized."

"This is why he would go home," Gallard replied and lifted the blanket to reveal Donald's face.

"Donald MacLean," Walter said in recognition. "But I do not understand why the death of his brother would move Andrew to risk capture by returning to his homeland."

"Look at his right forearm," the king said. Walter hesitated for a moment, then shifted his gaze as directed. He immediately recognized the DuFay mark.

"How can this be?" Walter asked, confused.

"I do not know," Gallard replied, looking down at Donald's body. "In all our years in Nordham, there has never been even a whisper of the DuFay name.

"You believe that the true DuFay line resides within your own kingdom?" Walter asked.

"It would appear so, though I find it most unlikely," Gallard responded. "I cannot fathom how that could be, yet the name would remain such a mystery."

"Either way, I now know MacLean's destination. He shall not escape me."

Gallard looked at Walter with an intensive eye. "This revelation changes our strategy. Donald has a son, and he would now be the true heir of DuFay. We cannot allow that information to become known. Your primary mission is now the boy. Do not risk failure by deviating from your mission or wasting time searching for MacLean. We know where he is going. Once you have the boy under lock and key you can return and take MacLean. Alive. We still need the sword. For all we know he may also have the shield. Now go and complete your task."

"MacLean has nearly three days on us," Walter said. "It will be difficult for twenty-five men to travel as quickly as one man, especially one man as motivated as he is. It is more than likely that he will reach Nordham before we do."

"Oh, I assure you, he will not be traveling alone," Gallard replied with a knowing smile.

"How do you know this?" Walter questioned in reply.

"Despite his unfavorable personality, Martin was a very thorough spy. He informed me that Andrew had grown quite close to a certain family, especially to the daughter, and especially after the father met with an unfortunate accident. I cannot believe that he would simply abandon them to whatever fate would be theirs on their own. You know well his sense of honor," Gallard answered. "He would most certainly lead them away from this bloody mess and at least take them to another place where they could live comfortably. And then there is Talbot's daughter. She spent no little time in Andrew's company as well and with her father gone, she would have nowhere to go and nobody to turn to for comfort and protection. Finally, when Donald's body was found, there were wagon tracks, not but a few days old, leading to and away from the cavern. A wagon would be needed for supplies and some comfort for a small band of travelers. No, Andrew MacLean does not travel alone. You should have no difficulty catching up to him."

"And if I do catch up to him?" Walter asked.

"Take him alive," Gallard replied. "Kill anybody with him."

"And what are your plans, Your Majesty?" Walter asked. "Will you remain here for a time?"

"There is no reason to remain here for an extended period of time," Gallard responded, looking around. "We came for the sword and the shield. I shall let our army rest for several days and recoup their strength, especially the wounded. During that time, I will search the castle and surrounding areas. Perhaps there remain secrets that would aid us in achieving our goals. Once the men and horses are rested, we shall resupply and return to Nordham. I trust that by the time I arrive you will have MacLean in your custody. You should leave before dark."

"I shall leave within the hour," Walter said as he turned to finalize his preparations.

"I will find you, MacLean," Gallard said maliciously as he twisted into a knot the robe he had taken from the dead king's body. "Run while you can. I found you once, I shall find you again. And when I do it will be the worst day of your life."

Epilogue

The soldier never knew what hit him. He had been walking a leisurely patrol near the tree line, outside of the castle, when the blow was delivered to the back of his head, robbing him of consciousness. Quickly making sure his assault had not been seen, the attacker dragged the man's limp body farther into the trees and away from whatever eyes might be in the area. Wasting no time, he removed the soldier's uniform and after removing his own clothes, donned the man's garments. The overgarment had a hood which he pulled over his head and then he donned the leather-style head covering. After a final self-inspection to make sure he would pass as one of Gallard's soldiers, the man left the woods and casually walked back to the castle, his head slightly lowered to help avoid eye contact with anyone he might pass.

Within a few minutes he was back at the castle's burned gates and without hesitating, crossed the make-shift bridge and entered the castle's large courtyard. Since no fighting had occurred within the castle's guarded grounds, there were no bodies lying around, no stench of death, just dozens of Gallard's men enjoying a respite from their long, arduous journey. This casual scene played into the hands of the imposter. He could roam the grounds without raising an eyebrow and he did just that for about fifteen minutes. The temptation to enter the castle was great, but he knew that to do so could raise the suspicion that he was seeking to avoid. There was nothing within those walls that he needed so desperately as to risk his life. He knew that the longer he stayed, the greater the chance that he would be discovered, so he was about to make his way to the front gate and away from danger when he spotted King Gallard and his military adviser standing in the courtyard by a cart with what appeared to be a body covered with a blanket. Gallard was speaking to Walter and while doing so, pulled the blanket down to reveal the face of the lifeless form. Taking a significant risk, the imposter worked his way to within twenty feet of the two men, his curiosity exceeding his sense of caution. He eaves-dropped on the conversation.

"MacLean has nearly three days on us," Walter was saying. "It will be difficult for twenty-five men to travel as quickly as one man, especially one man as motivated as he is. It is more than likely that he will reach Nordham before we do."

"Oh, I assure you, he will not be traveling alone," Gallard replied with a knowing smile.

"How do you know this?" Walter questioned in reply.

"Despite his unfavorable personality, Martin was a very thorough spy. He informed me that Andrew had grown quite close to a certain family, especially to the daughter, and especially after the father met with an unfortunate accident. I cannot believe that he would simply abandon them to whatever fate would be theirs on their own. You know well his sense of honor," Gallard answered. "He would most certainly lead them away from this bloody mess and at least take them to another place where they could live comfortably. And then there is Talbot's daughter. She spent no little time in Andrew's company as well and with her father gone, she would have nowhere to go and nobody to turn to for comfort and protection. Finally, when Donald's body was found, there were wagon tracks, not but a few days old, leading to and away from the cavern. A wagon would be needed for supplies and some comfort for a small band of travelers. No, Andrew MacLean does not travel alone. You should have no difficulty catching up to him."

"And if I do catch up to him?" Walter asked.

"Take him alive," Gallard replied. "Kill anybody with him."

The man had heard enough. Just as casually as he had taken position near the king and his military advisor, he retreated and made his way to the main gate. He could not resist one last look back at the castle. He saw Walter walk away from the king with a purposeful stride, leaving Gallard alone with a menacing look on his face. Knowing what he had to do, Angus turned his back on the place he had called home for over fifteen years and, choosing a northern course, headed for an uncertain future.

www.ingramcontent.com/pod-product-compliance
Lightning Source LLC
Chambersburg PA
CBHW050011120726
47903CB00006B/1719